FORGED FOR DESTINY

FORGED FOR DESTINY:
BOOK 1

ANDREW KNIGHTON

orbitbooks.net
orbitworks.n

This book is a work of fiction. Names, characters, places, and incidents are the product of the author's imagination or are used fictitiously. Any resemblance to actual events, locales, or persons, living or dead, is coincidental.

Copyright © 2025 by Andrew Knighton

Cover design by Alexia E. Pereira
Cover images by Shutterstock
Cover copyright © 2025 by Hachette Book Group, Inc.
Author photograph by Richard Wilson

Hachette Book Group supports the right to free expression and the value of copyright. The purpose of copyright is to encourage writers and artists to produce the creative works that enrich our culture.

The scanning, uploading, and distribution of this book without permission is a theft of the author's intellectual property. If you would like permission to use material from the book (other than for review purposes), please contact permissions@hbgusa.com. Thank you for your support of the author's rights.

Orbit
Hachette Book Group
1290 Avenue of the Americas
New York, NY 10104
orbitbooks.net
orbitworks.net

First published as an ebook and as a print on demand: April 2025

Orbit is an imprint of Hachette Book Group.
The Orbit name and logo are registered trademarks of Little, Brown Book Group Limited.

The publisher is not responsible for websites (or their content) that are not owned by the publisher.

The Hachette Speakers Bureau provides a wide range of authors for speaking events. To find out more, go to hachettespeakersbureau.com or email HachetteSpeakers@hbgusa.com.

Library of Congress Cataloging-in-Publication Data
Names: Knighton, Andrew, author.
Title: Forged for destiny / Andrew Knighton.
Description: New York, NY : Orbit, 2025. | Series: Forged for destiny ; book 1
Identifiers: LCCN 2024037532 | ISBN 9780316587877 (trade paperback) |
    ISBN 9780316581752 (ebook)
Subjects: LCGFT: Fantasy fiction. | Novels.
Classification: LCC PR6111.N63 F67 2025 | DDC 823/.92—dc23/eng/20241101
LC record available at https://lccn.loc.gov/2024037532

ISBNs: 9780316581752 (ebook), 9780316587877 (print on demand)

*To my dad, David Knighton, who turned me
into a fantasy fan and an avid reader. I promise, the
parenting seen in this book isn't based on you.*

Chapter One
The End

Valens and Fabia ran down Broadgate, chainmail jangling and swords swinging, racing the flames toward the heart of Pavuno. Ashes swirled through the air, routed by the wind. The smell of smoke was everywhere, and when Valens opened his mouth to speak, he tasted burning buildings.

"Which way?" he asked as they passed a cracked statue of the goddess Avgar, each of her four arms pointing down a different road.

"Right."

Behind them, there was an almighty crash, the third of the night, as the city walls gave way to the pressure of artillery stones.

When there had been one breach, they stood a chance of holding off the invaders from Dunholm. With enough good soldiers, enough shields and spears, enough of the dogged determination on which the Empire of Estis had been built, then maybe they could have held the line. It would have been a moment in which legends were forged, tales of heroism and sacrifice, great roaring verses full of inspiring bullshit. It would have been a night that lived in eternity.

Two breaches, though. Two breaches meant that the war was about to be lost and it was time for Prisca's plan, however bitter that thought was.

Three breaches was probably too late, but what else was Valens meant to do, go back to the wall and die for a lost cause? He believed in courage. He believed in strength. He believed in standing by his comrades in their hour of need. He even believed in heroism. There was a time and a place to put your life on the line, to make the noble sacrifice for all that you held dear.

And then there was a time to run like wolves were on your tail.

People streamed through the streets. Some carried their children. Some carried sacks filled with their worldly goods. Some only had the clothes they stood in. One of them grabbed Valens by the arm. He could have wrenched free of those twig fingers, but her desperation brought him up short. Her eyes were red-rimmed, spittle flying from cracked lips.

"Please, protect us," she screeched.

Valens stared. Didn't she understand? They were past protecting anyone. Today was lost. Only Prisca's plan gave him hope for tomorrow.

Fabia slapped the woman, the plates of her gauntlet leaving red ruts down a pale cheek.

"Stop fucking around." Fabia grabbed Valens's arm and dragged him after her.

Ahead, the stampeding crowd had stopped, panicked people clogging the street. Fabia thrust her way through. The smart ones got out of her way. The stupid ones got slammed aside by that gauntleted hand. Valens followed, and nobody was stupid enough to stand in his way.

They burst like a blade's tip from the crowd to face a thin line of Dunholmi warriors, the points of their spears glinting. Calling their tabards royal blue seemed a lie when the dye had faded from years in the saddle, and the spears were cheap work from a mass armoury. But a cheap spear would skewer flesh as well as a fancy one, and those spears pointed at the crowd, which meant they pointed at Valens and Fabia.

Valens didn't need Fabia's shout to tell him to keep running toward the enemy. It wasn't a matter of courage or recklessness; it was simply their best chance. Use surprise while they had it. Take on these six men and women instead of the thousands coming behind. Fight the foot levies instead of cavalry raised for the hunt.

The spear facing Valens rose. That was a mistake. He lowered his shoulders and swept his sword up, battering the spearpoint past his head. Another one hit his side, a bruising punch of an impact but not the searing pain that came with punctured armour. A swing of his blade knocked that strike away, then he was up close, putting his weight into a blow that split a Dunholmi's chest with a crunch of bones and a spray of blood. He punched a warrior in the face and kept running, leaving the survivors. He wasn't here to kill. He was here to live.

Fabia ran beside him. Blood trickled from a gash in her cheek. More dripped from her blade.

"Just like Tulabeck," she said with a grin.

"We won at Tulabeck."

"Apart from that."

There was no movement in the Square of Artificers, just abandoned belongings and scattered bodies. On the far side, the Clockmakers' Tower lay in ruins, its clockwork guts unwinding across cobbles, smashed open by an artillery stone. It broke Valens's heart to see the tower like that. People died all the time, as expected, but a place like the tower, it was special. That sort of place made their brief lives brighter. Now it would never bring anyone joy with its blaring mechanical chime ever again.

Valens pointed down a side street. Through the screams and crashes, his ears had picked out hoofbeats, a sound that haunted infantry. Blue-clad cavalry dashed back and forth, looking for something to kill.

One of them pointed at him.

"Faster." Valens sprinted across the square, heading for the long, narrow road that led out of the square to the Hill of Lost Names. Fabia could have outpaced him, but she didn't, and stupid as it was, he was grateful.

But as they reached the entrance to the street, hoofbeats echoed around them, the first eager cavalryman racing into the square from behind. There were dozens of Dunholmi soldiers now, each on horseback, each carrying their own gleaming blade.

Valens stopped in the narrow way.

"One of us has to hold them." He turned to face the oncoming rider. "You're faster."

"You're stronger." Fabia stood beside him, feet planted, blade raised.

"Fine, we'll do this the hard way. Left or right?"

The cavalryman was almost on them, his sabre the icy pale curve of a midwinter moon.

"Left."

The horse swerved. The cavalryman swung. Fabia's sword was faster than Valens's. She smashed the sabre aside, sliced through the man's arm and into the neck of the horse. The poor beast gave a pained huff and stumbled three strides before it collapsed, slamming its rider into a wall.

"I won." Fabia raised her sword as more cavalry trotted into view.

"You pushed him left. That's cheating."

"We don't have time to argue about rules."

They looked at each other, and a whole history passed between them. Days on the march and nights around the campfire; hangovers, blisters, and knife wounds; stories told, advice shared, promises kept and broken.

"I'm not leaving you to die," he snarled.

"But you thought I'd leave you?"

Hooves clopped across the square, slowly at first but building to charge.

"One of us has to go."

"And you lost the swing." Fabia jerked her head. "So go."

A weight like the fallen walls pressed down on Valens. If he left Fabia, he betrayed himself. If he didn't, he betrayed her. It was no way to end a friendship.

Hoofbeats sounded louder and faster. No time to argue.

Valens placed a hand on his friend's shoulder.

"Die well," he murmured.

"Fuck off and save the day."

Valens didn't look back as he sprinted toward the Hill of Lost Names. Not for the crash of blades. Not for the first screaming horse or its rider bellowing in pain. Not for the order to *fight harder, you bastards, there's just one of her.* Not as he turned the corner and lost his last chance to ever see Fabia again. Because if he looked back, then he would stop running, and both their deaths would be in vain.

Valens's chest tightened as he ran up the steep street. The destruction hadn't got this far yet. He was grateful for that. The shops on the Hill of Lost Names sold simple goods for simple people, plain things made to endure. He'd got his best bowl here, and the tankard he'd lost in a swamp the first bitter winter of the war. The brightly painted storefronts served people like him, not like the artisans on Sunrise Ridge, all working for people in the palace. These streets deserved to stand as long as possible.

He stopped for just a brief moment to catch his breath and turned to look behind him. From the top of the hill, he could see all the way across Pavuno, back to the fighting beneath the city walls, edges of steel glinting in the light of the attackers' torches. There was fire as well, war's constant companion. Flames rampaged through Shemside and Water Reach, the crowded timber houses of the poor flaring like tarred kindling. They marched up Emerald Hill, taking the mansions as slowly and steadily as an earl striding across the marshalling ground. They crept toward the Scholars' Spire, sending

FORGED FOR DESTINY

its inhabitants into a chaotic flurry; essence might keep a quill sharp for years, and the signs might spell out a man's fate, but armies carved a destiny of their own.

Valens rubbed his chest, armoured links clinking beneath his tabard. The temple of Laughing Loftus was gone, taking the bright panels that told Loftus's story. The Darting Drake Pub as well, with Valens's favourite table in the corner, and the notches in the wall from when Fabia learned knife throwing. Tellia's bakery with all its sweet treats. The wooden cat statue at the junction of Soft Street. Maybe even Fender's smithy. All gone to ash.

Valens turned back, the destruction hastening his need to see the plan through. He followed the last of the road onto a cobbled square in front of the foundlings' home. No one else was up here, in a dead end above dying streets. The dry ache of smoke made Valens's eyes run. Angry at his own weakness, he swept the tears away and strode to the door.

It had been a temple once, its carved stones honouring a god whose age had passed. A feathered head leered down from above a heavy oak door, which Valens hammered on with the pommel of his sword, the banging resounding across the hillside. A string of snail shells rattled against the wood.

Candlelight flickered in a window above the door.

"Open up, in the name of King Cataldo and Queen Junia!" Valens bellowed, hammering once more. "Open up or I'll break it down."

The door opened and a woman looked out. She was dressed in simple, patched clothes, her head wrapped in a fraying woollen scarf. She stared up at Valens, as most people did when they first met him.

7

"Are you here to kill us?" she asked in a hoarse croak.

"Of course not." He ran a hand across the stubble of his head, embarrassed at having scared this innocent woman. He tugged at his tabard. "Imperial legions, see? I'm here for a baby."

"Which one?"

"A healthy one."

She frowned. "I don't understand."

"And I don't have time."

Valens pushed her aside as gently as he could. She stumbled, then hurried after him as he strode down the stone hall that had once been a nave. His footsteps and her fearful panting echoed from the vaulted ceiling.

Valens had never seen so many silent children. They watched him wide-eyed from bunks stacked three high, ragged blankets pulled up to their necks. The oldest were near the entrance, the young and the sickly further back, like Prisca had told him. He needed someone healthy, but he also needed them to be young, so he kept walking.

The eyes of the children followed him. Those of their guardians too, this trembling pseudo-priesthood, men and women with poor prospects or good intentions who had committed their lives to looking after the lost. Right now, they seemed lost themselves, but Valens wasn't here to show them the way. Fabia's final words rang in his ears. She'd told him to save the day. He wasn't going to be held back by dead weight.

The babies were in rocking cots at the end of the hall. Every one of them had a snail shell on a string around their neck, a desperate charm of protection, weak magic for the poor. A man stood in front of them, clutching a broom handle. His shoulders were shaking, skin ashen, but he stood his ground, the sort of humble hero who dies to save the infant saviour.

"I won't let you sell them into slavery," the man said, the broom handle wobbling as he raised it like a sword.

"Me, a slaver?" Valens snorted. "Slavers won't be here for three days, maybe four. They don't come until it's safe." He nodded to the cots. "I'm here to save one of these kids."

"Really?" The man laughed. "Oh, thank you. Who are you here for?"

Valens stepped past him and looked into the cots. There hadn't been many children in his life. He'd never known his family, and his taste in bed partners meant that he wasn't going to make one by accident. Raising a family wasn't something you did while you were still fighting, not if you had any compassion for those you might leave behind, and these days, the people whose towns they passed through hid kids away rather than bring them to see the soldiers. He knew which end of a baby was which, but he hadn't a clue how to pick between them.

"This one." He pointed at one of the quieter bundles of wrinkled flesh and crumpled blankets. "Is she healthy?"

"Aquina?" The man smiled indulgently. "She suffers from some colic, poor thing, but—"

"What about this one?" Valens bent over the next crib and the kid inside started crying. "No, not them. Who's next?"

He needed to pick fast. Smart invaders would secure the lower streets first, but there were always some who got carried away with looting. It might be an hour before they arrived, it might be only minutes, and either way he needed to be gone.

"What is this?" The woman from the door stared at Valens, creases carved as deeply into her face as into the gargoyles looking down from the pillars.

"He's looking for someone," the man explained. "Is it your son, sir? Your daughter perhaps?"

"If we know the sex, we can help," the woman said.

"A girl would be better." Valens walked down the line. "But they need to be healthy and strong."

He peered at the children. Perhaps one was a soldier's kid, left behind by people he knew. Enough warriors had died this past year to fill a dozen foundlings' homes, and finding a warrior's child would honour the people he'd lost. More likely they'd grow up strong and brave too, taking after their parents. That would help with the plan.

"I still don't understand," the man said.

"You don't need to." Valens's voice rose. He didn't have time to waste, but he didn't know how to choose. "Just find me a healthy one."

Two babies started crying, which set more of them off. Soon, it seemed the whole world was wailing. Fitting for the night's business, but no help.

A door rattled. Valens spun around, sword raised, ready to fight his way out. Shutters rattled too, then subsided. It was the wind.

That was when he spotted a child wrapped in a yellow blanket, mouth open to laugh instead of to cry, one hand gripping tight on the edge of the cot.

"This one." Valens scooped the kid up. He half expected them to burst into tears, but instead they giggled and pressed one soft hand against his wrist, while the other clutched the string that held their snail shell. "What's their name?"

"That's Raul."

"I'm taking Raul." He should have just walked away then, but the fear and confusion in the guardians' eyes caught a weakness in him, the sort of stupid, soft sensation that could get a person killed, or that could get them to show kindness. "He'll be safe. He'll have a good life. I promise."

"What about the others?" the woman said. "Can you take them?"

"Can you take us all?" The man's trembling gave way to a bold burst of hope. "The older children can carry the younger ones, if you show us a safe way."

"Only this one." Valens settled the kid against his chest, holding it close with one arm. With the other, he pointed his sword at the adults. "Any of you follow me, you'll regret it."

He felt like a shit. He was a shit. But sometimes it took a shit to save the day. He'd have known that even if Prisca hadn't told him.

He strode back down the echoing chamber. They called after him, children and adults alike, high voices lost in the hollow vastness left by a lost god. He didn't listen, just strode out the door and away.

It was easier leaving the hill than approaching it, heading into the side of town away from the fighting. Smart people had left the city or were keeping their heads down, and the others hadn't reached that breaking point of panic where they'd form a desperate, running mob of fear and selfishness. He jogged alone through the night-draped streets, sword in one hand and baby in the other, down the Hill of Lost Names and upslope again, toward the gaping gorge known as Rack's Scar.

Valens stopped two streets before the Scar, sheltering behind a wagon. Warriors in blue lurked by the near end of the bridge. He noted without surprise the bodies of a few Estis men at their feet. A narrow bridge above a gorge only needed a few defenders, but when news came that the walls were falling, half of them would have run to save the city or save their skins, leaving the rest disordered and distracted. It didn't take a diviner to predict what would come next.

In his arms, the baby kicked and gurgled. It tried to take hold of his finger, but he shook it off.

"You'd better be bloody worth it," he said. "Though I don't see how you could."

The warriors roamed around the few bodies along the route to the bridge. Some of them were looting. Others stabbed the corpses with their spears, just in case. There wasn't much nobility in battle, even less in cleaning up after. Valens didn't eye those bodies in outrage, or to memorise their faces so he could avenge them. He looked in case he saw one in particular. If he did, then all was truly lost.

"It's all right, I'm here."

Valens whirled around, sword pointing at the source of the voice. Fortunately for both of them, Prisca had stayed a few steps back, a slender, unarmed figure in a city full of war.

"I saw that one coming," she said, head tilting to one side. "Where's Fabia?"

FORGED FOR DESTINY

"It's just me."

"Oh. My condolences."

It was an inadequate word, spoken with inadequate feeling, but it threatened to unleash a tide within Valens. He'd known Fabia since they were naive teenagers, standing in line with battered shields and their first blunt infantry axes. They'd trained together, marched together, bled and killed together, held each other up as their homeland collapsed. Losing her was like losing a limb. But grief wasn't something a warrior showed in public; certainly not in front of a royal minister. Valens had a job to do and he wouldn't shame Fabia's memory by letting feelings get in the way of that.

"You're late," he said, his voice flat as lead off a temple roof. He looked Prisca right in the eye. He expected her to put him in his place, to remind him that she was a minister and he a lowly warrior, to show him that some part of the empire remained.

"It's hard to find a precision blacksmith at the best of times," she said. "You try getting work done while the city's an inferno."

Valens frowned and shifted his weight. The baby squirmed. "It's your plan. Maybe you should have prepared."

"I needed more information. I still do, but I've worked with what I know."

Prisca jerked her head, sharp features reminding Valens of a hawk. He followed her along the street toward a burning building, probably set alight by the infantrymen on the bridge. Her ministerial robes were gone, replaced with hard-wearing trousers and tunic, a tinker's pack strapped across her shoulders. Out of sight of the bridge, she set the pack down and drew a slender iron rod. On its end was a flattened piece the size of a small coin, shaped like a half moon with a dagger through it. Holding the other end wrapped in cloth, Prisca thrust the branding iron into the building's flames.

"Bare her arm," she said. "The shoulder would be best."

"It's a boy, not a girl."

"Not ideal, but it'll do."

"You just said healthy, you didn't say—"

"I know what I said, but the words that free us at dawn can chain us at dusk. Not that I'd expect you to know your classics."

"I know chains." Having unwrapped the kid, Valens held it out, clutching the tiny pink body between his calloused hands. "There."

Prisca took the snail shell from around the baby's neck, drew the brand from the fire, and pressed its glowing end against bare flesh. There was a hiss, a stink of burning meat, and the kid started thrashing about, screaming at the top of its lungs.

"He even sounds like King Cataldo," Prisca said. "Wrap him up. I'll tend the wound later."

Valens flung the blanket around the wailing child and picked up his sword. "The soldiers at the bridge will have heard that."

He strode around the building, while Prisca wormed her way into the straps of her pack. Sure enough, warriors were heading their way, spears in hand and curious looks on their faces. In the flickering red light from the fire, it was hard to

FORGED FOR DESTINY

make out the colour of their tabards, and they squinted at Valens, trying to judge the same thing on him.

Now was a time for confidence, not cunning. Valens strode straight toward the warriors.

"Look what I found!" He grinned and held up the kid with one hand. "Looks like someone's growing up Dunholmi!"

The soldiers cheered. The closest one lowered her spear. Valens took the opportunity to charge, carving her open with a swing of his blade.

Spears were a great weapon in a battle, with a bit of distance and your mates around you, a wall of points to skewer anyone who approached. But this wasn't a battle, and Valens was already close.

He lopped off another warrior's arm at the wrist, left a third with blood spraying from the ruined side of his neck. The others backed off, shouting at him, shouting at each other, shouting for help from an army half a city away.

Valens ran through the gap where they had been. Prisca followed, her pack thudding and clanking. One more guard lowered his spear at the end of the bridge, then saw the size of Valens and thought better of it. He jumped clear, and the fugitives ran onto the bridge.

Rack's Scar was a void in the earth, a gaping chasm darker than night. There was no echo from the two sets of footsteps, just the roar of the river far below. Even the baby's cries became tiny as they were swallowed by emptiness.

Valens slowed to let Prisca overtake him, just in case. There was no sound of pursuit, but cavalry could come fast. The baby he held was important, but they could find another if

15

they had to. Valens himself was just the muscle: silent, steadfast, solid but replaceable. Prisca, though, she was special. Only she could hold the plan together in her head.

That was why he had said yes, when she came to him and Fabia with whispers of one last hope; why he gave up his duty to die on the walls; why he forced himself to flee as the kingdom fell.

Prisca drew her arm back and flung the branding iron. It spun through the night, catching the edge of the firelight, before disappearing into the bottomless shadow of the Scar.

They stopped at the far side of the bridge. There was no one around, just an abandoned tent and the blackened circle of a firepit. No one stood in their way, and no one was following them.

Valens looked back across Rack's Scar at the ruin of Pavuno, his heart heavy, his muscles aching from a long day of fighting and a long night of fleeing. Trees flanked this side of the gorge, and he leaned against one for support. The sky above the city was yellow and grey, fading out of the darkness of night. The trees stood as black silhouettes against its light, each one a stark sentinel.

"We'll die like heroes, or we'll triumph like them," Fabia had said, but Valens knew better: heroes lived forever in saga and song; the likes of Valens and Fabia were forgotten the day their bodies went cold.

Prisca wriggled her shoulders, settling the pack into place.

"Come," she said. "We need to be halfway to the hills by nightfall."

"It's barely sunrise."

"Then it's going to be a long day."

Valens wiped his sword on a clump of grass, sheathed it, then shifted the baby to that arm. It had stopped crying, and instead gurgled as it pounded him with tiny fists and feet. Looked like it was a fighter.

"Do you want me to take that?" Prisca asked.

Valens brought his hand around, ready to pass the warm bundle to her. A smaller hand wrapped around one of his fingers, like it was clinging to life itself. The baby looked up with vacant eyes and made a noise he didn't understand. It was so weak and useless, a stupid thing to rest the fate of a kingdom on. So pathetic.

"It's all right," Valens mumbled, pulling the yellow blanket tighter around the baby. "I'll look after him."

Chapter Two
Eighteen Years After

"You'll never beat me, old man!" Raul swung his sword in a short, direct arc. There was a crack as Valens's sword came up, wooden blade colliding with wooden blade.

"Harder," Valens said. "Strike like you mean it."

Raul went in again, high then low, trying to use Valens's own tricks against him. The sound of the blow reverberated from the steep hills.

"I said harder, not smarter. You're eighteen years old, a man in his prime. I should feel it when you hit."

Raul took a deep breath, blew blond hair out of his eyes, and took another swing. Again, there was a thwack of wood on wood.

"Gods' piss, lad, would you hold back like this against bandits?"

"They're not my da." Raul lowered his sword and looked sheepishly at Valens. "I'd feel terrible if I knocked your teeth out."

Valens laughed, briefly. It was a rumbling sound, to match a body that could have been made of boulders, as vast and weather-worn as any crag.

"Like you could hurt me." He turned away and his bare shoulders rose as he took a deep breath.

Raul knew that move as well as any in the fight. He'd first seen it when he was eight years old and lambing season forced Valens to tell him where babies came from. It wasn't explaining sex that made his da so uncomfortable. It was the bit after, about how he hadn't made Raul that way, how sometimes families came together differently.

He was sad, though Raul didn't know why.

Raul wanted to wrap an arm around his da's shoulders, but Valens was taller even than Raul and much wider—those shoulders took a lot of wrapping. Instead, he placed a hand against the side of his da's shaved head, felt the stubble and the scars as he drew that head down to touch his own. After a few heartbeats, just like always, Valens's expression softened into a smile.

"I'm proud of you, lad." Valens ruffled Raul's hair, almost knocking him over. "Prouder of you than of anything else I've done." He raised his sword. "Another round?"

Raul brushed his fringe out of his eyes and weighed the sword in his hand. He was lucky to have Valens, a proper hero who could teach him how to fight. Tallo's ma had died fighting in Earl Buscenti's company, and Ernestine's da liked to pretend, but no one had scars like Valens, or that way of talking about war where the whole bar fell silent, hooked on his words. No one else was learning to fight like Raul was, and he could happily have spent the whole day like this.

Andrew Knighton

But Prisca counted on him to be responsible when Valens got distracted.

"We should open the inn," Raul said. "The morning's half gone."

Valens glanced up at the sky, then nodded.

"You're right, lad." He took the wooden swords and wrapped them carefully in an old yellow blanket. "Come on."

Now that they'd stopped fighting, Raul felt the spring morning's chill. He pulled on his shirt, covering his wiry body and the half-moon birthmark on his upper arm, then pulled his woollen tunic over that. It wasn't a long walk home, but Valens had taught him to take his comfort where he could.

As they approached the tavern, greasy black smoke was trickling from the brewhouse out back, a simple but sturdy wooden building with clay pipes protruding from the roof, like a hundred others in the Winding Vales.

"Look, Prisca's home." Raul smiled. "I thought she was down the valley."

"She came in late last night."

"You could have told me."

Valens got that frown again, like the muscles in his forehead were trying to drag something from his brain.

"You know now."

"Do you want me to open up while you say hello?"

Raul knew that his parents weren't together in the way most couples were. It wasn't like Tanna's parents, who lived in different houses and had families of their own, or Jero's parents, who screamed drunkenly at each other on festival nights. Valens and Prisca were friendly, they worked together well, and they shared a home. They just didn't share a bed, or the sort of affection that went beyond friends. They were partners in the business of raising Raul, not two halves of a couple.

"You go see her," Valens said. "I'll open up."

"Are you sure?"

"Lad, you're as subtle as a rat with a mouth full of cheese. Go say hello to your ma, find out what she's brought back this time."

Raul ran to the brewhouse door and slid back the heavy bolt with a thunk. The charm above the door shook, needles tapping against a used horseshoe that kept roaming spirits from the vats.

"Is that you, Raul?" Prisca called out.

"It's me!"

"Come on up, then."

He scrambled up the ladder hidden behind the big barrels at the back, to the loft that was Prisca's special space. Here, smaller vats brewed things beyond beer. Pristine sheets of newly made paper hung from lengths of twine along one wall, and thick black ink trickled from a mess of pipes into a bowl. Prisca stood at a table in the middle, dressed in a tinker's simple tunic and trousers, goose quill darting back and forth across an offcut of parchment.

"How was your trip?" Raul asked, casting an eye across the table. Most of the manuscripts were familiar, but there was one he didn't recognise, a thin stack of pages wrapped in red leather.

"Busy. The lack of literacy in these communities baffles me, but it works in our favour. I scribed a dozen contracts and made a copy of Toybar's *Chivalric Virtues* for one of the lords."

"Just one copy?"

She smiled. It was a thin smile, as sharp as her eyes. "Of course not." A slender finger slid the leather-bound tome toward Raul, who grinned as he grabbed it.

Raul pulled out a stool and sat down, the manuscript open in front of him. The lettering was broad and jagged, using black ink on parchment, a copy of the book's style as well as its content, to preserve its essence.

"It's nonsense, of course," Prisca said, turning back to her work. She was writing in her own style, smaller and more flowing. "Toybar is pompous at best, wilfully misguided at worst. But you must learn to critique the concepts presented, not simply to absorb them."

"Will I need that to keep the books for an inn?" Raul asked, then joined in Prisca's inevitable retort. "Learning has value in itself."

Prisca raised an eyebrow.

"I'm starting to think that I raised you too smart, Raul. Or at least, too smart for my needs."

Raul beamed. Prisca was the cleverest person in the Winding Vales, so those words counted for a lot. As for learning, he would never complain about being told to sit and read. Most of his peers didn't even know how to make sense of letters, never mind whole books. His education, on the other hand, had revealed a world of wonders, people and places far beyond the Vales, some lost to the past, others over the horizon. There was so much more to the world than farms and fields, so many gaps in his knowledge he wanted to fill.

"Did you read the bones too?" he asked.

Prisca nodded.

"Runes, bones, the flights of birds. The omens aren't strong out here in the hills, but that doesn't make people any less thirsty to hear their fortunes."

"Do you ever wish you could do more than that?"

"More?"

Raul slowly turned the pages of the book, taking in the elegance of its close-packed text.

"That you could shape the essence of the world, make people's futures better instead of telling them how bad things will be?"

"Of course I would." Prisca drew the stopper from a pot of ink and dipped a fresh quill into it. "Back before the invasion, scholars' work in Pavuno was entirely about the future, trying to understand our essence based on the traditions we have and how it will affect us eventually. But my skills lie in reading, not shaping. I'll stick with omens and charms."

Raul turned another page. In place of the neatly scribed rows of letters, their slender backs bowed beneath the weight of so much meaning, he found a diagram: the emperors of Estis, down to two generations past, just before their family tree was felled by the army of Dunholm, before Estis itself became nothing more than the North March. Raul ran a finger down the connections, from parent to child.

"Do you really not know anything about my other parents, Prisca?"

It was an old line of conversation, but one he couldn't help following. One day, she might remember something she had seen or heard, or pick up some fragment of gossip as she roamed Estis. One day, perhaps, that thread would weave its way back into his life. And if not, it did no harm to ask. Prisca never seemed to mind.

"Your parents were lost before we found you, alone and abandoned in the ashes of Pavuno," she said. "That's all the enlightenment I can give."

"You really didn't see anything that could tell you who they were?"

She looked at him the way she looked at a newly presented manuscript, before she pronounced what parchment, ink, and quill she would need to copy it.

"One day, the truth will reveal itself," she said. "But not today." She looked out of a small window, watching a swallow flit past, a look that brought out the predatory sharpness of her face. "You haven't left Valens alone to open the bar, have you?"

Raul laughed. "He's been doing it far longer than I have."

"And he still makes errors every day." She waved toward the ladder. "I have work to do. Go make sure that he doesn't bankrupt us."

"Can I take this with me?" Raul held up the book.

"Keep it hidden. I put in too much work to see it confiscated."

"Thank you, Ma." He leaned around the table and kissed her on the cheek. Her face stiffened, then she patted him on the head.

"You're a good boy, Raul, but please, call me Prisca. 'Ma' is for old women slurping stewed fruit through the ruins of their teeth."

Clutching the book tight, Raul scrambled down the ladder and out through the brewhouse, sliding the bolt into place behind him. He nodded three times to the charm above the door, then hurried across the yard, past Jerky the rooster and his small harem of hens.

Above the back door of the tavern, a pair of dried rabbits' feet were splayed on an oak twig, paws welcoming visitors in. Out front there was a proper sign, a wooden board that Valens had spent weeks carving into something like a tankard. That sign invited in business; rabbit charms invited in the world.

Valens was in the taproom, its doors and shutters flung wide, welcoming the bright light and a warm wind out of the south. Timbers ten times older than Raul held up a ceiling stained with the soot of a long winter, waiting for Valens and Raul to whitewash it when summer came. A fire crackled in the hearth, beneath a cross drawn in ashes from last night's fire, to ensure that today's burned as well. Old Wellic sat by it, his stick leaning against a stool, a tankard of third-brew ale in his hand. No one drank Valens's ale quickly, not until the fourth or fifth cup, but everyone came to the tavern, and those with little else to do came early in the day.

"What you got there, boy?" Wellic asked, squinting across the room.

"Nothing," Raul said, setting the book down behind the bar, under the tattered yellow blanket that held the wooden swords. "How's your hip today?"

"It's got the spring tingles. Gets them every year since I broke it. That's how you get wiser with age, see, you learn to listen to your scars. Isn't that right, Valens?"

Valens shrugged and one of the pale lines on his face twitched. He moved earthenware tankards from one shelf to the next, the jet ring on his right hand clicking against their handles.

"He understands all right." Wellic winked broadly. "And we all understand too. Lots of good men and women's blood got spilled trying to keep us free, and those Dunholm bastards spill more every day."

Valens went very still, muscles standing out like ropes in the sides of his neck.

"No need to get bashful." Wellic waved his tankard. "We've all heard your stories about the fall of the city, about the battles before. Why don't you tell us one now?"

Raul gave Valens a pleading look. If Wellic wanted to listen instead of talk, that was something to be grateful for. But Valens didn't talk about the old days as much as he used to, and that strange sadness from this morning came back to Valens's face at the mention.

"Maybe later," he said.

The clopping of hooves drew their attention to the yard. Outside the small window, Raul saw that half a dozen riders had turned off the road, all of them dressed in blue tabards over chainmail. They reined in their mud-spattered steeds and headed for the hitching rail.

A tankard shattered in Valens's hand, pottery shards sliding across the surface of the bar. His tension froze Raul in place. Valens looked down, then hastily swept the broken pieces from sight.

"Bastards." Wellic spat in the rushes, then drew his stool closer to the fire, hunching over his cup.

FORGED FOR DESTINY

The riders stomped in. They had shortbows across their backs and quivers of arrows at their hips, next to curved cavalry sabres. On their chests, a white tree was stitched over blue, the symbol of the current governor in place of the royal crown they all used to bear. One of them wore a second belt of white cloth around her waist, with a silver dagger hanging from it.

Raul had seen cavalry patrols before, but seldom this close. The Dunholmi didn't often bother with the Winding Vales, leaving the locals to police themselves. When they did come, it had usually been when he was out of the tavern, sent on some errand by Valens or Prisca, so that he only saw them in the distance. Patrols meant trouble: rebels to be hanged, bandits hunted, books burned. The Vales thrummed with nervous tension at the sound of their hoofbeats.

He stared at them now, surprised by how ordinary they looked. A little paler, perhaps, than the people he had grown up around, but without the malevolence his imagination had painted across their features.

One of them stared back at Raul and raised an eyebrow.

"Can I offer you and yours a drink, Captain?" Valens asked, with a smile that didn't reach his eyes.

"Is it that bitter stuff you North Marchers drink?" the woman with the white belt said.

"Sorry." Valens shrugged. "It's all we have."

"Then it will have to do. But nothing too strong, we've got a long day ahead."

"Of course." Valens looked at Raul. "What are you waiting for, lad? Pour these good warriors their drinks."

Raul hurried behind the bar and gathered the tankards. He fumbled one, caught it before it hit the floor, and forced himself to slow down, to act with care. He was very aware of the crunch of rushes on the floor, the crack of a shard of broken tankard beneath his boot, the sounds of the soldiers half-hidden from him as he turned the tap on a barrel.

"What brings you up here?" Valens didn't lean on the bar, like he did when talking with the locals. He stood tall, feet shoulder-width apart, arms hanging by his sides.

"We've heard rumours of a scribe. We're out to catch them now, while the roads are muddy and slow."

"Folks up here need a scribe from time to time, for contracts and such. Can't pay your taxes if you haven't got accounts, and most of us can't write our own."

"Ah, but this scribe writes books too, and the law views that very differently."

Valens shrugged. "We're not big readers here."

The captain looked him up and down.

"No, I don't suppose you are." She waved a finger toward the gap at the end of the bar. "My troop are going to look around."

Valens tensed. There was a rustle and a creak, and when Raul looked over the bar, he saw that two of the warriors had their bows out, arrows nocked, strings not drawn but at the ready. The captain and Valens stared at each other, Valens clenching and unclenching his fists, the captain's gaze shifting across Valens's scars.

"Got your drinks," Raul said brightly, stepping into the gap by the bar. Ale slopped from over-filled tankards across

FORGED FOR DESTINY

his wooden tray. The warriors who'd been heading that way stopped, and one reached out a hand, then looked at the captain.

"It's been an awful thirsty ride," the warrior said.

"Search first," the captain snapped. "Ale after."

"This scribe." Valens placed his hands on the bar and looked at the spot between them. "Is there a reward for finding him?"

The captain held up a hand. Three warriors stopped to listen instead of shoving past Raul.

"Him?" the captain asked. "What makes you think they're a man?"

"So there isn't a reward?"

"There might be, if you know something worth rewarding."

Valens nodded slowly.

"Man came through here yesterday, first since the snows melted. Said he was a charcoal burner. Those stains on his hands, they were dark enough, but charcoal doesn't usually linger in the folds of your knuckles like that. Strikes me now, it's early in the year for charcoal burners."

"Yesterday?" The captain looked past her horses toward the muddy road. "Which way was he going?"

"He said northeast, toward Dellabant, but there are other places he could have gone, the way he was heading. Someone on foot couldn't check them all before he gets away. Riders, though, if they were fast..."

The captain looked at Valens, eyes narrowed.

"Why didn't you tell me this before?"

"Why didn't you tell me there was a reward?"

"There won't be, if we don't find him."

29

"I've earned my cut, if you do."

The captain waved her hand in a circle.

"Everybody out."

"But Captain..."

"Do you want ale or do you want silver?"

The warriors hurried out after her. The last man grabbed a tankard from Raul, knocked it back in two swift gulps, grimaced, and dropped it on the bar.

"For the road."

Then he was gone.

"Hope he falls in that road and breaks his neck," Wellic hissed, looking around from the fire. "Stains on the knuckles. You know how to sell a story."

Valens took two tankards off Raul's tray. He handed one to Wellic, then drank another in two big gulps, just like the warrior. He reached for a second tankard. His shoulders sagged as the sound of hooves disappeared toward the pass.

"Details are the whetstone of lies," he said. "Somewhere along the line, they started coming natural to me."

Details. One more lesson for Raul. He wasn't much of a liar, but maybe details would help. He sipped one of the ales and shivered with disgust at the bitterness.

Valens looked around, then emptied his second tankard.

"Go find Prisca," he said solemnly. "Tell her what happened. Then tell her I need to talk."

Chapter Three
Fescue and Wheatgrass

The wagons rolled into the yard, bright ribbons streaming in the wind, drums beating and flutes piping a merry tune. Some of the players danced beside them, bells jingling at their ankles, skirts flaring, and costume jewellery twinkling. Folk from half the vale followed, smiling and laughing, cheering at a spectacle that came only once a year.

Raul ran out to greet them, shouting excitedly. Even Valens was smiling as he stood in the door of the inn, sun shining off his freshly shaved head, watching the wagons arrive.

"Ladies, gentlemen, and all other folk!" Efron Dellest stood on the board of the leading wagon, arms spread wide, smiling beneath his bushy moustache. He wore the costume of a king, velvet tunic and puffed sleeves matched with a wooden crown painted to imitate the shimmer of gold. "You do us a great honour with this welcome, always the warmest we meet on our travels. It is a delight to once again be in the Winding Vales."

The crowd cheered. The last of the wagons rolled off the road and the players started unhitching the horses.

"Please, allow us one brief night of rest," Efron continued. "A fragment of time's shattered shard in which to recover from the road. A moment's peace, and then, tomorrow, we will perform for you all."

The crowd cheered again, then grew quieter as Efron leaned over, head turning this way and that, as if watching for hidden spies. A conspiratorial hush fell, everyone grinning.

"Would you care for a preview?"

Raul clapped as loudly as anyone. This was as much part of the performance as the following night's show, or as the poetry and songs the players would perform in the bar tonight, while protesting their desire for peace. The more the crowd clapped, the better it got.

"Then may I present the jewel of the roads, the vision whose fiery performance set the stages of Valdeblanc ablaze, my very own daughter, Yasmi Dellest!"

The canvas across one of the wagons rolled back, drawn by hidden strings, to reveal Yasmi standing on a platform, facing across the yard. Hair bright as the sunrise ran down her shoulders, across the simple grey outfit of the shifter, the company's leading role. Masks hung from her belt: a wolf, a monkey, an eagle, an ogre with green skin covered in warts. But it was Yasmi's face that drew the eyes of the crowd, as she tapped her foot three times against the boards, then held her hands out.

"The hour of the beast, you say?" Her voice seemed soft yet carried across the yard. The crowd leaned in, breath held. "Aye, perhaps, my lord.

FORGED FOR DESTINY

"Perhaps death itself is here and we poor mortals have not the will to hold it back. Perhaps war's red ruin is upon us, blood and fire, and the black of heartbreak at its end. Perhaps mountains will crack and the earth rip wide and swallow your kingdom whole."

Her voice rose and she seemed to swell, until there was no one else in the yard, no one else in the whole world.

"Those are terrible things, my lord, and the seer foretells them all. But those are things beyond our grasp. They are our fates, not our choices. The beast is a choice, and if you open that cage..." She pointed, and instead of the valley, Raul pictured steel bars and something terrible beyond. "If you open that cage, all that follows is on your soul." With one finger, she unhooked the wolf mask from her belt. A gasp of excitement ran through the audience. Raul shivered as Yasmi held it a hand's breadth from her face. "My lord, will you unleash the beast?"

She held for a moment, green eyes glittering above the mask, then swept down into a bow. The vale echoed to a riot of applause.

The moment the cheering started to subside, Efron leapt onto the stage.

"Tell your friends!" he proclaimed. "Tell your neighbours! Tell your enemies, if they have coin to pay and hands to clap! Be here tomorrow night, for the grand premiere of the latest offering from the Company Dellest."

Amid the hubbub that followed, the locals helped the players unload their wagons. Everyone wanted to peer into the boxes of props and the rolls of painted scenery, to sneak a peek at this year's story. While Efron went to talk with Valens, Raul dutifully played a more mundane part, stabling and feeding the horses.

It was quiet in the stable, so he heard the straw rustle behind him clearly.

"Shouldn't you be entertaining people?" he asked.

"Shouldn't you be serving them ale?" Yasmi wrapped him in an enthusiastic hug. "I've missed you, inn boy. Are you finally going to run away with me this year?"

Raul twisted around and hugged her back, resting his chin on the top of her head.

"I'm not much of an actor," he said. "Can't keep the lines straight in my head."

"How about if we run off to become rebels, then?" Yasmi took a step back and took on a duellist's pose, hand extended as if holding an invisible sword. "Defying the emperor himself, creating a land of freedom and beauty for all."

"I wouldn't be much of a rebel either." Raul brushed down one of the horses. "I don't have the strength for it."

"You look plenty strong enough to me." Yasmi squeezed the muscles of his upper arm. "These are bigger than last year."

"Not strong enough in here." Raul tapped his chest. "I'm not brave like the heroes in your plays, like Iron Hand storming the dark lord's fortress or Worad leading his people into the wild. I don't have the strength to face the schemes and the plots, to keep on fighting when the world has been twisted against you. The strength to break the rules."

"So you'll stay here your whole life, feeding horses and

shovelling their shit?" Her face contorted in disgust. "What a wretched fate."

"I like all this."

"Manual labour?" She shook her head. "Hard work? You're better than that, better than anything in this valley."

"Are you insulting my home?" He grinned, and she grinned back.

"Your home is a wretched hole."

"At least my home isn't the back of a wagon."

"At least my wagon doesn't stink of weak ale and piss."

She half raised her hand, and Raul did the same, but then they hesitated. She looked down at her feet, with an expression he'd never seen her use on the stage, and he withdrew his hand, rubbed it awkwardly against the back of his neck. A few years ago, a mock argument would have turned into mock fighting, the two of them grappling in the hay, but that hadn't felt safe for a few springs. He was getting too strong to wrestle someone half his size, and she . . .

"I've got something to show you," he said, brightening at the thought.

"I've heard that line before." She looked at him, and mischief glittered in her eyes. "But something tells me that's not what you mean."

He led her across the yard, which was quieting as folk returned to their work, and through the taproom, where players mixed with locals who'd taken the afternoon off. Efron was leaning on the bar, his crown sitting next to a bowl of stew, talking with Prisca but smiling at Valens, who smiled back, a small scar creasing at the corner of his mouth.

"...early draft went down marvellously in Valdeblanc," Efron was saying as Raul and Yasmi approached. "They loved hearing about Gestri's fall, and that promise at the end of something more..." He pressed his fingers to his lips. "Perfection."

"I don't know stagecraft," Prisca said. "It just seemed like an evocative story to me. If you can make it resonate with your audience, all the better."

"Have faith, good Prisca." Efron laughed. "Our show would leave the gods themselves in tears."

Yasmi leaned between them, dipped a finger in her father's bowl, and tasted the stew.

"Not awful," she said. "You're growing as a cook, Valens."

Raul's da shrugged, a slow surging of muscles like oxen at the yoke. His own bowl was empty already.

"Good work today, Yasmi," Efron said. "But the finish could still be improved. Remember, bring the energy down to draw them in, then up, for a thrilling climax."

His hands moved with his words, marking the lows and highs.

"Yes, Father." Yasmi nodded. "I'll do better next time."

"Good, good."

"I thought I might go for a walk with Raul."

"Oh, yes, why not. Spring is in the air." Efron shot a smile at Valens, then turned back to his daughter, wagging a spoon. "Don't be too long, though. We have rehearsals later."

While they talked, Raul rummaged under the bar. He unwrapped the wooden swords from their blanket, wrapped it around his new book, then thrust that into a satchel. When he straightened, satchel in hand, Prisca was looking at him.

FORGED FOR DESTINY

"What are you up to?" she asked.

"Taking Yasmi for a walk," Raul replied. "Unless you need me here."

Prisca looked from him to Yasmi, who smiled brightly. Prisca's finger drew a line through a spill of ale on the bar, and she peered at the pattern, reading omens in the wasted drink.

"We'll manage without for now, but you must wash the dishes when you return."

"I will. I promise."

"Be careful, there are patrols on the roads."

"We won't be going on the roads." Raul made for the tavern's back door. "Come on, Yasmi."

They headed across the yard, then out along the brook, past the beehives they kept to make honey for mead and over the ground where Raul and Valens sparred, then followed a goat trail up the side of the hill. Raul ran his fingers through the long grass and ferns to either side, let nature gently brush his skin.

"This one's fescue," he said, catching a stem between thumb and finger. "That one's wheatgrass. Wearing it as a bracelet on midsummer nights brings good crops the next year."

"If you're trying to impress me with your knowledge, then you're talking to the wrong woman," Yasmi said. "I dream of fine wine, braised fowl, and silk sheets, not woodlands and farming magic."

"I'm not trying to impress you." Raul blushed. "Not sure why I would."

"I bet you impress all the girls around here, though, with that tousled blond hair and those innocent eyes. I bet they love a bit of plant talk. 'Oh, my liege, how delicately your fingers caress that fern. Wilt thou also fondle *my* flower?' "

Raul blushed deeper.

"I don't really know the girls around here. Not well."

"Ah, so it's boys you're after? That explains a lot."

"That's not what I meant."

Raul frowned. He felt like his thoughts had gotten into his throat, forming a knot so tight that the right words couldn't get past. He used to say whatever he wanted to Yasmi, making these days each spring the easiest of his year. That was all he wanted now: someone to talk to, someone who wasn't Prisca or Valens.

"I don't really know other folks around here," he said. "I mean, I serve them drinks, we talk a bit, it's friendly, but they all act like I'm an outsider, like I don't really belong."

"You don't." Yasmi laid a hand on his arm, and the bite was gone from her voice. "You, Prisca, Valens, you're the only family in this vale that hasn't worked the same land for a hundred generations. Trust me, one outsider to another, you'll never really fit in."

"But it's my home!"

She shrugged. "Then make a new one. Come away with us. Bring your parents. We all know Valens would rather be in the big city."

"He would?"

"How can you know reading and writing, yet still be so dense?"

Raul didn't have an answer, so he made do with walking faster.

FORGED FOR DESTINY

"If you're trying to outrun me, you'll have to try harder," Yasmi said. "You have to be fit for a life on the boards."

"Oh yeah?"

Raul started running and she ran after him, the two of them laughing as they raced up the hill. There was a rustling as she headed into the long grass, trying to overtake him. He put on an extra burst of speed, drawing ahead, but then Yasmi's hand went to her waist, grabbing the wolf mask.

"Cheat!" Raul called out, but it was too late.

Yasmi pressed the mask to her face, and for a moment her whole body tensed, then she transformed. Grey cloth and yellow hair became a wolf's mottled fur. She flung herself forward, landing on all fours, and stretched out with clawed paws, charging up the hill in long bounds. As she got ahead, she turned her muzzle to look back, long teeth accentuating her triumph.

Raul laughed and kept running. The transformations never stopped amazing him, the moment of wonder when the shifter became the role they portrayed. He had seen Yasmi as a troll, a bear, a queen of faraway lands, and she dazzled him every time, not just her magic but how easily she fell into it. No wonder the Company Dellest were showered with praise.

She stopped at the top of the hill, waiting for him to catch up, then followed him down the other side, paws padding along the trail. He wanted to run a hand over her fur, like he'd run it over the grass, but that didn't seem right.

They walked into a wood, fragments of sunlight dappling the path, and stopped at the edge of a wide clearing. In it, rows of plants grew, spring leaves hissing against each other in the wind.

Yasmi raised a paw to her face. The mask came away and she stood human again. She sighed wearily and shook her head.

"The hemp field. You've shown me this before, and it wasn't all that interesting then. Unlicensed paper-making might stir a covert thrill in the sticks, but I see more exciting things down every street in Pavuno."

"We're not here for the hemp." Raul sat, his back against a tree, and opened his satchel. "I wanted somewhere secret to show you this."

"A book." Yasmi flopped down beside him. "How incredibly grand."

"I like books."

"I know, I know. What's this one about?"

Raul showed her the front page.

"No pictures. How am I meant to make sense of that?"

"It's called *Chivalric Virtues*. It's about heroes from history. Kings, lords, knights, overthrowing villainy and protecting their people."

"I have a hundred stories like that up here." She tapped the side of her head. "Memorised down to the last word of each speech, preserved and performed on a hundred stages a year."

"Does one of them feature a half-moon image?"

She narrowed her eyes. "What have you heard?"

Carefully, not wanting to leave a mark or a crease, Raul turned the precious pages, past long stretches of prose and three family trees, to the start of the final chapter. There, in the middle of the page, was an image of a crescent moon, pierced by a dagger. His shoulders tightened and the page trembled between his fingers as he stared at that shape, so familiar and yet so strange. Laying the book in his lap, he took off his tunic and rolled up his shirtsleeve until his shoulder showed.

His birthmark was pale against sun-browned skin, an inversion of the dark image on the page. Its edges were less clear, the moon distorted by the way his body had grown. But when he looked at the two shapes, he saw one.

"Do they look the same to you?" he whispered.

Yasmi traced the shape on his shoulder with the tip of her finger. His skin tingled at her touch.

"I'd forgotten this," she said. "Didn't make the connection."

"So they do look the same?"

"What?" She looked at his face, then at the book, and wrapped her arms across her chest, body turned away from him. "Could be. It's hard to tell, with all those stupid muscles you've been sprouting."

"They're hardly muscles at all, not compared with Valens."

Yasmi laughed. "A brown bear isn't muscled compared with Valens."

"Compared with the other farmers, then."

"You're not a farmer."

"I know." He held the book up, placing the page beside his arm. "Seriously, Yasmi, what do you think?"

She stood and adjusted the masks on her belt, so that each one overlapped the next on its left-hand side, half of each face visible to the world. She always looked so effortlessly elegant, whether wearing shifter grey or bright theatrical clothes, on the stage or in a hidden field.

"I think that you should come away with us," she said. "You'd be a terrible actor, but we always need people to lift and carry, to sew costumes and paint backdrops. You could use that reading and writing, find long-lost sagas for us to learn, or old stories for Father and Tenebrial to turn into plays, like Prisca's done."

Her voice was prickly as gorse. Raul didn't know what he'd done to upset her, but he was sorry.

"That's not for me," he said.

"You could see the whole world, not just the North March and the plains of Dunholm, but the canals of the Woven Lands, the minarets of El Esvadel, the sun setting over the Golden Ocean at Saditch. That's for everyone."

"I can't go. My family's here. My whole life. I don't know anything else."

"That's the problem, isn't it?" When she sighed, her whole body heaved. "We should go back. I have rehearsals, and you'll have a heap of washing up."

"All right, but can you stay human for the walk back? I want to hear about where you've been this winter."

Yasmi smiled, and the tension melted from Raul.

"Oh, I have been to some fabulous places..."

Chapter Four
Hanging from the Oak

"What a miserable place." Count Brennett Alder stared out across the city of Pavuno, a sprawling mess of wooden shacks and soot-stained stone. Hardly the city of scholars and priests that he had heard about in his youth, the great threat his people had crushed. "I suppose we work with what we are given."

A monument was rising at the edge of the old city, two towering triangular pillars built from the stone walls his great-uncle had torn down. There had already been changes over the years: more stables, wider streets, the demolition of the Scholars' Spire, statues to Dunholmi gods built to overshadow those of their Marcher cousins, but Alder wanted something grander, something inescapable. It wasn't enough to destroy the signs of the old order, to break their buildings and rename their land. You had to build something new on the ruins, to show everyone whose city it was. His predecessors as governor hadn't understood the need for such displays, and Alder was grateful for their failings. If he was going to earn the

Alder family the power they deserved, it wasn't enough to succeed—he had to be seen doing better than everyone.

He picked up the goblet perched on the balcony rail and carried it into the throne room. His chamberlain, guard, and three clerks followed, the clerks scurrying, the guard striding. Ketley Tur, the chamberlain, somehow carried himself with both pomposity and obsequiousness in the same crane-like steps.

Count Alder lowered himself onto the throne, blue silk robes arranged to expose the enamelled hilt of his sabre. With one arm, he propped himself up, while with the other he swirled the wine around his goblet. Red wine, of course: more dramatic when the conversation turned bloody, and drama was a channel for power. Surface mattered as much as substance.

The throne was cold and hard, as Alder's king intended. Governors of conquered provinces weren't meant to get comfortable in their posts, especially not governors from cadet branches of the royal line. Once they grew comfortable, they grew ambitious, or overly friendly with the locals, and trouble began. Alder had been sent to hold the reins of power on another's behalf. The king was in the saddle; Count Alder merely perched upon the throne.

He was still a stallion's stride more comfortable than the clerk who knelt in front of him, his robes dirty and torn, manacles on his wrists, his face bruised down one side.

"You have a fine hand," Count Alder said with a half smile, gesturing at the books piled on a table by the throne. "Very neat lettering. I'm told that the secret lies in how you cut the quill."

FORGED FOR DESTINY

The man just stared at the goblet. Off to one side, Chamberlain Tur pushed back his grey hair and peered at the books with disgust.

"A neat hand can be a virtue," Alder continued, fingers rasping across his stubbled chin, "when turned to virtuous work. Even the writing of books, under the licence of my cousin the king. But you don't have a licence, do you? And these books..." He tapped them with the foot of the goblet. "Categorisations of charms and ruminations on the essence of matter...These seem a lot like rebel books. Are you a rebel, Scaevus?"

The man hesitated, clearly choosing his words carefully.

"I am a scholar, preserving a proud intellectual tradition."

Alder opened one of the books. He knew its contents already, but if a point was worth making, it was worth making clearly.

"This one starts by listing rural charms," he said. "Heather on the bridal bed, preserving the first ear of corn, hanging fresh oak leaves above the stables. The essence of life bringing life. The author theorises that plants share an essence, and if we understand that essence, we can tap into the powers of growth and renewal. All very uplifting, until he suggests inverting the principle to blight an enemy's crops."

Alder set that book aside, picked up another.

"This one's my favourite. It runs from poultices and healing charms to killing a man a hundred miles away. All theoretical, of course, but what is the point of theory if you never use it?"

The man winced. "They're not all like that."

"Like what? Like something written for King Cataldo's

dark coven? Like you people were ripping power from the belly of the world?"

The clerk swallowed. His eyes, wide and bloodshot, focused on the goblet.

"Is this distracting you?" Alder ran a finger down the drinking vessel, across the curve of a brow, the socket of an eye as dark as his own, the ridged slits of the nose. "I wouldn't want you to be distracted."

From somewhere inside, the clerk found a remnant of a spine. It was almost impressive, how he straightened his back and stared at Alder.

"If you're going to kill me, then do it," he said. "You've stolen our land, but you won't weaken our minds. We remember. We learn. One day we will rise."

"Perhaps you will. Well, I should say perhaps your *people* will, but *you* will not." Alder nodded to the guards. "Take him down to the dungeon. Spend some time with him. If he talks about his contacts, heal him up and send him to the slavers. If not, he can burn with the books."

The clerk whimpered as they trotted him away.

"Shall I take these to the fire, my lord?" Tur reached for the books.

"Of course not." Alder waved his chamberlain back. "They'll go into storage with the rest, for our scholars to examine."

"Is that wise, my lord?" Tur looked at the books with disgust. "These are dangerous tomes."

"All the more reason to learn from them. I hear that the Stone Lords of Saditch have started an arcane library. How long, do you think, before their seers match what the North March did? How long before barbarians invade our plains again?"

Tur licked his withered lips and hesitated, on the brink of a response. If he'd had his way, then they would have burned every book on essence and the charms that evoked it. But he was too much of a coward to disobey an order, even if he might get away with it. Some days, Alder wished that he could breed more servants like Tur, but the thought of putting his chamberlain out to stud only made him laugh.

There was power in these books. Alder's grandmother had understood that. The king understood that. If Alder could show that he understood, and could add to their power, he would secure his position here, and a better position after.

"'We remember. We learn. One day we will rise.'" Tur recited the clerk's words like a mantra. "Have we heard that before?"

"Of course we have." Alder sighed and shut the book. "And others like it, from peasants talking about prophecy and a king to come. Someone is scattering this nonsense like seeds across the province."

"It doesn't matter what the peasants think, my lord, they can't change anything. Not all seeds bear fruit."

"Then let's make sure these seeds fall on stony ground."

———————————————— • ————————————————

Raul took a strip of cloth from his satchel, wrapped it three times around a branch of the old oak, and tied it securely in place. He tied another beside it, the colours of his new spring tunic and of Valens's hanging together. Prisca had shaken her head when he'd asked for a piece from her.

"Magic's good," she'd said, "but I don't need strength. Let the oak lend its power to others."

A breeze shook the green buds uncurling from the tree's gnarled body, made a hundred strips of cloth flutter and flap. Some were new like Raul's, local villagers and visitors from up the vale calling on the oldest tree they could find. Others were remnants from last spring, or before that, faded remains of old blessings. Some folks said that it was bad luck to leave them so long, others that it was bad luck to take them down. If Prisca was around for those conversations, they would turn to her expectantly. Her answer was only ever a shrug.

A pipit landed on a branch, tipped back its head to expose a pale feathered belly, and sang its high, piping song. Raul pressed his lips together and tried to whistle that tune. The bird looked at him, head tilted to one side, then fluttered back into the air, soaring gracefully away.

At the far end of the field, Longa was steering a pair of oxen through a gap in the hedgerow, dragging her plough behind. One of the inn's closest neighbours, she owned this stretch of land along the north side of the vale. As her plough passed through the hedge, its wheel stuck in the shallow ditch by the dirt road, and she cursed as she fumbled in the mud.

"Can I help?" Raul asked, approaching down the edge of the field.

"It's caught on something." Longa's efforts brought a healthy flush to her weathered face. "I can't budge it."

Raul crouched by the ditch, took off his tunic, rolled up the sleeves of his shirt, and slid his hands into the ooze. It slipped satisfyingly through his fingers, the earth parting for him. Moving carefully in case of splinters, he ran his hand down the curve of the wheel until it met an obstruction between the spokes, a flat point of rock. He took hold of it and tugged, but his fingers slipped off the smooth surface.

"Hard to get a grip, isn't it?" Longa said. "Might have to dig it out."

"I've got this."

Raul pressed his fingers deeper into the side of the ditch. The earth along this part of the vale was heavy, but not as solid as in the heights. Ploughs and spades turned it quicker and more seeds broke through. It was good earth. He forced his hand in until his fingertips found the back of the stone, curled around that edge, and heaved.

"You're going to give yourself a strain," Longa said. "Here, I'll get my shovel."

"I've got it."

Raul tensed his muscles, planted a boot against the side of the ditch, and pulled. He grunted, mud slurped, there was a trembling moment in which Raul and the earth hung in perfect tension, then he fell on his back, clutching the muddy rock.

"Told you," he said, slinging the rock into the roots of the hedge, where it wouldn't get in anyone's way.

With his help, Longa hauled her plough out of the ditch and steered the oxen into the field. Over a rise in the road, riders were approaching, six of them all dressed in blue.

"They've got lovely horses," Raul said, admiring the grey that led the way.

"Don't catch their eye." Longa pulled him off the road, into the field. "Here, make yourself busy until they're gone."

She set her plough blade to the dirt, then opened her satchel. In the top was an oat cake in the shape of the sun. Lots of farmers put them into the first line they ploughed, to add vitality and make the crops grow strong. She took it out, then hesitated as the clop of hooves stopped by the end of the field.

"You, woman." The warrior on the grey horse had one of those white belts with a shiny dagger, and pale streaks in his hair that matched the silver tree on his chest. He pointed to the oak. "What are all those ribbons for?"

Longa ran a muddy hand across her hair.

"Just decoration, sir. We do our best with what little we have up here."

"I'm not a fool." He climbed down from his horse and two of his warriors did the same. One of the others drew her bow. "We have charms where I come from too, nicer ones than those raggedy scraps. What are they for?"

Raul kept his eyes downcast, like Valens had taught him to. Hands in sight, back straight, don't make any sudden moves.

"I didn't..." Longa took a step back and bumped into her plough. The captain followed, pressing in on her, as his men drew their sabres. "It's just blessings."

"Oak blessings mean you're after, what...a long life, to last out the weather, maybe roots of your own?"

Some of the warriors snickered.

"Strength," Longa mumbled.

FORGED FOR DESTINY

"Strength?" The captain looked past her at the tree. "Sounds like something troublemakers would want. Are you a troublemaker?"

Longa shook her head. Her lips were trembling. Raul frowned. He didn't like to see his neighbours made scared over nothing.

"We need strength for farming," Raul said. "For harvesting and planting, for clearing fields and building boundaries."

The captain didn't look at him.

"If I want your opinion, boy, I'll ask you." He tipped Longa's chin back, forcing her to look him in the eye. "Next time I come past, that tree's going to be a stump, or I'll make you pull it down with your bare hands."

"It's the oldest tree in the vale."

"Now it's firewood."

The captain dipped his hand into Longa's satchel and took out the sun-shaped oat cake.

"Another charm?"

"For the field, not for us. To make the crops grow."

"I saw you people do magic on a field once. Teeth scattered in a circle. We rode through, and the ground opened like a great maw. Swallowed fifty good men and horses, then crashed back in and crushed them."

"I'm just a farmer. It's a blessing for the field."

"You people can't be trusted with magic." The captain stamped the oat cake into the dirt. "Let's see what else you're hiding."

He grabbed Longa's satchel, yanking her to one side. She tripped, banged her head against the plough, fell into the mud, half kneeling, half hanging off the handle. Her eyes crossed and her hand pressed to her forehead. She moaned.

"Hey!" Raul shoved the captain, who stumbled back, wide-eyed. "You could kill her."

Raul crouched, but before he could check on Longa, the captain recovered. With a snarl, he swung his fist. Raul caught the blow. The captain strained and Raul pushed back, teeth gritted, muscles tensed.

What was he doing? He was deliberately disobeying Valens's advice, standing up for the innocent like a hero out of the old stories. But wasn't this what a good person was supposed to do?

Hands grabbed him from behind, two of the warriors. He struggled and squirmed, but their grip tightened, twisting his arms behind his back.

"You dare raise a hand to me, boy?"

This time Raul was helpless. The punch slammed in and his stomach became a mass of pain. Another blow, and another. He would have buckled over, but the warriors were holding him up. A fourth blow, and this time he vomited, bile burning like shame. A whimper trickled out of him.

In the stories, the villains were aristocrats, archpriests, viziers, grand schemers twisting the fates of nations, or they were powerful monsters, beasts of wild instinct, fangs, and claws. It had never occurred to Raul that the real danger might be petty thugs.

The captain stepped back, shook his sleeve, and looked at Raul in disgust.

"Seems to me we've got a rebel here," he said. "Dabbling in

FORGED FOR DESTINY

dark magic, attacking the count's men. Maybe we'll hang one more charm from that tree before we chop it down."

He drew his silver-handled knife. Raul had thought that it was an ornament, but the pale morning light glinted off a strange symbol stamped into its cross guard and a blade as sharp as any he'd seen. The captain took hold of one of the ropes harnessing the oxen to the plough and severed it with a single swift slice. A second cut removed the rope at the other end.

The captain held up the rope in front of Raul.

"You ever seen a hanging, boy?"

"We weren't doing anything wrong," Raul said, his voice trembling.

"Then you shouldn't have resisted." The captain started tying a knot. "Maybe we'll do your friend too, make sure everyone gets the message."

Raul's legs were shaking. He swallowed, gulping back more words. He wanted to protest at the injustice, to cry out that this wasn't how the world was meant to work, that you couldn't go around hurting innocent people for the sake of an oat cake or a scrap of cloth. But he'd heard Valens's stories, and things never went well for those who pleaded and begged. Not with their captors, not with the audience. It took action to be a hero. He just wished that he knew how to act.

"That won't work," one of the warriors said, scratching her chin. "The rope's not long enough."

"What would you know?" the captain snapped, fumbling his attempt at a knot.

"I used to be an executioner's apprentice, before I took the

53

count's mark. You need enough rope for the noose, the drop, and the tree." The soldier looked at the tree, head tipped to one side. "Place like this, you'll need to tie it by the roots, then toss it over a branch. Not sure there's enough length on this whole plough team."

The captain flung the rope down in the dirt. He pulled out his dagger again. The corners of Raul's eyes prickled and he closed them tight, unable to face what was coming. He could feel his captors' breath on the back of his neck, hear the squelch of the captain's feet in the mud. He wished that Valens was there, then thrust that wish aside. He wouldn't want his da to die along with him.

If the world wasn't good, then at least he could be. There were worse ways to die than standing up for someone. He took a deep breath and braced himself to face his fate.

"Fuck it."

There was a click of metal tapping together. The pressure on Raul's arms ceased. He eased one eye open. The captain had put his dagger away and was waving his warriors back to their horses.

"This time's a warning," the captain said, glaring at Raul and Longa. "But I know both your faces, and if there's trouble here again, I know who to come for." He pointed at the oak. "That thing comes down by tomorrow."

He vaulted into the saddle and snapped the reins. Hooves clopped against the dirt road as the patrol continued on their way.

Taking deep breaths to steady himself, Raul held out his hand to Longa, who pulled herself to her feet. A trickle of blood ran from her hairline down her cheek.

"I should get an axe," she said, and her voice sounded heavy as she looked at the ancient oak.

"I'll help." Raul felt sick at the thought of chopping the tree down, but worse at the thought of what might happen if they didn't.

"You're a good lad." She patted him on the arm.

Raul's brow furrowed. If he was so good, would he have waited to intervene until the captain hurt her? Would he be felling a tree that had given their community strength for generations?

It had felt good, standing up to that brute, but maybe he could do better.

In the hedgerow, a pipit sang.

Chapter Five
Blood and Moonlight

The poultice was full of spring herbs, crushed grass, and soaked bread. Raul took a deep breath to get the full smell, then regretted it as the pain in his stomach intensified. He groaned and leaned over, which helped a little, and placed his hand against the bruises that were starting to show. That didn't help.

"You shouldn't have done it," Valens said, as he spread the poultice across a broad bandage that had once been part of a bedsheet. "Another captain might have cut off your head, or dragged you down to the slavers at the coast."

"I couldn't let them hurt Longa."

"Sometimes you let one person hurt to stop two dying."

"That's no way to live."

"It's the only way to stay alive."

Valens brought the bandage over. Gently, his heavy hands pressed it to Raul's sore flesh and started to wrap it around him. The cool damp was soothing.

FORGED FOR DESTINY

"I had to do something," Raul said. "They might have killed Longa."

"Don't pretend you thought it through. You did a foolish thing."

"I did the right thing." The more he was forced to explain it, the more certain he became.

"You're a serving lad in an inn, not a warrior."

"That doesn't stop the heroes in your stories."

"That's what they are, stories. Heroism isn't real. It's a word for when people get lucky doing foolish things."

Raul blinked, frowned, looked down at the ground.

"You don't believe that, do you?" he asked quietly.

Valens's breath came out in a slow growl. He tugged the end of the bandage and it pulled tight against Raul.

"I don't know what I believe," Valens said. "But I don't like seeing you hurt."

"Would they really have hanged us?"

"Yes."

"But why?" Raul's voice rose in frustration. "It's just pointless cruelty."

"Sometimes, for a conqueror, cruelty is the point."

Raul remembered the look on the captain's face, as wicked as the edge on his silver-handled blade.

"I've never seen them draw one of those officers' knives before. It cut through the rope like it was water."

"Hm." Thick, dexterous fingers twisted the edge of the bandage, then slid a charm of spiralling grass into a fold.

"It must have had a powerful charm on it," Raul continued.

Valens stepped back, looking at his work.

"It takes years of practice and just the right materials to make something that powerful," he said.

"Like the scholars used to do at the Spire in Pavuno."

"Occasionally, when they got lucky."

"And that's why the Dunholmi killed them?"

"That and politics."

"So all we have left is charms and signs?"

"It's all most people ever had."

The door to the kitchen creaked open, letting in the sound of players rehearsing. Prisca slipped through, then closed the door. There was fresh mud on her boots and on her knees. Her smile was strained. She leaned her staff in the corner, a lone figure in its solitary spot. There was a chip of flint embedded in a knot near its top, a piece of the road to stop a traveller getting lost.

"You look better," she said, and sniffed at the bandage. "Really, Valens, this is what you used in the wars?"

"It works."

Raul was used to these awkward moments between his parents, the tense silences and the carefully blanked faces. They didn't worry him anymore, like they did when he was small. There was enough comradeship to balance it out, to prove that they really were a family.

"I followed them past the gap," Prisca said. "They're proceeding into the next vale, looping toward the south."

Even without naming them, Raul flinched at the thought of the patrol. That small movement set his stomach aching again.

"Good." Valens nodded at the door. "Can't have this going on while they might gallop by."

"It's only a play," Prisca said lightly.

"Not if they know what they're looking for."

"And why would they?"

"Because they're smarter than you think." Valens pressed a thumb and finger against his forehead. "Or because you're not as smart as—"

"Let's take this outside." Prisca grabbed Valens's arm and dragged him away, though he was twice her size. She flashed a smile back at Raul. "Please put your shirt on, then find out if our guests want refreshments."

Raul did as he was told. In the taproom, Yasmi was standing by the fireplace along with two other actors. She was dressed in a bright blouse and loose trousers instead of shifter grey, but the masks still hung from her belt. She went abruptly silent as Raul walked in, her hand outstretched, full lips still.

"Come now, you can do better than this." Efron waved his hand. "'Faith, love, hope, none of these hold such power for me as—'"

"I haven't forgotten the line," Yasmi snapped. "This isn't one of Claudio's bungles."

"Hey!" one of the other actors exclaimed.

"You earned it. Now, isn't this rehearsal meant to be private?"

Efron looked around. Raul waved.

"I came to see if you want lunch," he said. "Maybe some ale?"

"Well, if we've paused anyway..." Efron's lips wiggled, and his moustache with them. "Claudio, Biallo, go find out how many want to eat, how many to drink. I have a guess as to which will be greater."

Actors headed up the stairs to the guest rooms and out into the yard, while Yasmi leaned against the bar, hair hanging across one side of her face, and looked at Raul with pursed lips.

"You look like you've been rolling in a ditch."

"Just reaching into one, to get a rock out." It wasn't a lie, and he didn't think that his parents would want him telling the whole truth. Not with how they'd responded to his return.

"Rural life really is an endless stream of joy." She sighed and the hair fell a little further across her green eyes. She peeked out through the strands. "What's to eat?"

"Bread and cheese. Maybe honey, if we have some left."

"Did Valens bake the bread?"

"I think so."

"It's one bit of cooking he's good at, all that punching and pounding the dough."

She squared her shoulders and her smile shifted into a perfect imitation of Valens's frown, as she grunted and beat the top of the bar with both hands. Her slender shoulders became Valens's mountainous bulk, simply through the way she moved. Raul almost laughed, but he didn't want to, not when Valens had just been taking care of him. He folded his arms and winced again.

"Why won't Efron let me watch the rehearsals?" he asked. "That's one of the best bits, seeing you work the play out together."

Yasmi stopped her impression and looked away.

"He's being a perfectionist. You know how directors get as they grow older."

"Not really."

FORGED FOR DESTINY

"Well, it's a thing." She looked at him. "As you'd know if you came away with us."

"Is there something special about this play?"

"Why do you ask?"

"Prisca and Valens were talking about it, and now you're acting weird."

Yasmi adjusted her sash belt, carefully judging its folds as she reworked the knot.

"It's probably because Prisca helped inspire it. Tenebrial's taken some old stories she told Father and turned them into an epic."

"An epic?"

"Truly epic. Villains scheme. Nations fall. Heroes rise. Love conquers all, or not. You'll see if you come along this evening."

"Of course I'm coming. I wouldn't miss it for the world."

"Good." She brushed dirt from his shirt, then shook her head at the other dirt underneath. "Please remember, it's just history. We keep the stories alive this way because people can't read them, and that can make the performance feel more important than anything else. But it's just a moment, it will pass, and there will be other stories."

"It's not like you to tell me that theatre doesn't matter."

"There's nothing more wonderful in the world." She hesitated, turned her head away. "But life isn't just about wonder."

The actors who'd gone to get lunch orders returned, calling out a string of names and what they wanted.

"Looks like it's time for you to get back to rehearsing." Raul took a count of how many mouths they had to feed, then headed into the kitchen. Someone closed the door firmly behind him.

There were loaves in a basket in one corner of the kitchen, light and fluffy inside, crisp and golden on the outside, but no one had brought cheese in from the cold house. He took a smaller basket down off a hook.

The sound of raised voices stopped him before he reached the back door. Valens and Prisca had never pretended that they agreed on everything. Valens said it was good to get these things out, though he usually said it with fists and teeth clenched while he stewed beneath the shadow of an invisible storm cloud. The idea that you could stand up to people, even ones you liked, had been drummed into Raul from an early age; one more reason why their response to his encounter with the soldiers had been so frustrating. But there was a difference between knowing that your parents argued and walking into the middle of it.

"He's not ready yet." Valens's voice was a rumble like rocks across the yard. "He's still only a child."

Raul frowned. Were they talking about him?

"We have to act *now*," Prisca replied, and Raul had to strain to hear her hiss. "The longer we delay, the more parlous the state of the country becomes. It's been eighteen years. People are starting to forget what we had before, to accept the new order."

"Eighteen years of wrongs to fuel their anger. Why not a few more?"

"You're not out there walking the roads. You don't see what I do. The tide is running out."

"Then drag it back in. That's what you do."

FORGED FOR DESTINY

"There is only so much leverage I can obtain without action to reinforce it. If we don't act soon, then the sacrifices we've made will go to waste."

There was a silence long enough that Raul almost stepped out of the doorway.

"What if it goes wrong?" Valens asked quietly. "What if Fabia died for nothing because we couldn't wait?"

"Fabia died believing in the plan. If we squander our opportunity, that's when she died for nothing."

Another silence. Raul shifted the basket from one hand to the other. It clunked against the wall, not hard, but loud enough to carry outside.

"Raul?" Prisca called. "Is that you?"

He stepped out, smiling. He didn't want to embarrass them by letting them know that they'd been overheard, and he was too confused to start asking questions. They were talking like they were planning something, but what? And why did they keep talking about Fabia, the friend from his da's war stories? It was all more than Raul could make sense of, so he smiled, just like always, and walked past them toward the stone-topped pit of the cold store, as if he'd been heading that way all along.

"I'm fetching cheese," he said. "The players are ready for lunch."

———————————●———————————

The yard in front of the inn had been cleared of everything except for two wagons at the front, with boards laid between them to form a stage and a rail behind to hang the scenery. Raul and Valens had brought all the stools and benches out of the inn and made more from barrels and planks. Some of the neighbours had rolled logs down the hill. Still, there weren't enough seats for everyone. Word had got around the Winding Vales that the players were making their annual visit, drawing in every farming family for miles around.

Torches burned in raised brackets at the ends of the scenery rail, and three more in cages at the front of the stage. Off to one side, a bonfire cast its own light, and kept the older members of the audience warm.

Prisca had a seat in the middle, to give her the best view of the play. When he was younger, Raul had sat on her knee, though she'd frown when he started squirming halfway through. These days, he stood at the back with Valens, where they wouldn't obstruct anyone else's view.

"Should be a good one this year," Valens said, looking at Raul from the corner of his eye. Around them, the yard was filled with chatter, fuelled by excitement and by the ale Valens was selling out of an open-topped barrel.

"They're always good," Raul said. "But Yasmi keeps getting better."

"She's got her father's gift, and more." Valens smiled fondly as Efron bustled past, heading for the stage. "Won't be long until we stop seeing her pass through."

"Really?" Raul's heart sank.

"Better money to be made on other circuits, or in one of the cities. Not Pavuno anymore, maybe, but one of the Dunholm ports, or further afield."

"Do you think she'd be happier that way?"

"You tell me, lad. You're the one she's friends with."

A hush fell across the crowd as Efron Dellest strode onto the stage. His moustache quivered as he ostentatiously cleared his throat, then spread his arms wide and addressed his audience.

"Good people of the Winding Vales, as always, you do us a great honour by being our first audience of the year. Tonight, we hope to honour you in return, with a performance rooted in the soil of this very land. No exotic adventure from far oceans for you this year, no bawdy comedy from the streets of Il Berran. Instead, I bring you a true story, a chronicle of the past, and perhaps, we can hope, an inspiration for the future. Good people, I present to you, in its international premiere, a piece penned by our very own Tenebrial Blackfinger, with assistance from myself, Efron Dellest. Starring Efron Dellest, Biallo Lavelle, and the shifter's shifter, Yasmi Dellest. Tonight, for the first time ever, feast your souls upon..." A drumroll emerged from behind the scenery. "*The True and Tragic History of King Balbianus.*"

Efron sailed off the stage on a wave of cheers, in which Raul clapped as enthusiastically as anyone, hooting and hollering in excitement. A moment later, one of the players strode on. He wore the outfit of the chorus, white cloth marked with black signs that could almost have been writing. His foot tapped the board three times, while the cheering dwindled to an expectant murmur.

"Four hundred years hence, you sit and watch our story," the chorus began. "Since when, long years have passed, our bones become dust and glory..."

It was a classic Company Dellest opening, with a short exposition followed by the arrival of the protagonist. Efron himself played King Balbianus, to no one's surprise, and he delivered soaring speeches with all the poise and grandeur his audience had come to expect. There was cheering when he united the Kingdom of Estis, and when he slew the villainous Earl Gastri in a duel. The fighting was nothing like the swordsmanship that Valens taught Raul, but it was very dramatic, and interspersed with a lot of sharp insults. Yasmi's appearances brought the biggest applause, her body shifted each time by the magic of the masks. She was the lion that led Balbianus through the forest; the troll that ruined his armies at Sonnal Bridge; the ferocious wolf that hunted him for the Lady of Woes. Each time, Yasmi was transformed in more than just appearance. She prowled as the lion, lumbered as the troll, stalked and slavered and howled as the wolf. She became those beasts fully, and Raul gaped at the sight of them.

As the play was approaching its end, King Balbianus staggered onto a moor, the canvas behind him showing rows of twisted black trees. Thick red wool hung from a gash in his tunic, as the king bled to death. The wolf was slain, victim of another dramatic fight scene, but it had done what it was summoned to do. The hero was approaching his tragic end.

The crowd fell silent. Somebody sniffed. Efron's feet thudded as he limped across the boards.

The scenery parted down the line between two trees, a trick none of them had seen before. There was a smattering of applause, which withered into intense expectation as Yasmi stepped out. She wasn't a lion, an ogre, or a bear. The belt of masks was gone. A murmur ran through the crowd as they reached a realisation: no moment of monstrosity or magic was emerging from behind the curtains that hid a shifter's transformation. It was just Yasmi, her own face and body, draped in anonymous grey, a young woman standing exposed. Power hidden in human form.

"Who is this?" Efron cried out, sinking to his knees. "Come you to staunch this wound, to save me from the destruction my pride has brought?"

"Nay, my king." Yasmi knelt beside him, speaking soft but clear, and as the actors leaned in, so did the audience. The world seemed to come closer, the black trees on the backdrop to loom larger. "I am a diviner. The omens brought me here to you, and I, in turn, bring an omen."

A flap of scenery slid down and a silvery half moon appeared in the deep blue sky.

"What say you?" Efron asked, with all the pride of an ancient king. "Is my empire to fall, now that I am gone?"

"Nay, my king. Like an acorn in the forest, your first seed has grown strong. For twenty generations, Estis will stand, and its strength will spread across the world. But one day, others will come, and the oak will be felled."

"Alas, all is ruin!"

"Not so, my king. There is a chance." She drew a dagger and handed it to him. "Spill the last of your own blood, let it flow into the soil of your kingdom. Leave your essence in the land, to rise again in that fallen generation. Through your blood, Estis will be born a second time, strong and free. The birch will fall and the oak stand once more in its place."

King Balbianus took the dagger from the diviner and held it aloft. A shiver ran down Raul's spine as its blade intersected the moon behind.

"A dagger in the moonlight." Balbianus shook his head. "Not how I wished to slide from this world, but if it takes one last slip of my wrist to save the nation I made, then so be it."

He thrust the dagger into his chest. Even Raul, who knew theatrical trick knives, gasped at the violence of the movement. Balbianus collapsed onto his side and a flap of his robe fell open, revealing a pale semicircle, like moonlight falling from above. The dagger lay across it.

"When this sign returns, so too shall our king," the diviner said, rising to her feet. She looked across the heads of the audience and met Raul's gaze. "Balbianus reborn, honour renewed, a nation restored. What was born of you, my king, lives immortal in your death."

She flopped across the king, and her hair fell across her face, so all that stood out was the symbol on his chest. The audience, well trained in the art of the finale, clapped and cheered for all they were worth, while Efron and Yasmi Dellest rose to their feet and took a bow, Efron exhorting the audience to tell their friends what they had seen.

Raul kept staring, the dagger and the moon emblazoned across his mind. The shape he had seen in that book. The shape of his own birthmark.

The symbol of Balbianus reborn.

Chapter Six
A Choice of Blades

All around Valens, people were clapping and cheering, their attention fixed on the stage. As the supporting players emerged to take their bows, the applause grew even louder. Efron's smile widened, an action that any other day would have filled Valens with warmth. Everybody was watching the stage, caught up in the thrill of the moment. Everybody except Valens.

In war, survivors learned to watch the world from the corners of their eyes, to catch the movement that would catch others off guard; though he was facing forward, he had seen Raul stiffen as the final scene played out, ready to fight or to flee. But neither of those was the boy's way. When Raul turned and ran through the back of the crowd, pushing past people to the door of the inn and out of sight, Valens knew he wasn't running from what he had seen, but toward the trap his parents had laid.

Prisca sat in the crowd, clapping with the rest, as if it was just another performance. Valens's lip curled. He spat in the dirt and turned away from her, wishing he could turn away from himself as easily. But one way or another, he had to face this.

"Going for more ale," he said to the man next to him, then pushed his way through the crowd toward the inn.

The taproom was empty, the fire burning low because no one had been in to tend it. Aside from the hubbub out front, the only sound was a creaking of footsteps on the boards above, someone pacing back and forth. Valens stared up at those boards for a long time, trying to find the courage to do the right thing, whatever that was.

"Don't tell me you're having second thoughts."

Prisca was at his elbow, wearing the pinched look she got when she thought he was being an oaf. Even with the extra wrinkles she'd grown in the past few years, the look was unmistakable.

"The boy deserves better," he mumbled.

"The nation deserves better. That's why we're doing this."

"We're lying to him. Again."

"Would you prefer to tell him the truth? That his parents died forgotten and he was destined for the same fate? That his whole country might die because one soldier doesn't have the courage to keep a promise?"

"It's not a good promise."

"Tell that to Fabia."

"Don't you dare speak her name." He turned on Prisca, muscles straining, one hand halfway to her throat. "She was a hundred times better than you or me."

"I'm not the one wearing her memory as an accessory."

FORGED FOR DESTINY

Prisca tapped his jet mourning ring. "I'm not the one threatening to give up on what she died for."

Valens pressed his thumb and finger against his forehead, which throbbed like he'd been drinking for a year. Prisca was right. He knew that. And yet, even though images of Fabia fighting off Dunholmi soldiers still haunted his nightmares, even though he yearned for the Estis of his youth, when Pavuno stood tall and his people's traditions were shown respect, he still didn't want this burden to fall on Raul's shoulders.

"I can't..."

"I know you can't." Prisca laid a hand on his shoulder. "You're not smart enough to think things through for yourself, any more than that boy is. That's why he needs the lie, and why you need orders. So follow them now and follow the plan."

"Can't we give him another year or two?"

"Is that what you want, another year stuck out here in the sticks, failing to run an inn while you listen to Old Wellic's farming stories?"

Valens shook his head. This place drove him mad. The life was so simple, so boring, and yet somehow he couldn't do it right. He was a worse innkeeper than he'd ever been a warrior, and some of the captains he'd served hadn't thought he was good at that. He couldn't keep this up. But admitting that, acknowledging he wanted out, made him feel even worse.

This was why there were no heroes, however hard you looked for them.

The door swung open and Yasmi walked in, still dressed in her shifter grey. She glared at Prisca.

"What are you doing to Raul?" she snapped.

71

"There are beverages and sweetmeats in the kitchen," Prisca said. "Enjoy your celebration. You were every bit as dazzling as you needed to be."

"Of course I was, but that's not the point."

"It's all the point you'll get."

Yasmi hesitated, and Valens hoped she had the sense to give in. He liked the girl—no, not a girl, a woman now—as much for her own sake as for Efron's, and while picking a fight with Prisca might show courage, it didn't show sense.

"Fine." Yasmi waved a hand. "I'm going back where I'm appreciated."

She stormed out.

Prisca turned to Valens. Her look reminded him of another day, eighteen years before. A storm had lashed his face as he stood on the walls of Pavuno. Every other guard had taken shelter, sure that no threats were coming that night. Most of the veterans who had earned palace duties didn't even stand out here, fobbed their wall duty off on some lowly youth instead. But the shield wall wouldn't hold if one man faltered, the camp wouldn't be safe if you didn't take your watch. So Valens stood in the storm and watched for the army they all knew would come.

Someone else had strode down the walkway, her waxed cloak flapping around her ministerial robes. She'd had to lean into the wind not to be blown away, but she'd made her way to him, and as the wind tore back her hood, Minister Prisca had stared into his eyes.

"You're Valens, aren't you?" she'd shouted over the wind.

"Yes, Minister." He'd hidden his bewilderment that any minister knew his name, let alone Prisca, the centre of every strategic argument Valens heard while he stood sentinel in the great hall.

"I've been watching you, Valens. I need you to help me with a plan..."

That had been eighteen years ago, in the heart of a glorious empire. Now, in this backwater inn, she looked at him with that same intensity.

"Ready?" she asked.

He sighed. Once you committed to a tactic, hesitation only made things worse. He wouldn't neglect his duty, however miserable it was.

"You lead."

"Of course."

He followed her up the stairs, poorly maintained boards creaking under their feet, and down a corridor to Raul's room.

"Blood for luck," Valens whispered, and stabbed the air with his finger.

"Blood for luck," Prisca echoed, then knocked on the door. "Raul, are you all right?"

The pacing of footsteps behind the door stopped, then started again.

"I'm fine."

"Really? You don't have anything you want to discuss?"

Footsteps again, then the door opened. Raul, his hair wild and his eyes wide in his slender face, stepped back, letting them in. He held a book bound in red leather, open to a page near the end. It showed that symbol Prisca had burned onto Raul back at the start: a dagger through the moon.

"What is this symbol?" Raul asked, and the strain on his

face filled Valens with shame. Normally, the lad smiled at everything. "Does it really mean what Yasmi said in the play, about a king being reborn?"

Prisca sighed and took the book from Raul's hand.

"I should take more care which books I give you," she said. "I was so excited to share, I didn't consider the consequences. I should have known that you were too smart not to put the pieces together."

Valens wondered whether she had found a book that already had that symbol in, or whether she added it during the copying. Maybe the whole book was one of her inventions, and copies were now circulating around Estis, scholars and collectors bidding against each other for a fake book by a fake author. Prisca was good enough to do any of those things, and to fit it seamlessly into the world.

"Am I...? Is this...?" Raul pulled up his sleeve, revealing the scar on his upper arm. The shape had stretched as he put on muscles the last few years, but their grisly handiwork was unmistakable, the shape clear. "Is my birthmark this symbol?"

Prisca nodded solemnly.

"It is."

"And does that mean...? Am I...? Do I have something to do with King Balbianus?"

Prisca perched herself on Raul's bed and patted the space next to her. He sat down, looking at her with those wide, trusting eyes, while Valens closed the door and leaned his whole weight against it, blocking out the world. That door blocked him in too, as he watched Prisca betray their son to save the kingdom.

"You know that I'm a diviner, don't you, Raul? That I read the omens for people, find fragments of their future, help them to follow the best path."

"Of course."

"Well, back before the war, I did that on a grander scale. I read the future for earls, dukes, even for the king. My advice guided a nation.

"Then Dunholm came, and their allies, and no amount of good advice could save us. They saw the signs too, and they countered the best moves we could make. They tore away our territories, then our homeland, and finally they marched on Pavuno itself, to kill King Cataldo and his coven, to smash the army Queen Junia had built. It didn't take a diviner to see that the nation was lost.

"Still, I kept looking to the future and to the past for signs. I learned about King Balbianus, about the prophecy that had been granted to him, and I began to hope.

"As the city was falling, a baby was brought to me. A son of Princess Aemiria, Junia and Cataldo's own daughter. A baby with a birthmark in the shape of a dagger through the moon."

Valens looked away. This part was too much, even for him. He'd seen Aemiria around the palace, struggling with the twin burdens of pregnancy and their looming doom. He'd heard the screams of childbirth gone wrong. He'd seen the grief of her family, the sad bundle brought out for burial in the rose garden. Aemiria's funeral pyre had still been smouldering when the last guards were sent to the city walls.

But it was the details that sold the story. The details would let people believe.

"As the city was falling, that infant was entrusted to my care. There was no way that the royal family could escape what was coming, but one baby, in the right hands, might have a hope. Valens and I brought you out of the city, as we had promised to do. We brought you here to raise in safety, away from those who might hurt you. We've kept you safe, but we...I..."

Prisca was no Yasmi, but she could act, in her own way. As she sniffed back the dry imitation of tears, her head hanging so that her dark hair obscured her face, Raul took her hand and looked tenderly at her.

"You saved me," he said, and looked at Valens. "Both of you."

"We did." Valens nodded. That part at least was true. He remembered a tiny hand reaching out of a yellow blanket, gripping his finger with a soft strength that seized his heart.

"And this..." Raul ran his fingers over the mark on his upper arm, tracing the pattern as he looked at the same symbol on the page. There was a seriousness in his eyes that broke Valens's heart all over again. "It means I can save the country? That I'm the one the diviner foresaw?"

"You are our best hope," Prisca said. "The entire time we've been here, I've kept up my divining, to foresee a path you could follow. It's not easy, and it would be dangerous, but if you listen to the signs, then you can save us all."

Raul stood, pushed his hair back from his eyes, and paced the floor again.

"Why didn't you tell me sooner?"

"Because you weren't ready. Because one wrong word could have put your life in peril. Because we wanted to shelter

FORGED FOR DESTINY

you, to let you live your own life as long as you could. But in the end, destiny has beaten us."

Raul clutched the book tight. The room was so small, and his legs so long, he could only pace three strides each way before he had to turn. The absurdity of those lurching movements made Valens want to grab him and sit him down, to give him the steadiness he needed. But Prisca had been clear. The real signs said that Raul must make his own decision, and their whole plan relied on Prisca's reading of those signs.

"I'm not just one more war orphan?"

"You're so much more."

Prisca's gaze flickered to Valens. There was a command in that look, and even if it hadn't been her place to issue orders, she was the only comrade he'd had for eighteen years. He had her back.

"You're our son," he said, and sank to one knee. "And our king."

Raul giggled, a sound quite unlike him, and pressed a hand to his mouth.

"You can't... This is ridiculous. Get up, Da."

"I will get up when you accept who you are." He couldn't look at the lad, but his downcast gaze only added to the image of a faithful servant honouring royal blood. Prisca knelt too.

"The sword," she said quietly.

"What sword?" Raul asked.

Valens sighed and stood.

"I'll be back."

He walked down the corridor, then up a staircase at the back of the inn, taking an oil lamp from a niche. Every step felt like dragging rocks. Outside, people were laughing, toasting the players. Someone was strumming a lute. Efron was singing, using that rich voice that made Valens tingle. Soon, the seats would be cleared and there would be dancing. One of the brightest days of the year. A moment of joy amid the dreariness of rural life, a night of fun for these simple farmers.

For the first time ever, Valens wished that he was one of them.

He pushed back a hatch and climbed into the eaves. Resting on a high rafter was a bundle, four feet long and wrapped in dusty blankets. He took it down, feeling the honest weight of steel. To a liar like him, it was an accusation.

The black of his mourning ring caught his eye. There were worse things in the world than lying. It wasn't like the boy was really his son, whereas he knew for sure that Fabia had been his friend.

"Die well," he whispered.

Fuck off and save the day, a memory responded.

He carried the bundle back down to Raul's room. The boy was standing by the window, Prisca beside him, whispering in his ear as they watched the revellers below. The lad seemed subdued, as though he had set down a great weight but still felt the weariness of it. Valens knew that feeling.

He laid the bundle on the bed and reverently pulled back the dusty covering, to reveal two swords. One was old and battered, its edge uneven from where he'd worn away notches, its leather grip lumpy around the strip of lead he'd used to improve the balance. A mass-produced sword from an earl's armoury, given character in the same way as Valens, through hard knocks and experience. He'd oiled it before hiding it away, and that gave its scratches a dark gleam.

FORGED FOR DESTINY

The other sword shone in the lantern light. It had been polished until it shone like silver, and swirling patterns were engraved on the flat of the blade just above the hilt, a moon at their heart. The leather around the grip was red and there was a ruby in the pommel.

"Balbianus left a blade," Prisca said. "A symbol that everyone could see, a sign of his authority."

"The one he killed the wolf with, in the play." Raul stared at the swords, his mouth hanging open, eyes shining with wonder.

Valens looked at Prisca, and she gave a tiny shrug. Why not make it that sword? An accidental detail to help the lad accept his new truth. They certainly weren't going to tell him about the armourer Prisca had visited on the White Coast, after learning of his skills and divining that old age would soon take his secrets to the grave.

"The very sword," Prisca said. "The first part of your inheritance."

Raul reached out, and Valens half hoped that the lad would pick up his own old blade, thinking that was more worthy of a king. A lad who chose honest, timeworn steel over polish and gemstones, that wasn't a lad he could have kept lying to.

But they'd stuffed Raul full of stories. All those books that Prisca brought back from her travels, all those tales of warriors and heroes that she'd made Valens tell in the inn night after night. They'd given Raul a sense of drama, and he picked the dramatic sword. The ruby in the pommel gleamed bright enough to match his eyes.

"I have a destiny," he proclaimed.

Chapter Seven
Only a Town

Raul could barely believe how quickly they left his home behind, once the decision was made. One morning, he was feeding the chickens and checking the spring vegetables for slugs. The next, he was packing his clothes and sword, ready to get on a wagon and ride away.

His sword. That one thing made all the difference, because it meant that he wasn't just leaving his life behind—he was setting out on a mission.

At first, he expected to ride out on horses, galloping for the capital like Balbianus in his prime, or to trek across the countryside, seeking shelter with friendly locals like in the story of Merin and Varn. But Prisca had other plans.

"We need to avoid drawing attention," she explained.

"Everyone pays attention to actors," Raul pointed out.

"To actors, yes, but not to their stagehands."

Efron seemed happy to have them along. He talked more about having an extra pair of hands than he did about the

FORGED FOR DESTINY

money Prisca gave him, and he kept smiling at Valens. Even if Raul didn't have a destiny waiting for him, it would have been worth doing this. And so, less than two days after a play had turned his world upside down, he looked back over his shoulder to see his home disappear around a corner of the road, wondering how long it would be before he returned.

If he ever returned. There was a thought like lightning through his chest, thrilling and terrifying in equal parts.

Raul enjoyed the swaying of the Dellest wagons as they rumbled down the roads out of the hills. It was soothing, like lying in a field while the grass bent in the wind, watching the clouds drift by, except that instead of clouds it was the whole world, full of people and places he'd never seen before. The woods they passed were less dark and dense, the fields larger and flatter, and there were big communal barns at the edges of the villages, their boards painted in proud, vibrant colours. Even the one that had burned down, at a quiet village they passed hurriedly through, had a grandeur to it, blackened beams standing strong despite their torment. Someday soon, he thought, a new barn would be built around those beams.

It was a good time to be travelling. The flowers were coming out, splashes of yellow, red, and blue scattered across meadows and draped through hedgerows. Bees trailed lazily from one flower to the next, and birds drifted overhead or flitted like magical spirits between the trees. A robin perched on a crossroads shrine, where rabbit bones and whittled figures lay at the foot of a square stone, offerings to help lost animals find the right trail and lost people find their path through life.

Raul laid a gift of his own at the foot of the shrine, a small clay cup he'd snatched up on the way out of the inn. That simple, familiar shape in his hands had helped him cope with leaving home behind, but now he felt like he could let go, as Valens had done when he'd sworn the inn over to Wellic's wide-eyed younger son. In that spirit, Raul set the cup down by the stone and filled it with water for the birds.

"This is yours now," he said, a lump in his throat as he stepped away from the cup. He wasn't sure who he was talking to: the birds, the land, whatever god guarded this road. Whoever it was, he hoped that they enjoyed the gift.

With a sigh and one last glance back across the Vales, he turned his footsteps to catch up with the wagons. He had a bigger life now.

Every night, if they weren't performing, then the players practised. Yasmi insisted, stirring the others from around the fire, drawing Efron's attention away from drinking with Valens or reworking dialogue with their playwright Tenebrial. They worked their scenes until Efron applauded and Yasmi smiled. Then everyone lay down to sleep beneath the stars, or beneath the canvas sheets that sheltered them from spring rains.

Two weeks out of the Vales, they crossed a low ridge where a scarecrow guarded the first shoots of corn, and looked down upon a riverside town. It was the biggest place that Raul had ever seen, bigger than any of the villages where the players had stopped to perform on their journey down through the hills, bigger even than the market town where Efron had bought canvas from a local merchant and Raul had helped paint a new backdrop for the play. This place looked like it

FORGED FOR DESTINY

wouldn't have just one merchant house, but a dozen of them, and who knew what else. A pointed spire towered over the north end of the settlement and the whole place was walled in by a wooden palisade on an earth rampart. There were enough hearth fires for a haze to hang above the rooftops, like a mist that had darkened with age.

"Is that Pavuno?" Raul asked.

"That?" Yasmi, sitting between Raul and Efron on the board of the leading wagon, shook her head and laughed derisively. "Of course that's not Pavuno! Pavuno's a city."

"That isn't a city?"

"Close your mouth, you're catching flies." She tapped his chin. "This is Laspeti. It's big enough for two performances, maybe three, then we'll be on the road again."

"Not the road this time," Efron said, flicking the reins to keep the horses moving past a lush clump of grass. "We will board cargo barges, wagons and all, and take the river straight down to Pavuno."

Yasmi's eyes narrowed. "What about the towns and villages between here and there? That's thirty performances at least, some of them in big squares, a penny each from the audience, not to mention the time to refine our act."

"Our focus is on Pavuno this year."

"Our focus, or Prisca's?" Yasmi, her voice still light and sweet, shifted her legs so that she sat a little further from Raul.

Efron shrugged. "Her money means that we can take this opportunity for a longer run in the capital. With all the rebuilding work, and the growth of the merchants' quarter, that might be the path to profit. We spent whole years there, before you were born, performing a fresh play each season to packed crowds. What once was may be again."

"Settle down in the city?" Yasmi raised her eyebrows. "Proper beds with proper sheets, no winters of cabbage and old corn? I could live with that." She leaned back and patted Raul on the shoulder. "You'll like Pavuno. It's full of bright colours and big buildings."

"And my destiny," Raul whispered to himself.

Without meaning to, he raised his hand to his upper arm, touched the place where his birthmark lay hidden. The sign of Balbianus, of the first king's essence, power emerging from the land in its time of need. He'd become obsessed with his responsibility—it was the first thing he remembered when he woke in the morning and the last thing he thought of as he drifted into sleep.

He hoped with all his heart that he could live up to it.

Approaching the town's gates, they were surrounded by the sound of hundreds of people all packed in together. There was a smell as well, sweat and smoke and sourness, like the tap-room at the end of a long winter's night. Valens frowned at the sight of the entrance.

"Those gates," he said. "Are they usually open like that?"

"During the day, yes," Efron said.

"But they lock them at night?"

"Bar them, I believe. To keep the wolves out and the pigs in."

"Hm." Valens ran his scowling gaze the length of the walls.

"Don't worry, my friend." Efron patted the grizzled old warrior on the shoulder, and his hand lingered. "You can leave any time you like. No one is going to trap you here."

FORGED FOR DESTINY

"That's what everyone thinks, until the trap is sprung."

"Trust me, the guards in this place, they want an easy life." Efron leaned over and his voice descended into a stage whisper. "Whatever you three are plotting, they'll never notice."

Valens shifted his grip on his walking staff and laid his other hand on the knife on his belt. He had hidden his sword securely under one of the wagons, and shown Raul how to do the same, but Raul didn't doubt for a moment that his da could protect them if trouble came.

The guards on the gate looked too cheerful to be trouble. Raul knew that he should be suspicious of anyone in the occupiers' blue, but it was hard to fear the round-faced woman in a butter-stained tabard or her colleague who was sleeping on his feet, wedged into the place where the gate met the wall, a horseshoe hanging from the wood above his head.

"Look who's back." The guard beamed and tapped her comrade with the butt of her spear.

"Wassat?" He rubbed his eyes and looked along the small train of wagons. "Is it that time of year already?"

"A delight to see you both again, my friends." Efron handed the reins to Yasmi and jumped down. He took each guard's hand in turn and pumped them vigorously. "Will you be coming to see us perform?"

"Wouldn't miss it," the buttered guard said. Her tabard was faded, its white crown symbol fraying; her comrade's was a brighter blue stitched with Count Alder's tree. "But if you're coming in, you'll have to pay the toll, same as always, to maintain the roads and walls and that. It's gone up since last year."

"It so often does." Efron sighed ostentatiously and pulled a pouch from inside his tunic. "How much will it be?"

While he counted out coins, the sleepy-eyed guard ambled over to the wagons.

"You're new, aren't you?" he said, looking Valens up and down, then up some more. "Reckon I'd remember a brute like you."

Valens stood very still. It was a dangerous sort of stillness, one Raul had seen in the moment before Valens decided which way to lunge with his practice blade, or whether he needed to throw out a troublesome drunk.

"He's mostly here to move scenery," Yasmi said. "And to play guards in the palace scenes."

"Makes sense. I'd think twice if I was an assassin and I saw him standing behind the king." The guard looked at Yasmi, and it was a very different look from the one he gave Valens, with a wider sort of smile. "Is there an assassin in it this time?"

"That would be telling."

"What about monsters? You playing a lion again? I loved that lion."

"Something even better." Yasmi pushed her hair back behind her ear as she leaned over, smiling at the guard. "Can you guess what I might be?"

Raul's stomach tightened and he looked away, toward Efron and the other guard.

"You know these aren't allowed anymore," the guard said, holding up one of his coins. It was silver, like the rest, but didn't have the triangular symbol that obliterated the monarch's heads on old Estis currency. "Got to be restamped at the North March mint in Pavuno before you can use them."

FORGED FOR DESTINY

"I'm terribly sorry, I don't know how it slipped in there." Efron pressed another coin into her hand. "Why don't you keep it, make sure it gets stamped, eh?"

"It would be the patriotic thing to do." The unstamped coin, still bearing Queen Junia's face, disappeared into the guard's pouch, then she carefully deposited the other coins in a box chained to a stump by the gate. "That all seems to be in order. You can go on in. There should be space for you to park down by the docks, next to the new stables they built for the count's messengers. If there's any trouble, you let us know."

"You're too kind, Sergeant. Have a wonderful day."

———————————— • ————————————

Yasmi tossed her head back and belted out the last words of the song, letting her voice soar on one final, piercing note. For a moment, there was no sound in the bar except for her. Then she jerked her head forward, stamped her heel on the table, and the whole room burst into applause. She smiled from the very centre of her heart, every fibre of her body trembling in response to the crowd's adulation.

"Again, again!" some of the drinkers cried, as others tried to start up a new song, one they could all join in on. Yasmi bowed, bracelets jingling as one hand whipped back with a small flourish and she jumped down onto the rush-strewn floor. *Always leave them thirsty for more.* Her mother had taught her that, along with so many other tricks of the trade. Now Yasmi had taken her mother's place, just as she had taken on her masks, and she took her guidance oh so seriously. Without books to tell stories, theatre had returned to its rightful place as the heavens that shone down upon the culture of this land, call it the North March or Estis, and she was its brightest star.

She accepted a cup of mead that someone was pressing on her, relished a sip of the sweet and heady drink. People gathered around, small-town folk with small-town tastes, impressed by anyone with half a finger of talent, dazzled by the likes of her. The only ones who weren't impressed were a pair of whores standing in a corner, one male and one female, both wearing embroidered veils over clothes fast falling out of fashion. Attention was the bait that hooked their clients, and she had stolen it all.

Among those crowding around was a man a little older than her, with shoulder-length blond hair and the sort of smile that could sell wagon wheels to ducks. Around his neck was a copper coin on a chain, like many merchants wore, part of their first profit; a charm to imbue them with wealth, or perhaps a way to show off. As any actor knew, one prop could serve many purposes.

"You have a beautiful voice," the merchant said, his voice deliciously rich. "It speaks of a passionate soul."

"And your presence speaks for itself." She pressed a fingertip against his chest, which was every bit as firmly muscled as she'd hoped.

"You're quite the dancer too, especially given the challenges of dancing on a tabletop."

"Do you dance?"

"I know how to follow the rhythm."

FORGED FOR DESTINY

"I'll be the judge of that." She smiled. "Perhaps they'll play a jig later, and you can show me your moves."

"I can't think of anything I'd like more."

The merchant's expression was too eager, too expectant. Where was the push and pull, the back and forth, the dance of words?

"I have to get back to my companions. Perhaps I'll find you when the band strikes up."

She slid past him. His hand shot out and circled her wrist. On instinct, her other hand went to the rabbit mask at her waist. There was a door ahead, another to the left, with an easy route through the legs of the crowd if she needed out.

"Don't disappoint me," he murmured, leaning in close. His breath was rancid, and now that she looked again, those muscles in his arms were knotted rather than sleek.

"I wouldn't dream of it." She pulled in her thumb and squeezed her hand out of his grasp. "Until later."

She worked her way through the crowd, enjoying the smiles, the compliments, the admiring looks and the hungry ones. It didn't matter whether they wanted you or wanted to be you, her mother had said, so long as they sang your praises. Folk had sung her mother's praises across half a continent, had lit candles in their windows when she died. One day, they would know Yasmi's name that well.

She flung herself down in a seat next to Raul. The stool's legs were uneven and it tipped back, so she went with the movement, leaning against the wall and pressing an arm against her forehead. Take the moment, find the drama, play with it.

"The stage is a fickle mistress," she announced. "So demanding. I am utterly drained. Do you kind gentlemen have anything to refresh me?"

"Seemed a pretty small stage for you," Valens said, pouring ale from a clay jug, thick fingers clumsy around the cup. "Sure you aren't losing your touch?"

The cup was earthenware, rough against Yasmi's lips, the ale a touch too bitter, but it refreshed as it went down.

"How do you do that thing with your feet?" Raul asked, blue eyes wide behind his ridiculous blond fringe.

"It's called dancing," she said.

"Very funny. I meant this bit, I've never seen it before..."

He pushed his chair back and tapped his feet back and forth for her to see. For someone who had never seen the move, he did a remarkable impression of it. He'd been the same with scenery painting, with packing wagons, even with the songs they sang on the road. His ability to learn was obnoxious, when compared with the work her father made her put in every damn day.

"Where did you learn that dance?" he asked.

"From my mother."

Yasmi polished off her drink, took the jug from Valens, and poured herself another. Valens raised his own cup, a swift movement as if about to do the same, but froze as its lip met the lips of his mouth. As if he was laying down a great burden, he set the cup on the table. By some trick of the candlelight, his scars deepened as he let the cup go.

"Do you miss her?" Raul asked. "Your mother, I mean?"

Again with the questions. Two weeks on the road, and he

still hadn't run out of them. If he was going to ask anyone, it clearly ought to be her, but did he have to keep on asking?

"I never miss," Yasmi said, striking an archer's pose as she summoned wordplay to fend off substance. "My string, stained by ancient hunter's blood, is the essence of accuracy, the taut line that my prey crosses from life to death."

"I know that one." Valens's brow crumpled. "From five years ago, that play about a civil war."

"*Sisters in Sorrow.*" Yasmi smiled and straightened the edge of her tunic. "Well remembered."

"I like the ones with wars."

"Of course you do. All that action and heroism."

"There's no such thing as heroes."

"How tragic. I hear whispers that the nation is crying out for one."

"Yeah, well, maybe one or two heroes. They're rare, is all."

Valens glanced sideways at Raul, while the boy looked oblivious down at his feet, trying to master the dance. That look from Valens was one Yasmi was starting to detest, as drenched in guilt as the great plays were soaked with blood. Whatever nonsense Prisca was dragging them all into, the man needed to lighten up.

"Who are those people with the veils?" Raul asked, glancing at the pair in the corner of the room.

Yasmi almost laughed out loud. A whore would be one way to lighten Valens's mood, but she didn't think her father would like that.

"They're entertainers," she said with a smile.

"What sort of entertainers?"

"They use their bodies."

"Like acrobats?"

"Bedroom acrobats, perhaps."

"Oh!"

Raul's mouth fell open. Yasmi watched him, curious to see how he would process this discovery. Valens seemed equally curious, and a little concerned. He clearly hadn't told his son everything that happened in armies on the march.

"I suppose that must suit some people." Raul shrugged. "I don't think I'd want to pay for it."

With his looks and his boyish charm, she doubted that would ever be an issue for Raul. The big city was going to be a revelation for him, if his parents ever let him out from under their gaze. Perhaps Yasmi should arrange something, a secret night out while Prisca was deep in her books and Valens drinking with her father, throw a few temptations Raul's way to see what took his fancy. And if, at the end of a night of drinking and dancing, he wanted something more, then it would only be right and proper to bring him back to her own room; she couldn't let this charming innocent fall prey to one of the city's wicked women.

She flashed Raul a smile and was pleased at the warm smile she got back.

"The barges leave tomorrow," she said. "A few more days and we'll be in Pavuno. I shall eat spiced lamb, buy a new silk blouse, and bask in the adulation of a public crying out for true art. How about you, Valens? You used to know the city. What are you looking forward to?"

"An armourer. Put a proper edge back on my sword."

"How terribly serious." She turned to Raul. "What about you?"

"I want to see all of it," Raul said. "The markets, the taverns, the temples, Rack's Scar, Old Gate, whatever's left of the walls." His expression turned serious. "And the palace, of course."

The palace. Now there was a thought. If they had half a year in the city, or maybe more, then she could work on getting the attention of courtiers, and with it an invitation to perform at the palace, where she could impress Count Alder. True, his support was a step away from royal patronage, but it was the step that could see her summoned to court, with all the fame and desire that brought. Tours of the great cities of Dunholm and its allies, where her very name would bring a riot of anticipation to those waiting before the stage.

"I won't just see the palace," she said. "I will perform there."

"For the conquerors?" Raul scowled.

"Who cares about the politics?" Yasmi shook off his appalled look and shook out her hair. "Art is for everyone. And speaking of art, I hear a jig starting up."

She hesitated. Part of her wanted to dance with Raul, to see what he could do with those feet and a little encouragement. But he was looking so serious, she could hear the questions piling up in his head.

"I have to go," she said, bracelets tinkling like chimes as she rose. "I promised a man a dance."

Chapter Eight
Choose to Do Good

True to Efron's word, they performed *The True and Tragic Tale of Balbianus* only once for the people of Laspeti before they packed up and made their way onto a barge heading to Pavuno.

The biggest boat Raul had ever been in before was a coracle for fishing in the high lakes. The barge was huge by comparison, big enough to carry the whole company of players, their wagons and possessions, and a cargo of wool stored beneath their feet. The vessel creaked and groaned from its tarred hull to the bulging triangular sails. But though it seemed novel and exciting at the start, it soon became as soothing as the wagons, drifting slowly down one river, then back up another broader one after the two joined.

The players took the opportunity to rehearse for the big city. Valens sharpened every knife he could find. Prisca spent hours scrutinising the bundle of books she'd brought along. But Raul was happy to watch the world drift by, from the simple cottages of reed cutters to the grand churning wheels of water mills. This was his country, his people, his destiny. He committed every passing face to memory, the faces of people he was going to set free.

And then, one morning, he emerged onto deck to see the river clogged with boats, the bank crowded with piers and huge wooden barns, the hillside so full of buildings that they spilled out of sight, up to the peaks beyond.

"Not bad, is it?" Valens asked, laying a hand on Raul's shoulder. "Even after everything."

"It's amazing." Raul stared open-mouthed as they slid between ships toward the docks. "Like a hundred towns put together."

He had imagined the city as something singular, hundreds of matching houses in neat rows with a few temples and taverns between, the ruined ring of fallen walls around the outside. The reality was messier and far more fascinating. There were walls of mud daub, wood, and stone; roofs made from planks, thatch, and slate; round buildings next to square ones, tall overshadowing small. They crowded together like a herd of sheep huddling for warmth on a winter's night, but with strange gaps in the flock, stretches of bare road or rubble like scars on the bark of an ancient oak. And rising from them, thousands of voices all shouting over one another.

Within an hour, the barge was moored. Raul was the first down the gangplank and onto the rain-slicked quay, rushing to see everything.

There were more people around the dockside of Pavuno than he had ever seen in one place, maybe more than he had seen in his whole life put together. There were the people on the barges, loading and unloading cargo, fixing sails and cleaning oars. There were the ones in the smaller boats, rowing passengers up and down the river or calling out for work. There were the people on the docks, carrying goods back and forth, arguing over heaps of barrels and stacks of clay jars. There were the runners, the customs collectors, the guards, the merchants with their coin medallions, the people passing through on their way to some other part of the city. In the precarious wooden buildings behind, men and women leaned out, calling down to the sailors. Up the hill behind those buildings, crowded streets ran to markets and squares.

There was sound all around him: the waves of chatter, the thud of boxes, the bumping of boats and creak of wagons. The smell too, ten times stronger than Laspeti, with notes that shifted with the wind and with the barrels rolling past, so that one moment there was fish amid the sweat and smoke, the next spices or fresh bread.

"Out of the way!" A warrior shoved Raul aside and a patrol rode through, all dressed in blue. Instead of the bows they carried on the roads up in the Winding Vales, these ones carried spears resting on their shoulders, a light spring rain running down the shafts. Following them came two more, crowns emblazoned on their chests instead of a tree. Everyone stepped aside and no one met their gaze.

Raul suddenly felt very conspicuous. He clutched his bundle tight, then thought better of that and tried to rest it casually on his shoulder, but the sword poked out from under the old yellow blanket. In the end, he wrapped his hand around the middle of the bundle and let his arm hang by his side.

Prisca and Efron walked up the sloped front of the barge,

FORGED FOR DESTINY

onto the dock. They were wearing hooded cloaks to keep off the rain.

"Still enjoying the spectacle, eh?" Efron said, handing another of the cloaks to Raul. "I can understand. After all these years, after all of her hardships and trials, Pavuno remains a wonder. I never tire of seeing her beauty."

"How could you?" Raul drew the cloak across his shoulders and pulled up the hood. "This is amazing! Look how tall the houses are! And did you see the acrobat over there? He was juggling fire!"

"I forgot how far out into the sticks you live." Efron chuckled. "Well, that's changing now, Raul. Come, see the city." He looked at Prisca. "I mean, if that's still the plan."

"You might change your mind five times a day, but I don't." She waved a hand. "Let's see this performance venue you've acquired."

They walked uphill away from the quay, into the crowds. To Raul's amazement, the people parted at every turn, creating a way they could get through, a path that closed in behind them. It was as if everyone knew where everyone else was going and planned their movements to avoid collisions. It felt as much like magic as the wards over doors and the small shrines at junctions.

This part of the city was new, full of wooden buildings that couldn't have been older than Raul. In places, new ones were rising on empty spots, or old rubble was being cleared. He saw a builder lower a bull's head into a foundation ditch, a charm to make the building sturdy and strong. Even the shrines at the major road junctions were new, their edges sharp and their stone pale, the gods on them strange figures carved in a flowing foreign style.

Up ahead, across a stretch of blackened dirt, were the remains of the city walls, huge square-sided stones, some nearly as large as Raul. Some lay where they had fallen eighteen years before, blocks stretching down the slope like ivy growing across bare ground. Others had been broken up, parts taken for new buildings, leaving behind irregular rubble and hard-edged grey splinters. Labourers roamed across those that remained, bringing ropes and pulleys and logs to roll the stones away.

"For the count's monument to the war," Efron explained. "Lest we should forget."

There was a twisted edge to his voice that Raul wasn't used to hearing from the jovial player.

"A governor must make his mark, if he wants to keep governing," Prisca said. "Though hopefully that won't be the case for long."

Efron looked around in alarm, surveying the people passing by.

"No one is listening," Prisca said. "I have read the omens, and we are safe for now."

Instead of carrying on toward the ruined walls and the old city beyond, they followed the upper edge of the riverside district, the boundary where buildings were rising like flowers into the spring air. Some of the buildings here were taller, better painted, with guards out front and wealthy merchants visible through the windows, while servants scurried back and forth from side doors. There was lots of traffic, but also lots of space, so they could easily step around the wagons full of timber.

"It's good to see life returning to the old place," Efron said. "The bounty of the gods blessing their people once more."

Prisca snorted. "This isn't life. These newly risen merchants are carrion feeding off a corpse. How many Estian voices have you heard since we arrived?"

Raul tipped his head to one side and listened more attentively. Many of the voices here sounded strange to him, compared with those in the Winding Vales, and some had accents he'd never heard before. Perhaps half of them sounded like Prisca or Valens, but as many sounded like the warriors who set fear running as they rode up the Vales.

He heard more voices like Prisca's, but less well-spoken, as they passed another building site. Labourers in patched trousers and sleeveless smocks called instructions back and forth to help them raise the wall of a house, its timbers darkened by the rain. Occasionally, a man with finer clothes and a Dunholmi accent shouted at them or waved a stick around. A pair of warriors stood in a tent on the other side of the wagon route, watching and laughing.

"Behold." Efron pointed downhill, past a half-built shop, to a large building with double doors open onto the thoroughfare. "Our new abode."

They trudged through the rain to the building, which towered over them, twice as tall as Raul's old home. Through the doors was a hall many times the size of the inn's taproom, with a high ceiling held up by square timber posts. To one side was a bar, and at the far end was a raised area, with a rail high on the wall behind it. Raul tipped back his hood and gazed around, trying to make sense of what he was seeing.

Why would someone set up an inn without tables and chairs? And why would it need all those ropes and pulleys at the back? Then he saw the hooked hoops on the rail, like the ones the players hung scenery from, and the pieces slid together.

"It's a house for acting in," he said, delighted by the realisation.

It had never crossed his mind that a building like this could exist, somewhere just for the performance of plays. Was there anything that couldn't be found in a city?

"This is no mere house." Efron leapt onto the stage and spun around to face them, arms spread wide. "This is a palace of dreams. We have a bar, a stage, a waiting room for the cast, and chambers above to rest our weary heads."

"How come it's here and empty?"

"A troupe of dancers of the night from Dunholm commissioned it, then decided not to make the sojourn to the city, given the tumults of the day. Under the circumstances, I was able to hire the place for a very reasonable fee."

Prisca narrowed her eyes.

"You've used my money to rent a whorehouse?"

"A would-be whorehouse."

Prisca hit one of the pillars with the side of her fist. It wobbled and sawdust spilled through a crack in the ceiling.

"Not even a well-built whorehouse."

"Nothing our crew can't make good. It is a prestige building, one that will bring us the attention and the audience we deserve."

"You're a dolt, Efron."

"Really?" His shoulders sagged, and so did his moustache. "Have I been an utter fool?"

"Perhaps, but there's not much to be done now, and at least it's somewhere to stay." Prisca scooped up the sawdust and let it run through her fingers. Her eyes grew distant, as they often did when she was looking for signs. "At least we'll fit plenty of people in to hear Balbianus's story, before the roof falls on them."

"Is that the plan?" Raul asked. "For us to join the theatre and help with the play, until..."

He hesitated. He wasn't sure how much Efron knew about what was happening, how much they could say in front of him. The other players thought that Raul and his family had come to the city in search of new opportunities, but Efron spent a lot of evenings with Valens, and sometimes talked with Prisca about the play.

"I shall check the chambers," Efron said, heading for a set of stairs by the bar. "You two can find me once you're done with family business."

Once he was gone, Prisca turned to Raul.

"A little more discretion, please," she said. "I know that I said the omens were good, but care is still important."

"Sorry." Raul licked his lips. "Is this what we're going to do, join the theatre? Yasmi will be happy, she's been telling me I should run off with them for years."

At least, he thought she would be happy. Her eagerness to talk had lessened now they were spending so much time together, but she still said she wanted to show him the city, and that seemed like a good sign.

"We'll use this as a cover, somewhere to sleep and an explanation for why we're here," Prisca said. "Officially, we manage supplies for the Company Dellest. That will justify our roaming the city while I gather the information I need."

"Information?"

"Records of past diviners, to help me navigate our best course and envision how you will liberate the nation. Many of the critical texts are banned, so we will need to acquire copies discreetly, or obtain them from the authorities' secure stores. And of course, we will remain watchful for new omens."

"Of course." Raul nodded. "Perhaps you could teach me to read the signs, so that I can help?"

"Perhaps. For now, I need you to fetch Valens from the boats. I want his honest assessment, before Efron fills his head with whispered fancies about this so-called palace."

Raul looked around and smiled. "I like it here. There's a bar in the corner, Da can go back to innkeeping."

Prisca's lips pressed together in a tight smile. "Don't tell him that yet. I wouldn't like to spoil the surprise."

Raul pulled his hood back up and headed into the rain, his blanket-wrapped sword tucked under the folds of the cloak. Valens had told him to be careful now so many people were around. He wouldn't let the blade out of his sight until they were safely settled in the playhouse.

He walked along a bustling street, heading downhill. He figured that as long as he kept going that way, he would eventually end up at the river, and so the docks. Finding the barges should be easy then, even in a place as huge as this. He ambled down the hill, weaving left and right to avoid bumping into people who seemed to effortlessly avoid each other, while the rain grew heavier, running from his hood and down his cloak.

FORGED FOR DESTINY

That rain cleared the streets and let him walk faster, as people retreated into shelter.

With his hood up, Raul almost didn't hear the cry of pain. It seemed distant through the drumming of raindrops on waxed cloth, but he stopped and looked around. In the Vales, such a plaintive cry meant a sheep trapped in a ravine, though he hadn't seen any sheep since reaching Pavuno.

Down a narrow street, a woman was kneeling in the mud, papers scattered in the puddles around her, cheap pulp dissolving as easily as the ink. Two warriors in blue stood over her. One was jabbing at the woman with the tip of his riding boot.

Raul walked toward them, his grip tightening around his sword.

"Please," the woman said, "it's for contracts, for shipping abroad. I'm a merchants' clerk."

"Likely story." One of the warriors stirred the papers with the tip of his spear, then spun its butt around to strike the woman in the chest, knocking her onto her side. "I see that charm on your belt. That's for divination. These pages are for a diviner's book."

"It's a charm my father left me, for good luck. That's all."

"You people say 'luck' a lot, when what you mean is 'magic.' I've heard about the luck you brought the rest of us."

"Are you arresting her?" Raul asked loudly, to be heard over the raindrops. "I think she'll come quietly. You don't need to hit her."

One of the warriors looked around.

"What's it to you?"

"You shouldn't hurt anyone unless you really have to."

The warrior laughed, guffawing like Raul had just told the most cunning joke.

"Yeah, well, I *really* have to do this. Get in my way, I might have to hurt you too."

The warrior brought the spear back, ready to hit the woman again. Raul grabbed hold of the weapon and clung on tight. The warrior's hands slipped down the rain-slicked shaft before he tightened his grip and turned, staring in shock and anger at Raul.

The other warrior lunged with his spear. Raul let go, side-stepped the attack, and stepped forward, bringing his arm up. He'd thought that professional warriors would be hard to fight, but his elbow slammed into the side of the man's head, and he staggered, the spear sliding from his grip.

Raul spun, cloak flying around him, and faced the one who was still standing. His hood limited his vision, but it also hid his face, and right now, that seemed like a very good idea.

"Let her go." His voice was edged with righteous anger, his skin flushed and muscles tensed. "She's not doing any harm."

"Resisting arrest." A voice emerged from one of the door-ways, followed by another warrior. She wore a captain's white belt around her waist. She carried a sabre and a shield. "Attacking His Grace's troops. Rebellion. You're both fodder for the gallows field."

Three more warriors followed her out of the building where they'd been sheltering from the rain. Raul couldn't fight them all with his fists, but he wasn't going to let them hurt this woman. He carried the essence of King Balbianus in

FORGED FOR DESTINY

his soul and the weight of the future on his shoulders. It was his duty to protect the people of Estis.

He wrapped his hand around the grip of the sword and let the blanket fall from it to the floor.

"Please," he said, as he took hold of the scabbard. "You don't have to be like this. You can choose to do good."

"I did," the captain said. "That's why I'm here. Get him, troop."

The warriors rushed at Raul. He drew his sword and shrugged off the fleeting disappointment when it failed to glint in the light. He dodged one blow, deflected another, caught a third on the blade, then twisted, turning the spear aside and stepping around so that he could go on the attack. A shudder ran up his arm at the impact of steel on flesh. The soldier he'd hit grunted and blood streamed down her side.

Raul's stomach churned and his throat tightened at the sight of that blood, at the strangely distant realisation that he had caused the moan of pain as she sank to her knees. Then the others were on him, and he had to push that feeling down to focus on the fight.

He darted and dodged, lunged and lashed out, used all the tricks and manoeuvres that Valens had taught him. Instincts took over, one movement leading into the next, as he responded to each threat in turn. He tripped a warrior, shoved him into another, drove a blow aside, drew blood with a stab to a shoulder.

The warriors were all around him. This wasn't like fighting with Valens by the brook, one-on-one, with the worst consequence a few bruises and some mockery over dinner. This was blood and pain and the threat of a noose at the end. He was in the centre of a maelstrom of blows in the pouring rain, his movements so frantic and his footing so unsteady that he was tiring already. He couldn't see what was happening at the corners of his vision, but he couldn't stop to pull back the hood.

In the chaos of the fight, the clerk ran away down the rain-slicked street. That was something, at least. Perhaps Raul could do the same. It wasn't heroic, but he had done what was needed. One more attempt to take them all down, one last chance to make Valens proud, then he would accept his limits and the lesson learned.

He feinted left, lunged right. It should have caught one of the warriors, but as the blow was falling, the captain's sabre lashed out from the blind spot at the edge of his vision. Raul pulled his blow back and the blade missed his arm but hit his sword hard. The sudden withdrawal put Raul's wrist at an awkward angle and the captain twisted her sabre to exploit that. Raul's blade was jerked around, the grip slipped in his hand, weight overcame the last grasp of rain-slicked fingers, and his sword fell into the mud.

Instead of a dramatic clang there was a splat, and his intricately decorated blade lay in the dirt, the ruby in its pommel muted.

"Nice sword," the captain said, kicking it away. "Someone comes from money. Wonder how much your parents will pay to keep you from swinging."

Raul's heart was racing, his sword arm trembling from fingers to neck. They had him surrounded, the captain with her sabre outstretched and her shield raised, the others grinning as they looked down to see this unusual sword.

FORGED FOR DESTINY

That gave him his moment.

He flung himself sideways, into one of the distracted warriors. The man's feet slid in the mud and he fell with a thud. Raul leapt over him, trampled the yellow blanket in the dirt, and ran, cloak streaming.

"After him!" the captain yelled.

Raul ran for all he was worth. He was fast, but that wouldn't be enough, not in a city full of enemies. He turned right down the next street, then left, taking twists and turns. No one had planned the rebuilding of Pavuno, they'd just flung buildings up wherever there was a spare space, and sometimes where there wasn't. With the rain driving people off the streets, it was easy to get lost in those twists and turns. The sounds of pursuit vanished into the rain and the artificial canyons of wood and stone.

The street was turning into a stream as he stopped to catch his breath. He looked back, but no one was coming.

The scabbard was still in his hand, wrapped in fine red leather to match the handle of his sword. His cheeks burned with shame at the reminder of what he had lost. The symbol of his heritage, of his mission.

He clutched his wrist, which ached from the blow that had disarmed him. So much for the chosen one. How was he meant to save the nation when he couldn't even keep hold of his sword?

"Then what?" Count Brennett Alder asked, turning the sword in his hands, watching the candlelight wink in the gem on the hilt. It might possibly be a real ruby, though Alder wasn't convinced. It certainly wasn't a good one.

"We called in other patrols," the captain said, not looking up from the flagstone floor. "Scoured the streets for three hours and sent riders to guard the roads out of town, but no luck."

Alder watched the water drip from the captain's cloak, forming a puddle that soaked into the knee of her trousers. She held herself well, for someone facing the consequences of a significant failure. Attacks on the warriors of Dunholm were rare; attacks by men who could afford engraved swords were unknown. Alder's father would have whipped the captain for letting the attacker get away or, perhaps, if he was in a forgiving mood, would have ordered someone else to do the whipping. But Alder's father had spent his life driven by resentment at not being king, a poison that had ruined his judgement and, in the end, his heart. Alder had learned what not to do from watching him.

"Hardly surprising that you couldn't find him, if you didn't see his face." He smiled at her. "A tall youth in a waxed rain cloak could describe hundreds of labourers in this town."

"Yes, my lord." The captain's shoulders, which until then had been braced tight, eased a little, and she let out a long breath. "We did our best. I'm sorry we didn't do better."

"At least you brought this to my attention." Alder tapped a finger on the flat of the sword. "It's distinctive and expensive. In the hands of someone more informed than you, it will help us to identify whoever is behind this attack and perhaps to rein in a rebellion before it can grow. This man thought he had found a soft target to begin his campaign. You and your soldiers did well to prove him wrong."

FORGED FOR DESTINY

He clicked his fingers. Ketley Tur slid out of the shadows at the side of the throne room. The chamberlain's shoulders were stooped, grey hair hanging past his cheek.

"My lord?"

"Arrange two days off for the captain and her troop, with good meals and some of the sweet ale from my stores."

When others heard that, they would be extra vigilant for signs of trouble. That was the sort of leadership Alder's father had never understood.

"Thank you, my lord." The captain bowed deeper. "Two of mine were injured. They've seen a physician, but..."

"They will see mine." Alder waved a hand. "Wait outside. Someone will make the arrangements."

"Thank you, my lord."

She strode out, head held high, while Tur crept over to the throne.

"Should I take that, my lord?" he asked, reaching for the sword. "I can start making some enquiries."

"I think I'll keep it."

Alder hefted the blade. It had a decent balance and a good edge, a sword that, despite appearances, was made for fighting. He preferred a sabre himself, but whoever chose this weapon knew their blades. He wanted to keep it close while he considered what else they knew, what they had planned, what they were doing in his city.

"I might start a collection." He tapped a gold bracelet on his wrist, which had once belonged to the chair of Estis's House of Earls. It had the weight of so much North March art, without delicacy or nuance, but he hadn't chosen it for its sophistication, as he explained to his underlings: "Souvenirs of a conquered country. My own small attempt to tap into the essence of the March."

"Very good, my lord."

"Still, something is stirring. Delayed tax payments, diviners in the hills, and now this. Send a description of the sword to our agents and offer a reward for information leading to its owner."

"Yes, my lord."

"And let's look again at arranging a grain dole for the poorer districts. My predecessors did nothing but aggravate the people, we need to start winning them around."

"Really, my lord? Do we have the funds for that?"

"How much does a small show of largesse cost us, compared with a rebellion?"

"These people are villains, my lord." Tur raised a skeletal finger. "Pandering to them will only—"

"We have been given a colt to tame. All it has known until now is the whip, but it will take kindness to soothe the steed."

"If you say so, my lord."

Alder looked sternly at Tur, who shrank inward, his robes hanging loose around his shrivelled form.

"I do say so, and you should learn to do the same."

"Very good, my lord."

Alder snorted. His lip curled in a derisive sneer.

"Very good will be when these people stop bucking against us. This is merely an adequate start."

Chapter Nine
Signs and Omens

The scabbard sat in the middle of the table, an accusatory red finger stabbing straight at Raul. The leather was darkened at the edges, where the damp hadn't quite dried out overnight. He should have taken better care of it, just like he should have taken better care of the sword.

All around them, the theatre was full of bustle, as the Company Dellest settled into their new home. Barrels rumbled across floorboards, crates banged up staircases, people shouted instructions or sang as they worked. Bundles of pungent herbs had been hung in the dressing room to ward off the moths, and more fragrant ones in the upper halls to deter spirits. While the company's footsteps thudded in the corridor, none of them came into the back room. The miasma of anger and regret would put anyone off.

"I'm so sorry." Raul sat with his arms tight against his sides and his hands under the table, fingers clasped around his aching wrist. Every time he looked at the scabbard, he felt that wrist twisting back, the pressure as the handle of the sword pivoted from his grasp, as his fingers slipped across the damp grip. He swallowed and looked away, then looked back again, knowing that he had to face his failings.

"It's only a sword." Valens laid a hand on Raul's shoulder. "It'll be all right."

"It's not just a sword! It's Balbianus's blade, handed down from generation to generation so that *I* could save his kingdom. You told me that yourself. If I've lost it, how can I be worthy of his legacy?"

"I'm sure Balbianus had other swords."

"Not like that one. I have to get it back." Raul looked across the table. "Don't I, Prisca?"

Prisca scratched her finger back and forth across a corner of the table. When she looked up, her eyes were narrowed.

"That sword matters," she said. "We must discover what happened to it."

"Prisca..."

Valens's fingers tightened on Raul's shoulder. This was the voice he used on someone drunk enough to disturb the inn's other customers, the voice from before he decided to throw them out.

"The sword matters," Prisca said again. "Are you going to tell him otherwise?"

Valens pressed his thumb and finger to his forehead. His lips pinched together.

"I need to read the signs." Prisca opened the satchel that sat on the floor next to her, and took out a small brass bowl. "Find me material to work with, preferably something from the Vales. Wine from the inn if we brought any, perhaps bones from that side of salted pork if we haven't finished it."

"I'll go ask."

Valens walked out, his footsteps joining the rest of the thuds and thumps.

"I haven't seen that bowl before," Raul said. "Is it made for divination?"

"It comes from the land that is now El Esvadel. I use it to achieve greater resonance."

Prisca turned the bowl over, revealing two sets of images engraved on the outside. One was an oak, shown first as an acorn, then a sapling, then in its full glory, and finally turned into the timbers of a house. The other side showed a baby, a child, a grown woman, and a grave. Flecks of green lay in the corners of the engravings, the patina of age not quite cleaned away.

"They're growing older," Raul said, looking at the images. "Are they meant to help you look through time?"

"In some ways you're quite insightful, aren't you?" Prisca said, running her finger across the image of the grave. "Yes, the bowl seeks to express the essence of time, to draw out our place within it. By tapping into that, we can reveal the aspect of the object or question that concerns us. A stronger connection brings us closer to the essence of the thing that we seek, and so will create a more reliable result. Do you understand?"

"Not really, but I suppose that's why I'm not a diviner."

"You suppose correctly, if incompletely."

She smiled at him. Prisca's smiles never had that crinkle around the eyes that Valens's did, but it was enough to make Raul relax.

"You'll use the bowl to find the sword?" he asked.

"I shall try."

"And then I can go and get it."

"We shall see."

Raul made a silent promise to the world. He would retrieve the sword that Prisca and Valens had entrusted to him, because it was the thing a hero would do, and because it would stop this guilty churning in his guts.

Valens stomped back in, carrying a jug and a stack of clay cups.

"Will milk do?" he asked. "It's from the company's goat. Efron swears blind he bought it in the Vales."

"We work with what we are given."

Prisca flipped the bowl right side up and sat it next to the scabbard. Valens poured milk into the bowl and into a cup for each of them, then sat down next to Raul.

The knife Prisca drew from her belt was short and slender, little more than a finger's width of iron with an inch of blade on the end. That blade had been sharpened and polished so finely that it was almost white. Prisca pulled up her sleeve and ran the blade across her forearm. Raul winced as skin parted and blood dripped into the bowl. As the milk curdled, Prisca slid the bloodied blade into the open mouth of the scabbard, tugged a cloth from her belt, and wrapped it around the wound. Her gaze became unfocused as she dipped her fingers into the bowl, then flicked them, leaving spatters across the table. She repeated the movement twice more, then sat back and stared at the results.

"Do you always have to do that?" Raul asked. "The blood,

I mean. I've seen you read the flight of swallows or the blowing of leaves, and that didn't need blood, but when you use the bowl, do you have to—"

"Hush, lad." Valens laid a hand on his arm. "Can't you see she's concentrating?"

Prisca leaned forward, staring at the pattern on the table. She took a drink from her cup, and then another. One finger trailed through the spatters of blood and milk, the curdled lumps and glistening liquid around them. When she had helped the Vales' farmers by reading the coming weather in the flight of birds, Raul had thought it was the most beautiful thing in the world. This had a hardness to it, blood-dark and brooding.

"The sword will come back to you," she said.

"Where is it?" Raul peered at the patterns. Was that one shaped like a tower, or a house? Did it mean something that those two were close together?

"It will reveal itself. For now, that's all that concerns us."

"But I can get it. Please, tell me."

She gave a frustrated shake of her head.

"For the third time, Raul, it will return. You will not endanger our endeavour in a needless pursuit."

First, she had been disappointed that he lost the sword, now she was disappointed that he wanted to go after it. He felt like he couldn't do right.

"Please," he whispered. "Tell me."

"Listen to Prisca," Valens said. "Don't put yourself in danger over this. There'll be enough trouble later."

"I suppose." Raul took a sip of his milk, then spat it back out. "Does it matter that this has gone off?"

Valens sniffed his milk and pulled a face.

"The boy's right, this has been out of the goat too long."

Raul leaned forward, filled with a new hope.

"Could that mean the omens were wrong?" he asked, pointing at the contents of the bowl. "Could we still find out where the sword is?"

Prisca looked into her half-empty cup. She sniffed and frowned, then shook her head.

"The reading stands, and we have other work to do." She pushed the cup away and stood. "Valens, put the scabbard somewhere safe. Raul, you're coming with me."

The sign above the dockside tavern was in the shape of a face. One side was painted white with black eyes and mouth, the other black with white.

"Who is she?" Raul asked, looking up at the sign.

"That depends on which face you ask," Prisca replied. "Like most people, she has more than one."

"Not people in the Vales."

Prisca gave a brief, sharp laugh.

"You're correct, of course. And that's why you are who you are. This country needs a leader of total honesty. But remember, for now, we can't admit your identity."

"Don't we need to tell people, to rally them to fight for freedom?" Raul thought back to the stories that Valens had told him as he grew up. "Otherwise how will they know to rise up?"

"First, we need to make sure that people are ready. Trust me, I've been thinking about this for a long time."

She pushed open the tavern door and they stepped into a cloud of smoke and sweat, the city air refined and concentrated into something even more potent. The atmosphere was very different from the inn back home. There was no welcoming charm above the door, though there was an eye carved into a beam above the bar. People sat forward over their tankards, leaning toward each other in the light from the small windows. Several heads turned as Raul and Prisca walked in, not to welcome but to watch. The conversations were as hushed as the whisper of reeds scuffing across the floor.

Prisca bought three tankards of ale from the barman, then led Raul to a table in the corner, where labourers in worn canvas clothes were sitting, thick gloves tucked through their belts. As Prisca approached, one of them nodded to the others, who got up and walked away, leaving their seats for the new arrivals.

"Good to see you, Appia," Prisca said, setting one of the ales in front of the woman. Like the other two tankards, it had a split face crudely drawn on one side, less an engraving than a series of scratches. "How are your people?"

"Half the docks are still empty, and the new merchants ride us ragged for clipped coin, but we find a way to provide." Appia looked at Raul from hooded eyes, then raised an eyebrow at Prisca. "Who's the straw-topped ship's mast?"

"This is my ward, Raul."

"Nice to meet you." Raul held out his hand. Appia eyed it for a moment, then shook. Her grip was firm, her palm calloused, worn even by farming standards.

"You too, I suppose."

Appia drew the tankard toward her, and there was a clink as something fell into her lap. She looked down, then drew a rectangular cloth-wrapped package from inside her tunic and set it on the table. "Our friend on the coast tells me this is the one you're after."

"You didn't check?"

"I was never much good at letters. Whole books full of them make my head ache."

"And the others?"

Appia sucked air through the gaps between her teeth.

"Well now, that's more complicated."

Raul tensed, set on edge by the way Prisca picked up the package and slid it into her satchel, every movement slower than normal. He wished that he still had the sword. Then, if someone betrayed Prisca, he could challenge them to a duel, teach them a lesson. He wasn't so sure that he could beat Appia with his fists.

"We had a deal," Prisca said, once the book was out of sight, and her stare hammered into Appia. "Break your word and I'll break your business."

"You think you're that well connected?" Appia raised an eyebrow.

"You think I'm not, after all these years?"

"My people do the hard work on these docks. I see everyone who passes through, meet most of the ones who matter."

"I travel the entire kingdom. The people you miss, I meet. People you never even see. People who matter. People who rely on my pen and my ability to read the signs. People whose business I've brought your way."

FORGED FOR DESTINY

"That's it, though, isn't it? It all boils down to business." Appia tapped the table. "Our deal was that I'd bring those books here from the Woven Lands, which I have, smuggle them past the inspections on the docks, which I've also done, and sell them on, which I will. But right now, the highest bidder for books is the palace, and I don't think that's where you want them to go."

"Count Alder is buying books?" Prisca leaned back. "I wasn't expecting that."

"Makes sense, doesn't it? Sure, he seizes some, but paying causes less fuss. This new governor's smarter than the last, and he doesn't like trouble in his town any more than I do."

"If you've been following the governor's habits, then you know where he's keeping these books, and the others they've been gathering since the invasion. That information could be invaluable."

"Maybe, and maybe we could make a deal on that. But right now, I've fulfilled the deal we have, and there was nothing in it about who I should sell those books to."

Appia swirled the ale around her tankard and a little slopped over the side. Prisca stared at the spill on the table, like she was reading something in it. Raul peered at the small puddle, but all he saw was a shape like the patches of a black-and-white cow.

"You don't want to sell to the palace," Prisca said. "Times are changing, and that would look bad when the change is done."

"I've found a balance point." There was a hardness in Appia's hooded eyes. "The scales of this city finally sit right, and my people don't have to worry where their next meal's coming from. If you're here to tip that balance, then we're going to have trouble."

Raul tensed, not just at the words but at her tone. Maybe it was a coincidence that, as Appia leaned forward, the barman reached under his counter and the woman two tables over leaned back, one hand halfway into her tunic. But maybe it wasn't.

"Change isn't always bad," Prisca said, as calm and collected as if she was sitting in their own tavern back home. "It brings opportunities."

"Opportunities for the few, pain for the masses. I know how this works."

"What if there was an opportunity to shift the scales, to take away one of the threats you face? To make a better deal for your people?"

"Dreams are for the night. I've got mouths to feed."

"And that's why you shouldn't sell those books to the palace. In time, they'll bring you far more profit elsewhere."

Appia sat back in her seat. She pulled a scrap of frayed string from her belt and, without looking down, started twisting it into knots.

"Tell you what, you pay me a bit extra, I'll make sure they get sold around town instead. My people get what they're worth, and the governor can grab his books for free later."

"Those books are important. They'll tell people about their history, where they come from, where their future lies. Those books will give them hope."

"Hope won't buy bread or beer, and that's what my people care about."

FORGED FOR DESTINY

Appia's fingers twisted around her scrap of string, the knots taking on the shape of a tiny person, like the straw dolls from harvest time. Prisca looked at Appia through narrowed eyes, then turned to peer out through one of the windows. There was a creak and a thud, followed by men shouting to each other.

"Raul," Prisca said, "Appia's colleagues are unloading a wagon. Why don't you take off your tunic and assist them?"

Raul stood. If lending a hand was the way to make friends, then he was happy to do it. He unbuttoned his tunic, draped it over his stool, and rolled up his sleeves.

"Back soon," he said.

"Wait." Appia stared at Raul's upper arm. She set her string doll aside, drew the hard-wearing gloves from her belt, and held them out. "These will help."

In the look of suppressed curiosity on Appia's face, Raul saw Prisca's plan. He made sure to reach out with his right arm, so that the sleeve pulled back further, revealing the half of his birthmark that wasn't already on show.

"Thank you." He took the gloves and headed for the door.

"Is that...?" Appia asked, watching him leave.

"What do you think?" Prisca asked.

It didn't take long to unload the wagon and roll the barrels to the back of the tavern. Appia's friends were even more experienced in moving barrels than Raul was, knowing when to push and pull, how to balance a barrel on its edge to get through a gap. By the time they were finished, Prisca was out front, wearing a narrow smile. A frayed string doll peeked over the edge of her belt.

121

"All done," she said. "Appia has seen all sorts of sense. Now we should get back to the theatre."

"You saw something in that spill, didn't you?" Raul asked as they walked away. "You knew how Appia would respond."

Down the dock, a crier was ringing her bell, promising news of which cargoes had come in from where. Beyond her, labourers unloaded the lumbering cargo barges, while travellers boarded sleek-hulled passenger boats.

"The world is full of signs, Raul. You just have to learn to look for them."

Chapter Ten

Histories and Violence

Raul hefted the axe, feeling the weight of it in his hand. He shifted his grip up and down the haft, working out where would give him the best swing. Valens had taught him how to do this while chopping wood for the inn's fires, but now he wondered if it had really been about hearths and ovens, or whether that had been a pretext. How much of his life had been preparing him to face his destiny?

"I've never really fought with an axe," he said. "I don't suppose you have any swords?"

Appia snorted and turned. For a moment, moonlight caught the edge of her own axe, before she drew its blade into the alley's darkness.

"Swords are illegal, remember? Unless you're running the place, of course."

"But you're smugglers, can't you bring them in anyway?"

"Why risk it when there are axes?"

Out in the street, a wagon was rolling past the front of a tall

123

house with a steeply arched roof and shutters reinforced with iron. As the wagon approached the alley, a shadow separated from those cast by its cargo of wool bales. The unmistakable silhouette of Valens stepped into the alley mouth.

"Three guards out back, right?" Appia said. "I told you."

"There were." Valens took a cloth from his sleeve and wiped the blade of his sword, the only one they had. "It's hard to get good guards these days."

He looked around. Half a dozen of Appia's dockers stood there, and even without the cloths across their faces, he could never have told them apart.

"Where's Prisca?" Valens asked.

"Here." A smaller shadow shifted toward him.

"You ready?"

"I am."

"Then it's time."

"Eighteen years of planning, and we start in a place like this. Can you believe it?"

"I believe in the plan." Valens's ring tapped against the hilt of the sword. "I believe in you."

He leaned down to press his forehead against Prisca's. Raul couldn't remember the last time he had seen his parents so close. He smiled, though no one could see.

"I believe too," Prisca said. "And I believe in Raul."

That made his heart swell until he felt like it was pressing against his ribs.

"All right," Valens said. "Blood for luck."

"Blood for luck," the older hands echoed, making small stabbing motions.

FORGED FOR DESTINY

Valens raised his sword. "Let's steal our history back."

When they had first talked about this, Raul had pictured the gang of them creeping up to the house that held the confiscated books, carefully cracking open a door and sneaking in. Valens had quickly made clear that wasn't how it would work. Speed trumped subtlety tonight, because they didn't know how long it would be before more guards came around. They would go in hard and get out fast.

They strode across the street, Raul and Appia leading the way. This was his first action as a freedom fighter, the beginning of the struggle he had been born for. He picked up speed, practically running at the door, axe drawn back. Then he brought it around in a two-handed blow, like Valens had taught him. Splinters flew as the blade slammed into the door, and a crack ran to the top.

"Gods, boy." Appia swung her axe, hitting the same spot as he pulled back. "You're stronger than you look."

One more swing reduced the wood around the lock to splinters. Inside, someone was shouting in alarm. Valens charged the door, turning his shoulder into a battering ram. The door crashed back into the wall and he strode through. Raul followed close behind.

The house had a grand entrance hall, with a tiled floor and a staircase running up the back. A pair of warriors in blue tabards stood behind the broken door, an overturned jug and palm-sized picture cards scattered by the chairs behind them. Three more were running in, spears levelled, shouting in alarm. The rush of air through the open door made blazing torches flare, throwing warped shadows up the walls.

Raul raised his axe and took a step forward. Valens shoved

him, and he stumbled bewildered to one side. Three arrows thudded into the wall where he had stood, while two more shot past Valens. One of the dockers grunted and slumped against the doorframe.

"Don't give them range!" Valens charged across the room, dodging past one of the warriors and knocking another into the wall. He thundered up the stairs, sword swinging at a band of archers.

Raul ran after him. Two of the warriors moved to block his way. He caught a spear on the haft of his axe, turned it aside, and stepped inside the warrior's reach. He mustn't hesitate, mustn't let the moment overwhelm him, like when he'd faced those warriors in the rain. He swung the axe hard, straight into the man's shoulder. There was a wet crunch as the blade cleaved through chainmail and sliced flesh to shatter the bone beneath. That sound, the scream that accompanied it, and the pale, pained look on the man's face made Raul feel sick, but he mustn't stop. These people were the conquerors. They had earned this. He pressed his foot against the falling warrior and pulled his axe free, ready to face the next one.

The other warrior stabbed her long-bladed spear at Raul, who sidestepped. The blow would still have hit, but Raul stretched out his axe and the blade of the spear screeched down its haft before catching the head. The axe was wrenched from Raul's hand and clanged to the floor.

"Got you, you little fucker." The warrior grinned.

Raul grabbed the haft of the spear with his left hand. With his right, he grabbed the hilt of the sabre hanging from her waist.

"Hey!" The warrior let go of her spear and grabbed the

FORGED FOR DESTINY

hand stealing her blade. Raul let go of the spear too and punched her in the face. It wasn't like when he'd scrapped with other kids in the Vales growing up, or even like the barefisted fighting at the harvest fair. He hit with all his strength, as if his fist could drive this woman from the world. Her head snapped back and she fell. The sabre, its pommel in Raul's hand, slid from its scabbard with a satisfying snick.

It had been a handful of heartbeats since they'd come through the door, and already Raul's head was full of things that he didn't want to think about. The wet thud of the axe. The breaking of bone beneath his fist. A warm spatter across his cheek. This was heroism. This was what was needed to save the world. He looked up to see Valens striding up the stairs, sword clanging against the archers' sabres, and he swallowed the bile rising in his throat.

He could do this.

In the moments that it had taken him to beat two enemies, the room had descended into a brutal melee, dockers in grey rags and warriors in bright blue fighting in the twisting torchlight. Shadows lurched across the walls. Cries of pain and of anger echoed around the room. There was a thud as Valens flung one of the archers off the stairs, and a scream as an arrow pierced the man behind Appia.

Into the chaos strode Prisca, as calm as if she was walking through a meadow. She paused in the middle of the room, looked left and right, then up the stairs, her hand resting against her satchel.

"There." She pointed up the stairs. "Raul, come with me. Appia, you can deal with this."

"Can I really?" Appia hit a warrior with her axe, then

turned to defend one of her gang from a spear. "Don't let these fuckers get out."

Valens was at the top of the stairs, the last two archers retreating in the face of this towering mass of muscle. Both had abandoned their bows, drawing their sabres instead. As Raul and Prisca reached the top of the stairs, one of the archers flung himself at a closed window, but the reinforced shutters were too sturdy and he bounced off, falling onto the bare floorboards. Valens brought his foot down hard, there was a crunch, and the man lay still.

Raul stared. He felt like a weight was dragging on his insides. He had seen bodies before, not just farm animals but people too. Diovanno, who got caught in a snowstorm and was found frozen in his own orchard. Selia, her legs crushed beneath a wagon, blood soaking into the soil. But there had been no intention in that. It had just been the way the world worked.

Except that this *was* how the world worked. This was how you fought for freedom. He clung to that thought as he clung to the sabre and tried to ignore the damp spot sliding down his cheek.

"Here." Prisca glanced around, then stepped cautiously into another room. Through the doorway, Raul caught a glimpse of shelves and niches filled with books and scrolls. Those shelves had Prisca's whole attention, her gaze dragged toward them like a trout on a line.

The door creaked. A figure in blue stepped from the shadows behind it and pressed a curved knife against Prisca's throat.

"Stop right there." Wide eyes stared past Prisca at Raul. "One more step and I'll slit her throat."

The man was slimmer than the soldiers downstairs, his long

FORGED FOR DESTINY

scholar's robe hanging off a body that seemed little more than lightly covered bones. His skin was pale and there were bags under his eyes. Raul wasn't sure that he could have swung a sabre, let alone fought one off, but the way the dagger wobbled at Prisca's throat didn't make it any less deadly.

Raul swallowed, trying to think of a way to deal with this. What could he say? What could he do?

"I've got this." Valens's hand settled on Raul's shoulder, and immediately he felt steady.

"No," Prisca said. In spite of everything, her voice was clear. "You check the rest of the floor. Raul can save me."

"Don't be a fool, Prisca." Valens's fingers tightened, pulling Raul back.

"Yes, *Prisca*," the man with the knife said, emphasising the name too hard, failing to assert control. "Don't be a fool."

"We'll deal with you soon enough." Prisca's voice was infinitely calmer and steadier than the knife at her throat. "Now, Valens, remember the plan."

"I won't lose another—"

"Which of us sees the signs?" Prisca's eyes went wide, and Raul saw a gleaming intensity that had never been there before. "Trust in destiny."

"Fuck destiny."

"Then trust in our son."

Raul could hear the grinding of Valens's teeth. That hand squeezed so hard Raul thought his shoulder bone might break. Then the hand was gone and Valens stormed away.

"Stand back," the man in the scholar's robes said, his voice no steadier than his hand. "You're going to let me go."

Moments before, fear and tension had threatened to overwhelm Raul, but there was no time for that now. Prisca believed in him, and she needed him.

He lifted the sabre, feeling its weight, considering all the ways he could attack. If there was one that didn't end with the scholar's knife slicing Prisca's throat, then he couldn't see it, but he could still keep her safe.

There was a clang as his sabre hit the boards.

"Let her go," he said, raising his hands. "Take me instead."

"Why would I do that?"

"Because I'm a more valuable hostage."

"How?"

"You're a historian?"

The scholar nodded.

Raul shrugged off his tunic, letting it fall across the sabre, and rolled up his sleeve.

The scholar frowned. "Why do I know that mark?"

"Balbianus," Raul said.

"Why would anybody have Balbianus's sign branded on them?" The scholar's eyes darted back and forth. He licked his lips. "Fine. Come here."

Raul walked slowly over, hands raised to chest height, palms out, showing he was unarmed. He turned and backed through the doorway, toward the scholar and Prisca.

The scholar shoved Prisca into one of the shelves. He lunged with the knife. Raul sidestepped, but not far enough. There was a jolt of pain as the blade slashed his exposed arm.

Raul grabbed the scholar's wrist and twisted. The scholar screeched and the knife fell from his hand. Raul stuck out a leg and yanked on that arm. The scholar tripped over Raul's foot and his head hit the doorpost with a crack.

"Excellent work," Prisca said. "Now quick, before reinforcements arrive."

Opening her satchel, she strode toward the shelves.

Raul looked down at the unconscious scholar, then at his own arm. He'd bled before; accidents were inevitable when cooking and farming, tiring work with sharp tools. But this pain was deliberate; someone had tried to kill him. He shivered. A few inches to the side and it could have been his chest. A nail's width deeper and it could have been a vein.

"Raul," Prisca snapped, pulling a sack from her satchel. "The shelves."

Raul glanced at his ma, then down at his arm. It wasn't bleeding much, and heroes weren't meant to worry about these things, were they?

He tore the sleeve off his discarded tunic, wrapped it hastily around his arm, and tucked the end in. That would stem the bleeding until they were done.

Then he looked around the room. He'd never seen so much paper and parchment before, not even in Prisca's loft above the brewhouse. Rows upon rows of books, rolls, and scrolls. Small heaps of loose pages. His wound was forgotten as he gaped at it all.

"We're after Vadrion's *Histories*, Gasparo's *Principles of Essence*, and Drescuttia's *Chronicle of the Kings*," Prisca said. "Anything with Balbianus's mark or the word 'prophecy,' take that too. It's all about foreseeing our next steps."

Raul scanned the shelves. He wasn't a bad reader, but he

wasn't fast like Prisca, whose whole life had been learning. It was hard to concentrate when he could hear groans and a sound like wet wood being chopped on the landing.

"Here." He pulled a set of matching books in pale leather bindings off the shelf. The name "Vadrion" was written down their spines.

He turned to Prisca, who was rearranging a heap of loose papers. She set them down and held out the sack for the books.

"Drop them in," she said.

"Shouldn't we be more careful?" Raul asked. Books were rare and precious things; Prisca herself had taught him that.

"More warriors could be here at any moment," she said. "Just drop them in."

Raul took a breath, then did as he was told, wincing as the sack thumped on the floor.

"There." Prisca handed him the sack and pointed at the shelves behind him. "Check the front pages of all the books with the red spines. Take any histories of Estis, even if they call it the North March."

The sound of chopping was joined by the flapping of pages as Prisca and Raul raced through the shelves. Then came a sound from outside: the clopping of hooves, first slow and steady, then one set breaking away at a gallop.

"Time's up, book lovers." Appia stood in the doorway, axe resting on her shoulder. "Warriors are coming to the front. I've told our friends to scatter."

"I'm only half done," Raul said. "I need more time."

"We'll have to make do." Prisca cast a handful of papers on the floor. "Come."

FORGED FOR DESTINY

Raul grabbed the sack and followed Appia onto the landing. Down in the hall, someone was shouting that they should put down their weapons and raise their hands.

Appia snorted. "Too late for that."

She led them into a room at the back of the house, where Valens stood by the ruined shutters of a window, axe in hand. He grabbed the sack and tossed it out, then pointed.

"Jump."

Raul looked out. A cartful of hay stood moonlight pale amid the darkness of a street. He vaulted over the window ledge and landed in the hay, then rolled clear. He was followed by Prisca, then Appia, and finally Valens, the cart creaking under the impact.

Valens grabbed the sack of books.

"What about the guards?" Raul realised that he had left his axe behind, and the sabre he'd used in its stead. Angry voices were approaching, the clop of hooves and the stamp of boots in the mud. He was ready to fight unarmed if he had to, but he didn't want the others to die because he was unprepared.

"Mostly at the front still," Valens said quietly. "Amateurs. Come on."

He led them between two buildings, into the city's narrow back streets. Raul flinched at every shifting shadow, raising his fists in a futile defence against foes who weren't there. Straining to listen for the sounds of pursuit, he turned his head, then almost tripped on a rut in the road.

"Calm, boy," Appia whispered. "Don't give yourself away when we're almost clear."

The footsteps and raised voices receded as they crept

through the streets, those same streets where Raul had so recently lost his sword, where he had been forced to run from the oppressors he was here to overthrow. It was hard to stay calm when that moment kept flashing through his mind, when he could hear those same oppressors on his heels now.

Except that they weren't on his heels, were they? The sound of them faded further with each turn of the streets, and as those sounds grew quieter, so did the hammering of his heart. He grinned, though no one could see it in the darkness.

Tonight, he had beaten the Dunholmi. Sure, he had run again, once more leaving his weapon behind. But when he laid this weapon down, it was a choice. When he left, it was a retreat, not a defeated flight. A sack of books hung over Valens's shoulder, and Prisca was still with them, thanks to Raul.

Maybe he really could be the hero his people needed.

Chapter Eleven
Rehearsing Lines

Yasmi ran her fingers down the silvered edge of the mirror, and its polished beauty gave her a happy shudder. People said that you should put a scratch into a new mirror, so that it couldn't capture your whole essence and steal your soul, but Yasmi couldn't bear to scratch this one. The mirror's beauty brought out her own, something she would never mar.

They could never have had treasure like this out in the provinces, moving from town to town day after day. It would have been too unwieldy, scratched and dented within a month. But here, the star of the show could have a floor-length mirror, and apparently they could afford it, despite the shows they had missed by skipping towns along the Elvin Way. She had been so frustrated by that, by missing the roar of those crowds and the looks on their faces, the rapturous expressions of backwater simpletons exposed to the wonder of high art. But it was worth it to be in a place with a permanent stage, with standing room to match any rural town square and seating for the rich in balconies above. A place where she could foster a following, fanatical theatregoers who came to see her over and again, who sang her praises and spread the word. A place where she could stay in the same bed for more than three nights and see the same faces each morning.

She took a sip of wine, licked her lips, and stepped back to get a proper view. The trousers were good, the tunic exquisite, with sunburst slashes in its red sleeves, but the outfit wasn't quite perfect. The whole was just a little too much. She removed a set of engraved Saditchi bangles and set them down on the windowsill, along with her wine cup. Yes, that was it. She blew herself a kiss, then walked out of the room.

Most of the others were waiting by the stage, the players flinging lines back and forth. The playwright Tenebrial perched possessively on a stool, constantly correcting. Claudio hung from a rope ladder, Biallo below him, the two of them adjusting cords that controlled the scenery sheets. Her father was in the doorway, talking with a stoop-shouldered stranger who looked as if he was about to wither into bones, leaving behind only a set of elegantly cut blue robes.

"Shall we begin?" Yasmi leapt onto the stage and glanced at her father, but he wasn't watching. She snatched the wolf mask from her sash and held it out. The wolf was her favourite, every movement of its muscles a delight. The monkey was fun, the lion beautiful, the snake a fascinating challenge, but the wolf stirred her soul. "I'm feeling feisty today."

The players cheered and moved to their places for the start of act one, but her father held up a hand.

"Yasmi, Tenebrial, a moment of your time."

The other players watched and whispered as she followed the twitching playwright to the door. It was only now that her eyes fell upon the two warriors in blue standing behind the robed figure. One of them was handsome in a burly sort of way, and Yasmi was pleased to see him smile at her arrival, but the other was ugly as a corpse dragged out of a swamp. Yasmi twisted the wolf mask on the end of its string and glanced around, making sure that the back exit was clear.

"This is Master Ketley Tur," Efron said, "Count Alder's chamberlain. Master Tur, this is my daughter, our troupe's shifter, Yasmi Dellest, and our playwright, Tenebrial Blackfinger."

Yasmi smiled, ready to suffer the old man's attention as the price of being her, but instead he turned to Tenebrial.

"You created what they will perform?" Tur's tone was shrill. His eyes kept darting around, like he expected someone to spring out of the wings at him.

"That's right." Tenebrial clenched his hands together, but he couldn't quite stifle the twitch at the corner of his eye.

"Why?"

For a master of the carefully crafted phrase, Tenebrial was an utter embarrassment where conversation was concerned. Yasmi sighed, but still they weren't paying her attention. Her father seemed distracted, glancing from Tur to the players, his fingers twisting around each other like eels in a basket.

"I am here to check the content of this play," Tur said. "To determine your licence to perform. You will sit with me while the cast go through it, and you will tell me about any deviations from your words."

"This would all be a lot easier if you let us have scripts,"

Tenebrial said. "Then I could give you a copy to read and mark for edits."

"Are you suggesting that the laws of the land are wrong?" Tur raised a sharp eyebrow. Now his eyes settled, nailing the playwright with an accusing glare.

"Of course not, but what I am saying..."

He might murder small talk, but Tenebrial could split a philosophical hair so fine it became invisible. As he started arguing with the chamberlain, Yasmi tugged on her father's sleeve and drew him out of earshot.

"Why are we suddenly being censored?" she hissed.

"Oh, they've always done this." Efron patted her on the arm, but his eyes were on the argument. "I just didn't like to bother you with it. I know you take after your mother in detesting administration, and I'd rather have you focused on your performance."

"Have you gone mad?" Yasmi glanced at the stage. What she really wanted right now was to feel the boards beneath her feet and the attention of the company falling upon her, but she couldn't rehearse like this. "There's no way that an official approves our current play."

"It'll be fine. We'll tone things down while we perform for him, make the chamberlain less scheming and the foreigners less bloodthirsty. He'll demand a few little changes, which we'll sadly forget once we have a real audience."

"You think that will work?"

"It always has in the past."

"In the past, we didn't have a purpose-built theatre and a play about a lost king prophesied to return." She pressed her

FORGED FOR DESTINY

hands against her face, a feeling close enough to a mask to bring her comfort. "You never should have made Tenebrial listen to those heroic stories Valens tells. We could have been performing another comedy, or that musical he was working on about a living forest."

"I would have enjoyed seeing how you played a talking tree, but don't you think that this is better? And by far the best role Tenebrial has given you. I wouldn't want to waste such a performance."

Yasmi gritted her teeth. Her father was right, of course, but she was here to impress Count Alder, not to get strung up by him for treason.

"Say we put on something toned down now," she said, "then perform the real play for audiences. What happens to our performance licence once this dusty old scarecrow finds out?"

"It'll be fine. It always is."

"Argh!" She flung her hands in the air. "This is Valens's fault. He put these ideas in your head."

"Actually, it was Prisca who suggested—"

"Don't you dare tell me she's the one you listen to. You and that old warrior have been playing hide the sword every spring for three years, and I've seen that little grin you get when he flexes his muscles."

"Really, my queen of the boards, I don't think that's relevant." Her father at least had the decency to blush. "Besides, Prisca is helping fund our season."

"Meaning that she gets to put treason on our lips while we sit in the shadow of the palace?"

139

"I will admit, it's not an ideal situation, but it will all change when Prisca's plans—"

"La la la la la." Yasmi slapped her hands over her ears. "I don't want to know what that old mountain goat has planned. Pleading innocence through ignorance might save me from a noose one day, understand?"

Efron nodded.

"Good." Yasmi took her hands from her ears. Her belly was a ball of stress. She needed to get up onto the stage and get her mask on. "You take Master Skin-and-Bones and his guards on a prestige tour of our new building, while the rest of us work out what we can safely perform. We'll get through the day, then make some proper decisions about this mess later. Understand?"

"Yes, dear."

Yasmi hated taking charge almost as much as she hated a poor performance. In that much, at least, she was quite unlike her mother, who had governed the company with a fist of stone. The problem was, that had kept Yasmi's father from the grit and grime of important decisions, and his failings forced these moments upon Yasmi.

"Go, deal with it." She ushered him toward the blue-clad figures, then hurried to join the other players. "Gather around, everyone."

These people had been listening to her since she was an infant reciting her first verse, and it was easy to manage their attention now. In theory, all were equals in the troop, but no one could dominate a room like her.

"We're going to put on a special performance for our

guests," she said, as her father led the chamberlain and his guards out of the room. "We need to get it just right." She waved the players closer and tilted her face into a shadow. Light was for revelation, darkness for deception, or so the traditions said. "We're ditching the middle two scenes of act three, and that first one from act four—Claudio, slip something into scene three to explain what happened to the duchess. We can't keep the finale how it is, so I'll improvise around my final speech, make something that implies a glorious future under Dunholm. The good thing about not having the canvas up yet is they won't see that business with the moon and dagger. Biallo, I need you to strip out the patriotic parts from your murder scene, so that—"

"No, no, no!" Tenebrial broke in indignantly. "You can't do this. Every scene is precisely structured. Every moment matters. All this rough chopping will ruin it."

"What do you normally do?"

"Sit down with Efron, make a few changes to the dialogue, quietly run through them with the relevant cast members, see how they work in rehearsal."

"We don't have time for that. The censor's here now."

"Give me an hour, then."

"We don't have an hour! We need to get up on that stage and practise the transitions, so that we don't accidentally talk treason while someone from the count's retinue is watching."

"I really don't think—"

"Good, because we're out of time for thinking." Yasmi jumped onto the stage and took the elk mask from her belt. She tapped her foot against the floor three times for luck.

"We're going from the last minute of act three, scene three, near the end of the hunt. Places, everyone."

Most of the cast stepped back to watch, while those in the scene spread around her. She looked across her audience, imagined the hundreds more who would pour in every night, and smiled as she raised the mask. She felt its power, the essence of athleticism and elegance, the noble lord of the forest. The worries of the world faded away as she prepared to embrace the story and the shifting.

Then Prisca walked through the door.

"Yasmi, where is your father?" the diviner snapped.

Yasmi froze, every muscle clenched. She should just move the mask another inch, sink into the role, let someone else deal with this.

"Yasmi Dellest, I asked you a question."

How was it that one woman's voice could so perfectly set her on edge? Everyone was looking at Yasmi, but their admiration had curdled into uncertainty.

She lowered the mask. "What do you want?"

"I have a suggestion for the play."

Tenebrial leapt up and his stool clattered on the floor. "No, no, no! No more butchering my words."

"Can't this wait until later?" Yasmi asked. "We're rehearsing."

"The perfect time to try a variation," Prisca said, as if it was the most reasonable thing in the world.

"No, no, no!" Tenebrial waved his finger back and forth, pointing at each woman in turn. "How many times must I say no?"

"Apparently I was wrong." Yasmi jerked her head. "The

FORGED FOR DESTINY

rest of you, practise the transitions we discussed. Tenebrial, Prisca, we'll talk."

She dropped off the stage and strode over to Prisca, dragging the playwright with her. Gods and ruin, this was turning into the worst day ever.

"Right." Yasmi straightened her tunic, then rested her hands on her masks, one finger tapping against the wolf. "Tell us your idea."

Prisca's calculating gaze flitted around the room.

"Father's busy," Yasmi snapped. "Talk to me."

"Very well." Prisca drew a book from her satchel and Tenebrial's eyes lit up. "I have completed further research into the story you're working with, exploring divergent accounts. There's a transformative moment in the finest versions of the story, a turn that your audience would find particularly dramatic."

"Transformative?" Yasmi's throat tightened. If this was going where she thought it was, then there would be trouble.

"Indeed. It might benefit from a change of costume, or even an unmasking..."

"No." Yasmi crossed her arms. "Absolutely not."

"It's a simple matter of shifting. You do it behind the stage all the time."

"Exactly. Behind the stage. Never on it. That breaks the magic."

"It could enhance it. Imagine the response of an audience, most of whom have never seen one of your transformations, none of whom have ever seen it in a play. This single moment of vulnerability, heightening the veracity of events, the emotional weight of the finale."

Tenebrial had opened the book to a page marked with a ribbon.

"I can see value in it," he said, and his cheek stopped twitching as his eyes glazed over, listening to words that were only in his head.

"Why not just ask me to perform naked?" Yasmi said. "It would be less outrageous."

"And that outrage will make it unforgettable." Prisca's smile didn't reach her eyes. "Everyone will be talking about you. Everyone will want to see you perform."

She was right, curse her. Yasmi could imagine the gasps, the cheers, the cries of outrage, the roar of an audience unable to contain itself. And with a bigger audience, the transformations would be more powerful, adding to the drama of the moment. She would go down in legend.

The old witch almost got her.

"You mean everyone will want to hear your propaganda," Yasmi said. "No, thank you." She turned. "I have to get back to rehearsals."

"Remember who is paying for this place," Prisca said quietly.

Yasmi whirled around. "Remember who's hiding you and your criminal family. Don't think I didn't see the bandage on Raul's arm yesterday."

They glared at each other. Between them, Tenebrial's shoulder twitched as he clutched the book between thin fingers.

"...and here we are back at the stage," Efron announced, striding in with the chamberlain and his guards. "Hopefully by now, we're ready for your performance."

FORGED FOR DESTINY

He looked at Yasmi, who sidestepped in front of Tenebrial and the book.

"Almost there, Father," she said brightly. "Why don't you find seats for our guests?"

"Perhaps I could watch as well." Prisca stepped out around Yasmi, whose blood ran cold. Across the room, her father went pale.

"Who is this?" Master Tur asked, one eyebrow rising.

"This is one of our patrons," Efron said, the smile rushing back to his face. "And this is Master Tur, Count Alder's chamberlain."

"I thought as much." Prisca bowed her head. "An honour, Master Tur. Are you here to judge the play?"

"Indeed."

"Good. It's so important that the masses are exposed only to the right ideas. Peasants are so easily led."

"I could not agree more."

"And all the more critical that the plays are judged correctly when they appear in such a grand venue as this." Prisca swept a hand around, taking in the echoing room with its balconies above. Her voice carried like she was born for the stage. "It would be terrible if so many people saw the wrong play because it hadn't been judged by someone with the right background and education, someone of noble birth."

Tur's hand clenched on the sash around his waist, knuckles whitening. His eyes darted across the stage, the seating, the players, then his own guards, before settling on Efron. He swallowed.

"On consideration, I have decided not to see your play

today," Tur said. "You will send someone to the palace to recite it for Count Alder himself, so that he can make sure it is appropriate."

"Of course," Efron said. "I could come, and after perhaps..."

"I'll do it." Yasmi bowed to the chamberlain. "It would be my honour to perform for the count."

This was it. Her chance to shine. This day might be a rutted mud road swallowing the wheels of theatre's wagon, but she was ready to stride down another shining path.

The chamberlain's eyes drank her in, and he nodded. "Yes, I believe Count Alder would like that. I will send instructions once arrangements have been made."

Without a word of farewell, the chamberlain stalked out, hands still clenched tight around his belt. The guards strode after him, the handsome one winking at Yasmi as he passed. There was a muffled conversation, then the sound of hooves disappearing up the street.

The whole troupe let out a sigh of relief.

"Why did you do that?" Yasmi asked quietly as the players bustled back into life. "Surely the last thing you want is the count's personal attention on your play."

"What the count has permitted, no guard will check, no official will question. I'm sure that you will give him a performance he can only approve of." Prisca's smile was narrow as a razor blade. "Isn't a palace performance what you wanted?"

Some small part of Yasmi wanted to deny it, just to stop Prisca getting her way. But it was only a small part.

"Can we rehearse at last?" She strode toward the stage,

pulling the elk mask from her belt. "I need to make this performance perfect."

———————————— • ————————————

Count Alder stared from his balcony out across Pavuno, toward the monument rising from the ruins of the city walls. They should have built something like it years ago, but his predecessors as governor had lacked the imagination. Nearly two decades in this place, and they'd done little more than gather books and send soldiers on patrol. No wonder trouble still welled beneath the skin of the North March, waiting for the one wrong cut that would make the country bleed.

He turned the captured sword in his hands, looked at how the light gleamed on the engravings. The artisans he'd spoken with said that the work was new but in an old style, though if it was a forgery they didn't know the original. One of them had a strange look in his eye, like he wanted the sword to reveal something more. Alder had considered holding him for questioning, but it didn't feel like they were at that point yet. A curious sword was no reason to unsettle people of value, as long as they could be kept cooperative with cash instead.

Familiar footsteps stuttered tentatively across the throne room.

"How was the theatre?" Alder asked, holding the sword up to catch the light.

"As it always is, my lord," Ketley Tur whined. "Wastrels playing at kings."

"And the play? How much can we let them get away with this time, to give people their safe little thrill of dissent?"

"I don't know yet."

Alder turned, the sword held in a low fighting stance. Tur, shoulders hunched and head bowed, dragged his gaze from the blade to the governor's face.

"I have arranged for one of them to recite the script here, my lord. For your personal approval."

"I have better things to deal with than stories and clowns." Alder pointed the sword at Tur. "I don't need you wasting my time."

"There's a young woman who will provide the performance, very comely, apparently she's popular with audiences."

"If I wanted a woman in my life, I'd find one of my own class." Alder strode past Tur and seated himself on the throne. "And if I wanted a whore, then I'd find one whose tongue had practice with the swords of men, not words."

Tur's laughter was rasping and paper thin.

"Indeed, my lord. Very witty. Still, these players have occupied the new dance house above the docks, they will have large audiences, so I thought it best for you to give your personal approval."

"You mean you didn't want to take responsibility." Alder picked up his goblet. It held milk, not wine. The city was agitated, shifting beneath him, and he needed to stay in the saddle. "You're more of a mule than a stallion, aren't you, Tur? A plodder, not a galloper."

"If you say so, my lord." The chamberlain bowed his head. "But my plodding has led me down an interesting trail."

"Oh?"

Tur reached into a pouch hanging from his sash belt and drew out a roll of parchment.

"In moving documents from the house that was attacked by rebels, we found some that we didn't know we had."

"More theoretical texts?"

Alder held out a hand, took the parchment with its cracked edges and age-blurred lettering. There couldn't be many texts on the theory of essence still hiding around the city, especially not ones by the old Estian scholars. Finding one among the documents they already held would earn him the king's appreciation, and further shame his predecessor, currently the royal advisor on trade, a position that could provide great influence to one of Alder's younger relatives or perhaps a loyal friend. The ladder of politics held space for only one climber at each height; sometimes it was worth greasing the rungs.

"Mostly history," Tur said. "With a very specific prophecy."

"Prophecies are like pigeons, far too common and the useful ones are rare."

Tur reached forward, closer than Alder liked, and tapped the page. Beneath his finger was an image of a crescent moon, pierced by a knife. Its style was similar to the engravings on the captured sword.

"Our local-born scholars were very interested in this," Tur said. "Almost agitated."

"And we didn't know we had this before the raid?"

"Indeed not, my lord."

Alder laid a hand on the pommel of his solid, practical sabre.

Another vein of mystery running through Pavuno. He had been afraid that the city would bleed, but it seemed that he might have to slice it open himself, to clear the wound in the province's side before its infection spread.

He missed the open plains of home, good company, and good music. He missed the courtly dances, the manoeuvring of bodies and of whispered words, politic played out in flesh. The pleasures of this place still evaded him, but it was offering an interesting challenge, with power as a prize at the end.

He looked again at the blurred letters on the page, so similar to other old documents he'd seen. Where had these pages been hiding for so long?

Chapter Twelve
The Bridge at Rack's Scar

There weren't as many animals in the city as Raul had expected. Most streets had chickens pecking in the dirt and cats stalking the rats. There were some pigs too, roaming between the buildings, and an occasional goat tied up outside someone's door. But for a place with so many people, they wasn't nearly enough livestock, and no cows at all.

"How do they feed everyone?" he asked as they walked along the street, Prisca beside him and Valens slightly behind, carrying the walking stick that was as close to a sword as he could openly carry.

"They purchase it," Prisca replied.

"With what?"

"Goods they make, or taxes paid to the governor."

"What sorts of goods?"

"Cloth, pottery, shoes, anything you can think of. Cities are the perfect places to turn raw material into refined products."

"Is that what you're doing to me, making me more refined?"

Prisca laughed. "In a way, I suppose."

Outside an apothecary's shop, the count's warriors were tearing down an arch of branches interwoven with blood-red ribbons, a charm to bring health and fertility for all who walked through the door. The apothecary and her neighbours watched in sullen silence as the offering was ripped apart and trampled in the dirt. Prisca walked on past, not looking or commenting, never even changing her pace, and Raul did his best to match her, not to show how appalled he was. Someone must have put days of work into that arch, to carry spring's essence into summer, to maintain life and growth. Hours to make a thing, moments to tear it apart, to make the world a worse place.

He was going to change all that. Like the arch, he would help his country to grow strong.

"While you're improving me," he said, "there's something else I'd like to learn."

"And what's that?" Prisca asked.

Raul looked around, watchful for anyone who might be listening. He still hadn't got used to the fact that, in the city, the more people there were, the safer it was to talk. The sheer volume of them meant that his words would be lost to anyone except his ma and da.

Still, he lowered his voice.

"Divination."

He had expected her to be enthusiastic about the idea. After all, divination had provided the prophecies that told them his destiny. It had helped them to find the house where the governor was storing his gathered books, and to find the right

FORGED FOR DESTINY

time to attack. Surely it would be helpful if Raul could do this too? But Prisca made the same noise she'd made when he asked to spend a summer with the herders in the high hills, the noncommittal noise that said she was working out how to say no.

"Divination is a difficult thing," Prisca said. "To comprehend its complexities takes years of study. Even to read the surface signs, you must scrutinise a hundred connections at once, to work out which matter and which are coincidence."

"Why?"

"Because it is about the intertwined, about seeing how disparate elements share an essence, how one is reflected in another."

"I can do that."

"All right, then. If you can explicate the meaning in the next animal to cross our path, then I'll try to teach you."

They walked on, Raul looking left and right. A cat watched them from a doorway, and a rooster strutted past, but they didn't cross in front of them. Raul was relieved. Between disdain and arrogance, neither seemed like a good omen.

With a creak of harness, a wagon rolled across the junction ahead, drawn by a heavy horse with blinkers over its eyes.

"Well?" Prisca asked, stopping while they waited for the wagon to pass.

Raul considered the horse. It was working hard and there was a tirelessness to its movements as it plodded along, tail swishing away the flies that followed. But the blinkers blinded and limited it, which of course was the whole point. Maybe instead of looking for good or bad omens he should look for

153

something more complicated; except that complicated was harder to work out, and now he stood gaping in the street, all because of one horse.

"Given up?" Prisca asked, motioning him on.

"I'm thinking."

"Then the time isn't wasted. Thinking is sparring for the mind."

"I'd rather be sparring with the body," Valens said, swinging his stick.

"You'll face combat soon enough."

That thought made Raul's stomach lurch, as he remembered the sound of an axe sinking into flesh, the smell of blood, finding a red spatter down his face when he got home. Never mind divination, if he was going to fulfil his destiny, then he needed to develop a stronger stomach.

Houses gave way to workshops as they headed downhill. Raul didn't know what exactly Valens and Prisca were looking for, but he was happy to be out with them, seeing the city. He couldn't get over how many buildings there were, and the size of some of them. They'd seen a stone building that could have held their whole village, and that Valens had said was a temple. Then Raul had spotted what he thought was also a temple on one of the other hills, only for Valens to say that it was a foundlings' home, giving Raul a look that he didn't understand at all, like he was expecting something more. Scattered among lower buildings were the tall, new houses occupied by merchants who had grown rich under Dunholm's rule, their timber-frame walls painted in every colour of the rainbow, their compounds guarded by spiked fences and prickly guards. But the most amazing sight had been the brick kilns behind the mud flats along the lower river, like a row of giant beehives with smoke swarming from their stacks.

The rows of workshops grew thinner. They passed a squat warehouse where a pair of merchants were haggling over prices, and a building draped in bright bunting where men and women in veils leaned over a balcony rail, calling sweetly to passersby. Then they were at the edge of the new city, the part that grew between the lower river and the fallen walls. In the uneven ground where the rivers met, slender new birches and poplars were growing, a small patch of growth clinging at the fringe of what people had made.

"That's useful," Raul said. "Planting new woods."

Valens snorted. "Only because they chopped the old trees down during the siege. Look."

Sure enough, stumps stood between the new trees, low undergrowth, and chunks of stone. Some of them were fire-blackened.

"Why not build there?" Raul asked.

"The ground is uneven," Prisca said. "And tree roots are needed to stop the rivers wearing it away."

"So why not let that ground go?"

"Because then the waters will erode land people actually want, and we can't have that." Prisca raised an eyebrow. "Have you worked out your omen yet?"

"I'm thinking about it. Maybe you could show me how you read the signs, as an example?"

"That wasn't the deal."

"Go on, show him," Valens said. "The lad needs to learn about the world if he's to lead."

Prisca raised a finger like she was about to tell Valens off, then thought better of it. She led them up the broken ground, to look down the steep embankment of the River Rack. To their left, the ground rose sharply toward the mountains, the upper city, and the slender bridge across Rack's Scar.

"If a person is already connected to a place, then they carry it in their essence. Signs in one may reflect the other." Prisca pointed to the bridge. "You were born near here, Raul, and when the city fell, we carried you out across that bridge."

"I carried you out," Valens said proudly, prodding his chest with his thumb.

"Well done, you carried a baby." Prisca leaned forward, peering at the water. "With the three of us here once more, this place may reveal truths about who Raul is and what his future holds. The chaos of nature is ripe with omens, so we look to the river."

Raul stared at the deep waters, which rushed and tumbled between rocky banks, but he couldn't make any sense of what they might be saying. It wasn't that there was no pattern. There were so many patterns, how could he tell which were important?

Prisca's breath became slow and deep, then caught in a gasp. She pointed at the water.

"It calls to you," she said. "The man of the city. The hero of Estis and its people. You will snatch life from the maelstrom, bring it safe from the rapids to the shore. But an omen of the past emerges, a lie to be revealed."

She took a step back, blinking.

"Are you all right, Ma?" Raul asked.

FORGED FOR DESTINY

"Don't call me that," Prisca snapped, her hands pressed to her head. "Blasted boy, always demanding my attention."

Raul felt as if he'd been slapped.

"I..."

"I'm sorry." Prisca grabbed his hand. "I didn't mean it. I just... What I saw, it overwhelmed my mind for a moment. Really, Raul, I didn't mean it."

"I know, Ma." Raul wrapped his arms around her. She seemed small and frail in a way that she never did when she was speaking. He was shocked to find that she was shaking.

"I should check my books," Prisca mumbled into his shoulder. "Maybe I had it wrong." She pulled out of his embrace, then drew a charcoal twig and a scrap of parchment from her satchel. "I must write things down, while I remember."

Raul and Valens moved to flank her, hiding what she did. Not all writing was banned, but one piece of paper led to another, and any could raise questions. They looked across the top of her head, and Raul saw his own confusion mirrored in Valens's eyes. Since when did Prisca doubt that she was right, or need to make notes to remember anything?

A cry of alarm snapped both their heads around. A figure was falling from the bridge across the Scar, her scream cut brutally short as she hit the water.

"Gods." Valens shook his head. "Poor fucker. Hope for her family's sake they find the body."

A dark shape bobbed in the frothing current as the river swept toward them between its jagged banks.

"I see her," Raul said. "She could still be alive."

He scrambled down the bank, jumping from one rock to

the next, heading for the river. His knee jarred as he landed awkwardly and he nearly lost his footing but flung his arms out wide to steady himself.

"Raul, stop!" Valens bellowed. "Those waters will kill you!"

"They can't." Raul tore off his tunic and kicked off his boots. "I have a destiny, remember?"

"You don't understand. Stop! Now!"

Two months before, those words in that voice would have frozen Raul in his tracks. That was before he learned who he really was. If he had to do terrible, stomach-turning things in the name of freedom and destiny, then he could do noble ones too.

The black shape came rushing toward him, tumbling over rapids, veering back and forth as the current churned between spiked teeth of rock. He dived into the river thirty yards ahead of it, water parting with a splash, then closing behind him. His hands hit the bottom and he was seized by a force more powerful than his own momentum, a current that swept him down and to the side, away from the bank.

Raul had swum in mountain streams, but never one as powerful as this. It tossed him this way and that, slammed him hard against a rock, flung him up just long enough to grab a desperate breath before he was carried under. In that moment, he saw the dark shape on the water and was sure it was a person. That made the ache in his ribs worthwhile.

With the strongest strokes he could manage, he pulled against the current, trying to reach his goal. But the current was pushing him downriver as fast as her. He hit rock again, a jarring impact that sent shudders of pain up his back, and

FORGED FOR DESTINY

he almost opened his mouth. With one hand he grabbed the rock, managed to hold himself in place, to lift his head out of the water for a gasp of air and to see what was happening. That other body swept toward him, a dark shape in the foaming current, face down in the water. The river was carrying her toward the far bank, away from him.

He planted his feet against rock and let his hand slide away as he pushed off. The current seized him, pulled him off course, but he had enough momentum to reach her, to grab an arm, to pull her in. He wrapped his arms around her, dragged her head to the surface, and clung on tight.

There was no fighting the current now, not with his arms full. He couldn't guide them, only protect her. The current dipped, then rose. His back scraped across a rock, then another, leaving him stinging and scared, sure that the wound would hurt a hundred times worse once he wasn't cold and numb, so very numb.

His pulse was pounding in his ears. He wanted to twist his head around, to see the rocks coming, except that he didn't, and those two impulses crushed him between them as surely as his skull could be crushed against stone. He clutched the woman tight, like they might somehow save each other.

The currents swept over them, dragging them back under the water. He had no breath left, no strength to drag himself to the surface. His chest was aching, ears ringing. The cold world of the river grew dark.

There was a jolt as something struck him. Another rock. No, fingers. A hand around his arm, then an arm around his shoulders. Pain flared at the pressure against skin flayed by rocks, waking him enough to try to struggle free, but he was clasped by a strength far greater than his own, dragged up against his exhausted will.

Cold air hit him like a fist as they burst through the surface of the river. His first gasp turned into a string of desperate breaths as his lungs found what they had longed for. He still had hold of the woman, and someone—Valens, of course—had hold of him.

Raul started kicking, trying to help.

"Stay still," Valens said. "We're almost there."

The waters slowed. There was splashing and a crunch of gravel. Valens hauled them onto the shingle at the end of the trees, just above where the two rivers met. He took the woman from Raul, and she flopped like a baby in his arms. He slapped her back and water sprayed from her mouth.

The woman groaned.

With trembling arms, Raul pushed himself into a seated position. Prisca was running toward them along the river-bank, and other people with her. They shouted and pointed.

A wind whipped in like a lash across Raul's back and every inch of his skin there stung. He tugged at his shirt. It fell off of him, the back in tatters. Dripping wet and naked from the waist up, he stumbled to his feet.

There were people all around, crowding in, shouting, and pointing. Nothing they said sank in. The cold of his body was seeping into the edges of his mind, as the exhilarating terror of his rush through the river wore off. At least the numbness flattened the pain in his back and the ache where his shoulder had slammed against the rocks.

FORGED FOR DESTINY

Someone slapped him on the shoulder, and a jolt of pain cut through the fog. A woman was shaking his hand, a man trying to hand him something. There was cheering and clapping, shouts of excitement as more people approached.

He made out the woman he had saved through the tumult of the crowd. She'd hit her head, somewhere in the maelstrom, and blood seeped through her hair on that side. Valens was handing her to others for support. Raul pushed his way to her, and she looked up.

"Are you all right?" he asked, raising his voice to be heard.

It was such a stupid question, and he was a stupid boy from the country, but he didn't know how else to ask.

The woman looked at him in confusion, then down at his arm.

"Moon boy," she mumbled, running a finger across his birthmark. "You saved me, moon boy."

"We did." Raul raised his chin and smiled at Valens.

"Damn right you did!" a man shouted, and held up a flagon. "Here's to the hero!"

"What's your name, lad?"

"Where are you from?"

Others cheered and jostled around Raul. He moved closer to the woman he'd saved, while Valens tried to hold the crowd back enough for them to talk.

"I found something, moon boy, when I was drowned." The woman held out her other hand. In it was a metal rod, slender and misshapen with rust, a warped disk at its end. "You should have it."

Raul took the rod. Its surface was rough, unpleasant to the

161

touch, but the weight was satisfying. It felt significant, like the power of the current sweeping him along.

Prisca reached them, elbowing her way through the throng.

"Look at me, Raul," she said. "Follow my finger."

He did as he was told, but while his eyes followed, his mind was on the weight in his hand.

"Is this an omen?" he asked, holding it up for her to see.

The whole world seemed to freeze, or perhaps just Prisca did. She grabbed the rod.

"Not an omen, just junk." She flung it away with a vehemence he'd only seen when she was talking about Dunholm. There was a distant splash as it went back into the river.

More and more people arrived, more and more noise. A lot were fussing around the woman, but just as many were interested in Raul. Questions hurtled at him from left and right— who was he, where had he come from, how did he survive the Scar? People pointed and prodded at his birthmark, while others brushed up against the raw pain of his back, making him clench his teeth. Valens jostled them back, but even his scowl wasn't enough to drive them away or quiet them down, while the story of what had happened grew and spread around them.

A pair of warriors in blue appeared, their horses raising them up above the heads of the crowd. Prisca frowned as they trotted closer, the crowd reluctantly parting to let them through.

Valens took off his tunic and handed it to Raul.

"You're shivering, lad. Best cover up."

"It'll get stained. My back..."

FORGED FOR DESTINY

"Better a stained tunic than a fever. Put it on."

He did as he was told, even though the tunic was soaking wet and it hurt where it pressed against his rock-flayed flesh. Valens combed thick fingers through his hair, squeezing out the water.

Prisca was fussing around the woman Raul had saved, drawing attention to her. While the crowd was distracted, Valens set a hand gently but firmly around Raul's arm and drew him along, pushing a path through the crowd away from the riders. Valens ducked his head, and Raul did the same as they wormed their way out through the throng, past the people who'd seen him to the ones demanding to know what was happening, the crowd that came just because there was a crowd. The further they got from the centre of it all, the fewer people paid them any attention, so that by the time Prisca joined them and they emerged between the new trees at the edge of town, they were just three more people in the street.

"I left my boots behind," Raul said as mud squelched between his toes. "Sorry."

"I'll fetch them later," Valens said. "Or get you new ones."

"You said when you bought them last summer—"

"Never mind that, lad. You saved an innocent life. That's worth more than boots." Valens smiled. "I'm proud of you."

The warmth inside Raul couldn't chase away all the cold the river had left, but it helped.

Ahead, a wagon crossed their path. Raul suddenly laughed as a thought unfurled through his delirium.

"That horse," Raul said. "I worked it out."

163

"Huh?" Valens looked at him in confusion, but Prisca's expression was sharper.

"Really?" she asked.

"It wasn't an omen at all, was it? You said that animals are signs because nature in all its chaos brings out omens, but that horse was too tied up in human things to bring me a sign."

"Well done, Raul. Sometimes I forget how insightful you are, in your own way."

"The river, though, you read that right. It called to me, and I snatched life from it. I brought someone safe to the shore." He rubbed his chin. His fingers were cold, and they left flakes of rust. "I don't know what the omen of the past was, though. Maybe the lie will be revealed later."

"Maybe." Prisca looked away. "Visions are complicated, imperfect, incomplete, the essence of one thing confusing another. Some elements we never truly understand."

"But I got it right, the meaning of my animal. So now will you teach me divination?"

Prisca bit her lip, then nodded.

"Why not? I should warn you, though, it will take a very long time."

Chapter Thirteen
Dreamers

Valens had always had a soft spot for the statue of Balbianus in Dreamers' Square. Sure, no real warrior held their sword like that, and thrusting out your chin above your shield only exposed your throat. But the statue wore a pack, like a real soldier would, and centuries of weathering had given it something like scars. He'd often sat at its feet late at night, sharing a jug of ale with Fabia and the statue.

This was where Prisca had first explained the details of the plan. She'd pointed up at the statue, talked about symbols and heroes and the cycle of history, while rocks crashed against the city walls half a mile away. That hadn't been the last time Valens had drunk with Fabia and Balbianus, but it had been close. Valens twisted the mourning ring around his finger, remembered Fabia's laughter echoing around the square. She could laugh at anything. He still envied that.

The plinth was empty now. All that remained of Balbianus was the heel of a stone sandal, where the statue hadn't broken away cleanly, and chisel marks around where he had stood. Strange how there'd been no marks like that on the statue, which must have taken a lot of chiselling. Maybe that was what made good art: the ability not to leave a trace. Like when Valens watched the players, and he could almost forget that it was Efron on the stage, not some ancient king. Not that he would ever want to forget Efron...

There were chisel marks on the doorframe too, right next to where Valens was leaning, half listening to the tense tones of Prisca and the priest of Yorl. A few simple strokes in the shape of a mountain, to give the building stability and strength. The stone around them was worn from generations of worshippers touching that spot, hoping to absorb that strength and stability, on their way in to ask the one-eyed god to reveal their future. Maybe it had worked, maybe it hadn't, but Valens felt stability, continuity, endurance as he looked out at Raul sitting on Balbianus's plinth, talking with a passing tinker. The boy was where he should be.

Prisca, just like always, was trying to get where she shouldn't.

"You're quite right," said Holy Cirillo, the High Priest of Yorl. "It is the place of Yorl's chosen to reveal hidden truths, but not all truths are for everyone."

"Didn't the prophet Salmae say that the one eye should be open as wide as it can?" Prisca replied. "All I request is to have my eyes opened."

"She did say that." Holy Cirillo adjusted the patch over his left eye. "That is why we share our truths. What makes you think that we have anything hidden away?"

FORGED FOR DESTINY

"I had a friend who saw inside your vaults, back before..."

Prisca gestured toward the square, where warriors in blue were riding past a temple significantly grander than Yorl's, a horse god carved in bright new marble over its main arch. A group of young men and women in velvet tunics had stopped close to Raul and the tinker, filling the space around the empty plinth with their laughter and expansive gestures. The newcomers wore ostentatious medallions in the style of merchants' lucky coins, though Valens doubted any of them had ever done a day's trade. The warriors glanced at the youths, then rode on.

"Your friend misled you," Cirillo said. "We have no vault."

"Everyone keeps secrets."

"Not from Yorl, and not from the governor's men. Our temple stands at his pleasure, and could easily be turned over to a foreign god if we angered him."

"If you fear that I'm the governor's spy, you needn't worry." Prisca's finger stabbed at the air, too fast for Valens to follow, like she was writing a string of invisible letters. "My interests lie elsewhere."

The priest kept his eye turned pointedly away from Prisca's darting finger.

"Whatever your interests, I want no part of them. I won't be drawn into putting my congregation at risk." He scowled. "I met a royal minister who looked a lot like you, back before the fall, a woman with little respect for the independence of the temples. I thought that she died with the rest of the royal court. If she's still alive, I hope that she has the good sense to stay away from the city, because no one wants to see her here."

In the square, the expensively dressed youths had gathered around the nervous tinker, who laid a defensive hand on her pack. One of them was tugging at her sleeve, another messing with her hair. Raul stepped toward them, all smiles and gestures of peace, ready to calm any trouble. He was a good lad.

Valens pushed himself off the doorframe and lumbered over to Prisca and Cirillo. An attendant filling a brass bowl glanced at him, then hastily turned her eye away. Holy Cirillo stared at Valens, his expression stern.

"What?" he snapped. "Are you going to make me talk?"

Valens snorted. He could threaten the priest. He would, if Prisca told him to. Shit, he could snap the guy's wrinkled old neck as easily as he could swallow, or squeeze him until his face went red and he begged to talk, but the talk you got from that wasn't worth it. Torture got you more lies than truth.

"We should go." Valens laid a hand on the eating knife that sat where his sword should be. "This is a waste of time."

"Patience," Prisca said. "There is too much at stake here for us to precipitately abandon our interests."

Valens pressed his thumb against his forehead. She always used more long words when she was feeling obstinate, which made it doubly difficult to deal with. First he had to make sense of them, then he had to work out why they were wrong. Nine times out of ten, he couldn't do either.

"You don't need their prophecies," he said through gritted teeth. "You've found plenty already."

Or made them for herself, when she needed to. Before he lived with Prisca, Valens hadn't even known there was a difference between ink made now and ink from five hundred years ago.

Cirillo took a slow step back.

"If you have documents of prophecy," the priest said, "then I do not want to hear about it. Leave, now."

It wasn't the priest's command that made Valens look around. It was the sound of raised voices, the dying away of the crowd's chatter, the swift scuffling of feet across dirt. Sounds that made him grip the handle of his knife.

In the square, the tinker stood behind Raul, clutching her pack. One side of the pack had torn open, scattering pots, spoons, and small bags of herbs. Raul's fists were raised, and one of the rich kids in the velvet tunics lay at his feet, clutching a bloodied nose. The others were circling, flexing their arms, calling out jeers and insults. Pack tactics, instinctive and uncoordinated, but enough to surround Raul if he wasn't careful.

Before Valens could make a move, Prisca's hand gripped his forearm.

"Wait," she hissed.

"But he—"

"Believe in him."

Two of the rich kids charged at Raul, one from either side. He swung at one of them, ducked past her punch, grabbed her by the collar and belt, and hurled her into the other one. The two of them went down. Another tried to grapple Raul from behind, but his elbow slammed back and they stumbled away, clutching their chest.

One of the attackers, angrier than the rest, drew a knife so long it was almost a sword. Raul held up his hands and called out something that was lost amid the onlookers' excited shouts. The blade flashed as its edge caught the sunlight, but that was all it caught. The attacker had clearly spent his money on clothes and enamel-handled weapons, not fencing lessons. Raul sidestepped, wrapped his arm around the knife hand, and twisted. There was a crunch that cut through the crowd noise. The knife fell in the dirt.

The attackers backed off, forming a huddle around their injured, pointing and glaring at Raul. A few of the crowd cheered as the attackers scurried away, their velvet tunics dusty and dishevelled.

Raul helped the tinker gather her fallen goods. The crowd watched and some of them pointed at him. Valens thought he recognised a face or two from the riverbank. The high priest was also watching, his hand pressed against his chest.

Once the tinker was safely gone and the crowd dispersing, Raul headed up the temple steps. Valens stood taller, seeing the boy he had raised coming to them victorious.

"Sorry," Raul said, one hand rubbing the back of his neck. "I didn't mean to cause trouble, but they were trying to steal from her."

"The righteous need make no apology, and the transgressor knows not the words," Holy Cirillo said. "Do you know who those young people were?"

"Sorry, no, I'm new to the city."

"The one whose arm you broke is Senius Tisco. His mother has the contract to supply fodder for the barracks, the palace, and the teams transporting materials for the governor's memorial."

"Does that mean there's going to be trouble?" Raul looked at Prisca, then at Valens.

"From whom?" Holy Cirillo snorted. "The Tiscos are

FORGED FOR DESTINY

bullies, as cowardly as they are proud. Young Senius won't face the youth who hurt him, and he won't admit what happened to his mother or her friends at the palace."

"They work for the conquerors?"

"Where power runs, coin follows. Would you still have fought him if you had known?" The priest stared at Raul with an intensity set to scour away lies, to expose his moral sinews.

"I think so." Raul shrugged and gestured with an open hand at Valens. "My da taught me to stand up for what's right, no matter who it's against."

"You're his father?" The priest raised an eyebrow.

"I am." Valens stood so tall and proud, he could have taken that lost statue's place. All the other things he'd made in his life had been awful, mostly dead bodies and bad beer, but he'd got one thing right, and the result stood in front of him.

"Come with me."

They followed Holy Cirillo through the temple, past pillars carved with recurring images of waves, wheat, and clouds. One showed prisoners taken in war, a harvest of labour for the mines. At the front was an altar in the shape of a bull, illuminated by an ornately framed window and fat, smoking candles on iron stands. Attendants scattered and then regathered like startled flies. One of them handed Cirillo a rolled animal hide, while another set down a brass bowl and a matching jug. The high priest unrolled the hide, goat or something like it, the fur and the skin below so pale they were almost white. He poured red wine into the bowl, then held it out to Raul. An attendant draped an embroidered scarf across the boy's head, covering one eye, to Raul's clear bemusement.

"No blood drawn fresh from sinners anymore, but this will do well enough," Cirillo said. "Dip your fingers in the bowl, then scatter the droplets on the hide."

Valens watched, arms folded, chest aching with tension. What if the priest saw something he shouldn't? Why wasn't Prisca stopping this? She was the one who had shown Valens how powerful divination could be, yet she watched now as if simply curious. His fingers clenched tight on his upper arms.

The droplets pattered across the hide. Cirillo's eye shifted this way and that, surveying the red stains.

"I see a snake," he said.

"A snake, or a river?" Prisca asked. She leaned forward, and so did Raul, turning his head to study the pattern from different angles. Cirillo frowned as he looked at the lad.

"Your back." He pointed at a dark, damp stain just above Raul's belt. "What happened?"

"Oh, that." Raul laughed. "Funny thing, that *was* a river. I got battered on the bottom helping someone out. The bandage must have come loose."

"He saved a woman from drowning," Valens said. "Down by Rack's Scar."

"That was you? A river, then…" Cirillo smiled at Raul, then turned back to the droplets on the skin. "Strength, power, the unstoppable force of time, the water of life and the current that sweeps it away."

He tapped a cluster of wine stains on the skin. To Valens, they looked a mess, same as the rest, but Cirillo nodded and his brow furrowed.

"Destruction," he said.

FORGED FOR DESTINY

"I'm sorry," Raul whispered. "That's not what I want."

Cirillo reached out with a bony finger and tipped Raul's chin back, so that he looked straight at him. Any other young man would have withered before the intensity of the priest's gaze, but not Raul.

"Destruction is inevitable, young man. Yorl needs the empty socket as much as the piercing eye, to make space where visions can grow. The death of winter frost is the harbinger of spring's green growth, and sometimes a storm must sweep through to bring the trade wind that follows." He looked at Prisca. "I tried to explain that to the minister I met, but she would not accept the omens."

"Perhaps she has learned since then." Prisca bowed her head.

Cirillo took a deep breath and stepped back to take in the view of the hide.

"Is this you, young man?" he asked. "The strength of the river and the destruction it brings?"

"I hope not. I want to build something better, not destroy."

"Our desires and our destinies are seldom the same."

Cirillo's finger snaked across the hide, taking a winding path from one side to the other, hesitating at one point as if uncertain which way to turn. He glanced at the stain seeping around the edge of Raul's tunic, and he shook his head as if shaking off a fly. He grabbed the edge of the hide and rolled it quickly up.

"Here." He held out the hide to an attendant. "Burn this."

Part of Valens, the part of him that had struggled to balance an inn's costs for so many years, was appalled at the waste. It

Andrew Knighton

was a perfectly good hide, and these things didn't come cheap. There were a dozen ways they could have used it. But this was a temple, and the priests had authority.

"Come." Cirillo took a candle as thick as his forearm from an iron stand and beckoned them after him to a side door, down a set of well-worn stone stairs, into a cellar, a space with only one entrance, good for defending but bad for escaping. Its walls were carved with wide niches, the sort that might have held bones in any other temple. Here, they were empty.

"This is where we kept records of prophecies and divinations," he said. "Most of them are in Dunholm now, gathered up and swept away straight after the fall. Some were burned. I know which ones, and what they held." He tapped the side of his head. "I am told that theatre keeps our stories alive, but theatre warps and distorts, it fits real people into the spaces performance needs. There are other ways to preserve what we had, ways that are truer to the signs, to the essence of the world." He held out a hand. "Each of you give me a hair."

Valens ran a hand across his scalp.

"I ain't exactly got..."

"It doesn't have to be off your head."

Prisca was doing as she had been asked, and Raul following her lead, so Valens pushed up his sleeve and pulled a hair from his arm. It hurt more than he expected, but that was life, wasn't it?

Cirillo plucked one of his own grey hairs, twisted it up with the others, and dropped them into the candle flame. There was a brief crackle and a charring smell that seemed too intense to Valens. Cirillo dipped his finger in the wet wax at

FORGED FOR DESTINY

the top of the candle and drew with it on the wall. The shape of a key gleamed on the muted stone. Then, with a click, the wall swung open.

The room beyond was older, crudely carved, its niches small. As the priest went around lighting candles, they illuminated the books and scrolls in those gaps.

"The oldest and most precious records of Yorl's chosen," Cirillo said. "At least, the oldest you're going to see around here."

The door silently shut against Valens's back, leaving him trapped in the cramped space with documents staring down at him, a legion of incomprehensibly dangerous foes. Prisca smiled a thin smile and Raul looked around wide-eyed, but Valens had never felt so out of place.

Cirillo bowed his head and lowered his voice in prayer.

"Where the storm raged, let his eye show us calm seas; where there was drought, a time of rain." He rolled up his sleeves. "Let's see what the future holds."

Chapter Fourteen
An Audience of One

Raul hummed as he nailed together the parts for the stage tree. He'd asked Efron why they didn't cut down a real tree and bring that in, instead of faking one. The master of the players had explained that sometimes reality wasn't as convincing as illusion. Raul wasn't at all convinced about that, but Efron had to go talk about scene changes with Tenebrial, so Raul was left building by himself, trying not to obsess about the contradiction. Humming made for a good distraction.

"Is that meant to be 'The Prophet's Bower'?" a voice called indignantly from the balcony.

Raul stopped humming and looked up to see Yasmi, a mask in her hand and a mocking smile on her face.

"You recognised it, didn't you?" he called back.

"Only just. I don't think you had the right notes, never mind putting them in the right order."

"I'm not the leading lady of the new age," he pointed out.

"Just an amateur scenery maker. Why don't you show me how the song's sung?"

"If you insist."

Her smile made him smile even wider, and he flushed with anticipation as she spread her arms wide, took a deep breath, and started to sing.

The sound of her voice was as pure and clear as anything that Raul had ever heard. It flowed like a mountain river in the spring thaw, a force that washed his heart clean and left him feeling renewed. The walls of the theatre weren't enough to contain it, and as she sang, passersby walked in through the front doors, while players emerged from the wings. Yasmi sang about the past and the future, about the seeds that fell in the autumn and the promise of new life for the spring. She sang of lost love and anticipated comfort. Her voice rose in power and urgency until it reached one final peak, and then, as suddenly as life itself, it stopped.

Silence.

Then applause, the respectful appreciation of fellow professionals and the raw, heartfelt gratitude of ordinary people. Raul clapped as loudly as any of them.

Valens appeared at his elbow. "Prisca wants you."

Raul set down his hammer and headed backstage, to the room that his ma had made her own, like a thrush building its nest, but lined with papers and parchments instead of twigs and moss.

"Can I help with something?" Raul asked.

It seemed unlikely, though he'd tried. Alongside her, he'd read the documents they took from the governor's men, and the ones she had copied at the temple. Raul understood the words on the surface, but their deeper meanings eluded him until Prisca pointed them out, and she seemed more interested in watching his responses than in shaping them.

"This." She tapped the open cover of one of the books. "Did you see others like it?"

It was one from the raid. The cover was a thin wooden board, holes drilled down one side to take the twine that bound the pages. These were an older sort of books, Prisca had told him once.

"Some," Raul said. "Are you only after ones bound in beech?"

"What? No, idiot, not the wood. The symbol on it. Did you see others with it?"

Raul took a step back. She'd never called him an idiot before. Had he done something wrong?

Prisca looked up, frowned. Her eyes closed for a moment, and when they reopened, her expression softened.

"I'm sorry," she said. "I'm tired. This analysis is almost as draining as divination itself."

"I'm sorry. I forget, because it doesn't look like hard work." Now it was Raul's turn to regret his words, face crumpling in shame. "I mean, not that it's not hard, but it's not physical work, so you can't see it, and..."

"I understood." She tapped the book. "This symbol, have you seen it?"

The symbol was an hourglass with crenellations at the top, like a crown. Raul closed his eyes and thought back to the house they had raided, with its bulging shelves.

FORGED FOR DESTINY

"It was on the spines of some newer books, with leather covers. Why?"

"Someone was making a...a..."

Her knuckles went pale as her hand gripped the edge of the table.

"Are you all right, Ma?" Raul asked, and laid an arm around her shoulders.

"I'm fine." She shrugged him off. "I'm just...What's the word, for when you have a lot of things, and you put them together?"

"A collection?"

"Yes, that's it, a collection."

Raul laughed. "You're usually the one teaching me words."

"Yes."

Prisca lowered herself into a seat. Her fingers rubbed at trembling lips.

"Are you sure you're all right?" Raul crouched and took her hand. "You don't seem well."

"It's nothing." She jabbed at the book with her finger. "Someone was assembling a collection." She put extra emphasis on the recovered word. "Someone with impeccable taste. If there's more that interested them, then we need it."

"I'm sorry." Raul let go of her hand and looked again at the symbol. "I didn't know that you wanted those ones."

"We'll find a way to get them, I'm sure."

She looked up as Efron, Yasmi, and Tenebrial walked in, Valens behind them.

"You wanted to speak with us?" Efron asked.

"Indeed. I would like to talk about..." Her voice strained,

like a tree creaking in a storm wind. She straightened her back, clasped her hands together, and turned her full attention to Efron. "I want to talk again about adding a moment of heightened drama to the climax of the play. A physical transformation that will drive the larger truth home for the audience."

"An unmasking." Yasmi crossed her arms. The fingers of one hand plucked at her sleeve, making it puff out. "You're still pushing for this."

"An unmasking. That is what I mean."

"I think it has potential," Tenebrial said. "Imagine, humanity emerging from the world, one shape unravelling into another, just as Balbianus's fate is transformed, and our world with it."

"It's disgusting." Yasmi shook her head. "Practically pornographic. I won't do it."

"It would be memorable." Efron stroked his moustache.

"Really, Father?" Yasmi glared at him. "What would Mother think?"

"She always liked a big spectacle."

"This isn't a spectacle, this is—"

"Groundbreaking." Efron's eyes widened. "Unforgettable. The sort of performance people would talk about all across the country."

Yasmi froze, a fresh complaint halfway to her lips.

"What do you think, Valens?" Efron asked, his voice a little quieter as he looked around.

"I'm a warrior." Valens shrugged. "Don't know how theatre works."

FORGED FOR DESTINY

Prisca cleared her throat. Valens's brow drew in.

"I suppose Prisca's right," he said. "It would be dramatic."

"The common man speaks," Efron said. "Common in a good way, I mean, not that I, um, that is to say, Raul, what do you think?"

Everyone looked at him, Prisca's expression expectant, Yasmi's challenging. He wouldn't have known what to say even if he hadn't been caught between them. He'd seen Yasmi mask and unmask dozens of times, when it was just the two of them, but the world wasn't so simple that you could act the same way everywhere. Prisca and Valens had seen him naked when he was a child; that didn't mean he would strip off in front of Yasmi, and that thought made him feel even more awkward.

"Should Yasmi decide?" he asked. "She's the one who has to do it."

"Thank you," Yasmi said. "A voice of reason at last."

"No, no, no!" Tenebrial's hands jerked into the air. "We can't let the players decide the story—all we'll have is three hours of monologues, crotch jokes, and tragic deaths." He waved a finger under Efron's nose. "This is a matter of principle now. We unmask, or I leave."

The playwright turned on his heel and stormed out of the room.

"Well, if we do have an unmasking, then *I'm* leaving." Yasmi tossed her hair.

"Don't be absurd," Efron said, shaking his head. "You wouldn't give up this grand chance to perform before the whole city. Whereas Tenebrial..." He shrugged apologetically. "You know what he's like."

181

Yasmi glanced at the door, at the window, then at Raul. He wished that there was something he could do.

"This isn't fair," she whispered.

"I'm sorry, my queen of the boards, but life is seldom fair." Efron patted her on the shoulder. "Look on the bright side: you're going to be very, very famous."

Very, very famous. Those words echoed in Yasmi's head as she followed Chamberlain Tur along hallways and stairwells from the gatehouse into the heart of the palace. Of course that fame appealed, and the adulation that came with it. She might have gone from backcountry taverns to a regional palace, but there was still much further to rise, and an infamous spectacle could help. It would draw crowds into their theatre, there was no denying that. She imagined their gasps and cheers, maybe even a shocked scream or two. It was everything she wanted. But at what price? Could she bear to make herself that vulnerable, to let herself unravel and re-form in front of strangers?

Her father and Tenebrial had offered to come with her to the palace, to be there for the reading. They had practically insisted. In response, she had dug her heels in and denied them that choice. They might force their will on her for the final play, but tonight, she would show them that she still had some power.

Construction was under way in the main entrance to the palace, some defensive work that Tur refused to discuss and that Yasmi only asked about for politeness's sake. Rather than clamber through scaffolding and step around workmen, they

FORGED FOR DESTINY

took an indirect route to the throne room, down corridors that ran through the outer walls, past stables and storerooms and steps into darkness. At one point, they walked through a cold tower whose bolted door must surely have opened onto the cliffs. A back route out, perhaps. A way to discreetly escape if she disgraced herself.

As they walked deeper into the palace, such dull details were replaced by accommodation suitable for nobles and courtiers. The rooms became warm, the air scented with incense and sweet herbs. There were clean-burning oil lanterns instead of tallow candles, tiled floors instead of trampled rushes. Tapestries and banners decorated the walls, some of them clumsy depictions of war and adventure, others elegant portrayals of courtly life, the finely dressed and refined company that Yasmi dreamed of keeping. Heavy curtains and sturdy shutters kept the wind from coming through the windows, protecting her from the cold of the outside world.

They ascended a last set of stairs, with a marble rail down the side, and crossed a hall whose high windows showed the starlit sky. The guards that had flanked her and Tur the whole way through took hold of the doors in front of them. Reinforced oak swung open into the throne room.

Yasmi paused for a moment, straightened her sash belt, ran a finger across her masks. Should she have kept on the gold bangles? They had made her feel ready for grand surroundings. But no. Tonight she would impress with words and performance, not shining trinkets. She was wearing her finest silk trousers and tunic, with birds embroidered down her right side. That would be enough.

She walked in with head held high, smiling for her audience.

Count Alder sat on his throne, elegantly dressed and perfectly poised, alone except for a guard by the small door behind him, barring the only other exit. This was what the troupe had asked for, so that as few people as possible would know the play before opening night, but Efron hadn't expected the count to listen. Apparently, the previous governor had always invited a dozen of his closest allies, a chance to entertain them, to show people how special they were.

Without a crowd, it was harder to judge her position, when she was getting too near to her audience. How close did she dare go to this one man, his cavalry sabre hanging beside his slashed silk robe, that sardonic half smile beneath short dark wavy hair.

"My lord." A dozen strides from the throne, she stopped and bowed.

"Mistress Dellest, I assume?" Count Alder gave a small wave. "You may stand."

She straightened and stood facing him. She wanted to check her tunic, to tug out the wrinkles that always formed when she bowed, but to do that in front of him would be a disaster. She didn't dare look away as he stared at her, dark eyes scrutinising, judging.

"I hear that you are good at what you do," he said. It was a good voice, one to match his looks, smooth skin offset by enough stubble to turn him from boy into man.

She mustn't hesitate, mustn't become distracted. This was her chance.

"I am the best, my lord."

FORGED FOR DESTINY

"Then this should be an enjoyable evening; I've missed real entertainment."

He took a goblet off a table beside the throne, one in the shape of a skull. No—upon another look, Yasmi realized it was a *real* skull. She was enthralled and appalled in equal measure. There must be a story behind it. What enemy had he slain to take that trophy?

"Please, proceed," Count Alder said.

Yasmi drew her hair back across her shoulders, tapped her foot three times, and held out her hands.

"Four hundred years hence, you sit and watch our story." It was a line for the chorus, not the shifter, but tonight she played all the parts. "Since when, long years have passed, our bones become dust and glory..."

No player could be at their best alone, performing for three hours straight, without set or props or costume, reduced to reciting lines. It didn't help that some of those lines had been changed, whole scenes removed, other parts more subtly altered, a barbed play neutered to satisfy the censor. She couldn't even don her masks, much as she wanted their strength, their shelter, the extra skin of confidence that came with truly becoming someone else. But she was Yasmi Dellest, idol of the stage from here to the border. She gave a performance worthy of a throne room.

Count Alder watched patiently, his dark eyes fixed on her. From the sides of her vision, she saw Tur craning his neck, guards shuffling down the room to better see and hear. Even the skull goblet seemed to watch her with its empty eyes. She stood taller, inflated by their attention, lifted up by their admiration. This was what she lived for.

185

At last, mouth dry and throat aching, she took her bow.

Count Alder set his goblet down. The fingers of one hand tapped against the palm of the other, the faintest applause she had ever received.

"Bravo," he said. "That was rather good, wasn't it, Tur?"

"Indeed, my lord," the chamberlain croaked.

Yasmi slumped. Rather good? Was that the best that she had managed? She had finally reached the halls of real power, and she had disgraced herself.

"There's no need to pull that kicked-puppy face," Alder said, with a crooked half smile. "I grew up at the royal court, watching the very best. A formal recital from a provincial little troupe was never going to compare."

Provincial. Little. The words were daggers slicing at her heart.

"Gods' blood, someone bring the poor girl a drink, she must be parched."

Alder walked down the steps from the throne. A servant hurried over, refilled the count's goblet, and put a silver cup in Yasmi's hand. She took a sniff, then a sip. It was the best wine she had ever tasted.

"You're the troupe's shifter." Alder walked slowly around her, assessing her like she was a horse waiting for auction. He smelled of new leather and fresh straw.

"Yes, my lord." She stood tall, tilted her face to better catch the light.

"My grandmother was fascinated by shifters." Alder tapped a finger against the rim of his grotesque goblet. "Wanted to use them in war. She recruited a legion of volunteers for it, brave and wily warriors, and half a score of craftsmen who claimed that they could carve weirdwood masks. Can you guess what happened?"

"They must have failed, my lord, or all the world would have heard."

"Indeed. So tell me, Yasmi, why did it fail?"

Yasmi took a sip of her drink and peered at the count over the cup. Which strand of the truth was he trying to tug free? The role of the shifter, perhaps, trained from childhood to transform without ruining their body. The masks, carved not just with unique techniques and materials but with an eye to who would wear them. The audience, maybe, how their belief in a certain truth powered the transformation, even when they were an audience of one. Timing even, the way that the seasons and the hours helped or hindered. Which of these was Alder after?

If the count's grandmother had worked on this, then she must have learned the practicalities of her failure, why her plan was near impossible. Which meant that Alder wasn't looking for that. He'd fed her a line to see if she knew the next one, the theory behind her powers, this matter of essence.

"I don't understand how shifting works myself." There was no need to act. She had her instincts, and that was enough. "I follow my heart and a lifetime of training, but without that..." She shook her head. "Magic is a strange business. I can pretend to understand it when I play a scholar, but that's all. You'll have to find your explanation elsewhere."

Alder looked at her, just a trace of laughter crooking the corners of his lips.

"A good answer," he said. "As good as I'll get, I'm sure."

"Thank you, my lord." She took another sip of her drink, tried not to tremble.

"You have good masks." His tone was lighter but Yasmi knew an act when she heard it.

"My mother commissioned some. Others are from further back in the family."

"Good shifters are even rarer than good actors, as my grandmother proved. Are you any good?"

"I think so, my lord." An hour before, she had been certain of it. An hour before, every audience had loved her. Now she had met the audience that mattered most and learned how little she knew.

"Show me."

He faced her, only a few feet away, fingers curled around that skull as he sipped his wine, dark eyes twinkling. The man could have been a player himself.

This was it. Her chance to make up for her disappointing performance. Her chance to really impress. She reached for the wolf, and touching her favourite mask made her feel confident again.

She stopped, the wolf in her hand. Her mother had told her never to give the audience what they asked for, whether that audience was a theatre crowd or one man alone. To impress took anticipation, it took surprise. Give them what they thought they wanted and they would never be impressed. Give them what they asked for and you weren't even the one making the show.

"I'm sorry, my lord, but that's not what I'm here for," she said. "I'm sure that a cultured man like you knows that a

FORGED FOR DESTINY

professional won't shift in front of her audience. Even a provincial professional."

Her heart hammered at the dread and the daring of it all, of denying anything to a relative of the royal family. When she had learned tightrope as a child, every step had felt like it risked a terrible fall, and now that dizzying sensation returned. She raised the silver cup to her mouth, took a deep drink, and slowly licked her lips. Keeping her hand steady was her finest performance so far.

Alder's lopsided smile crept just a little higher.

"Very good." His goblet tapped against her cup. "I shall have to keep an eye on you, Yasmi Dellest. With the right trainer, you might become one of the greats."

He turned from her and walked toward a set of shutters at the side of the room. Guards opened the window and a wind swept in across a balcony, ruffling his hair. Yasmi had relished the comforting warmth in the palace, but now that cool touch came as a blessed relief.

"Tell me, Yasmi, do you sing?" Alder asked.

"Yes, my lord." Her world had felt blown around and battered before, but it seemed to have settled.

"Would you sing now? Something civilised, not this country's rough songs?"

She took a drink. He was giving her another chance. Saying no once had been daring, twice would be too far. Besides, singing was easy. She didn't need to remember a whole play, or to take on a body that wasn't her own. She just had to let her essence take hold.

"My throat is a little dry, my lord, but I will do my best."

189

"I would expect nothing less."

She thought of her performance earlier, and of watching Raul before that, listening to the awful noise he made while he was working. She couldn't have called it a tune, but it made her smile. She remembered the look in his eyes as he watched her sing, and she didn't feel inadequate anymore.

"The Prophet's Bower," then. An encore.

She clasped her hands in front of her, took a deep breath, and let the first note rise. Alder leaned against the balcony, framed by the stars of the sky, his cup sitting forgotten in his hand as his smile grew wider with each note.

This was it. The audience she had looked for, a handsome noble and the promise of glories to come. A thrill ran through Yasmi as she opened her heart and let her song soar.

Chapter Fifteen
A Charmed Life

The city was so much louder and lighter at night than the Winding Vales had ever been. It seemed to Raul that every second street they passed had someone shouting or singing, though it was near midnight, and those who were still awake would surely miss the first light in the morning. Those people seemed so cheerful, even if the intensity of their conversations could be intimidating and their songs were slurred with drink. Warm light poured from the doorways of a hundred inns, all ready to welcome weary travellers. Maybe one night, once the kingdom was free, he could stay up late and wander, watch the patchwork of light and shadow, listen to the songs, step through some of those doorways and meet new people. Maybe then, it wouldn't feel so overwhelming.

Not tonight. Tonight he moved in shadows, a new axe in his hand, a dozen people with him. Valens, Prisca, Appia and three of her dockers, others from the growing number who showed up at the theatre for hurried conversations with his parents, who looked at Raul with hope or doubt or desperation. When their eyes met, a sense of responsibility fell upon him, and he stood taller for it. Their expectations gave him strength.

A door opened, the light from within cutting through the darkness ahead. Raul froze. Valens grabbed his arm and dragged him two stumbling steps before he found his feet again, striding through that light and on.

"I thought we weren't meant to be seen," Raul whispered.

"You think a crowd lurking in the shadows would be less conspicuous?" Valens asked.

"I suppose not." Raul would have to remember that, when it was time to do these things without his guardians guiding him, whenever that happened. A hero couldn't shelter under his da's cloak forever.

The end of the street brought them to the edge of a cleared area, near the top of one of the hills. Here, the governor's half-built memorial towered above the rubble where houses had once stood. Even in the gloom of a half-clouded night, it stood out, two angular peaks, dark against the background of sky and snow-capped mountains.

"Fucking obscenity," Appia growled, and spat at her feet.

"Good to remember the dead," Valens said.

"Their dead, not ours."

"We're all the same under the armour." Valens glanced at Raul. "I mean, except that we're in the right."

"To the left," Prisca whispered. "The tents. You see them?"

Sure enough, three squares of pale canvas squatted in a cleared patch on the gentler side of the rubble-strewn slope.

FORGED FOR DESTINY

The moon emerged from behind the clouds that were gusting past on an easterly wind, and everything stood out starker. Dark stripes against the side of one tent showed a pair of guards on duty, but Raul had learned a lot since they came to the city, and those weren't going to be the only warriors.

"You sure the books are in there?" Appia asked.

"I saw a flight of crows swerve in their path across this part of the city, and then swallows do the same," Prisca said. "When I caught one of them and cast the entrails, I saw signs for knowledge, for secrets, for freedom. The books are in there."

"I'd put them somewhere with solid walls."

"They've already got to guard this place," Valens said. "Putting the books here saves on warriors."

"Still reckon we should torch it once you've got what you want."

"Those papers belong to our people," Prisca said. "I won't see them destroyed, even if we can't liberate them all."

The rebels gathered in the dark, clutching their weapons and watching their leaders. Raul felt the weight of expectation, of people waiting to see what he was worth. His mouth went dry thinking about whether he could do this. Was it the same for everyone? Did doubts hold his comrades back?

"I know it's daunting," he said, just loud enough to be heard. "Not knowing what we'll face. Wondering whether you're ready to fight. When that doubt creeps in, think of your comrades and the faith they've shown, by fighting alongside you. They believe in you, just like you believe in them. Trust their judgement and let their faith hold you up. We are stronger in this together than we ever would be alone."

193

The words sounded weak, nothing like the grandeur Tenebrial threaded through his speeches. Yet there were nods, quiet murmurs of assent, a stiffening of backs that spoke to stiffening resolve.

"Blood for luck," someone whispered, and others followed suit. Raul joined in the words and imitated the gesture that came with them, like he was stabbing an unseen opponent with his finger. That seemed to please them even more.

"Well done, Raul," Prisca whispered.

She pulled a scarf up to cover her nose and mouth, and Raul did the same. Around them was a soft rustling as the rebels pulled on disguises, pulled out weapons, and kissed charms for protection. The grain of wood pressed against Raul's palm as he shifted the axe in his hand, adjusting his grip, though he could never get it quite right. He took a deep breath, puffing himself up to feel a bit bigger, to chase away the tingling of his skin and the flutter like flies' wings in his belly. He wished he had a charm, a rabbit's foot perhaps, or a feather he'd found on an auspicious day, but he'd never found his own luck.

"Wait," Valens whispered, tilting back his head. "Wait... wait..." Another cloud slid in front of the moon. "Now."

They ran across the broken ground, no one speaking a word. Raul stumbled on unseen rubble, flung out his arms, more fell than ran forward, but found his balance and kept going. A thud told him that someone else hadn't been so charmed.

It was barely a hundred strides to the tents, just long enough for a guard to turn at the noise and peer into the darkness.

"Hey, what's—"

FORGED FOR DESTINY

Valens's blade cut her words as surely as her throat. The other guard brought his spear around, but Appia grabbed the shaft while he was squinting into the darkness, and one of her men hacked him down. The guard let out a squawk of alarm between the first blow and the one that finished him.

With two swift slashes of her gleaming knife, Prisca cut a triangular hole in the side of the tent. She stepped through and Raul followed, while the others ran on around, hunting guards.

The tent was full of construction supplies: ropes, mallets, scaffold poles, the pegs to join them together, anything that might have suffered from being left out in the weather. Raul flung open the lid of a chest, but inside were metal spikes, not the scrolls and books he'd hoped for.

Prisca pushed a flap aside and strode out the far side. A body's length away, the flicker of a newly lit lantern shone from the next tent. The night was full of thuds, clangs, cries of alarm.

Raul pushed past his ma, axe in hand, and into the tent. A warrior with a captain's white sash stood by an oil lamp on a barrel. There was a chair behind her, a saddle for a footrest, and a blanket tossed to the ground. She blinked sleep from her eyes.

"Who are you?" Her hand went to her sabre.

"You don't need to get hurt," Raul said, hefting his axe. "Just let go of the sword."

"I don't think so, boy."

She drew and lunged in a single swift movement, blade hissing through the space between them. On instinct, Raul stepped back, even as he brought his axe around. He'd thought to catch the blade on his haft, but the curving path of the strike shifted, came around, caught him on the shoulder. Shocked by the impact, he stumbled back again, though the blow was more bruising than blood-letting.

The captain kept up her assault, a flurry of blows coming in from every angle. Raul parried one, ducked another, deflected a third. She was fast and agile, her feet constantly moving, position shifting to find the best angle of attack. He knew enough to understand why she was beating him, but not enough to stop it.

Another slash hit his forearm, cut the shirt, and sliced the skin beneath. Blood trickled along the bottom of Raul's hand, though only a little. He smiled as he dodged her next attack. He saw it now. All these attacks were so swift because they had no force. This was fighting for show, not to kill. It seemed so intimidating, but what use was that against what Valens had taught him?

Raul hurled himself forward, axe swinging. It wasn't an elegant blow. It didn't need to be. It broke the captain's rhythm, sent her stumbling, eyes wide. Her mouth opened to shout, but her feet hit the saddle, she fell, and the ground knocked the breath from her lungs. Her fingers reached for her fumbled sabre, but Raul stamped on her wrist, then brought his axe around. The flat of the blade hit the side of her head with a sound like empty barrels knocking, and she went limp.

Raul bent over to check that she was unconscious. As he tipped her head, a shield-shaped lead charm on a leather cord slid around her neck and into the dirt.

FORGED FOR DESTINY

He turned, looking for signs of other soldiers. The only movement was Prisca, stooped over a selection of chests. She was drawing something from her satchel.

"What's that?" Raul asked.

"The wrong book," she said, placing it in one of the chests. "My mistake. Bring the lamp closer to find the ones we need."

Raul took the lamp from off the barrel and held it high, so that it illuminated inside all the chests. Prisca crouched in front of them, scanning their contents.

"Those there." Raul pointed to the middle chest. "The pile at the back. They're the same size as the ones I saw before."

Prisca lifted out the topmost book. Sure enough, it had the symbol of a crenellated hourglass on the spine, the one they were looking for.

"You have an excellent eye for details," Prisca said. "One day soon, you'll learn to see the bigger picture." She handed him a sack. "Put them in this, I'm going to check the others."

Raul set the lantern down and picked out books, just the ones with that symbol on them. There were more than he had expected. Behind him, Prisca rummaged through another chest.

"Do we need all of these?" he asked.

"Of course not." Prisca's voice was sharp. "But this is no time to sort through them."

"Sorry, I was just curious."

She took a deep breath and her voice softened. "It's good that you pay attention to the world, Raul, but perhaps we could save the questions for later?"

"Yes, Ma."

"Don't call me Ma."

The tent flap was flung open. Raul jerked to his feet, but it was Valens, blood spattered across his face and dripping from his sword, like a hero at the end of a great adventure.

"Alarm's been raised," he said. "Time to go."

Raul grabbed his axe and slung the sack over his uninjured shoulder. The corners of books jabbed into his back. They got heavy when there were this many of them, as if all the ideas they held added to the burden.

"Want me to take that?" Valens asked, holding out a hand.

Raul shook his head. This was his part of the mission, and he didn't want anyone to think that he couldn't do it. He strode out into the night.

The air around the construction site smelled of blood and worse. In the light leaking from the tent, Appia was holding up one of her people. Another was clutching a rag to their own arm. Beyond the tents and the rubble, more windows and doorways were lit up than before, more voices rose from the shadows. The most voices came from the northeast, where someone was shouting in the far-off streets.

Valens looked around, then pointed. They all started running downhill, Raul and Appia in the lead, Prisca in the middle, Valens bringing up the rear. The moon was hidden, the ground uneven, and Raul struggled to keep his footing as he picked up momentum. His toes hit a chunk of brick, his ankle turned, he started falling.

Fingers clamped around his arm, kept him upright long enough to stretch out his leg, find balance again, keep moving. Then Valens let go and they were running together, side

FORGED FOR DESTINY

by side off the wasteland and into the streets, like they'd run across the hillsides back home.

The buildings closed in, hiding them from the moonlight that seeped through thinning clouds. Appia, still supporting her injured comrade, led them this way and that, through the twisting chaos of the city. Within moments, Raul was completely lost, but so were the sounds of pursuit. The rebels slowed to a walk.

"Good work, lad." Valens laid a hand on Raul's shoulder. "I saw that captain you felled in there."

Raul smiled. His arm had almost stopped bleeding, the books had settled nicely against his back, even his bruised shoulder felt better beneath Valens's palm. Most importantly, they'd got what they came for and gotten away.

Maybe he did have a lucky charm after all. Maybe he'd had one his whole life. Not a rabbit's foot or a found feather or a lead shield on a leather thong, but something far more potent.

He had his parents.

Chapter Sixteen
Signs in the Mud

Raul sat beside Prisca, copying lines from books, reading through others with the meticulous, word-by-word care he'd had when she first taught him his letters. He felt like that child again, basking in his ma's attention, grasping at the tasks she gave him, determined to show her how smart he was. Just like then, he was dissecting the words to draw out meanings that had recently lain hidden, though now he picked at metaphors and repetitions instead of the tricky business of "th" and "ph" and "gh." His legs were too long to swing underneath his seat, but he tapped one foot against the floorboards and hummed quietly as he read.

"Hush, please," Prisca said. "I'm trying to concentrate."

"Sorry." That moment was pleasingly familiar too, unlike the itch in his bandaged forearm, which was annoying. He scratched at it.

"Is something the matter?" Prisca's hawk-like gaze turned to his hand.

FORGED FOR DESTINY

"Itches a bit."

"Is anything seeping or inflamed? Even the slightest wound can putrefy if poorly tended."

"Just a rough edge on the bandage. I'll re-tie it later."

"Very well, but if anything's amiss, you have Valens look at it."

"Yes, Ma."

"I don't want you getting an infection."

"No, Ma."

"I've told you before, 'Ma' is an old woman sliding into senility."

"Sorry, Prisca."

"That's better."

He smiled and started tapping his foot again, remembering just in time not to start humming.

The room they were working in had become a lot like Prisca's hidden room above the brewhouse back home. Books and bound parchments mixed with fluttering scraps, copies of classics alongside documents for customers and friends. She had even assembled a small ink still, which bubbled away in one corner, its crucible heating over an oil flame. Amid the astringent smell of the ink, Raul could almost believe that if he looked out the window he'd see the rolling green Vales and not the cramped city streets. But if that had been real, then he would have been hearing birdsong, instead of the tumbling, jumbling chatter of a thousand human voices.

He turned a page, yawned, rubbed his eyes. Barely midday and he was flagging. It seemed absurd, when he wasn't even fetching and carrying, just sitting like Old Wellic by the fire in the inn. Perhaps only his brain was tired, not his body, and he should go make scenery while his mind rested. He could paint quietly, without interrupting Yasmi's rehearsals.

Two words drew his attention back to the page: "spiked moon." That was how many texts referred to Balbianus's symbol of a dagger through the crescent moon. Raul ran his finger back up the page and read again:

When the red eye watches over Rack's Gate,
When lie marches in truth's shoes and falsehood becomes fate,
Through shadow and earth shall walk the people's sword,
Come from the wilderness of green, a nation to restore.
The spirit of the spiked moon shall stride into haunted hall,
The song of the heart shall rise and the false lord shall fall.

He tapped his finger against the fifth line. Something there was familiar. He reached for his notes from a previous book. Sure enough, there it was: *Haunted hall is palace? Haunted royal ghosts, or governor as false spirit?*

The spirit of the spiked moon could be the essence of Balbianus, which was to say Raul himself. He was meant to go to the palace. That was hardly a surprise, it wouldn't be much of a revolution without taking back the throne, but this seemed to say more. Was it telling him when to act?

He turned a page, feeling its rough edge, scanning every mottled inch of the paper, but the book was a collection of old poems and prophetic texts, and none of the others related to this one.

"Prisca, I have a question." His voice was too loud in the

FORGED FOR DESTINY

small room, so he lowered it. "The city used to have a lot of gates through the walls, right?"

"That is correct." She didn't look up from her book. "Queen Junia had two of them closed to wagons, to facilitate the efficient collection of tithes, but five remained in full use."

"Were any of them called Rack's Gate?"

"No..." Her voice trailed off and her brow crumpled, then she nodded. "Rack's Gate refers to the pass between two of the mountain peaks, the Old Dog and Watcher's Height."

"And do you know anyone with a red eye?" His foot tapped faster on the boards. "Or maybe one of the earls had a red eye for this symbol, and he's out there somewhere, not seen since the invasion?"

This was how he had to think about the prophecies, not to find the most obvious interpretation, but to look for something more.

"The Red Eye is utterly unsuitable for heraldry. It is one of the most ominous signs in the sky, a star that appears in its own shifting cycle. Its chaotic essence has often heralded times of change and darkness."

"Change can be good, right? And it might not be dark for us?"

"What has got into you? You're shaking the table."

Raul thrust the book in front of her.

"Look! This is about Balbianus coming back, about the palace and taking on a false lord. Then see here, it's meant to be when the red star—"

"Yes, yes, I see." Without looking around, Prisca pointed to a shelf behind her. "See if there's a volume of astronomical tables."

Raul grabbed one book after another off the shelf, yanked them open, and slammed them shut, looking for an opening page that mentioned stars or astronomy. Some were so strange or abstract he didn't even understand why Prisca had chosen them. What did *The Principles of Logistical Essence* have to do with their work? This was why Prisca made the plans and he followed them: his ma saw connections he couldn't.

"Tesmodon's *Articulation of the Ever-Cycling Heavens*?" Raul asked, taking down a leather book with the arms of the Woven Lands stamped on the front.

"Perfect."

Prisca accepted the book and rapidly turned the pages. Each one was a mass of curving lines and symbols that crisscrossed in strange tangles. Raul felt as confused as he had those first few times learning to read. He stared at the marks that meant so much to his ma, but their meaning remained hidden from him.

"There." Prisca tapped the page. "The Red Eye will appear over Rack's Gate in twenty-three days. That must be our moment." She turned her thin smile upon Raul. "This is our opportunity. The prophecies have spoken. We move then and victory will be ours."

"What about this stuff with shoes and fate?"

"We can worry about that later." She raised her voice. "Valens! Where are you?"

"Maybe you shouldn't shout when the players are rehearsing?"

"They'll live. Valens!"

Heavy footsteps pounded the boards and Valens ran in, sword in hand. He looked around, then lowered his blade.

FORGED FOR DESTINY

"Thought something was wrong," he mumbled, setting his sword down on the table.

"On the contrary, something is very right." Prisca tapped the page of prophecy. "Raul has discovered what he must do, and when."

"Oh, he's found that, has he?"

"I have." Raul beamed.

Valens didn't seem as pleased as Raul expected. He looked slowly from Raul to Prisca, his expression blank, then took a slow breath, like he was working up to saying something. His fingers found the black mourning ring, and as he turned it, he nodded.

"Well done, Raul." Valens's brow furrowed, and he smiled sadly. "Suppose we'd better get ready, hadn't we?"

———————————— • ————————————

The sacks of grain were the size of a man's head, large enough to be useful, small enough to spread largesse without hurting the city's reserves. Alder smiled as he stood on the back of the swaying wagon, handing those sacks down to the poor as he rolled through the streets. It was no way for a nobleman to travel, but a good way to be seen.

"My lord, do we really need to be here?" Tur, kneeling next to Alder, gripped the side of the wagon tight with one hand while gingerly handing grain out with the other. "We could have given this task to labourers or guards. There are legal cases you need to hear, supplies to be arranged, correspondence to address..."

Andrew Knighton

Alder dropped a sack into the hands of a mud-smeared peasant, tossed another to the beggar behind her. More people were following in their wake as word spread of what was happening. Alder smiled, waved, dropped more grain to the crowd.

"Do you know how long my father petitioned the king for this post?" Alder dropped two more sacks into grubby, grasping hands. At least one of those fellows was on his second round. If Alder had told the crowd, they would have leapt on the man, demanding fair shares, but the last thing Alder wanted was to cause a fight. This was meant to be a happy occasion. He gave the man his grain and watched him scurry away.

"A decade, at least, my lord," Tur said. "I distinctly remember helping to scribe the first petition."

"And when did the king agree?"

"Last winter, after your late father passed."

"Not just after. The moment he was in the dirt, I received my commission. What does that tell you?"

For the first time that afternoon, Tur focused on handing out the sacks, his face crumpling in concentration that Alder didn't think was about balance.

"Answer me," the count said.

"I don't know." Tur looked with a frown across the hungry faces trailing after them. "It is hardly my place to judge the thoughts of a king."

Alder raised an eyebrow. Tur couldn't be this naive after his years around the court. There was one political lesson he had clearly learned, that sometimes it was better to feign ignorance.

FORGED FOR DESTINY

"The king knew I was the best choice for this post," Alder said. "He wanted me here, but he couldn't be seen to give my father anything, after the bad blood between them."

The cart bumped over a rut in the road. Alder kept his balance, arms wide, while Tur sprawled across the grain sacks. The driver shouted an apology and the guards riding alongside them closed in, but Alder waved all of that away. He held a hand out to help Tur up, then went back to doling out grain.

"Sometimes, show matters as much as substance," Alder said. "So we come out here, the governor and his chamberlain. We slow down this work, which labourers could do better, and we work late tonight on the tasks we should have done now. For all of that inefficiency, we will be praised, and people will talk about how well we rule."

Alder picked up two more of the small sacks. People behind the wagon stared up at him in gaunt hunger as he held the corn aloft, showing his bounty to the watchers in the windows and the street. Then he lowered those sacks into the thin and desperate hands of the poor, making sure he was seen by those same eyes.

———————————•———————————

"Do a lot of places sell lanterns?" Raul asked.

"Enough," Valens replied, looking around the Blood Market, trying to work out which street would take him to the right sorts of artisans.

"So how will we know which to buy from?"

"By looking." Valens tried not to let his impatience show. It wasn't really the lad's questions that were bothering him, and he knew it. It was every other thing about this situation. Problem was, everything centred on the lad, so that was where his impatience broke through.

"We'll need someone who makes a lot of lanterns, if we're leading people into the palace through tunnels. Even if most of them stay outside ready to rise up after we—"

"Hush, lad." The words finally sank in, dragging his attention from the streets to his ward. "Don't talk about that in the open."

"No one's listening. They're all busy with their own business."

"You don't know that. Now come, this way."

Valens wished that he could wear his sword around the city. He felt like he was constantly being watched, like every person they barged past on the way through the market might be the one who recognised him from back in the day, or who saw something strange in him and Raul. Every warrior they passed could be the one who decided they were suspicious or who wanted to impress his comrades by picking on the locals. Things could turn sour at any moment, but the weapon that would have got him odd looks in the Vales would get him arrested here. Even axes or stout sticks, though legal, risked marking them out as trouble, and the closer their time came, the more important it was not to draw attention. All he carried was the knife on his belt, sharpened beyond what it needed to cut his food, and an eye for his surroundings, picking out the narrow gaps, the high ground, the potential weapons everywhere they went. Being ready to leap in and give his own

FORGED FOR DESTINY

life for the boy. It was what Fabia had done. Valens wouldn't shame her by doing less.

"Piece of pork belly, sir?" A butcher held out his wares. "It was slaughtered at the fat of the moon, so you know it's going to be good and tasty."

Valens ignored the offer. He loved a city market, the bustle and busyness, the sheer variety. Whatever cut he wanted, it would be here—like that pork. Spices to cook it in. Bread and wine to go with it. Two streets over there was a woman who'd do the cooking for him, get the meat just perfect, so the juices oozed out with every bite. You couldn't get that in the Vales. But this afternoon he had to stay focused, even though he'd not eaten yet. This afternoon was about sliding pieces into place around Raul, about building him up, like Prisca had planned.

Except that Raul was gone from his side.

Valens whirled around, reaching for the sword that wasn't there. He relaxed as he spotted Raul standing in front of one of the stalls, staring at a hunk of meat.

"Come on." Valens tapped Raul on the shoulder. "We're not here for beef."

"Look at it." Raul pointed at one of the cuts. "What shape does that look like to you?"

"Steak-shaped."

"Not moon-shaped?"

Valens shrugged. He'd never been one for poetic comparisons, and he didn't understand this one. "I suppose."

"There's a dagger through it."

"It's a butcher's spike. They use it to..." Valens's voice

trailed off as he realised what the boy was getting at. A moon shape with a spike through it. Prisca's talk of seeking signs had got to him, and it had gone too far. Valens needed to keep the lad grounded in reality. "It's just meat, a coincidence."

"Or maybe the world is sending us a sign."

"That's not how the world works."

"Isn't it? Then why are we out looking for lanterns?"

Valens frowned. When had the boy learned to use questions like they were accusations? This was what happened from too much time around Prisca.

"Speaking of lanterns…"

"Look."

Raul crouched, peering at the dirt by the foot of the stall. A woman jostled him with her basket as she passed.

"Watch what you're about there, you fool," she said. "You're going to give someone a tumble, get your own back broke while you're about it."

Valens stepped behind Raul, sheltering him from the flow of pedestrians. They might miss the crouching youth, but no one ever missed Valens.

"What would you call that shape?" Raul asked.

Valens squinted over the boy's shoulder.

"It's a mess of blood and dirt, like battlefield mud."

"But doesn't it look like a lantern shape?"

"Maybe, if you squint."

"And this one next to it, a bird maybe?"

"Sure, it's a bird." Agreeing had become a habit while he was in the army: agreeing with captains and earls so he wouldn't get punished, agreeing with his comrades because

FORGED FOR DESTINY

what they shared mattered more than what held them apart. Agreeing worked on Prisca too, when she was in one of these moods. He might as well try it on the lad. "Come on, we've got business to do."

"Are you buying or just gawping?" the butcher asked, staring over her stall at them.

"Leaving." Valens tapped Raul on the shoulder, the one that wasn't lumpy with bandages and poultices under the tunic. "Come on."

At the end of the marketplace, three people stood on a raised platform, two of them men and one a woman. Their hands were bound, their legs joined with shackles, and their filthy shirts had been torn open to expose their backs. Half a dozen armed warriors stood around the base of the platform, and another was up there with the prisoners, lashing their backs with a horse whip, one at a time. One of the prisoners cried out as the whip bit, leaving a red line across the pale skin of his back.

"What is this?" Raul asked, his voice edged in horror.

Valens hesitated, trying to work out what to say. He couldn't just tell the lad that this was what conquerors did, pain to keep the conquered in line. He was meant to be teaching him why they were in the right and these people in the wrong.

"Those three run one of the big city granaries," said a woman next to them, eager to show that she knew the gossip. "They mixed eggshells in with the grain, like folks used to do, to protect it from rot. Count Alder don't like us using magic, so he called it sabotaging city supplies, had them arrested."

"Reckon it would have been all right if they just put the

eggshells in," a man said, pursing his lips. "But they drew runes on them, tried to expand their essence, and that's when it goes from charms to magic."

"That's what the Dunholmi want you to believe." The woman snorted.

"Don't matter much to these people, does it? They won't survive two months of this every day."

"Two months?" The anguish in Raul's voice was as clear as the crack of the whip. He leaned in close and lowered his voice. "Da, we have to do something."

"Yeah, we should leave. Too many guards."

"No, I mean—"

"I know what you mean, and you mean well by it, but we'd be outnumbered. Even if we won, the city's swarming with patrols, they'd trap us in minutes."

"We can't leave these people!"

"They've got more chance this way than trying to fight their way out. Now come on."

Doubt furrowed Raul's face, and Valens could practically smell the guilt coming off of him. The lad wasn't just good, he was too good. They had to get this business done before he got himself killed and all their plans broke along with Valens's heart. So he walked, and Raul followed, the habit of obedience dragging him away from danger.

In the old days, Valens would have headed straight to the Hill of Lost Names for the goods he needed. That place had always attracted his sorts of artisans, making functional things for those who needed them. From what he'd heard, the Hill was still like that, but he couldn't bring himself to walk where

FORGED FOR DESTINY

Fabia died, to face the ghosts of that night. Instead, they headed east out of the Blood Market, down a street that turned from butchers through potters to a mix of artisans' shops. These were places where the smithing or the wood turning happened out back, so that craft wouldn't get in the way of commerce. Valens grudgingly admitted that there was something honest about the way they worked in the Vales, where he could see new cups being made before he bought them for the inn, but the way things worked here was so much easier.

They passed a mound where rubble from the city's fall lay overgrown with ivy, nettles, and rough grass. All the good stone had been reused in rebuilding, but not everything could be saved, and once the rubble piled up, some patches weren't worth the bother of clearing. Between the dirt and roots he glimpsed clumps of crumbling brickwork and stones with scorched undersides, signs of the city's fall clinging on through eighteen years of rains. He wondered if any of those bricks had once been part of the Darting Drake, where he and Fabia spent so many happy evenings; whether that cracked piece of carved stone had once overheard his prayers at the temple of Laughing Loftus.

For all the melancholy that memory brought, there was more creation than destruction in this neighbourhood, more than enough to serve their needs. Five shops sold ironwork in this street alone. If they bought a couple of lanterns from each, they should avoid drawing attention. Raul could wait out here and hold the lanterns as Valens got them. Shame they couldn't get swords too, or proper fighting blades for their axes. Maybe Appia knew someone who could help.

"Look."

Raul pointed at the sign above one of the shop entrances. Each of the ironmongers had one like it, a metal sculpture that showed off the skills of the smith. One was a model of a horse, another a tree, a third a castle. This one was an eagle, thinly made with articulated wings and carefully hung on chains so that it bobbed in the breeze, those wings flapping in slow motion.

"A bird, like I saw in the entrails," Raul said, his hushed tone speaking to an unexpected awe.

Valens stiffened. Not more of this.

"It was just blood, not entrails," he said.

"It was still an omen."

"You can't go living your life by omens."

Raul looked at him for a moment, eyes wide, and Valens realised what a damn fool thing that was to say, the frayed end of a thread he couldn't risk unravelling. He frantically tried to think how he could take the words back.

Raul burst out laughing.

"You almost got me, Da, you sounded so serious."

"Yeah, well..." Valens sighed. They had to start somewhere, why not this place? "Let's go in, then."

The shop was smaller on the inside than Valens had expected, rows of pans and cauldrons, racks of knives and spoons, looming at them from every angle. There were hatchets, handsaws, drills, all manner of useful tools, the work of a serious professional serving other serious professionals. Every piece was made with skill and care, the rough edges smoothed off, the imperfections hammered out. Near the front were horseshoes, stirrups, and bits, wares to appeal to the purses of the occupiers.

FORGED FOR DESTINY

"Can I help you, gentlemen?" A woman emerged from the glowing back room in a billow of hot air, sparks cooling on her leather apron, sweat gleaming on the muscles of her bare arms. She pulled off her heavy gloves and thrust them through her belt.

"We're looking for lanterns," Valens said, watching her warily. Was she friendly with the Dunholmi, or just eager to take their money?

"Then you've come to the right place." The blacksmith pointed to a high shelf. "I've made a special shutter you can shift around, lets the breeze in without letting it blow the flame out. They cost more than most, but they're worth it, like everything I make."

Valens reached for the lanterns, but Raul stopped him with a wave of the hand, a gesture reminiscent of Prisca.

"You have other lanterns, don't you?" Raul approached the blacksmith, looking past her at something on the wall. "Better ones."

"Ah, you were referred by one of my *other* customers." The blacksmith opened a chest in a darkened corner of the store, took out a lantern, and ran a finger across the sun shape engraved on its back. The lantern started glowing. "The essence of the sun's light, bound into metal. That's hard to do, takes a special sort of iron, and only one in ten works, so there's a lot of waste. Makes it costly, you understand?"

Valens took the lantern and turned it in his hands, staring in wonder at that light. Estian scholars had been working toward amazing things before the nation fell. Prisca talked about it a lot, in the early days after the fall, about drawing the essence of one thing into another, about dissonance and

215

complementarity and boundaries, the sort of talk where one word in five meant nothing to Valens, and the rest didn't sound like they belonged together. He'd seen strange things too, when the scholars from the Spire brought their skills to war, when they seemed to change the weather or the ground the armies fought across. That was meant to be the beginning of something new, something huge, something that left a cold, heavy feeling in Valens's guts. But he'd never held a thing like this, so simple and practical, magic to improve day-to-day life. Here was a blacksmith working wonders that would have made scholars weep.

"Why don't you just sell these?" he asked. "However much you ask for, you'll get."

"The same reason people don't sell books on the streets: Dunholm doesn't trust us with magic. I could lose my hands, never mind my business, for a thing like this, but..." Her voice trailed off and she took a step back. "Remind me, who recommended my work?"

Her hand snaked out of sight, around the doorframe, to where Valens would have kept a hammer handy, if he had a forge he might have to defend. He set his hand where his sword ought to be.

"We're not just here for the lanterns." Raul, his eyes unfocused, laid a hand on a wooden wall panel. The blacksmith tensed. Raul's fingers ran across a dark mark, an image of a lizard drawn in old blood. How had Valens not noticed it before? He felt like he hadn't even seen that panel, but now the image was clear as day.

The blacksmith brought her hand up, holding a hammer,

FORGED FOR DESTINY

and swung at Raul. Valens lunged, bringing the lamp around, and she lurched back. The hammer hit the wall instead of Raul, and splinters flew. Something gleamed in the gap behind the broken plank.

Valens drew his knife as the blacksmith wrenched her hammer free.

"I fought at Old Breck and on the last night of the wall," Valens growled. "I'll gut you before you even swing."

"I've been hammering steel fifteen years and I'm still half your age," she said. "I'll smash your skull before you touch me."

As they tensed, ready to go at each other, Raul slid a hand through the hole and heaved. A whole panel came away. Behind it hung a row of swords.

"We'll buy these too," he said.

The blacksmith waved her hammer. "How do I know I can trust you?"

Valens gripped his knife tighter, looking for his moment to lunge. Then Raul stepped in front of him and sank to one knee, hanging his head, and Valens's heartbeat thundered like cavalry across the plains.

"You can smash your secret out of my head," Raul said, his voice shaking just a little. "Or you can help make a world where you won't have to hide your wares."

The blacksmith looked from Raul to Valens, and she wavered, like she could see a great hammer hanging over her. But the lad had a way with people that Valens could only envy.

"All right." She lowered her hammer. "You, muscles, close and bolt the door, then we'll talk prices. I like your words, but I've still got a business to run."

Chapter Seventeen
New Moon Rising

Raul swung the sword once more through the air of the storeroom, getting his arm used to its weight. It wasn't as good as the sword he had lost, but it was more satisfying than the wooden training blades, and a lot better balanced than a woodsman's axe. He didn't know much about blacksmiths, but judging by these and the lamps, Drusil was good at her job.

He slid the sword into the scabbard hanging next to the axe on his belt, then closed the lid on the chest of weapons and piled up baskets of costume on top. He donned the black cloak he'd found in one of those baskets, a shield of darkness hanging from his shoulders almost to the floor.

It was time.

The theatre was quiet, its inhabitants long ago gone to bed. Even Prisca had snuffed her lantern and left her books for the night. As Raul crept down the corridor and out past the stage, lighting his way with one of Drusil's magical lamps, he was as

FORGED FOR DESTINY

alone as he had been since they first arrived in the city. It was a little unnerving, but exciting too.

"What are you doing?"

He spun around and shone his lantern at the voice. His other hand went to his sword. Then he saw Yasmi sitting on the edge of the stage, one leg crossed over the other, rubbing the ball of her bare foot, and his heart stopped its frantic hammering.

"Me?" he asked. "What are you doing awake?"

"I just got back from the most wonderful tavern. The wine was adequate, but the food was exquisite, and the company outrageous. I haven't laughed so hard in months."

"Is it safe to walk around alone at night, with all these warriors about?"

"You think warriors are the threat in a city?" She shook her head. "I'm well equipped to chase off any predators." She patted the masks hanging from her belt. "As Denladius says in *The Prince of All Tides*, 'What footpad would cross his foil with the fangs of a beast?'" She dropped from the stage, slid her feet into her shoes, and walked over to him. "Your turn now, what are you doing?"

This close, it was awkward to keep the lantern pointing at her, so instead he turned a catch and shutters shifted, scattering the light into a broad pool. The angles of Yasmi's face stood out in that soft light: the curve of her lips, the spark of her eyes, one brow raised in a gently mocking arch. She smelled of red wine and oranges.

He hesitated. This was meant to be a secret, his chance to stand on his own two feet, to prove to himself that he didn't need Valens's help or Prisca's guidance to be a hero. But bringing Yasmi along wouldn't be giving up on that; she'd never shielded him from the world. And besides, he hadn't seen much of her the past week, between his tasks and her rehearsals. Having her so close yet never there made him miss her in a way he hadn't when they were apart all year.

"I'm going to help some people who are in danger. Do you want to come?"

"More of your great adventure?" She ran fingers down the edge of his cloak, feeling the cloth, then straightened it. "Why not? It might be fun to play at heroics, just this once. But if we're hiding, then we shouldn't wear black."

"It's good for hiding in the dark of night."

"No, dark grey is good for that, black is too intense. Trust me, tricks of the theatrical trade."

She jumped up to the stage, as agile as the small deer that ran across the western vales, and disappeared into the wings. Raul glanced around uncertainly as rustling noises emerged, and then she reappeared, dressed in drab browns instead of her usual bright colours, carrying a pair of deep grey cloaks.

"Here." She threw one at Raul. "Switch to that."

He set aside his black cloak and turned the grey one, looking for the hood and fastening.

"What's this?" Yasmi patted the hilt of his sword. "Are we playing at warriors now?"

She snapped to attention, arms by her sides, face like stone. Then she waggled her eyebrows, and Raul burst out laughing.

"Perhaps we should get one for you as well," he said.

"I do like a game of find the weapon." She laid a finger on

FORGED FOR DESTINY

his chest. There was mischief in the sparkle of her eyes. "That could be even more fun."

Raul, his cheeks hot and his pulse quickening, took a step back. His words were as jumbled as his thoughts, getting in each other's way as they tried to escape the logjam in his throat.

"We should...They're in...the back room, that is, we've got..."

"I don't need a sword." She patted the masks on her belt. "Monsters fight as well as heroes."

She took the cloak from his hand and wrapped it around him. As she fastened the catch at his throat, he caught that smell of wine on her breath.

"Are you sure I can't persuade you to try a different sport?"

There was the spark in her eyes again, and Raul knew just what she meant, wanted to say yes, didn't know if he would know what to do, didn't want to spoil what they had, wanted to reach out, wanted to push away, wanted to just close his eyes and feel the warmth of her hand against his chest, it was all too much, too many thoughts, too many words, his pulse too fast, he couldn't, he didn't...

His hand clenched on the pommel of the sword, and that cut through. He had a destiny. He had to help people.

"If you're coming, then come." He spun around and headed for the door. Yasmi snickered, then followed.

———————————— • ————————————

Once Raul had found out where the prisoners were kept, it had made perfect sense. Using a granary to hold people who had meddled with a granary could have been something out of a story, the memorable detail that made an incident stick in people's minds, and the public whippings that Raul had seen were certainly meant to be memorable. The sight and sound of them were seared across his mind, a vision of cruelty, a reminder of what he fought against.

Three warriors of Dunholm stood in front of the granary. They had the plain blue tabards of infantry levies, like most of the troops given guard duty, and none was wearing an officer's sash. One leaned on his spear. The other two had propped theirs against the wall and were playing knuckle bones in the dirt, one of them cursing as he fumbled for pieces in the moonlit gloom. Raul's whole plan, if he could call it a plan, relied on the fact that he could take down all three on his own, but now that the time had come and his clammy palm pressed against the hilt of his sword, he was glad that Yasmi stood in the alleyway beside him, ready for the fight.

"I'll sneak around the buildings to the left," Raul whispered, remembering stories of ambushes Valens had told him, how important it was to surround an enemy. "While I'm doing that, you shift into a lion or a wolf. Then we can charge them from both sides at once."

"It's a charming plan, but might I suggest something more nuanced?"

"Huh?"

She discarded her cloak, unfastened the toggles of her tunic, and adjusted the edges of her shirt, exposing a V-shape of skin from her collarbone down to the centre of her chest. A simple necklace, artfully positioned, drew the eye.

FORGED FOR DESTINY

"I'll distract as many as I can, you sneak up on the rest. A surprise attack works better if they don't see us coming."

Raul swallowed. It did sound like more of a plan, and he was struggling to think of anything else.

"All right." He gripped his sword tight. "Let's do it."

Yasmi stepped out of the darkness, a silk scarf trailing from one hand, hips swaying as she prowled down the street. She could have been made of moonlight, it so perfectly shone from her.

The leaning guard looked up, then nudged one of his companions with his foot. The third guard whistled. Raul didn't like the way they looked at Yasmi, wished it wasn't too late to change his mind.

"What you doing out here, love?" The middle guard rose to her feet, rested her hands on her belt. "Little late for a nice girl to go out alone."

"Who says I'm a nice girl?" Yasmi tilted her head, and her hair shifted across her shoulder. She raised her silk scarf across her face for a moment, forming the briefest imitation of a veil. "Maybe I don't want to be alone."

The third guard licked his lips as he gathered the gaming pieces. "I can help with that."

"She's going to cost you," the middle guard said with disdain.

"I can afford it. Got your money, remember?" He rattled the gaming pieces in his hand. "How much?"

"Let's talk about that somewhere private." Yasmi strolled past the guards. "Away from your judgemental friend."

"She's not judgemental, just jealous." The guard followed Yasmi into the darkness between two buildings.

"And I'm not his friend!" the other one called after him.

The eyes of the remaining two guards had followed Yasmi's departure, and they watched that darkness still, looking away from Raul. Slowly, silently, he slid from the shadows and crept toward them.

"Why is it Ratleg always gets the girls?" the guard with the spear asked.

"You think that counts as 'getting the girls'?" The other guard snorted. "You're a dolt, Cag."

"I must be, standing here wagging my chin with you, while he's in there getting that sweet filly."

Raul raised his sword. Could he use the flat to knock this man out? He didn't want to kill anyone he didn't need to. Listening to their gossipy conversation made them human, made it harder to do the worst.

"That sweet filly is going to empty his purse and leave him with an itch that won't stop."

"You're just jealous that you're not the one who can afford her."

"Screw you, Cag."

"You're not my type."

Cag snickered and turned from his companion, just as Raul finally brought his sword down. Instead of hitting the back of the guard's head, the flat of the sword glanced off his temple and into his shoulder. He staggered, shouted in pain and alarm, gripped his spear in both hands.

Now Raul had no choice. He rammed his blade straight into Cag. The guard's eyes went wide and he gasped, then Raul pulled the sword free in a spray of blood. Cag fell to the ground.

FORGED FOR DESTINY

In those critical few seconds, the other guard grabbed her spear. She jabbed it at Raul, who jumped back to avoid one blow, then deflected another. He stepped in to get past the point, but she swung the shaft around and almost tripped him. He swung wildly, a strike that ran along her arm and into her hand. A crunch. More blood. A grunt of pain. The spear drooped. She opened her mouth wide, but before she could shout, Raul stabbed, thrusting with all his strength. His arm shuddered as he pushed through flesh, over ribs, and out the back. She stared at him, their faces inches apart, then her eyes rolled back and she fell, taking his sword with her.

Raul stared at the bodies, the grotesque mess he had made. Wasn't this supposed to get easier? How was it becoming worse? He yanked his sword free with a terrible scraping, sucking sound.

Yasmi emerged into the moonlight. She looked down at the bodies, at him, back at the bodies. For the first time, Raul realised the gaping chasm between inviting her along on a late-night adventure and showing her the grim reality of his new life.

"I did what I had to," he blurted out.

"Of course." She stood stiff and alert, carefully adjusted the collar of her tunic and set to fastening the toggles. When she looked at him again, her expression was softer. "Are you all right?"

He nodded, straightened, tried to look as calm as she did. He was the hero. The hero didn't have doubts, didn't get sickened by the deaths they caused. The hero was strong and certain.

"The other one?" he asked, pulling out a rag to clean his sword and give his hands something to do.

"'Brick to the back of the head, gets them every time,'" Yasmi said in a voice that wasn't her own. "Tenofon in *The Maze Builder's Dream*. Not one of Tenebrial's best, but it makes an audience laugh." She glanced back. "That one won't be laughing come morning, but he's better off than his friends."

Raul pushed his guilt aside and turned to the granary tower. The wall was mud brick plastered with daub, solid and seamless. There was a wooden hatch in the base, and a bar holding it shut. A sturdy iron lock fixed the bar in place. None of the guards they'd taken down seemed like the sort who got trusted with keys, and he didn't want to search the bodies.

"Better do this the quick way," he said. "Hold this and keep an eye out in case anybody comes."

He handed Yasmi the sword and pulled an axe from his belt, almost fumbling it with his shaking fingers. He got a good grip on the haft, a log-splitting grip instead of a warrior's hold, and swung. Three blows—*thud, thud, crack*—and the bar snapped. He flung the larger, unlocked part away and opened the hatch.

"Come out, quick," he said, leaning over to speak through the opening.

Someone shuffled around inside.

"Please, not again." More whimper than words. "Luca can't take it. His back's still bleeding from yesterday."

"I'm not here to beat you, I'm here to rescue you." Raul leaned in, caught a dusty breath, and coughed. It was even darker inside the granary, no hope of seeing the prisoners. "Come on, quick, before more guards arrive."

FORGED FOR DESTINY

That got them moving. Shuffling steps, then the first of them crawled out. She turned to help the second, who whimpered as he moved, his back a mass of dark and sticky streaks. The third hurried out, looked around, kicked Cag's body, and spat on it.

Everyone looked at Raul expectantly.

"Where are you taking us?" the first prisoner said.

"I..."

Raul hadn't thought beyond liberating them. He'd assumed that they would have somewhere they could go, but now he thought about it, that made no sense. He couldn't hide them in the theatre, too many people coming and going, too many questions. The woods by the river weren't well enough grown to hide anyone. Back home, he would have known a dozen places, caves and bowers and wooded spots between hills. Where would you hide someone in a city, with people all around?

"Do you have trusted friends?" Yasmi asked. "Here or out of town?"

The bleeding prisoner nodded. "My cousin. She might..." He took a sharp breath, let it out through gritted teeth. "She might help."

"Then go to her," Raul said. "Stay hidden, stay safe. Soon, a time will come when you can walk free again."

One of the others grabbed his hand.

"Thank you," she said. "With all my heart, thank you."

"I'm just doing what has to be done." Raul took a deep breath. He needed to say something heroic, something inspiring, something that could spread the word of revolution, give people hope for what lay ahead. "Tell your friends that a change is coming. A new moon is rising, and it brings freedom."

"We'll tell them." The woman bowed her head over his hand. "Thank you, my lord."

"I'm not a lord, just one man trying to do right. Remember my example, when the time comes."

The prisoners hurried away. Raul looked down at the bodies.

"Let's hide these," he said. "The longer before they're found, the more time those people have to get away."

" 'A new moon is rising.' " Yasmi granted him a sidelong smile. "That was good. Tenebrial's work?"

Raul shook his head. "Just something I came up with. Hope it sounded right."

It wasn't far off dawn when they got back to the theatre. Yasmi's hands were sticky with blood, though she'd wiped off as much as she could. The smell was still on her, though not as badly as on Raul, who was spattered with the stuff. He didn't seem to mind. Why would he? He was the hero.

She had questions about what he was doing, but more important was why. This seemed to be her chance to ask. Her memories of what they'd done were an open wound, one she wouldn't want to touch once it started to heal.

They paused in front of the stage. Yasmi really wanted to bathe, but that meant lighting a fire, fetching water, making enough fuss and noise that she was bound to wake someone, and she couldn't face them yet. She reached for Raul, then

FORGED FOR DESTINY

thought better of it. Raul the inn boy had been someone she could tease to the edge of her bed and still feel she was in control. Raul the warrior was like a statue; handsome but hard, an intimidating figure towering over her.

"I've never been an accomplice to murder before," she said, and hid the trembling of her voice behind laughter. "I think that once is enough."

Even as she said it, she knew that it wasn't true. She'd seen the way the people they rescued looked at Raul, and the way he had responded. *One man trying to do right*, he'd said, and she'd felt those words to her bones. Even with the stink of blood and the stickiness of her hand, with the memory of the impact of that brick against the guard's head, if Raul had said he was going out again now, she would have followed him. She could have challenged the inn boy, but she couldn't have said no to this Raul.

That was why she mustn't ask the questions racing through her mind. The more she knew, the further she would be drawn in, swept along by currents deeper than either of them. She could play-act the rebel, but she wasn't ready for the reality.

"I should go," she said. "To bed."

He nodded slowly, staring at the stage. The tree at the back was just visible, cast as shadows by the starlight through the windows.

"Thank you, Yasmi," he said. "I couldn't have done that without you."

She laughed again, the sound too shrill, like she was thirteen years old and trying to prove that she understood a dirty joke.

"You could, and you will." She patted him on the arm, then forced herself away. "Good night."

Chapter Eighteen
Burning Down a House

Count Alder brought his sword up, caught his opponent's attack on the blade, and slid it down to the guard. He twisted, almost wrenching the sabre from her grip, and she stepped back, spurs clicking against the floor. Before she could find her stance again, he went on the offensive. Swift blows, low then high, up around her shield and back down. A clang as he hit her greave. She retreated, with a loose blow to ward him off. He knocked it aside, grabbed her arm, and was in, the tip of his blade pressed against her belly.

"Yield!" she exclaimed.

"Very wise." Alder stepped back. "I would hate to waste a good captain."

"Thank you, my lord." She bowed her head. "Again?"

There was a high-pitched cough from the doorway, the sort of noise that Chamberlain Tur mistook for polite interruption.

"Sadly, no." Alder bowed his head to the captain. "Go back to your duties, my own have come to plague me."

FORGED FOR DESTINY

He walked to the throne, swishing the engraved sword through the air as he went. Getting to know this captured blade had confirmed three things. First, that it was very well made, for someone who planned to do battle. Second, that it hadn't seen proper use, as its pristine steel only now showed nicks and scratches. And third, that he needed practice with a variety of weapons. The guard captain had almost had him twice today, and if he was caught without his sabre, then he didn't want to be at that sort of risk. He had suspected all of these things before, but it was good to be certain. A dozen nobles back home stood ready to pounce on his slightest failing, to take his governorship, his lands, his life. Politics had no mercy for mistakes.

"What do you have for me now, Tur?" he asked, draping himself over the throne.

"I am afraid that trouble is stirring in the city, my lord." Tur hunched over, rubbing his hands together. "Many signs of discontent."

"What sort of signs?"

"Moons, mostly, painted on walls where many will see them."

"Moons?"

"Indeed, my lord. Rudely daubed in many cases, but unmistakable."

"Some sort of magic? Rebels trying to tap into the essence of the moon? To, what, illuminate the city, or make it vanish for three days?" Alder straightened in his seat, gripped the sword ready for action. "Could this be a threat?"

"Perhaps, my lord, though I doubt it is meant as magic."

Tur's twig fingers crept inside his robe, drew forth a book, opened it, and held it out. A symbol stood solid amid a feathery mass of text: a moon with a blade through it.

"Where is this from?" Alder asked.

"Our collection of confiscated texts. It was among the documents our archivists missed until the recent raids."

"Missed?"

"Indeed, my lord."

Alder had found many things to dislike about Tur, but there were some to admire, and intelligence was among them.

"You think something's wrong."

"Our archivists are skilled and patient, their cataloguing thorough. For them to have missed one such document was surprising, but a dozen, a score, more..." Tur shook his head. "These criminals aren't just stealing, they're leaving things behind."

"Planting evidence."

"Indeed, my lord. Evidence that has unsettled our native archivists. There have been mutterings, and two disappearances."

"Desertions?"

"Indeed."

Alder leapt from his seat and down the steps to the floor of the throne room. He needed the blood to flow. It was easiest to think in the saddle, with the world flying by and his whole soul engaged, but at least on his feet he could trot back and forth, could find something of himself.

"What does the moon mean to these people?" he asked, raising the sword to fence the empty air. He flowed through

FORGED FOR DESTINY

attacks and defences, feet darting, blade dancing, familiar movements clearing his mind.

"It can mean many things, my lord, but in association with a blade it is most often a sign of Balbianus, and of the founding of Estis."

"A lesson in history?"

"And one for the future." Tur's lip curled. "Their prophets have long predicted Balbianus's return, but their works were ephemeral and disconnected. These documents weave those frayed threads together, turn them into something more cohesive, more strident."

"I see." Alder had found his rhythm. Slash, thrust, parry. Slash, thrust, parry. Slash, thrust, parry, thrust again. "How old are these documents?"

"Some appear to be very old, but appearances can be deceptive."

"They certainly can." Three thrusts, the first two feints, the third a lunge at gut height. "If I was looking to start a rebellion, I might use prophecy to get people past their fears."

"My thoughts exactly, my lord."

"I might use it to rally them around a leader."

"Indeed."

Alder advanced on Tur, sword outstretched.

"Don't flinch like that," he snapped, and tapped his finger against the flat of the sword, near the crosspiece. "Look at this."

Tur craned his neck, trying to peer at the blade while keeping away from it. He snickered when he saw the shape Alder had picked out.

"A moon," Tur said. "My, my. I believe some texts mentioned a sword."

"Of course they did. Now tell me, how many people outside of our archivists see the confiscated documents?"

"Very few, my lord, until they're shipped home."

"But word is getting out?"

"I believe so, my lord."

"And yet, most people won't hear about these documents until a revolt is done, until they retake their books?"

"I assure you, my lord, the rebellion won't succeed."

"I know that, you know that, but they have to play like they're winning, and that means planning the next step." Alder tapped the moon engraving. "This isn't just for us, Tur. Someone is playing a long game."

"Very well observed, my lord. But for the short game, what would you have me do?"

Alder walked to the balcony and looked out across Pavuno, the sword resting against his arm. The city was a miserable place, soot-stained and ruined, even the parts that grew back cramped together, ugly heaps of rock or rickety wooden frames. There were no promenades, no riding parks, no roads wide enough to race, barely a scrap of green before the river's edge. It was full of devious rebels and ungrateful peasants, but it was his. He had outmanoeuvred a dozen cousins, aunts, and unrelated nobles to become governor, but some fool thought that they could outplot him with their clumsy scheme.

"These moons in the streets, when did they start?"

"That is unclear, my lord, but there has been an increase in the past three days."

FORGED FOR DESTINY

"Since that business at the granary?"

"Indeed, my lord."

"They must be expecting a clampdown: more patrols, more guards, more arrests."

Tur nodded. "That would be the obvious response."

"Then we'll give it to them." Alder grinned. He'd enjoyed playing the good governor, dispensing justice and grain, but it was time to give this country its head. "I'm curious to see what they have planned."

───────────●───────────

"Ready in the wings?" Efron's voice resounded around the theatre.

"Yes, play master," Raul called out, his voice joining that of Yasmi, who stood on the far side of the stage, behind the rope ladder that ran to the scenery beams. She gave him an encouraging wave, and the slender bracelets on her wrist tinkled like chimes. He waved back enthusiastically. He'd never been a player before, and the prospect of his few short lines made him grin.

"Ready in the audience?" Efron bellowed.

"Yes, play master!" the rest of the troupe roared from their seats.

"Very well, then. To bless this stage for our new production, I present *The Shortest Play*, starring..." Efron turned his head. "What do you want?"

Raul peered around the scenery hangings, saw Tenebrial at Efron's elbow, giving a twitchy wave toward the stage. Efron frowned, blew through his moustache, then turned to face them.

"Raul, your parents call for you."

Raul sagged. So much for his first steps onto the stage. It might just be a six-line story of doomed romance with a joke at the end, but he'd been practising those lines each day, making sure he had them just right. Here he was, in a costume to match Yasmi's, ready to begin, and his moment was snatched away.

"Father." Yasmi brushed the rope ladder aside and stepped onto the stage, one hand on her masks. "Can't he do this first? It's good luck to include an amateur."

"And bad luck to cross Prisca." Efron shook his head. "Biallo, you know the lines, you're up."

Raul turned away so that no one would see the redness in his ears or the frown he knew he shouldn't wear. If his ma was summoning him, it would be important, and he was too old to be sulking, though he really didn't want to miss out.

He hunched over and walked quietly backstage, to a corridor near the rear of the theatre. Prisca's and Valens's voices reached him a dozen paces before the door.

"Why now?" Valens asked. "Why so fast?"

"The Red Eye is coming. We have to act."

"Yeah, but the Red Eye—"

"The count is giving out grain, buying favour. As many people sing his praises as curse his name."

"You think they're not suffering enough?"

"We're losing support."

"And gaining as much from the families of those he hangs. What's really going on?"

FORGED FOR DESTINY

"I told you, the signs show that—"

"The lad ain't ready for—"

"He is quite well enough equipped to—"

"—fake it now, we've got to fight, and—"

"—irrelevant, the omens are in place, and we must—"

"You wanted to see me?" Raul stepped into the room. To his relief, his parents fell silent.

"Sorry, lad." Valens took a step back. "We were just talking."

"Discussing the prophecies," Prisca added.

"Is something wrong?" Raul asked, a knot forming in his stomach.

"With this?" Prisca pointed at the papers on the table. "Not at all. But I've been hearing more about your recent escapade. Is it true that you tried not to kill Dunholmi warriors?"

The knot in Raul's stomach tightened. They'd been proud when he'd told them about the rescue, once their initial shock passed. He'd hoped that they might also be proud when he told them about trying not to kill, but Valens's stone-faced reaction hadn't been what he'd hoped for. And now this...

"I don't want to kill people if I don't have to," he said.

"There are times when it's right to kill," Prisca said. "Fighting for freedom is one of them."

"You taught me not to hurt people unless I have to."

"And now you have to."

"I can't..." Raul ran a hand through his hair. "If I become like the people we're fighting, then what's the point?"

"The point is that they are cruel, vicious conquerors who stole our country."

"If I become cruel and vicious, aren't I as bad?"

"Context matters. Circumstances matter. Yours are very different."

"Killing is killing."

Prisca waved a hand in front of Valens. "You have a try."

Valens rubbed a thumb across his forehead, like he was trying to drive out the wrinkles.

"It's like in the stories," he said. "Sometimes you've got to smash something old to build something new."

"Hasn't there been enough of that? Just look around Pavuno, at all the ruins, the broken walls, the spaces where royal statues used to be. You told me this city used to be magnificent."

"And it will be again." Prisca tapped the table. "Raul, you must get past this nonsense. You have managed to oversimplify an already simple issue. We don't have the time to... to... Fire and fury, what's the word I'm after?"

Her hands pressed against the table and she scowled like she was staring at Count Alder himself. Her tension sent a new doubt through Raul. Was he doing something worse than he thought when he started this argument? He must have upset her deeply to get such a reaction. He looked to Valens for guidance, but his da looked unsettled, and that made everything worse.

"Ma, are you all right?" Raul asked quietly.

"Yes, yes, I'm just..." She looked up at him, and her expression softened. "Raul, how many times must I ask you, please don't call me Ma."

Valens laughed in relief. "That's more like it."

Footsteps approached. Raul looked down the corridor to

FORGED FOR DESTINY

see Appia approaching, along with a bald man in threadbare scholars' robes. He stepped aside to let them into the room.

"Prisca, Valens, this fancy windbag is Pomponius," Appia said. "The scribe I told you about."

"Ah ah ah." Pomponius wagged his finger in the air. "There are no scribes outside the palace. The odd clerk, perhaps, but I am an accountant."

"An accountant who writes things for people."

"And thus stays inside the law."

"Not too far inside it, I hope." Prisca opened a chest at the back of the room, one marked with a hooded eye to deter attention. She took out a bundle of papers and parchments, then handed them to Pomponius. "Will these be adequate to your endeavours?"

Pomponius leafed slowly through the pages, examining each one in turn. They all looked old, like so many of Prisca's documents, but were blank, and Raul couldn't work out what the accountant was looking for. After a few minutes, Pomponius nodded and carefully placed the papers in his satchel.

"You have inks as well?" he asked.

Prisca held up four clay pots, each stoppered with wax.

"First we discuss payment."

"Of course." Pomponius waved a finger. "Appia tells me that you seek service rather than coin?"

"You can make multiple copies of the same document?"

"I can, as long as it is legal and will be used discreetly."

"I want copies of these. Hundreds of them."

Prisca placed two sheets of paper on the table. Both were new, and each had the symbol of the moon pierced by a dagger in its centre. Raul laid a hand protectively on his upper arm as he read the large letters:

A NEW MOON COMES! BE READY TO RISE!
THE NEW MOON HAS COME! ESTIS, RISE UP!

"Simple enough for most people to read, I believe," Prisca said. "If not, I can adjust them."

"These are neither legal nor discreet," Pomponius said, shaking his head.

"And you intend to use these legally?" Prisca shook the ink pots, then pointed at his satchel. "Or those?"

"How I use specialist paper and ink is my business."

"And who I supply it to is mine. I don't have time for mass production, and you don't have another source. So, do we have a deal?"

Pomponius curled his fingers in, pressed the knuckles against his mouth, took a deep breath. The whole time, he stared at the bottles of ink.

"Very well." He snatched Prisca's illegal pages and stuffed them into his satchel, then held out his hands. "Two hundred copies of each by the end of next week."

"Five hundred." She handed over the ink. "And remember, there's more where this came from."

"I'm sure there is." Pomponius hurried out, taking Appia with him.

Prisca sank into a seat. A blob of thick ink had fallen onto the table. She ran a finger through it, sketching something like letters on the bare wood.

FORGED FOR DESTINY

"Five hundred. Along with the street painters and the play, that should be enough fuel for our fire, now we must finish laying the kindling..." She looked up and blinked. "Where were we?"

"Killing," Valens said, and touched his ring.

"Ah, yes."

Prisca tapped her finger a moment longer in the ink, then took a scrap of wool from next to her ink pot and wiped her finger, working the wool into the creases around her nail. When she was done, the digit was dry, but a dark stain remained. Raul waited, questions about Pomponius and their deal forgotten as he struggled to work out what he could say to please her.

"What if we weren't asking you to kill?" Prisca said. "What if it was burning down a building? Would you do that?"

"If there was no other way, just like I'll kill if there's no other way."

"But how will you know that there's no other way?"

Raul frowned. It was a good question. So far, those choices had been instinctive, the moments of unrestrained violence coming out of necessity. Could he have made the same choices in a moment of calm? How would he have decided?

"It seems to be about time," he said. "If I have time, I'll try to find another way, until I run out of time and have to break something or someone."

"Then you're wasting time, while other harm might fall."

"It might not, though, and I can see the harm I'm doing." He nodded. Yes, he had it now. "It's all about time."

"Good grief." Prisca pressed her face into her fingers. "How are so many people so stupid?" She drew her hands away and looked at Raul in a way she hadn't done in years, the way she used to when he was small and broke the rules, rules he later learned were there to keep him safe. "I have strived for eighteen years, without respite or thanks, to prepare the liberation of this kingdom. Eighteen years. The least you can do is what you were raised for."

Her stare was a weight pressing down on Raul, squeezing him into an unfamiliar shape. She had done this when he was a child, and it had made him who he was now.

His feet took control of themselves and he paced back and forth, hands twisted together by his belly.

Valens's hand settled on Prisca's shoulder.

"Pris," Valens whispered. "Look at him."

Raul glanced around. Prisca's frozen expression softened, just a little.

"Appia is doing what's needed," she said. "Pomponius too, regardless of his motives. And you, you've done so well so far. Just try to become what you ought to be."

"I'll try," Raul said, nodding eagerly.

But in his heart, he knew he was misleading them, and it tore at him. Because he knew he was right, and if he had time to find another way, he would never burn that house down.

Chapter Nineteen
Acting the Hero

Yasmi leapt from the wings of the stage, her teeth bared, howling beneath the glowing half globe of a paper-lantern moon. She was the wolf: its lust, its longings, its hunger. She was ferocity unchained. She was the wild at the heart of the world, and in the heart of humankind. As she drew breath for another howl, she was invincible.

The audience gasped, then cheered, such a noise that the rafters of the theatre trembled. No, that wasn't just their cheering, that was the stamping, hundreds of feet hammering the floorboards, until the whole theatre vibrated to the rhythm. They loved her.

She'd never had an audience so large, or so enthusiastic. Their attention, their belief fuelled the magic of her mask. Her fur was sleeker than it had been in the provinces, her claws sharper. The stage shook with her every step.

She prowled across the boards, flung her head back, and howled a third time. It was only meant to be twice, and

Tenebrial was precious about every last sound, the rhythm of noise as much as words. But this was the greatest moment of her life, and she wasn't going to let it go.

A man in gold-trimmed robes held out one hand to block her passage, while with the other he raised his blunted sword high. He smelled of sweat and of exhilaration, not the fear of prey. Her belly rumbled. What would it take to make him even more delicious?

"Hold, beast!"

The lines, though familiar, jolted her, brought her to a halt, as they were meant to do. The rhythm of the words that followed was meant not just to excite the audience but to soothe any overexcited shifter. Normally, she didn't need them. Normally, they didn't have an audience like this: so many of them, in a space that echoed back their excitement, watching a play that their whole lives had prepared them to love.

Efron's words were still flowing. The rhythm of rehearsals drew the right response without a need for her to think. The wolf backed off from the king's threats and the power of his presence but was whipped back into rage by his righteousness. A terrible downfall, to die because he was a good man.

"...and so I say, beast, let us together find our peace."

That was her cue. She bared her teeth and howled once more, not a noble sound this time, but a dread, discordant roar. For the first time in three hours, the audience fell truly silent.

"Alas, this wolf will not to righteous man become a friend, so draw my blade and bare his claws, and we'll fight to the end."

She and her father leapt at each other, and for a moment

FORGED FOR DESTINY

she was afraid that she would lose herself, as the wolf came howling out of her heart. Not a real wolf, those scavengers and opportunists, those furred families she had seen watching the mountain passes. This was the wolf of dreams. The wolf of nightmares. This wolf was a monster.

The audience cheered again as king and beast clashed. They roared in excitement as he hit her, howled in fury as she knocked him down, screamed in exhilaration as he rolled out from between her feet, brought his blade down, and won. Fists waved in the air as she staggered and fell. Even the people in the balconies were on their feet.

A scenery curtain fell across them. She leapt up and bounded to backstage while, in front of a paint and canvas forest, the king's loyal friends sought him in vain. Out of sight, she pressed a paw against her chin and pulled off the mask.

There was a moment of uncertainty as she forced her body back to its true form. There were two safe shapes: her own body, and the one a mask gave her. She had met a former shifter once, a man who played on past his prime and one day lost control of those shapes. The ruin of his body would live in her mind forever.

The mask came off, as it always did, and she became herself once more, dressed in simple shifter's grey. She hooked the mask back onto her belt, and with fingers that were slower than they should have been, she unhooked another.

It was the first time in years that they had commissioned a new mask. The work was exquisite, an intricate whirl of knots and veins that felt more like real wood than the weirdwood it was carved from, fracturing at the edges into tendrils like branches and roots. Paint blended from brown to green, hinting at leaves that would have been too crude an affectation. Most of her masks were inherited from her mother or selected and adapted to her from the carvings of a craftsman in Dovrept, familiar icons like monkeys, lions, and snakes. But this one had been made specially. That was how important she was, how much audiences loved her, how much her father admired her work. It was beautiful and precious and came at a huge cost.

"Yasmi." Tenebrial's arm was stretched out, tapping her shoulder from a safe distance. "We need you out there."

She swallowed, clutched the mask tight.

"Do I have to?"

"The play needs you."

"The play is just a story."

"The audience needs you."

She took a deep breath and got to her feet. For the audience. To feel their adulation again.

She walked out onto the veiled stage and took her place near the back, amid the fake trees that Raul had helped build. Beyond the curtain, imitation noblemen were reaching the end of their quest, the moment of surrender. She could hear the audience murmuring, interested but not immersed. This was filler, buying time for the leads to recover and reset. Still, she hesitated, knuckles white as she gripped the mask.

"Yasmi," her father hissed from the wings. "Quick!"

For him. For the audience. For her mother's memory. She tapped her foot three times against the boards, then pressed the mask to her face.

The magic of the mask flowed through Yasmi, the power of the theatre and of the audience, directed through weeks of careful preparation. Her body hardened to bark. Her limbs twisted and tangled. Her roots slid across the stage and her branches rose to the ceiling, as she became the mightiest, most real oak in a forest of fakes.

The nobles reached their last line and plodded off, to mild applause. The curtain rose.

Her father, still Balbianus, staggered through the forest, bleeding red wool. The hushed audience watched. Somebody sniffed. Someone else sobbed. Efron's feet thudded as he limped across the boards. Yasmi let that drag on until he was in the centre of the stage, until he had taken one, two, three rasping gasps, until the tension had risen as high as it could go, the audience like a drawn bow shaft that must either spring back or snap.

She brought a branch around and lifted her mask.

The audience watched in rapt silence as the grand oak transformed into a beautiful woman. None of them would have seen the like of it before, least of all by a shifter of her skills. It was her moment of triumph, and it was as hollow as the mask. She felt as if her skin had sloughed off and the cold air of judgement pressed on her bare heart. No barriers. No shelter. No characters. No feigned anger or false smiles. Just her.

She had never felt so scared.

"Who is this?" Efron cried, raising himself on one arm. "Come you to staunch this wound, to save me from the destruction my own pride has brought?"

"Nay, my king." Yasmi knelt beside him, speaking soft but clear. As she and her father leaned in, so did the audience, drawn to her every word. "I am the essence of your nation, the child of your life's work. I am Estis itself, flesh risen from the dirt. The omens brought me here to you, and I, in turn, bring an omen."

The lantern moon descended silently from the ceiling as, behind the scenes, Tenebrial turned its well-oiled winch.

"What say you?" Efron asked, putting on that grand voice he thought all royalty used. "Is my kingdom to fall, now that I am gone?"

"Nay, my king. Like an acorn in the forest, your first seed has grown strong. For countless generations, Estis will stand, and its strength will spread across the world. But one day, others will raise their axe, and the oak will fall."

"Alas, all is ruin!"

"Not all, my king. You have a chance." She drew a stage dagger and handed it to him. "Spill the last of your blood here, let it flow into my soil. Bind our essence together, and I will hold yours close, until a fallen generation cries out your name. Through your blood, Estis will be reborn, strong and free. The birch will fall and the oak stand in its place."

King Balbianus took the dagger and held it aloft. For a moment, she feared that they'd got the angles wrong, that it wouldn't catch the moonlight. But their stagehands were as professional as the cast. The dagger turned and the light came, silver on the blade.

"A dagger in the moonlight." Her father shook his head, hamming up the grief. "Not how a king should take leave of

FORGED FOR DESTINY

this world, but if my people's fate hangs on one last slip of my wrist, then let me buy their lives with mine."

He thrust the dagger into his chest, the blade vanishing into the hollow handle. The audience gave their loudest gasp yet as they watched Balbianus collapse, a flap of his robe falling open at a hidden twitch of Efron's fingers. It revealed a pale semicircle, like moonlight falling from above. The dagger fell across it, blade sliding back out. Above them, a cord unhooked, and a dagger shape of black cloth fell across the glowing moon.

"When this sign returns, so too shall our king," Yasmi said, rising to her feet. The audience was enraptured, not a single face downcast or turned away. She had never stood so tall. "Balbianus reborn, honour restored, a nation renewed. What was born of you, my king, lives immortal in this boon. Balbianus's people. Balbianus's blood. A blade through the heart of the moon."

She flopped to the stage, falling across her father's face, her hair hiding her own features, so all that stood out was the symbol on his chest.

The audience went wild.

———————————•———————————

Inns in Pavuno were different from the one Raul had helped run back home. There, everybody knew everybody else, so everybody talked to everybody else. There might be a few cautious minutes when a stranger arrived, a traveller passing through the Vales, but the locals would soon work out what sort of companion they'd gained, and everything flowed from there. The only people no one talked to were the Dunholmi patrols, and they didn't stick around for long. In the city, people were more cautious, disinterested, divided into their own tables. There were no charms above the doors welcoming them in, encouraging them to know each other, though Raul had spotted the hooks and nail holes where they used to hang. Perhaps that was why it took an effort to coax people into conversation, because they had been denied welcoming magic. But if Raul was meant to unite them against the invaders, to bring the magic back, then sitting beside a warm fire with a cup of ale was surely a good place to start.

"Show me again," he said, as one of his new friends moved upturned cups around the table.

"All right." The man held up a hazelnut. "This goes under the middle cup, see? Now I move the cups around, back and forth, back and forth... You seem like a smart lad, you're keeping track of it, right?"

"Of course."

A few people had gathered around. They looked amused, which was good, but if they wanted to win, then they ought to watch the cups instead of Raul.

"Which cup is the nut under?" the man asked.

"That one."

Raul tapped a cup and the man lifted it, revealing the nut underneath.

"Well done. Want to try again, and this time make it interesting?"

"You mean add more cups?"

FORGED FOR DESTINY

The man laughed. "No, I mean put money on it."

"I'll have a go." A woman placed a coin on the table. Raul thought she might be friends with the cup man: they didn't talk, but they'd exchanged a look just now. People here weren't all unfriendly with each other, even if they showed it in odd ways.

"I can't," Raul said. "I don't have any money."

"You could borrow some off your father." The man gestured to Valens, who was leaning on the bar, listening to an excited woman who had just rushed in.

"He wouldn't want to spend money on this."

"You could bet something else, then. What have you got?"

"Nothing I'd want to risk losing." Raul smiled and shook the man's hand. "Thank you for showing me the game."

Someone laughed and slapped the man on the back.

"Better luck next time, Gorgo."

The man was about to say something more, but his eyes went wide and he turned the cups over. The hazelnut vanished from the table.

"We have to go." Valens tapped Raul on the shoulder.

"Why?"

"Trouble in the city. Best not to be caught out."

Raul got up and waved to the people around him. "It was nice meeting you all."

He followed Valens out of the inn, each of them reaching up as they passed to touch the goat carved into the doorframe, fingers brushing well-worn wood as they sought a safe journey home.

The market square was better lit than when they had gone into the inn. A fire was blazing in the middle, and people were gathering around it, calling out to each other in fierce excitement. Some of them carried tools: mallets, picks, spades. Others carried sticks or stones.

"Is it a festival?" Raul asked, as something was flung onto the fire amid a round of cheers.

"It's trouble." Valens gestured up the street leading to the theatre. His other hand rested on his knife. "Come on."

The streets were busy, people rushing back and forth, some carrying torches to light the way. They were shouting, and Raul caught the words "dagger" and "freedom." One of the torchbearers stood by while a woman with a jar of paint daubed a giant moon across a house front.

"What's going on?" Raul asked as he hurried after Valens.

"Prisca's play. It's gone too well."

From the end of the street came shouts of anger and cries of pain. Flashes of blue revealed Dunholmi warriors mixed in among a swirling mob of women and men, an ugly, chaotic brawl that Raul couldn't follow, though he could see its casualties sprawled and groaning on the cobbles.

"Is this it?" he asked, pushing himself up on his toes. "Has the uprising started?"

"This is a mistake." Valens grabbed Raul's arm and dragged him into a side street.

"We should join them. If these people have the courage to throw off—"

Valens swung Raul around and his back hit the wall. Hands gripped his arms so tight that he was afraid they might break. He stared, shocked and bewildered. His da had never treated him like this.

FORGED FOR DESTINY

"Those people have no leader, no weapons, no strategy," Valens growled. "They're going to die."

He let go of Raul and took a step back. This street was small, quiet, just the two of them, though the flicker of firelight flitted in at one end, along with voices and hoofbeats.

"Sorry." Valens hung his head. "Shouldn't have done that. It's too much like..." He clasped his hands together, twisted the black ring around his finger. "This isn't the time for heroics."

"In the stories, sometimes they have to—"

"There's a lot the stories don't say. I'll show you."

Raul nodded and followed Valens down the twisting, narrow streets, back in the direction they'd come.

"Are we—"

"Watch and listen."

Valens stopped in the shadows of an alley mouth, close to the inn where they'd been drinking, and Raul stopped beside him. In the square, the flames were stretching higher. The crowd cheered as something was thrown onto the fire.

Hoofbeats again, beneath the shouts. They grew louder, and part of the crowd turned as riders burst into the square.

They were terrible and magnificent, not the Dunholmi warriors he had seen guarding and patrolling but the ones out of war stories. They galloped into the square, tabards bright, armour gleaming, sabre edges arcs of silver against the night sky as they let out a battle cry.

The riders smashed into the crowd, battering them with the weight and the speed of their horses. Bodies were flung to the ground or into the fire, crushed beneath hooves. Sabres fell like scythes, reaping a harvest of humanity. The united excitement of the crowd became a fractured mass of terror, a place of screams and wet thuds. Some of them were illuminated by the fire, others mercifully silhouetted, vanishing into the darkness as they fell. A woman ran screeching, her hair and tunic in flames.

"We have to help." Raul drew his knife. Valens slammed him back into shadow.

"You think you can stop this with that?" His hand squeezed Raul's fingers around the grip of the knife.

A dozen strides from them, a rioter stood proud, mallet raised, facing down a galloping warrior. He brandished his weapon, face full of grim determination. The horse swerved, a sabre flashed, and the man fell. There was a crunch of bones snapping beneath hooves.

Raul sagged. He felt like something had broken inside his chest too.

"I'm meant to be the hero."

"You will be, when the city's ready." Valens took the knife from Raul's numb hand, slid it into its sheath. "Best not go back to the theatre. Let's go to Appia's until this dies down."

Chapter Twenty
To Be Muted or to Be Hanged

Raul's stomach tightened as he rounded the corner and saw the state of the theatre. Its pale new planks were blackened with stripes of soot, grey flakes fell on the wind, and heaps of charred timbers lay in the street. Despondent performers skulked around the entrance, speaking in hushed and broken murmurs.

"They burned it!" he said, staring in horror.

"Look again."

Valens walked on down the street, his shadow stretching in the early-morning light, one more dark shape among many littering the ground. Raul looked past him, took in the buildings standing nearby, two of them with their fronts burned away, another reduced to a blackened skeleton. There was nothing like that at the theatre. Its black was soot blown from other buildings, but none of the structure was damaged; an onlooker to the carnage, bloodstained rather than bleeding.

"Where's Prisca?" Raul asked, now more curious than alarmed. His ma was tough enough to roam the Vales alone and canny enough to plan an empire's fall. A night of rioting wouldn't touch her.

Sure enough, a familiar figure emerged through the theatre's front doors, lean and purposeful. Her hawkish gaze caught them and she gave a curt nod. She was followed a moment later by Efron Dellest, his purple silk shirt flaring as he waved his hands.

"...most abject state of misery, our home the epicentre of a human storm, our neighbourhood as black and barren as the heart of Duke—"

"I understand, Efron." She cut him off with the sharp edge of her voice. "You have had a difficult night. That is no reason to abandon a trail that has brought you so far."

"We will be blamed for what happened. Our play—"

"Was the catalyst for existing tensions. Not your fault."

Raul moved closer, as did the unsettled players. Claudio was chewing on his lip, Biallo twisting a scarf between white fingers, Tenebrial twitching like a flea. Only Yasmi, dressed in her shifter greys, stayed in the dirt by the door, legs crossed, cradling a mask in her lap.

"Of course it is not our fault!" Efron flung his hands in the air. "This is your doing!"

"Mine?" Prisca glared at him.

"Yes, yours! You were the one who wanted this story told. Look at how people have responded."

"You made your choices." Prisca pointed at Tenebrial. "You wrote it." Her finger stabbed an inch from Efron's nose. "You

FORGED FOR DESTINY

commissioned it." She whirled around to take the others in. "You all performed it. Take responsibility for your actions."

"Oh no! You don't get off so easily. You planted this worm of a story in my head, kept dropping hints about how noble and glorious it would be. Why, even the unmasking was your idea."

"I gave you ideas. You chose to use them."

"And you think that will save us from the scaffold when Count Alder learns where the riot started?"

"Is this the thanks I get, after all the funds I've poured into your endeavours, you ungrateful, pretentious, talentless—"

The actors gasped and Prisca froze. She took a sharp breath and raised a finger as if summoning her next point.

"You funded us because of your..." Efron waved his hand at Raul, who shrank from the anger in the actor's eyes. "Your agenda."

"You should consider where that agenda ends, whether Count Alder is the one whose approval you need."

Many of the actors looked at Raul, and he furled further in on himself. He'd hoped that when the time for action came, these people he'd lived and worked with would be among the first to back him. Right now, he wasn't so sure. He wished this moment could end and they could go back to making scenery together.

"The risks here are too great," Efron said. "We will go back to the script the count approved."

"No, no, no!" Tenebrial held out his hands, snatching at something swept away in the current of time. "That version is muted, neutered, devoid of power. We might as well put on a farce."

257

"Better to be muted than to be hanged," Efron snapped. "As for you..." He turned back to Prisca. "I'm sorry, but I must ask you to find other accommodation."

"I pay the rent here."

"You paid it. Now we have our first night's earnings, which will see us through while our art earns our keep. I can't have dissidents living in our props room when the authorities come calling."

Prisca's terrible stillness went all the way to her eyes. She was like a raptor watching a rabbit hole, talons bared.

Raul looked at the ruined buildings and the litter of charred wood, the ashes that kissed the players' cheeks as they blew down the street. Those pale faces beneath the ashes, shaken and bewildered, trying to make sense of what they had endured.

"Maybe Efron's right, Ma," he said. "I saw the rioting last night, and the warriors putting it down. It was terrible. We can't bring that to our friends' door."

Murmurs of agreement from the players.

"How many times must I tell you, don't call me—" Prisca cut herself off, took a deep breath, straightened her back. "Raul, you are too young to understand. This is more complex than—"

"The lad's right." Valens's words were like slabs of stone slamming down between them.

"There may be an appropriate moment for you to start thinking for yourself, but this is not it."

Valens rubbed a thick finger across his forehead, while his eye squeezed tight shut. Next to him, Raul stood rigid with

FORGED FOR DESTINY

tension, shocked by his ma's words. Yes, she got angry some-times, but this, here, now...

"None of us have slept much," Valens said. "Let's go rest, come back together when we're thinking clearly."

"I am thinking just fine," Prisca snapped. "Apparently I am the only one who is, the only one capable of remembering what is at stake."

"That's it." Valens grabbed her arm and dragged her toward the theatre door. "Efron, wait here. We'll be back."

Raul stood uncertain. He didn't want to watch his parents argue, didn't want to stand here either, with more and more eyes turning to him. The only ones that didn't were those that could have given him comfort, as Yasmi kept staring at her mask. In the end, the pressure propelled him through the door.

Inside, the theatre looked eerily normal, without a trace of destruction. Most of the audience stood through a play, so there weren't many seats to be overturned. The only damage he could see was a garland of spring flowers, which the players had hung to bring them good health, lying trampled amid the rushes on the floor. Raul picked it up, tried to straighten the bent leaves.

Valens and Prisca stood in front of the stage, under the moon-shaped lantern. He was hunched, hands clasped, twisting his ring around. She stood stiff-backed, arms folded, chin raised.

"This is what we came here for," she said. "You've known that the whole time. Don't get squeamish on me now."

"It wasn't meant to hurt our friends."

"In war, people get hurt." She tapped one of the scars pro-truding from beneath the sleeve of his tunic. "You know that better than anyone."

"I chose that life. They didn't." He gestured toward the door.

"It's a cruel world and innocents suffer. That's why we need to give them a hero."

Valens's laughter sounded more hurt than amused.

"You know what a hero is? It's what you're left with when you cut away half the story, when you spill blood, then hide it under the rushes. Wars aren't just glory and courage, they're sickness and starvation, a hundred suffering victims for every warrior who rides home triumphant. Heroism's a lie we tell ourselves so we can live with the loss. There are no heroes in the real world."

"That can't be true." Raul stepped out of the shadows, the wreath clutched so tight that a needle-edged holly leaf pierced his palm. "What about the heroes whose stories you told me? What about Presida on the plains, or Treganus against the stone ogres? What about Balbianus?"

Valens looked at him, mouth open, then turned his gaze away, chin pressing against his chest.

"Yes, Valens," Prisca said, eyes narrowing. "What about all the stories you told Raul?"

She spoke oddly, each word a tiny blow, and Valens stepped back beneath the onslaught. Both hands pressed against his forehead and his breath came in long snorts, like a bull.

"Don't vex yourself." Prisca's voice became softer. "This is about the righteous fight, and that's what you live for. The thrill of battle. The chance to overrun the enemy and set the world to rights."

"It's not what I'm here for." Valens shot a furtive look at Raul, then looked back at the ground.

FORGED FOR DESTINY

"Of course it is. You committed your life to this cause, just as surely as Fabia did. Don't let your work be for nothing. Don't let her sacrifice be in vain."

Raul had heard Fabia's name before, in war stories his da told on ale-soaked nights at the inn. But he'd seldom heard Prisca mention her before, and never seen his da respond like this. Valens lunged at Prisca. Muscles bulged in his neck and his teeth bared in a snarl.

"How dare you!" His hand stopped an inch from her face, fingers shaking. "Your mind must be going, old woman, if you think that you can use her name like that."

"My mind is none of your cursed business. We have all made sacrifices to reach this point, and now we must face the finale. I will not let you ruin it."

The two of them stepped back. They were like wrestlers at the harvest fair, bruised and battered, tensed and waiting for the next round. Where had Raul's parents gone?

They were intensely focused on each other, poised and waiting to strike, oblivious to anything beyond the cloud of resentment that roiled between them.

Something flickered in Prisca's face. She glanced fleetingly at Raul, then turned her gaze back to Valens. Her body relaxed and her voice softened.

"I'm sorry," she said. "Sorry to both of you. I understand your frustrations. We are in a difficult situation, nothing is as we imagined, because nothing ever is."

She looked down at her hands, then out the door, toward the street.

"If there is such a thing as heroism, then those actors

showed it," she said. "They put on a play about our first king under the noses of our oppressors, gave people hope at a time when they desperately need it. They might not have done it for heroic reasons, might be more interested in art and fame than the future of our homeland, but how many ever choose to bear the weight of the world? Fabia scorned the idea of heroes, but in my heart, I believe that she was one."

"That she was." Valens nodded. "And she'd slap us both for saying it."

"We have forged something to save this land, a chain to drag it out of the dirt. Every link in that chain is important, and when we see a weak one, we must repair it, not scream about its cracks."

For the first time, Raul recognised something he had been struggling to see since they left the inn. Prisca hadn't meant to reveal his destiny to him when she had, and while he knew that she had been planning for it, he had never acknowledged how much she had done. All those years, all those travels, she had been preparing a way for him, a chance to build a better world. How could he let doubt take hold when she had committed her life to his cause?

Maybe some heroes were made by accident, but he could make a choice.

"What do we do now?" he asked.

"Bring our friends in," Prisca said. "I'll manage this."

Raul did as he was told, and the troupe shuffled in, soot-stained and bleary-eyed, Yasmi clutching her mask.

"Are you all right?" Raul whispered to her.

"Hm?" She looked up but he didn't think she saw him. "Oh, yes. I'll be fine."

FORGED FOR DESTINY

Prisca stood in the middle of the stage. She'd found King Balbianus's wooden crown and was turning it in her hands.

"Friends," she said. "Hosts. First let me say thank you. You took us in for the long journey to the city and for the time we have stayed here. I am grateful for that, and it grieves me that I haven't shown proper appreciation."

She leaned over to set the crown down, and when she straightened, she did so slowly, with a grimace, one hand against her back. For the first time Raul could remember, she looked her age.

"I know that you're scared," she said. "Last night you put on a play that started a riot. If I was in your shoes, I would be wondering what comes next."

The players made noises of concern and discontent.

"You're pissing right we would," someone called out. The mood in the room ranged from tense through nervous to outright hostile.

"I would also be proud," Prisca said, raising murmurs of confusion. "Your skills, your gift, your writing, crafting, performing, these things came together in a spectacle so moving that it set the city ablaze. How many troupes can say they have done that?"

There was reluctant laughter, even a couple of muted cheers. But some grumbled still or watched her with silent glares.

"I understand why you might want to give it up," she continued. "I would. But then, I'm not an actor. I've not felt the boards beneath my feet or the audience's eyes on me. I don't know whether it's worth the risk for the response you got last night. Maybe you can get the thrill of that performance, of

263

that response, some other way. Perhaps another of your plays will do. I don't know."

This time, the sounds were thoughtful, players whispering to each other, expressions shifting, weary eyes brightening. Someone started to protest but was hushed by the player next to her.

"I do know this: people out there want to see this play. How many attended last night?"

Prisca looked at Efron, who looked at Tenebrial. Every eye turned to the playwright.

"Two thousand," he said, waving an ink-stained finger. "Give or take a hundred."

Whispers rushed around the room. Half the places they performed on the road didn't have populations that big. The impact of their new playhouse, and of their new play, were starting to sink in.

"Is that a lot?" Prisca asked, catching the eye of the loudest complainer.

"Of course it's a lot," he called back. "Piss and blood, you ignorant scribe, don't you know anything about theatre?"

"Forgive my ignorance, you're the experts here, not me." Prisca made a show of counting on her fingers. "Two thousand in the audience, and yet ten thousand rioted for it." She raised her eyebrows. "That's eight thousand who'll want to know why they felt like they did, and two thousand who'll want to feel that excitement again: not the riot, but its precursor passion. How many more will flock here, as word streams through the city?"

A lot of nodding now, louder murmurs of agreement. Efron

FORGED FOR DESTINY

smiled. Even the man who'd called Prisca an ignorant scribe was thoughtfully stroking his chin.

"Will you give up on that play?" Prisca asked, standing tall, hands held wide. "Will you give up on the greatest performance this city, this country, this world has ever seen?"

She had them. Some were reluctant still, shaking heads or murmuring uncertainly, but there were too many grins, too much chatter, too many shining eyes to turn back.

"What about the neighbours?" someone shouted, a last attempt to turn the tide. "Won't they be mad that we got them torched?"

"A valid point," Prisca called out. "Which is why we will go out today and help them rebuild, all of us, the people of this theatre. We will show them that we mean no harm, that we can be good for them. And we will invite them to tonight's performance: you can be sure that they'll tell their friends."

Laughter. "Tell your friends" was Efron's great exhortation to people leaving his plays. No one there could deny its appeal.

"Come, then." Efron waved a hand. "Let us go to the streets and undo some damage. Then sleep, eat, recuperate, for we have a performance tonight."

The chattering crowd of actors poured into the street. No one commented on how Prisca had folded her family back into their home, in the "we" going out to repair. Raul supposed that conversation would come later.

"How did she know there were ten thousand?" he asked Valens as they watched the troupe leave.

"What?"

"Ten thousand rioters, how did she know?"

"She didn't. Sometimes truth's not as important as the point you make."

"Oh." Raul scratched his head, unconvinced.

"Come on, lad." Valens slapped him on the shoulder. "It's been too long since we did an honest day's labour. I'm looking forward to this."

"Me too, Da." Raul, his heart lifting, followed him toward the door.

On the stage, Prisca picked up the crown, spun it around her finger, and walked away with a smile.

Chapter Twenty-One
The Maker of Secrets

It wasn't the worst inn Valens had ever spent time in, but it was no substitute for the long-lost Darting Drake. The rushes were old and sparse, the plaster between the wall beams crumbling, and there were stains on the tables too dark for wine or ale. A rough place for rough business. At least it had a private room, with its own back door, and an owner Appia trusted, or perhaps could control. That made it as safe a place as they could meet.

There were wards too, for whatever they were worth, carefully crafted to avoid prying eyes. A cup left casually by the door, with a little ale for the spirit of the street. A hooded eye so artfully carved it could have been mistaken for a knot in the door beam. Some scratches on the wall that might have been a goat, if you squinted at them right. Would the magic even work when it was hidden like that? Valens didn't know, but he was glad of it all the same. It felt like the old days.

He stood with his back to the wall, watching each arrival,

looking for what weapons they carried, both open and hidden, whether they skulked or looked away beneath his gaze. He didn't have any reason to expect betrayal, but he didn't know these people well enough to trust them either. Not with so much at stake.

Raul greeted each one as they came in, smiling, shaking their hands, asking questions in his genial way until they smiled too, some a little, some a lot. Prisca had got Efron's wardrobe mistress to adjust the lad's clothes, so that he looked more the heroic part. Tunic tightened in places, loosened in others, the sleeves removed to show off the muscles beneath the cloth of his shirt. Thin enough cloth for a hint of his birthmark to show, and that caught everyone's eye once they got close enough. Word was spreading. A new moon rising indeed.

Appia arrived first, with two other labour gang leaders, one from the mines and one from the fields. People who influenced large groups of tough workers, who'd knocked heads together to get those positions. People Valens could understand. After her came Drusil the blacksmith, and a tanner she'd introduced to the group, one who'd lost fingers to Dunholmi law and who knew leather armour. Holy Cirillo, the High Priest of Yorl, shouldn't have been a surprise, given his hidden books, but Valens hadn't taken him for a man of action. It took all sorts to serve a god.

They each took a seat at the table, and a cup of ale or of goat's milk as suited them. Valens closed the doors and took his own seat next to Raul. The lad had dealt with the niceties, had warmed them all up with his charm. They were smiling,

FORGED FOR DESTINY

relaxing, nodding along. That was good. It meant that Valens could knock back his drink and get straight to business.

"How are we set for arms?" Valens asked.

"I've made most of what you asked for," Drusil said. "Though I'm still waiting on the High Widder iron."

"I thought we had a boat to move it." Valens looked at Appia. She was knotting strands of old string into dolls, building a community of frayed hemp on the tabletop.

"We've got plenty of boats," Appia said, fingers working while she looked his way. "What we can't control is the guard shifts at Tantia's Bridge. A friend of ours takes over as captain in two days. I won't risk my people before then."

Valens's brow furrowed as he thought about where those places were, how they connected to each other.

"Can't you bring the ore down the Rack?"

Appia snorted. "Only if you want it at the bottom of the river. There's no boat can carry cargo down the rapids."

"I swear there used to be boats for running the Rack." Valens scowled. Was this one more thing the invaders had wrecked, in their fury at Estis?

"There were, for those hurt badly in the mines, but the rapids drowned nearly as many patients as the royal physicians saved."

"So you don't have one of those boats."

"I didn't say that." Appia looked at him from hooded eyes, then flicked a string doll across the table. "My friends have all sorts of boats, but the Rack boats weren't built to carry ore."

Valens clenched his fist under the table. They had enough weapons for the main strike, but he'd wanted more. Arming

269

people made them think like fighters, made them ready to rise up. He'd wanted to put a blade in every hand that would take it, but it was too late to change plans now.

"We need a way into the palace," he said, picking up the string figure and turning it between his fingers. "And when we find it, we'll need folk to come with us. Some of your best."

"Thought you wanted us on the outside." Appia twisted another strand of string. "Seize the city. Contain the troops. What did Prisca call it?"

"Chain the body while we remove the head," Holy Cirillo said, his one eye staring at each of them in turn. "Like Treganus among the ogres."

"Somebody has to be the executioner's blade." Raul had been reading again, or maybe listening to Prisca, his head filling with fancy phrases. Luckily, this lot seemed impressed. "The sharper the blade, the cleaner the cut. If we have your best, then we can capture Count Alder quickly and force the troops out before they damage the city."

"Capture him?" Appia raised an eyebrow. "Surely just..."
She ran a finger across her throat.

"Not if we don't have to."

"Bargaining power," Valens added. "With his troops, and with his king."

"I suppose." Appia had the weary tone of a woman bowing to the inevitable. "I'd still rather string the fucker up, for everything he's done. For the people we've lost."

"Maybe that'll happen." Valens tapped Raul's arm under the table, silencing the protest that might have come. The lad

FORGED FOR DESTINY

was smarter than him, where it was about books and words and big ideas, but he was proving painfully slow at learning what not to say. "First, we've got to win our freedom, and the time for that's not far off."

"It's true." Cirillo placed a parchment on the table. "Righteous folk inside the palace managed, at great risk, to extract this from the confiscated documents. More signs that Prisca's divination was right. We must act when the Red Eye rises."

He unrolled the document and started reading, explaining the meaning of some old prophecy. Sometimes it talked about Balbianus's blood, or the one who was coming, and these people around the table—these tough, experienced, worldly men and women—looked at Raul like he was something they had never known before.

Valens wondered whether this was one of the real old prophecies that Prisca had woven into her web, or one of the ones she had invented, with her perfectly worn parchments and her carefully coloured inks. It was probably crap either way, prophecy was like that. What mattered was what people believed.

"Excuse me," a strange voice said.

Valens leapt from his seat and across the room. He plunged his hand through the slim gap between door and frame, grabbed a scrawny throat, and dragged its owner through. Red-faced, he slammed the door shut. How had he not heard the bolt shift? How had he not seen this man come?

"Who are you?" He pressed the point of his knife against the man's side. "How'd you find us?"

"Followed her," the man croaked, pointing at Drusil.

The blacksmith was on her feet, like everyone else, and Valens was pleased to see that they all had weapons, even the priest.

"His name's Quintae." Drusil slapped a hammer against her hand, and the muscles in her arms bulged. "Carpenter three doors down from me. Makes cupboards and chests."

"Not just." Quintae tried to shake his head, which was tough with Valens's hand around his neck. "Can help. But first..." He pointed at the door. "Guards coming."

"You saw them?" Valens narrowed his eyes.

"Following the priest. Waiting across the street now. Heard them talking about reinforcements, I did. Thought I'd warn you."

"How do I know that this isn't some trick?"

"I..." The fallen look on Quintae's face said he hadn't thought that through. Carpenter or not, he was seconds away from a knife through the heart.

"Bring him with us," Raul said, opening the back door. "He might know more."

Valens glanced at Drusil, raised an eyebrow.

She frowned, then shrugged. "Always seemed like a harmless little rat to me."

"Fine." Valens shoved Quintae across the room. Survival first, questions after. "Drusil, you're with us. Everyone else scatter."

"We'll make some fuss, draw them off," Appia said, gesturing to the mine leader.

"Won't be the first time," her companion said, grinning, and the two of them strode out.

FORGED FOR DESTINY

Pushing Quintae ahead of him, Valens hurried down back streets and alleys. Somewhere behind him, people were shouting, but he only looked back to make sure that he had Drusil and Raul.

"My place," Drusil said. "It's the closest safe spot."

The shouting faded into the hubbub of the city as they made their way uphill, past the stables where the Scholars' Spire had been, across the Blood Market, and down the artificers' street. They approached the smithy from the back, where fewer people would see who came and went, straight into the forge instead of the shop.

It was gloomy in there with the shutters barred. Drusil had banked the coals before she left, but the place was still warmer than the streets. An orange glow pierced the gaps between the coals, cast soft shadows, picked out fragments of their faces. Valens sat Quintae on a stool, laid the carpenter's hand on the anvil, and picked up a hammer.

"Close the door," he said, low and menacing.

"Not needed." Quintae shook his head, held his hands out in front of his chest. "Came to help."

"Persuade me." Valens hefted the hammer. "While you can still follow your craft."

He hoped that Raul and Drusil had the sense to stay out of this. Torture didn't work the way people wanted it to, but the threat of it could shake words loose, and for that he needed Quintae's attention.

"Da." Raul wrapped his hand around the head of the hammer. "Please, let me talk to him. There's no need for this."

Valens gritted his teeth. He tried so hard to raise Raul as a good lad, it never occurred to him that he might have raised him too soft. The boy needed to toughen up for Prisca's plan to work.

No. That wasn't right. He wasn't going to break his son, not even to save a kingdom. Besides, there was a place for the soft touch. Raul's charm might help here as much as the hammer.

Valens took a step back, picked up a fire iron, and spread the coals. Released from darkness, the fire's glow bathed Quintae and Raul.

"Go on," Valens said, "but if he lies, I'll be ready."

"Won't lie," Quintae squealed, his face pale, scraggly hair shaking. He tapped a finger against his lips. "Promise, won't lie."

Raul crouched in front of the strange little man, with his long face and his narrow fingers.

"How did you find us?" he asked.

"Followed her." Quintae pointed at Drusil. "Quiet, careful, wanted to see."

"To see what?"

"New moon."

Quintae reached inside his tunic, drew out a sheet of paper, which he carefully unrolled; one of the pages Pomponius had penned and that Appia's people had scattered around the city. The dagger-pierced moon with words around it:

A NEW MOON COMES! BE READY TO RISE!

Quintae handed the sheet to Raul, then ran a finger down the lad's upper arm. Sweat had stuck the shirt to Raul's skin, making the mark more visible.

"New moon," Quintae whispered, eyes wide.

FORGED FOR DESTINY

"You want to join the struggle?" Raul asked.

Quintae nodded. "Must change. No more."

He tapped the side of his head. There were scars between the clumped and scraggly hair. Someone had made a mess of Quintae, and Valens suspected that someone wore the colours of Dunholm. Still, he had to be sure.

"How do we know we can trust you?" he asked.

"Keep secrets." Quintae tapped himself on the chest, then pointed at Drusil, who stood by the door, hammer at the ready. "Keep her secrets."

"Liar." She snorted.

"Secret sword cupboard."

"How d'you know about that?"

"Made it."

"Germian made it."

"You see it made?" Quintae shook his head. "No, because I make secrets, and Germian makes deals. Hidey holes, secret passages, hidden rooms, in houses and boats. I make them."

Valens slapped the fire iron against his hand. He was inclined to believe this, but it paid to keep up the pressure.

"Why not take credit?" he asked. "Why hide behind this Germian?"

"Safer in secret." Quintae tapped the paper. "But now, new moon rising, I think this has secrets, think it needs to keep them. I can help."

Valens looked at Drusil. The fire was rising in the forge, enough light to pick out the lucky silver nail protruding from the wall behind her. The same light shone red in Drusil's eyes, lit the sneer of her lip.

275

"You trust him?" he asked.

"I don't trust Germian anymore," she said. "But given she and I need to talk, I can ask what she thinks of him."

That, it seemed to Valens, was as good as this was going to get. Killing Quintae would bring complications, not least Raul's response. Besides, the man might be useful. The closer they got to the Red Eye's arrival, the more secrets they had to hide. An army needed engineers, and what was Quintae if not the engineer of a secret war?

"Go talk to Germian," Valens said. "We'll wait until you're done. And Quintae?"

The carpenter looked up from Raul's arm. "Yes, master?"

Valens laid the fire iron on the anvil with a clang. "You'd better not be lying to me."

Chapter Twenty-Two
The Performance of a Lifetime

"One would think that you'd never ridden a horse, Tur," Count Alder said as he rode down from the palace, a trail of chosen warriors behind him.

"My lord?" Ketley Tur's shoulders shifted and his fingers tightened on the reins. There was a good chance that the fool was going to get himself thrown.

"Stop wriggling. Sit up straight. We are servants of the royal line of Dunholm, so hold yourself like one."

"Yes, my lord." Tur stiffened. He still looked more like a rotting tailor's dummy than a proper horseman, but he did come from peasant stock. The steeds he was used to were probably fly-ridden mules and lumbering carthorses. Alder would have to have the man trained before he brought him out again.

The locals watched as they passed. Along the sides of the

road, the obsequious and the obedient, trying to get his attention, to tell him their petty problems or to offer him goods unworthy of his lowest servants. Behind those were the faces of surly acceptance, the weary eyes and pale, resentful scowls. How many of those expressions would hold a hint of accusation, if he got close enough? How many hid rebellion behind the mask of obedience? Enough to have burned down a stable and five merchants' houses, killed three of his men and sent forty to the physician. Enough that he felt as though he was riding through a wasps' nest, waiting for the whisper of those tiny lives to rise into an angry buzz. That was all these rioters were, stinging insects, and like those insects, they would be gone by summer's end. The question was, how much damage could they do while their moon shone, to his city and his reputation?

Tur tutted. "We must do something about this."

"About what in particular?"

"This." Tur thrust out a bony finger, pointing over the heads of the crowd.

"A tavern?"

"The carvings on the door. Magical. That goat is for luck in travelling. If I may, my lord, I will send one of your men to have it removed."

"You may not." Alder leaned forward to stroke the neck of his horse, which had become agitated by some movement in the crowd. "We cannot stop every little piece of magic these people use. It's woven into the fabric of life."

"Indeed, my lord. But such charms lead to more powerful arts, and we cannot allow those to rise again." The

FORGED FOR DESTINY

chamberlain's voice struck an uneasy note between anger and pleading. "Everything your uncle did, everything our people bled for, relies upon keeping those arts suppressed."

"Indeed, but there are limits. We cannot deprive them of knives because they might learn to make swords, and we cannot destroy their charms because they might learn to master essence. So we take down anything big and public, punish prominent offenders, prevent anyone from reaching for too much power, while letting them have small everyday things."

"My lord, your own warriors have been—"

"I won't risk my men's resentment by muzzling them, any more than I'll build my policy on their worst instincts. There's a balance to be struck here, Tur, and it's a delicate one. If we make life impractical, then we will drive things underground, turn more of these people into rioters and rebels."

"I fear, my lord, that they already turn."

"Which is why we ride out." Alder waved to the crowd, and his robes slid back to reveal the chainmail beneath. "To remind them of our strength, and to lay down the law."

The street opened out into the cleared ground around the half-built monument. There were already warriors here, lowly infantry levies with spears and shields. They stood straight as Alder and his noble warriors rode by, hooves clopping against packed dirt. There were corpses too, rioters killed in that night of turmoil or hanged since. All hung, limp and pale and naked, flies buzzing around their bodies. Alder wished that more had been caught. This display would have to deter the others instead.

The monument they were riding toward rose at a high

point in Pavuno's former defences. Two steep pyramids of stone, one for the fallen and one for the future. Scaffolding rose around the first, and masons worked its smooth sides, chiselling the names of women and men lost in the long war. The other was blocky, a heap of stones waiting to become something more refined. If these people wanted magic, then Alder would show it to them.

Just like in an army camp, those around Alder had two reactions to a lord's arrival. Some stopped and stared, waiting expectantly. Others focused on their labours, working harder and faster than ever. Tur was one of those, constantly trying to impress. It was exhausting to witness, but useful.

Alder reined his horse in and dismounted. Tur had more trouble, his horse uncertain how to respond to his timid handling. One of the chosen stepped up to take the chamberlain's reins and help him down.

"The rioters didn't attack here?" Alder walked slowly around the monument, observing progress. His hand rested on the hilt of his sabre.

"Indeed, my lord." Tur scurried after him, stoop-shouldered, one corner of his unevenly belted robe trailing in the mud. "After the attack on the supply tents, we doubled the guards, and that was enough to deter any criminal. This is one of the safest places in the city."

"I'm sure."

Alder stepped under the scaffold. A mason stepped back, her head bowed. Alder laid a hand on the monument, felt the cool of the stone, the crisp edges of fresh carvings.

He knew many of the names engraved here: nobles' names

written large and low so that everyone would see them, those of knights and common soldiers receding in smaller scripts up the side, decades of the fallen immortalised in stone. Here was a distant cousin of his, lost in the crossing of the Tulivon twenty years before. Time had wiped all but the haziest memory of her from his mind, and he'd never liked her much, but that was hardly the point. The people of the North March must be made to remember their crimes, every last bloody moment of them.

"This is fine carving," he said. "The North March's reputation for craftsmanship is well earned."

"Thank you, my lord." The mason bowed her head deeper.

"Here." He took a jingling pouch from his belt and handed it to her. "Share this with your fellow artisans. Some people only destroy, but you grant the world beauty. That should be rewarded."

The mason glanced down the hill to the hanging bodies. These people were like a wilful colt. You needed to offer them a whip with one hand and oats with the other. That would break them in soon enough.

Alder strode back to his horse, Tur and the chosen guards striding after him.

"Mount up," Alder said.

"Already?" Tur's face fell.

"Of course." Alder took hold of the saddle and set one foot in the stirrup. "We've quashed the symptoms of trouble, now we need to root out its cause."

Noonday light streamed through the window, making Yasmi's hair glow. She rather liked the effect, enhanced as it was by the blur of the mirror, a blur that mercifully hid any signs of tiredness. It had been another restless night, unnamed anxieties waking her every hour. But a star could not admit to exhaustion; she must burn bright and beautiful for all the world to see.

She assessed her outfit a final time and removed one of the small coloured scarves tied around her arm. Pleased with the result, she opened her door and headed into the theatre's back rooms. She needed something tasty to waken her senses and give her energy for the day ahead.

A certain amount of bustle was to be expected in a building full of players. Though their days were less busy without the toils of the road, unpacking every night and packing up again in the morning, her father always found tasks to keep them occupied. The theatre was improving day by day, with new backdrops and props, decorations around the pit, plans to expand the galleries for wealthy patrons, bringing more coin and more applause for her at the end of the night. But today the place was quiet. Perhaps the troupe were out helping the neighbours rebuild, as they had done each day since the riot. Perhaps Tenebrial had made changes again and they were learning new lines.

She found a bread roll in the kitchen, not fresh but close enough, and some goat's cheese, tangy and soft, rolled in herbs to mellow its taste. Nibbling on her breakfast, or perhaps her lunch, she walked out onto the stage.

By the theatre's main doors, half the troupe were huddled, silently staring up the street.

"He's coming this way," someone hissed.

"Who is?" Yasmi asked, jumping down into the pit.

"The count." There was a tremor in her father's voice. "He's been talking to the neighbours, and now..."

Half the players scattered, rushing to the shelter of the low galleries, while others froze in place, then bowed at the waist. Yasmi tossed her bread over her shoulder, straightened her tunic, and stood smiling as Count Alder strode in.

The count had held himself with an air of power when she met him before, but it was easy for a man to do that in his throne room: the stage was set to his advantage. Walking in now, he made clear that his authority came from more than props. His back was straight but not stiff, his stride confident, and he scanned the theatre with a casually possessive eye. One corner of his mouth quirked up as he spotted her.

"Mistress Dellest." He gave the smallest nod.

"My lord." She bowed gracefully, one leg stretched back, then straightened to face him. "You honour us with your presence."

"I do."

"This is my father, the master of our troupe, Efron Dellest."

"My lord." Her father tipped forward until his moustache almost drooped to the ground.

"Rise, Master Dellest. I can't talk with you while you're facing the dirt."

Others had come in behind the count: his chamberlain, Tur, like a spider made from dust, and half a dozen armed men, hands on their swords, faces set with menace. Alder approached the stage and a beam of sunlight fell across him, illuminating the beautiful blue of his robes. To a casual observer, they might look like the robes he had worn in the throne room, but these were cut to drape artfully over armour, to complement the warrior beneath.

"I hear that your play has been a success," the count said, looking up at the moon lantern. Yasmi was relieved to see that its dagger symbol had been furled away.

"Indubitably, my lord." Her father was bringing out his collection of grand words, always good for impressing small-town mayors, but were they right for a count of Dunholm? "The people adore a good story and are much enamoured of those who tell it."

"As well they might be, given your performers." Alder smiled at Yasmi. "You are the talk of the town, at least the parts still standing. The unmasking in particular has people impressed."

Yasmi maintained her welcoming smile, but her heart was pounding. Only three days, and he already knew that they had changed the play. Three days, and he had come here. So much for Prisca's assurance that showing him the safe version would hide the truth.

Yasmi glanced at the back door, but one of the count's men stood there. The walls of the theatre closed in, less of a home now than a cage.

"A masterstroke by our playwright," Efron declared, barrelling on through a situation he only half understood.

Yasmi's search for the right words was slowed by her sleepiness. If only her mother was still here. But if her mother was here, then Efron wouldn't have quenched his loneliness

FORGED FOR DESTINY

with Valens, and they wouldn't have been roped into Prisca's schemes. Now Yasmi was too slow to stop her father making another mistake.

"There was no unmasking in the version I saw," Alder said. "Or did I miss that part of your performance, Yasmi?"

"No, my lord, but—"

"Plays change in the rehearsing," Efron said, stepping forward, the words coming too fast. "Even in the performance. We adapt as we see an opportunity to heighten the drama, to touch the soul of the audience, to raise our art to a more dizzying peak."

"I am entirely in favour of art." Alder's finger tapped the hilt of his sword. "Riots, on the other hand? Those we could all do without. I hear that the recent disturbance started here."

"In the neighbourhood, perhaps, but you know how cities get. Passions become heated, frustrations swell like rotten fruit, and in the end, they burst forth at the least touch. Who can really tell where the trouble begins on such nights?"

"A score of informants can, all of them pointing this way."

"And how reliable, really, are such people?"

"They have lived in this city longer than me. Longer than you too, Master Dellest. They know where the rotten fruit falls." Alder looked straight at Efron. "I make certain of the facts before I throw accusations."

Efron shuffled his feet and gave a high, hollow laugh, as empty as it was inappropriate.

"An unfortunate mishap, perhaps," the actor said. "Passions inflamed by the power of our play, an audience unprepared, many of them drunk, we have shut the bar since, which is unpopular, of course, but I feel a proportionate, even a necessary step if we are to retain the integrity and power of the piece while...while..."

Efron stuttered to a halt beneath Alder's piercing gaze.

"Drunks." The count tapped the hilt of his sword again. "You don't think that your choice of stories might have played a part?"

Efron glanced at Yasmi, who had no more of an answer than he did. Telling the count that she had been uncomfortable with their story from the start was hardly a defence when she had persuaded him to approve their work. That she had refused to shift in front of him, then done it in front of an audience of two thousand, only added to the shroud of guilt draped across the theatre.

For the past three days, bodies had been hanging in markets and at road junctions, a reminder of what happened to those who broke the law. Like the rest of the players, Yasmi had convinced herself that she was safe from that fate, just as she had convinced herself that they could get away with this play. It was a tale she wanted to believe, and for a storyteller, that was hard to resist. But sometimes even the most appealing stories fell flat.

At least she would make a prettier corpse than most. Perhaps she could convince the executioner to match her noose to her best dress, get her accessories right to the very end. She stifled a bitter laugh, laid a hand on her wolf mask to steady herself.

"I didn't know much about Balbianus until Yasmi's recitation." Alder walked away from them, prowling around the

FORGED FOR DESTINY

perimeter of the pit. It was how Yasmi would have performed the part of a hunter, but seeing through the mask made it no less menacing. "It turns out that I learned little even then. So many details that Tur has told me since, details that slipped in during your rehearsals. Adaptations to add to the power of the play, I suppose?"

"Yes, my lord." Efron spoke more quietly now, clutched his hands together.

"Why did you choose this story?" The count's tone came close to genial, but not too close for a noose to slip through the gap. "And why these particular adaptations?"

"There are so many stories, my lord, it's sometimes hard to tell. I believe an acquaintance of ours may have suggested Balbianus as a story under-represented in the modern theatrical canon."

"Well, that makes sense." Spurs jingling, Alder walked up the steps at the side of the stage, then looked around the galleries from his new vantage point. "This acquaintance, was it one of the guests you have staying?"

"My lord?"

Alder strode to the edge of the stage, his boots thumping against the boards. He glared down at Efron.

"Guests. A large, scarred man. A tinker woman. A youth with a gormless grin. Your neighbours tell me they've been here as long as you have, that they come and go at all hours and keep confusing company. Is one of these the acquaintance who inspired this play?"

To Efron's credit, he wasn't fool enough to look down, to openly play the part of the criminal caught in the act. But sweat shone on his brow and his arms pressed tight against his stomach.

Yasmi didn't want to cast Raul as a troublemaker, nor Valens, not even Prisca. But they had brought this on themselves, and she wasn't going to let them drag her troupe to the gallows with them.

"They're a family from the Winding Vales," she said. "Their inn is usually our first touring stop. This year, they asked to travel with us to the city, and offered to pay for lodgings here."

Not the whole truth but no outright lies. Her performance must be perfect, in words and in tone. From the corner of her eye, she saw her father's look of disappointment as she dropped Valens into the count's path, but what choice did she have?

"The woman, is she a clerk?" Alder asked. "A diviner perhaps?"

"I believe so, my lord."

"You believe which, clerk or diviner?"

"A bit of both, if I understand her trade." Yasmi shrugged. Her hands were clammy and she fought back the urge to press them together. "We're so busy with rehearsals and performances, I haven't paid attention to what they do. If it's any help, the young man nailed together some of our scenery."

"And his mother nailed together your plot?"

"She made suggestions, things we wouldn't otherwise have included. In retrospect, we were foolish to listen to her."

"You certainly were." The count crouched at the edge of the stage and lowered his voice. Yasmi took a step closer. "Between you and me, we've been hearing rumours of dissident scribes roaming the hinterlands, using legitimate work as a cover to spread forbidden texts."

FORGED FOR DESTINY

"Really, my lord?" Yasmi widened her eyes, brought her hand up, not touching her chest, that was too melodramatic, but a move toward a shocked stance.

"Really. So tell me, what is this woman's name?"

This was the terrible moment, but what else could Yasmi do? Pretend that she didn't know the name of someone she lived with? Give the count a false name, only for him to find out the truth from a neighbour? For all she knew, he had the answer already and this was a test, one that could see her and her father hang.

She was as close as she had ever been to true fame, to a noble patron who could take her all the way to court. Prisca had no right to ruin that with her schemes. It wasn't a betrayal, it was simply what must be done.

"Her name is Prisca."

Tur's scratchy voice came from close to the door. "Prisca Servita?"

"That could be. She mostly just uses the one name."

Count Alder looked at his chamberlain, one eyebrow raised.

"A minister for the previous regime, my lord," Tur said. "An associate of King Cataldo's coven. We didn't know if she died in the conquest or escaped."

Alder rose. He towered over Yasmi and her father, a warrior with a face like thunder and a sword at this hip.

"You have given shelter to traitors," he said. "Have spread their word through your performances. All of that ends now."

Yasmi shook. The most important performance of her life, and she had got her lines wrong. The noose was coming.

"Your theatre will be closed, as will all performance spaces in this city. I will not give rebels a chance to agitate the populace."

Alder jumped off the stage and strode toward the doors, his warriors closing in behind him.

"That's it?" Yasmi blinked, trying to make sense of what she was seeing.

"You expected something else?" Alder spun around, and she wished that she had stayed silent.

"I just..."

"As I understand it, you were foolish rather than treacherous, tricked into helping a cunning saboteur. You didn't know, did you?" He looked straight at Yasmi. "Did you?"

"No, my lord." A lie she could be nailed to, but the only answer she could give.

"Well then. I can't allow this to continue." He waved a hand at his surroundings. "But a talent like yours shouldn't go to waste. Think about what you could do next. I look forward to finding out."

He strode away, his entourage with him.

Into the echoing silence that followed, Efron flung up his hands.

"It's a disaster, our beautiful theatre, closed! Ruin, I tell you, woe and ruin!"

"We're still alive." Yasmi sagged against the stage and gave a light-headed laugh. "Isn't that enough?"

───────── • ─────────

Alder rode away from the theatre, past smoke-blackened buildings, frightened faces, people frantically trying to wash painted half moons off their walls.

FORGED FOR DESTINY

"Do you really think that they are innocent, my lord?" Tur asked.

"If they are, then they're hopelessly naive," Alder replied. "But how much intelligence is needed to make believe for a living?"

"So they're guilty?"

"We'll work that out later. For now, we hunt the fox we know about, and chase the other trails tomorrow."

He set his heels to his horse's flanks and it picked up speed, galloping through the city. His chosen men raced after him, while peasants scattered from the streets ahead. The wind whipped at his hair and the sun of summer's first day kissed his skin.

Count Alder grinned. He was going to enjoy putting these people in their place.

Chapter Twenty-Three
Hidden Places

Raul had just been getting used to the way people moved in cities, the way that a chaotic jumble of movement hid a spiky sort of order. Now he saw a proper pattern again, like a normal town only larger: farmers rolling their near-empty wagons out the far side of the square, leaving behind a few trampled vegetables, while entertainers and wine merchants emerged to set up for the evening. Unlike the farmers, the folk of the night fair had brightly painted carts, with signs on poles above them, and they argued animatedly over pitches. Some were foreigners, with the pale skin and hair of Saditch or long Esvadelian coats. Like the farmers, most of them left offerings at the statue of four-armed Avgar or that of Harl the Hunter, the Dunholmi god whose marble sculpture pointedly towered over Avgar. Small coins and splashes of beer joined cabbages and carrots, trading with the gods for a prosperous night.

"This person Appia wants us to meet," Raul said, "is she with the night fair?"

FORGED FOR DESTINY

"Perhaps." Prisca ran a finger along the grain of the bench they sat on outside one of the square's inns. "She might have arrived already, with the farmers, or simply have liked this as a meeting spot, with all the people coming and going."

"She might not turn up at all," Valens growled from Raul's other side. He was scowling even more than usual and had refused to have his empty cup refilled.

A group of warriors, wearing the count's white tree on blue, ambled along the edge of the square, spears over their shoulders. They stopped by one of the wine carts and its owner poured them each a drink, saw his hand left empty when he held it out, and raised a rude gesture at their backs as they walked away.

"Should we move?" Raul asked. "The guards are coming."

"Why move? We're just a family enjoying a drink." Prisca sipped her ale. "Besides, they don't look interested in starting trouble."

As the guards came closer, one of them nudged the white-belted captain, who looked over at their inn.

"Calm," Prisca murmured from behind her cup. "They've probably just spotted their next chance to scrounge a drink."

As the guards approached, a figure in an oversized cloak and a floppy hat emerged twitching from a street behind them.

"Is that Tenebrial?" Raul asked.

"Looks like he's dressed in the dregs of the costume box," Valens said.

"He's coming this way."

Except that he wasn't. Tenebrial caught sight of the guards, froze, looked in alarm from the uniformed warriors to the inn. He frantically waved his hat, then disappeared from view.

"Still think it's all fine?" Valens set his cup down.

"Calm, remember."

Prisca lowered her cup as the warriors approached. Several had taken their spears from their shoulders and held them in both hands.

The captain examined Raul and each of his parents in turn, settling in the end on Prisca.

"What's your name?" the captain asked.

"Jovia of Lower Vispunti." Prisca smiled her thin smile. "I've brought my family here for the cattle market."

"Cattle market's tomorrow."

"It's a long journey, we didn't want to miss out."

The captain nodded slowly, looking along the line of them. "Stand up," he said.

"Why?" Raul asked.

"Because you're coming with us."

"Why?"

"Because you look like the people we're after."

"What people?"

"Rioters. Rebels." The captain drew his sabre and the warriors behind him lowered their spears, points gleaming. "People who murdered our comrades."

"How awful." Prisca put her cup down. "There's clearly been a mix-up, but we'll come along, won't we?"

There were two other guard patrols in the square, and at a wave from the captain, they'd started heading for the inn.

"'Course." Valens stood and Raul followed his example. "Just let me finish this."

Valens raised his empty cup, then flung it at the captain,

FORGED FOR DESTINY

hitting him in the middle of the forehead. In the time it took the others to react, Valens had grabbed the nearest spear and head-butted its owner.

"Run!" he roared.

Prisca was on the move. Raul went with her. When he looked back, Valens was following, spear in hand, four guards on his heels, more trailing behind.

"Keep running!" Valens bellowed as Raul turned, ready to help like a hero should. But long years of obedience overcame his best intentions and he flung himself after his mother, out of the square.

The street they ran down was bustling with people for the night fair. Prisca dodged around an ale merchant's cart and Raul followed. Valens vaulted the cart, kicking a pile of cups down with a crash, then turned and flung the spear. Their pursuers ducked behind other carts.

"Quick!" Prisca turned down a side street and the other two followed. A man with a basket full of laundry protested as she barged past, then protested again as Valens thundered through.

"Sorry!" Raul said as he dodged around the man.

From the sounds of protest and shouts of command, their pursuers weren't far behind. Prisca turned down another street, apparently at random, then another. She pushed a door open and walked into a house.

"Do you know someone here?" Raul asked

"Hey!" A woman scrambled down a ladder beside the door. "Who in Yorl's eye are you?"

"No one." Prisca tossed the woman a jingling pouch. "Because no one was here, understand?"

The woman looked into the bag, then out the door, where a hubbub of voices was approaching. She slammed the door shut.

"Back alley takes you to the brick kilns."

They hurried out the back door and down a space that was more gutter than street. At the end, it trickled across a stretch of ruins and into a filthy brook, on the far side of which the clay domes of kilns stretched down to the river. There weren't many people around, just the kilns and the smoke trailing up from them. Raul was already flushed from the chase, but his body ran with sweat as they wound their way through the heat haze between the stacks.

"Here." Prisca stopped by one of the few kilns that wasn't smoking. She sank to her knees and crawled inside. "It will do until night falls, then we can head to that warehouse where Quintae's building a safe hole."

It was cooler inside the kiln than out, its walls protecting them from the others' heat. It didn't take light for Raul to know that his hands were smeared with soot.

"Here's that heroics you were after," Valens muttered as he squeezed his way in. "Hiding in an oven."

Raul wasn't sure if that was directed at him or Prisca.

"Heroes often hide in the stories," he said. "And get chased. The big fight only comes at the end."

"True enough." Valens snorted. "The big fight's most everyone's end."

The hiding hole was bigger and more comfortable than Raul had expected. Hidden behind a false wall in the end of a long,

FORGED FOR DESTINY

thin warehouse, it had enough space for two narrow cots, one above the other, and storage beneath them. He sat on one of the cots, Valens crowded into the corner behind him, while Prisca perched on the one above. The smell of wood shavings was familiar and pleasant after the stink of sweat and dirt that was the city streets, but that couldn't do much to lift Raul's spirits.

"I don't feel very heroic right now," he said. "Hiding in a kiln, skulking through the night, hiding here all day while other people take the risks."

"Welcome to the real world."

"Valens," Prisca snapped, "that is not helpful. Think about the example you're setting."

"This isn't helpful either." Valens raised his fist, as if about to thump the wall, then looked at Raul and lowered his hand. "At least it's keeping us alive."

"Alive isn't enough," Raul said. "We need to be out there helping people."

"Let them help themselves for a bit."

With a click, the door slid open, revealing a hooded eye carved into the frame. Appia came in, dressed in her usual canvas work clothes. The door closed itself behind her, sliding smoothly along waxed rails until the hidden panels took their place in the wall. Raul wanted to ask Quintae how it worked, but he wasn't sure that he would understand the answer, the carpenter's broken words often providing more confusion than clarity.

"My brother made these." Appia set a head-sized bundle down next to Raul and untied the knot, revealing a selection of bread rolls made with seeds, herbs, and pieces of cheese. "Thought you might be hungry."

"Thank you." Raul passed rolls to his parents, then took one for himself. It was warm from the oven and the scent made his mouth water. "We've got food already, but these smell amazing."

Appia shrugged and pulled out a scrap of string, which she started twisting into knots.

"I've had to hide out before. You need things to stop you getting bored or you start taking risks."

Raul watched in fascination as the jumble of knotted string turned into an animal with four legs and a long head.

"Do you keep those?" he asked.

"I give them to my nieces. One of them pretends she has a farm, the other one fights them against each other. Kids, you know, they've all got their own obsessions."

"They must be proud of what you're doing."

Appia shook her head.

"They don't need to know what I do, not at the docks and not here." She tucked the finished dog inside her tunic, pulled out another piece of string. "They're smart kids. I've bought them apprenticeships for when they're older, with a stonemason and a seamstress. They're not going to haul bales and fight thieves like I do. They're going to have a better life."

"We all are, once the country's free."

She looked at him, her fingers still working the string. After a moment, she nodded.

"I really hope you're right, and right now, I reckon that hope's worth fighting for."

FORGED FOR DESTINY

There was a tapping, three fast knocks then two slow ones, the signal for a friend. Appia stepped out and the door slid silently shut behind her.

Raul reached for another bread roll, then thought better of it. If Appia was right, then he'd be glad of having one of the different rolls to try later, and if not, he didn't lose anything through restraint.

After a little while, Appia returned.

"Someone to see you," she said quietly. "Best if you all come out."

Warily, the three of them followed her past stacks of bundled sheepskins. Halfway down the warehouse, there was a gap between the stacks. There, Yasmi stood, flanked by burly dockers with clubs in their hands. She was dressed in plain clothes and no jewellery, her reddish blond hair bound beneath a headscarf, one hand clenching and unclenching where her mask belt should be. There was a bulging sack by her feet. A thick band of cloth covered her eyes, and someone had painted it with two crosses of thick black tar.

"Didn't want her to know where we are," Appia said. "Best for everyone."

"Are you all right?" Raul asked, rushing over but stopping shy of touching her. Yasmi looked strange without any of her theatrical decorations, pale-skinned and exposed.

"A little underdressed." Her laugh would have been convincing, coming from anyone else. Her head tilted down. "And you?"

"We got chased by guards, but we're safe now."

Yasmi shuffled her feet, toes trailing in the dust. "I'm sorry.

I think they already knew some, but I told them who to look for."

"You?" Valens's growl was like a caged beast. His fingers curled like he was crushing her between them.

"Your fault?" Prisca asked, calmer and clearer.

"No." Yasmi swallowed, stood straighter. "You chose that play to stir people up, and you got what you wanted. I wasn't going to let them hurt my people for your sakes. Would you have let them hang one of you?"

"For the good of the people of Estis?" Prisca asked. "Yes."

"Well, I'm not as good as you. Or perhaps your mask is better."

Appia drew a long knife, raised an eyebrow, and Raul stared in alarm. Prisca shook her head.

"Why are you here, Yasmi?"

"I brought these." She knelt, felt around the mouth of the sack, and opened it, revealing all the books and documents they'd gathered since coming to the city. "I considered burning them, to get the incriminating evidence out of our home, but I know they're important to Raul."

She ran a finger under the cloth binding her eyes.

"Don't," Prisca snapped.

"Don't worry, this is one mask I'm not taking off." Yasmi scratched her cheek. "An itch is a small price to pay for not knowing what happens here."

"You could be part of it." Raul stepped forward. Unable to catch her gaze, he took her hand instead. It was soft and warm, and she clung to him like he was her last hope. "You came with me once before. You're smart and you're great with people. You could really help."

FORGED FOR DESTINY

She shook her head.

"Heroism is one mask I can't wear, Raul."

"It's not a mask. It's something you feel."

"Perhaps for you, but I would be feigning. It's not a role I know. Let me stick to my monsters." She let go of his hand and took a step back. "Check the sack. If there are any I've missed, then I want to know now, not to see the count's warriors pull them out of our prop chests."

Raul started unpacking the sack, passing each book or document in turn to Prisca, who sorted them into neat piles. In between, he glanced at Yasmi, reassuring himself of her presence, however brief it was.

"A mask," Valens mumbled.

"What's that?" Raul looked around, saw his da slowly nodding.

"Nothing." Valens walked over to Yasmi. He didn't look so angry anymore, and for the first time in days, his shoulders weren't tensed. "How is it out there?"

"The Dunholmi made a pyre of the night market," she said. "Some of the warriors got it into their heads that the entertainers and ale sellers were hiding you, so they burned all their carts."

The energy drained from Raul as he thought of those beautiful, brightly coloured carts going up in smoke.

"There were beatings too, of course. I don't think they killed anyone this time, but it's hard to tell, with those rioters still hanging in the streets."

"Anything else?" Valens asked.

"The count's closed the docks and his people are searching

any wagon coming in or out of town. No ships are allowed to leave, and those coming upriver are being held by the guards."

"Golden Ocean consortia won't like that."

"I'm sure that the count will make it worth their while. Contracts to rebuild, perhaps?"

Valens ignored the edge in her voice. "Anything else?"

"Isn't that enough?"

"You told him about us. So, anything else?"

She sighed and lessened somehow. There was a presence she showed everyone else in the world, that Raul had only ever seen subside when they were on their own, sitting on a hillside in the spring. That presence left now but what remained was different.

"They're tearing down performance spaces. Not ours yet, but I don't know what we'll have to do to keep it."

"You have a way in with them?" Prisca's eyes narrowed and she smiled her slender smile.

"I'm not playing your spy." That presence was back, Yasmi swelling to fill the space around her, voice rising through the quiet of the warehouse. "My troupe have been through enough because of you."

"It's all right." Valens patted her on the shoulder. "This is a time for action, time to stand up and show the world who we are. Time to be the heroes the stories taught us about. Right, Raul?"

Raul thought of the bright handcarts burning; of the theatre being torn down; of bodies swinging in the streets. He remembered a birch whip cracking against the backs of people who wanted to look after their grain. Then he thought of all the ruins still standing around the city and how much more they would hurt someone like Valens, who had seen them in their prime.

This might not be like the stories as he'd imagined them, but that meant that heroes were needed all the more. The sort he might not have called a hero a few short weeks ago.

"They tear down the things that matter to us," he said. "Let's tear down something of theirs."

Chapter Twenty-Four
Family Ties

The building site stank of death. Even without the sun's heat warming them, Raul smelled the bodies of rioters, heard the creak of one turning on the end of the noose, the sound of the final door closing on a life. Above them, the star-speckled sheet of night was ripped open by towering shadows, Count Alder's half-built monument rising like a pair of black blades.

That stone message of cruelty and conquest grew taller and more intricate every day, as blocks were raised and details carved. Raul didn't blame the masons who worked on it. They had families to feed, a craft to follow, and when armed men demanded their services, how were they meant to say no? But their work couldn't be allowed to continue.

Other smells oozed in, low and heavy. The smells of oil and of tar. By the tents where the site's guards dwelt, voices were rising, confused and uncertain. It couldn't be long before they became alarmed.

By then, it would be too late.

FORGED FOR DESTINY

Uphill, at the far side of the site, fire flared out of the darkness, casting stark shadows across the front of an abandoned house. It ran across a row of barrels lying on their sides, lids open, contents draining across the dirt. There was a series of crashes as storage jars shattered in the heat, and the flames rushed down the hill on a tide of oil and tar.

"Fire!" The scream went up from one of the tents. "Everyone out! Fire!"

Warriors raced from the tents, some of them instinctively clutching their spears, the more alert ones carrying buckets. Others rushed from their posts standing guard around the edges of the site. They wore the plain tunics of Dunholm's infantry levies. The count might love his monument, but guarding it was no duty for his cavalry elite.

"It's an attack!" someone shouted, and the cry was taken up elsewhere. Spears and bows pointed into the darkness. An arrow flew through the flames.

"Where are they?" someone shouted. "Who's doing this?"

On one side, a bucket chain formed, while others kicked dirt and heaved rocks to divert the flow of flammable liquid. Some guards were too slow, and flames reached the ropes of a tent, then ran up its canvas.

"Now?" Appia whispered in the darkness.

"Not yet," Valens replied from Raul's other side.

There was a hiss of arrows. One of the guards fell. Another clutched her leg, screaming. Figures in dark clothes, their faces hidden by hoods and scarves, emerged into the flickering light, carrying clubs, axes, and swords. Each one had a single strip of white cloth tied around their upper arm. Some of the guards formed a line facing them, while others struggled to stifle the advance of the flames. The ones in charge argued among themselves, uncertain how to respond. The attackers shouted and the defenders shouted back. All the guards had their attention turned to that side of the site.

"Now," Raul said.

He ran out of the street where he had been hiding, and twenty others came with him. Valens, Appia, and a band of her comrades from the docks, wearing heavy gloves and carrying ropes. They sprinted up the hill to one of the monumental pyramids, the one that was closer to completion, and swarmed up the scaffolding that covered it. Around the base, the monument was intricately carved, the names of conquering Dunholmi chiselled into the stone. One woman spat on those names as she climbed.

With swift, sure movements, the dockers slid ropes over the stones and tied them together, forming a cradle around the monument. Appia checked the highest knots while Raul kept watch. The distracted guards hadn't noticed them yet, but that could change, and they only had so long before reinforcements arrived. The crackle of flames and crash of weapons made that inevitable.

At a signal from Appia, the dockers dropped down the monument, grabbed the ends of the ropes, and ran to one side. Raul joined them, the rope rough even through the gloves he had been given. Valens was there, his face as stern as the stones.

"One, two, three, heave!" Appia said.

They pulled on the ropes, a score of individuals turning into a single straining muscle.

FORGED FOR DESTINY

"Heave!"

Raul did as Appia commanded, the muscles in his arms bulging as he pulled with all his strength. There was a scraping sound, slow and menacing.

"Heave!"

"What's that?"

One of the guard captains had noticed, but it was too late. Raul, Valens, and the dockers stepped back, dragging the ropes with them. Stones slid, tipped, toppled. There was a crunch as the topmost stone bounced off those below, and a thud as it hit the ground. Another fell, then those that remained came down with a crash that drowned out all the flames and the fighting.

The dockers cheered, exultant. The guards, caught between two armed gangs, backed toward each other and the burning remains of their tents.

"This heroic enough for you?" Valens grinned as he drew his sword.

A warm glow spread through Raul. *This* was rebellion like he'd imagined it, warriors side by side, taking on the world.

"A new moon rises!" he yelled, raising his sword in the air. "For Estis!"

They charged, Raul and Valens and the dockers from one side, the masked rebels from the other. At the edge of the guard band, a woman raised a bow, drew the string. A rock flew out of the darkness and hit her in the head. She struck the ground a moment before the rebels slammed into her comrades.

It was a brutal fight, dozens of fighters lurching and lunging through the shifting shadows. Raul charged in, almost hacked at the woman closest to him before the flames illuminated the white cloth around her upper arm. He shifted his strike, slashed the man she was fighting, slicing open his side. The man fell screaming and Raul moved on through the fight, sword up again, blocked a sabre, kicked its owner, stabbed him in the guts.

This wasn't like duelling Valens with wooden swords, but all that experience helped. Raul responded instinctively to the cuts and thrusts, parrying and dodging without having to think. That gave him vital seconds to pick out friends who needed his help, to save a masked docker here, a worshipper of Yorl there, his familiar allies, this rough army in the fight for freedom.

An arrow shot past his head, inches from taking an eye. He turned to look where it came from, but Valens was already running the archer through.

In the distraction, a spear thrust caught Raul off guard. He swayed back just in time, so that it only clipped his forearm. The stinging pain brought him clarity as he swung his sword around, but his opponent kept them at spear's length. Raul dodged a thrust of the spear, tripped on something in the darkness, fell to one knee. The Dunholmi loomed over him, spear raised.

Appia's axe smashed into their back. The spear fell and the body on top of it.

"That's how we do it, boy." Appia grinned and wiped blood from her cheek. "Make the fuckers pay."

A whistle tore through the air, a warning from their lookouts.

FORGED FOR DESTINY

"That's it!" Raul shouted, scrambling to his feet. "Go!"

They scattered into the night, taking their injured with them, leaving only a trail of bloody footprints. When the guards came, they would find bodies and burning tents, but no trace of the rebels. Most of all, they would find the monument to their aggression flung down into the dirt.

Throughout the city, the cry of the new moon would spread.

———————————— • ————————————

"Where are we tonight?" Raul asked as he and Valens jogged through the starlit streets.

"Yorl's temple," Valens said.

"That's a good omen." Raul pointed at a cluster of stars. "That constellation is his plough, isn't it?"

"That it is. And over there, that's where the Red Eye will rise, when the time comes."

Raul slowed, stared at the gap between the mountains. Not long now. A week, perhaps. Prisca told him that he was ready, but how could he be sure? So much depended upon him.

"You did well in the fight," Valens said.

"I did?"

"You don't stop anymore, don't stand staring at what you've done."

Raul shrugged. "We have to stop them."

"That's right, lad." Valens patted him on the back. "That's what heroes do."

They crossed Dreamers' Square, past the statue-less pedestal, looking around in case they were seen. A soft knock and the door of the Temple of Yorl opened, a passage into a world of sheltered candlelight. They slipped inside and the door closed behind them, shutting out the menace of the night.

A drop of blood fell from Raul's blade onto the floor.

"Here." Holy Cirillo handed him a cloth. "Clean that. You have a guest."

The two of them cleaned and sheathed their weapons. Raul hadn't even noticed the spatter of blood on his face until Valens reached out with a cloth.

"Got to look presentable." Valens laughed softly as he wiped away the blood. "Can't go letting people think we're killers."

The cloth came away red. Valens set it down next to the collection plate. Raul wondered what Yorl would think of that offering, blood given to him alongside coin. He did ask for sacrifices, but surely that was just for divination.

"I still feel sorry for them," Raul said quietly.

"For who?"

"Those warriors we killed. They were doing what their leaders told them to do, fighting for their homeland. They didn't mean to become villains."

"No one ever does."

The door creaked. Raul spun around, sword halfway out before he recognised Prisca.

"What are you doing here?" Raul asked.

"One of the temple attendants came for me, said that it was important." Prisca looked Raul and Valens up and down. "It went well?"

"Well enough." Valens looked at Prisca and his tone

changed, became stronger, more confident, like when he told one of the old stories. "You should have seen Raul carving his way through them. Like a king out of legend."

Raul blushed. "I was just doing what you taught me."

"You were the best of us." Valens clapped a hand on his shoulder. "As is right from a man born to lead."

Raul held up one hand. It was as steady as the rock the city was built on.

"It's getting easier," he said.

Holy Cirillo emerged from the depths of the temple, the hem of the high priest's robes whispering against the floor. He gestured for them to follow, past the bull-shaped altar, through a door carved with fish swimming through a net, and down familiar steps into the cellar.

The room was better lit than before. Candles sat in many of the formerly empty niches on the walls. At the far side of the room, in front of the wall that concealed the hidden library, a woman in an embroidered red dress sat on a cushioned wooden chair. She drew back a veil, revealing hair dyed a striking blond, a face carefully made up, a silk scarf wrapped around her neck. She was clearly older than she looked, even older than she wanted to look, but she didn't have the air of desperation Raul had seen on some others in the city as they tried to hide their age. Muscled servants stood on either side of her, cudgels in their hands, both wearing veils of their own.

Prisca looked at the woman for a long moment, her forehead crumpling into a frown.

"Is it so long, Prisca?" the woman asked. "Have the years really done such horrors to me?"

Prisca's eyes went wide and she sank to one knee. Valens was already there, his head lowered, fist pressed to his chest. Raul imitated the gesture but found it hard to keep his head bowed while looking at the strange woman.

"I thought that you were dead," Prisca said.

"I am, I must admit, terribly close." The old woman coughed, touched a lace-trimmed piece of silk to her lips, then lowered it into her lap. "I was almost a grandmother back then, and time kills as surely as any blade, if not as mercifully." She shifted in her seat. "It turns out that life in a brothel is not as life-giving as that in a palace."

"You haven't been..." Prisca looked up, alarmed.

"Of course not. Who would pay for this?" The woman waved a hand. "For my status, perhaps, but I couldn't tell that to anyone, could I? Not when the whole family was meant to be dead. No, I've been running the place. The skills of managing a court or a country are much like those for managing whores, flattering egos between twisting arms. And of course, the veils are helpful if one wants to remain unseen."

"Why not leave the city? You had friends in El Esvadel. It would have been safer."

"Desert my family's seat while they remain unavenged?" Her voice, so serene, became jagged. She clutched the side of her seat. "Never."

Raul's knee hurt from kneeling on the cold stone and his side was aching from the fight. He shifted, switched knees, and the rustle of his movement drew the woman's attention. He gave up on lowering his gaze, looked straight at her. She was clearly somebody aristocratic. He leaned forward, the better to see her.

FORGED FOR DESTINY

"First I hear of trouble stirring in my city." The woman pointed at Prisca. "Then I hear that the invaders are hunting someone with your name. And then the holy father brings me word of a boy, one born to save the nation…" She fixed Raul with a stare of ferocious intensity. He smiled at her. "Who is he?"

"He goes by the name of Raul," Prisca said. "Raul, this is Her Imperial Majesty, the Queen Consort Junia."

Raul's eyes went wide. Queen Junia, the wife of the last king of Estis? Hadn't she died in the invasion, like the rest of the royal family?

He tensed, not sure how he was meant to act in front of a queen. There was bowing, and only speaking when he was spoken to, he knew that much from the plays, though there might be less scheming and shouting around real royalty. He bowed his head again, lower this time, and tried to keep his aching body still.

Then another thought hit him. This was his grandmother. He smiled down at the floor.

"This Raul leads your rebellion?" Junia said the word "leads" strangely, like it wasn't quite what she had been after.

"Yes, Your Majesty."

"Why?"

"May I?"

Prisca shifted, and Junia waved her to her feet. Prisca stepped in front of Raul, bent over, and unfastened the thick leather tunic that he wore to protect him in fights.

"Keep quiet," she whispered, so soft that he barely caught the words. "Remember, she is a queen. I can answer your questions later."

Raul kept himself still. He wanted to impress his grandmother almost as much as he wanted to please Prisca.

She dropped his tunic on the ground, then rolled up his sleeve.

"This is why." She pointed at the birthmark on his arm.

Junia raised an eyebrow. "Perhaps age is taking its toll on my mind."

"As you may remember, there was a prophecy that, in our time of greatest peril, Balbianus's essence would return to us. And so, as the city was falling, a baby was born. A special baby. A royal baby." Prisca looked directly at Junia for the first time. "You thought that you were the only one to survive the city's fall. Remember Princess Aemiria's son."

"How dare you." Junia glared at Prisca. "To use my daughter's name like this." Her hands clenched on the sides of her chair. Her servants stepped forward, cudgels at the ready. "To rip open that grief."

"You lost a daughter," Prisca said, her voice hard as stone. "But think what it would mean for the kingdom to know that your grandson survived." She placed a hand on Raul's shoulder. "Maybe you will live to see your vengeance after all."

Raul struggled to stay still. He had thought that his grandmother would be pleased to know that he was alive, just as he was delighted to know that she lived. Perhaps if he told her about what they were doing...

Prisca's fingers tightened on his shoulder, pinning him in place. In her chair, Junia sat like a statue, staring at Prisca. It seemed like the shock of what was happening had overwhelmed her. After everything he'd been through, Raul could understand that.

FORGED FOR DESTINY

The queen's eyes narrowed and she tapped a finger against her seat.

"Well?" Prisca asked.

"I understand." Junia stood, slowly and stiffly, then gestured with one curled finger. "Raul, come here."

Prisca's grip fell away and he rose. He could hear Valens's heavy breaths, hear his own cautious footsteps, hear the pulsing of blood like a drumbeat in his ears. He stood half an arm's reach from the queen, looking down into her eyes.

She ran a finger across his birthmark, then along his cheek.

"Handsome," she said, and squeezed his arm. "Strong. Smart?"

"Smart enough," Prisca replied.

"Smart enough." Junia nodded. "You seem like a good boy, Raul. Were my Aemiria still alive..." That last word caught, broken, on her lips. She swallowed and looked away for a moment, before meeting his gaze. "Were my Aemiria alive, she would be proud to have a son like you. Come."

She drew him into her arms, and he hugged her back, bending so that his body formed a shield around her. She was thinner than she looked, bones sharp through the folds of her dress. Little of the queen remained.

"I'm sorry that you lost her," Raul said. "That we lost her."

The queen's grip on him tightened, fingers clawing at his back.

"I miss her every day," she said. "I miss all of them." She stretched onto tiptoes and whispered in his ear, "Be careful who you trust."

He wanted to tell her that he understood, that they watched

315

constantly for the count's men and only told their allies as much of their plans as they must. But the rasping quiet of her tone made him hold on to those words.

She let go and he took a step back. She turned away from him, toward one of her servants, who held a wooden box on the palm of her hand.

"I brought something," Junia said. "To help, if your endeavour proved worthwhile."

She opened the box and took out a bronze sculpture the size of Raul's thumb. Candlelight illuminated the shape of a moth, its wings drawn in. An image of a pair of lips was embossed on its back, with a deep scratch splitting the image in two.

"The most powerful charm my late husband ever made," Junia said. "Watch and listen."

She tapped her foot, a steady rhythm, then plucked at the sides of the moth. Delicate bronze wings unfurled. As the second wing opened, the sound of her foot faded away. Raul couldn't hear Valens's breathing anymore, the footsteps from Prisca as she came closer, or the words as his ma's lips parted. He looked down, and Queen Junia's foot was still tapping silently against the ground.

Raul swallowed, resisted the urge to reach out and touch the moth. He'd never seen magic so powerful; it put even Drusil's lanterns to shame. This was the magic the scholars of the Spire had worked toward, magic that could change the world, and Queen Junia had brought it for him.

She folded the moth's wings away and sound returned.

"A madam must sometimes move around her brothel

FORGED FOR DESTINY

unheard." She placed the moth in the box and handed it to Raul. "I shan't need it much longer, but perhaps you can make it useful." She gestured to her servants, who followed her past Holy Cirillo to the foot of the stairs. "Good luck to you all. You are going to need it."

Then she was gone.

Raul clutched the box tight, a gift from his grandmother. All those times he'd asked about his birth family, he'd never even dreamed that the answer could be something like this.

"That'll help," Valens said, staring at the box as he rose from his knees. "When the time comes."

"It will," Prisca said. "I'm curious, what did she say to you?"

Raul hesitated.

"She told me she loved me." He smiled just imagining how that would feel, and the smile hid the cold, creeping tension inside of him.

He wasn't even sure why he lied to his parents. Junia was his grandma, and she had meant those words only for him, but it was more than that. The strange meeting, the tense exchange between her and Prisca, the feeling that he had only half understood what was being said. And then those whispered words...

With one hand, he gripped the pommel of his sword, and some of the certainty he had felt in the fight returned. He was the chosen one, descendant of kings, essence of Balbianus. As the prophecy said, he was going to save the kingdom.

Wasn't he?

Chapter Twenty-Five
Different Masks

"My lord." Yasmi bowed, arm extended, leg stretched back, a bow full of flourish and style. "Thank you for seeing me."

"One moment."

Count Alder kept his back to her, leaning over a table while one of his captains spoke. All of them had dirt spattered up their riding boots, flecks of ash on the blue of their surcoats. One wore spurs that clinked as she stepped closer. Yasmi didn't hear what they were saying, though the words she caught had a terrible inevitability: "rebels," "swift," "fire," "end it."

Alder shook his head. A muscle twitched at the corner of his mouth.

"They think that they can goad us with this strike," he said through gritted teeth. "That by desecrating the memories of our fallen, they can drive us to desperate acts."

"What else can we do?" someone asked, slamming a hand against the table. "Let them get away with it?"

"What do you suggest?"

"People living nearby must have seen who did this. Round them all up and lash any who won't talk."

Alder took a deep breath.

"I understand your rage, but I need a city still standing when this is over." He tapped the map that lay unrolled on the table. "I won't be drawn into antagonising the people I govern. Examples will be made, but only the right examples. Go eat, think on it, come back to me when hunger isn't sharpening your tempers." The other warriors left, and Alder turned to scowl at Yasmi. "You may stand."

She obeyed, with a sense of relief. Her thigh had been starting to cramp.

"I realise you must be busy, my lord."

"True." Alder leaned against the table. He was artfully framed by the bright sky in the window beyond. "But I always have time for exceptional people. What can I do for you?"

Exceptional. In spite of everything, that was how he saw her. She might make it to the royal palace yet.

"It's what I can do for you, my lord."

Alder laughed bitterly. "Can you double my troops or tell me where the rebels are hiding?"

Yasmi had never been more glad of her ability to hide her feelings.

"Not exactly, my lord, but there is another way that my troupe can help."

"Really?" Alder walked up the steps to his throne and sat down. At a wave of his hand, a servant emerged from the shadows, unfolded a stool, and set a loaded tray down on it. "It seems that I have some entertainment to go with my meal. Please, go on."

He picked up a small pastry with one hand, a goblet with the other. It was the skull goblet she had seen before and its hollow eyes sent a shudder down her spine. The bodies were piling up around the city; occupiers, rebels, and those caught between. Would the count be adding any of their skulls to his collection?

She braced herself. Her safety was never enough. Life must bring fame and spectacle, or what was the point? Apart from food and drink, fine clothes and handsome men, song and dance and the beauty of a sunset or a silk...

Stay on script. She was here for good reason, a chance to save the troupe's faltering fortunes, if she could just persuade this one man. She touched the wolf mask on her belt and gave the count her most winning smile.

"My lord, it pains me to know it, but my troupe and our play have caused you difficulties."

"Difficulties? You started a riot, which is fast running into revolt."

"And you wisely closed the theatres to prevent the problem spreading."

"It might have been wiser to hang the lot of you and make my point clear."

She lowered her gaze, let her sorrow show. She never should have let Valens and Prisca talk her father into this business. True, there had been magnificent possibilities, and the response of the crowd had been unparalleled, but so were the consequences. There were better ways to get a nobleman's attention.

"Our necks are, of course, at your disposal," she said. "But

I'm here to suggest an alternative, a way to undo the harm we've done."

A way to turn against Raul, a rebellious part of her own mind whispered. But Raul was a grown-up, in body at least, he had made his own choices, and it wasn't like she was here to tell the count about him.

Not this time, at least.

"Go on." Alder took a sip from his skull. "If nothing else, this should be amusing."

"There." Yasmi pinched thumb and forefinger together, as if catching his words out of the air. "You have found the point already, my lord."

"Have I?" He chuckled hollowly. "As you grow older, Yasmi, you'll learn that too much flattery can seem insincere."

She winced at that one. Did he see her as only a girl, a child to be humoured? He wasn't so old himself, flesh not yet wrinkled like Prisca or sagging like her father.

"Then to the point, my lord. Our talents stirred the people up, why not use those talents to calm them? Last year, we performed a very well-received comedy, about a pair of merchants on the Coral Coast. It had the audience roaring with laughter. How much less likely are they to rebel if they are content? Particularly if that contentment comes with an announcement at the beginning that it was supported and endorsed by you?"

"You've set my city in flames and you want to fix it with a comedy?"

"It's the least we can do."

"On that, we agree."

He swirled his goblet, downed the last of its contents, then held it out for a servant to refill.

"I suppose that you would want to reopen your theatre for this?"

"It is the best venue, my lord."

"And charge for attendance?"

How else were they meant to equip and feed a troupe of players? She wouldn't be made to feel guilty for looking after her own, not by Raul and his family, certainly not by this man.

"If we may, my lord. And a part of the proceeds could go toward your rebuilding efforts."

He chuckled again, with more warmth this time.

"A bribe? You might make a courtier yet, Yasmi, though that would waste your talents as surely as keeping the theatre shut." He leaned forward in his seat. "How do I know that your play won't stir up more trouble?"

"We will perform it for you now, my lord. The troupe are waiting."

"We went through this the last time."

"This time there will be no changes during rehearsal. The play is set, and we will keep our best seat free each night so that someone you trust can check on us. Perhaps there are even alterations you would like to the play, which we can make."

Tenebrial would hate her for suggesting that, but better to be hated by him and loved by their audience than known by no one at all.

Alder reached for another pastry. An antique gold bracelet slid down his wrist. The whole time, he kept his eyes on her,

FORGED FOR DESTINY

as did that ghastly goblet of his. Yasmi hardly dared breathe, in case the sound offended him.

"Fine," he said. "Call your people in. Truth be told, I would like to see you perform again."

"Yes, my lord."

A command performance. The theatre reopening, but not their competition. And then, who knew where the count's favour could take her, if she could keep it this time. Yasmi smiled as she turned away, straightened her tunic, and headed for the door.

* * *

Yasmi flung the door of her room open, stepped inside, and spun in front of the mirror, masks and silks flying out. She had done it! Courtiers roaring with laughter. Guards slapping their thighs. Even the count wearing a smile the whole way through. A triumphant performance on the basis of two days' rushed rehearsals, and tomorrow they would reopen. She would hear the crowd's roar again. She would be the toast of the town.

The door swung shut, revealing a dark shape behind it. Yasmi jerked back, knocked the mirror, which hit the floor with a clang. She opened her mouth to scream, but a hand pressed it shut.

"It's me," Raul whispered. "Please don't make a sound."

Yasmi nodded slowly, then peeled his hand off her face.

"I'm not saying that I haven't imagined a moment like this." She ran a hand down his other arm to where his hand rested

323

on her side. "Though you were better dressed, and considerably less smelly."

"Sorry." He stepped back and pulled aside the scarf covering half his face. "I didn't want to put you at risk by being seen with me."

"So you came to my room?" She shut the door, then sat on the bed, legs crossed, back against the wall. "It's not your stupidest moment ever, but I'd put it in the top ten."

For all that she had mocked his appearance, Raul was looking good. The ruggedness of his leather tunic and sturdy boots balanced the youthful good looks that had always risked tipping into pretty, and he held himself more like a grown man, chest out, hand on his knife, ready to take on the world. Not quite one of Balbianus's chosen band, but as close as most men could get. The only sign of uncertainty was in his eyes, which flitted from side to side.

The boy was trouble, so much trouble that she'd just spent half a day trying to put it behind her. Still, she couldn't resist patting the bed.

"Come on, hero. Sit down. Tell me what's bothering you."

He did as he was told. That was Raul for you. There were stone markers along the road that changed more between one spring and the next.

"I was worried about you," he said, cupping his hands in his lap. "Is it true that you were taken to the palace?"

"I went to the palace," she said. "The difference might be subtle, but as Tenebrial will tell you, there's only one letter's difference between 'sword' and 'word.'"

"Does spelling matter now?"

FORGED FOR DESTINY

She sighed, caught herself licking her upper lip.

"It's sweet of you to leap to my rescue, but as you can see, I'm absolutely fine."

He looked at her, and she was glad that she still wore her best outfit from the trip to the palace. He got that look in his eyes, like he was struggling to squeeze the words out. Her heart beat faster at the thought that she could be arrested just for having him here, in the room, with her. She brushed a finger across the back of his hand, tilted her head to one side. It had been a good day. She deserved to celebrate.

"What is it?" she whispered.

"I...I think I might be doing the wrong thing."

"There's nothing wrong with it. It can even add to the fun of a friendship. Just look at Efron and Valens. A night or two together once a year makes them happy."

"I'm not...Do they...? I didn't..." Raul jerked to his feet. "It's not that sort of thing."

"Then what is it?" She folded her arms across her chest.

"It's about what we're doing here, about all of it, I..."

He hunched in, face screwed up with frustration. For the second time in a matter of minutes, he had become someone she never knew. But while that Raul filled her with excitement, this one drew pity.

"You can tell me," she said softly, leaning forward. "Whatever it is, I won't tell."

Those were the words he needed to hear. She could work out later whether they were true or not.

"Somebody said something to me, and it's got me worrying about everything I do."

"Who said it?"

"I can't tell you."

"Well, what did they say?"

He hesitated. "I can't tell you that either."

Yasmi sighed. Young men could be very frustrating.

"I thought you wanted to talk about this."

"I do, I just..."

He rubbed his eyes. He didn't look like he'd been getting much sleep, which wasn't surprising given the state of the city. Raul had always had a certain fragility to him, a tension that showed when his view of the world was challenged. He could never find peace until he'd fitted new knowledge into what he knew. Right now, he looked like someone had poured new knowledge in, and he was about to burst from it.

"What if the things I'm doing are more harm than good?" he asked.

"You mean out there?" She pointed to the window. "All the fights and sabotage people are whispering about? If that's you, then a lot of people might agree."

"But it's what I'm meant to do. The omens guide us. They show us where to strike, and how, what will weaken—"

"Stop!" Yasmi flung up her hands in a panic. "What I don't know, I can't betray. Please, please don't tell me."

"I need to tell someone. While I'm with the others, I keep it inside, where it can't mess things up, but time's running out, and soon we..." He stopped, hand outstretched like a beggar pleading for alms. "I can't tell you that."

"No, you can't."

Yasmi stood, the masks on her belt clacking against each

FORGED FOR DESTINY

other. She took his hand between both of hers. The skin was hard, cracked, more worn than when he'd been hauling barrels each day at the inn. His face was worn too, dark under the eyes, but he was still Raul.

Outside of the troupe, he was her best friend in the world, perhaps her only friend. He'd been in her life forever, though they only saw each other for a few days each year. Now his life was at risk for a task that was tearing him apart, and tomorrow, she would start the work of undoing his support. Summer was here and they were in the city together. They should be sitting by the river, basking in the sunshine, or drinking wine under moonlight while they watched the jugglers at the night fair. They shouldn't be doing whatever this was.

"You don't have to play the rebel," she said. "Run away with me. We can take the troupe with us, disappear into the countryside, perform crude plays for inns full of drunken farmers. I'll act and you can paint scenery, and when the show's done, we can sit out on hay bales and watch the sun rise."

What was she doing, giving up an audience of thousands for the sake of one boy? He didn't even care how good her performance was; he would applaud her for whistling while she patched her clothes. Her gifts were wasted on him. Still, she leaned in closer, placed a hand on his chest, felt his heart beat through the leather of his tunic. A smile lit up his face.

"That sounds wonderful." He sighed. "But I can't."

"Why not? It would be perfect. The city's turned into a swamp and it's going to drag us both down, but out there we could be free. You, me, the open road, not just a few days at the inn but the whole year around."

327

"It's not who I am."

"It can be. It's just like shifting. You put the mask on to start with, pretend to be somebody else, and after a while, the mask becomes part of you."

"I'd be abandoning my family."

"They can come with us. My father would love to have Valens along, and Prisca could help Tenebrial with his plays."

"Not just them. Others."

Gods, no. Was he taking on responsibility for the whole world now? Buying into some idea that all the city was his kin? He had to understand that it didn't work like that once you left the sticks behind.

"Come on." She pressed a fist against his chest. "Do it for me."

"I can't. I'm sorry."

Her shoulders slumped. Her gaze fell. Why was this bothering her so much? She could find some other farm boy, out there on the road, or here in the city. Everyone who saw her perform adored her. She was the idol of the modern stage, able to win around even Count Alder. She wasn't going to end up lonely. She wasn't even sure which part of it all she was mad at losing, the friend or the boy. What mattered was that, whichever way she looked at it, he didn't want her, and that was what she craved. To be wanted.

"You should go." She hugged him tight while she could, letting her resentment melt away. "I've got to rehearse, and you have unspeakable acts of dissent to hatch."

"I'm sorry." He hugged her back. "It was a lovely idea."

"Maybe next life around." She sighed. "When we're both wearing different masks."

Chapter Twenty-Six
Love and Sacrifice

The warehouse was dark and quiet, the windows boarded shut so that no one could look in. Valens sat on a wool bale, one of Drusil's magic lanterns half-open next to him, eating cold stew from a wooden bowl. He could hear the others gathering on the far side of a stack of sheepskins. It would soon be time.

Appia walked around the corner and sat down on one of the bales. It was the black bale, the first wool of some farmer's shearing, bound with a strip of dark cloth to single it out. Lucky wool that was supposed to bring the wearer prosperity, that would go for three times the price of the rest. The merchant who'd stored it here would throw a fit if she saw how Appia used it, but mistreatment of goods was the least of their crimes.

"They hanged three more last night," Appia said.

Valens looked up from his bowl. It was almost empty already, so it didn't matter much if he lost his appetite now. He'd been getting back into the habits of campaign, eating quickly in case he was interrupted, eating all he could in case there wasn't more later. Habits he'd spent years bringing under control. Habits that told him his life wasn't his own anymore, that he was marching to someone else's drum.

As if he needed his stomach to tell him that.

"Three of yours?" he asked.

"One of them," Appia said, clenching her fist. "The other poor fuckers were in the wrong place at the wrong time." She took a deep breath, then unclenched the fist. "Lucky for us."

"Lucky." Valens tapped his ring against the bowl. "Right."

"Better them than us."

"They're from Estis. Our people."

"I'd rather be one body down than three. Gives us all a better chance when the boat hits the dock."

Valens ran his spoon around the inside of the bowl. It turned out that innocents dying wasn't enough to put him off his food. He'd have starved to death on his first campaign if it was. Still, the thought worried at him, like a loose nail in a shoe. They were drawing people into this mess based on some vision of a grand, heroic moment, standing for right and for freedom, for country and for king, albeit one long dead. But could people really live with the idea when they saw that their own were dying for a cause they had no say in? Could *he*?

Appia had pulled a tuft of wool from the bale and twisted it into a string. Now she was knotting it into one of her little dolls.

"What is that?" Valens asked, struggling to make sense of the fluffy shape.

"A bear." Appia held it up. "Big belly, broad shoulders, low head, see?"

FORGED FOR DESTINY

Valens nodded. He might have to squint to see it right, but these things were made for kids, who had a magical way of seeing the world. He remembered how young Raul had seen dragons in the clouds and ogres in lumps of stone. To Appia's nieces, this would be the world's best bear.

"Which is it for, the army or the farm?" he asked. Appia had only talked about these figures once, but the details had stuck in his mind. Stuff about kids did that these days, in a way it hadn't when he was young.

Appia's fingers went still. Valens frowned. He hadn't meant the question as a criticism. He had comrades-in-arms again, for the first time in many years, and he wanted to know them better, not to cause offence. Appia's nieces wouldn't care whether a bear belonged in their collections. Whatever she wanted to make for them, they would love it.

"I'm guessing army," he said. Appia was a comrade, she needed to know that he was on her side. "It's hard work training a bear to fight, but better than having one near your sheep."

Appia looked up. The corners of her eyes glistened.

"I had a nephew too," she said quietly. "He liked forest animals. Then a fever swept through town last spring, and without the old king's coven, there was no one to stop the disease." With trembling fingers, she set the bear down next to her. "I'm still doing this for Nino." She waved a hand, taking in the warehouse and all its secrets. "All of this."

Valens clutched his mourning ring so hard his fingers ached. What could he say? It was one thing to lose a friend in war, but losing a child to something so purposeless and indiscriminate, there was no making sense of that. Nothing anyone could do to make it better.

Then there were footsteps and he was saved from having to find the words.

Quintae, the rat-faced carpenter, came in, and Drusil behind him, her blacksmith's hammer hanging from her belt, one of her lanterns in each hand.

"Well?" Valens asked, drawing their attention while Appia drew herself together.

"Prisca was right," Drusil said. "The omens showed us the way. There's a cave halfway down Rack's Scar with a hidden tunnel at the back."

Omens. Valens snorted at that word. Prisca knew about the tunnel because she'd been part of the court's inner circle. Someone had shown her that tunnel, or perhaps she'd had it made herself, ready for a moment like this. Saying that the omens showed her made other people feel like fate was on their side, like they could believe every other word that came from her divination. But while Valens had gambled his life's work on Prisca's grasp of omens, he preferred to lay his actual life on the firm ground of facts.

"Well hidden." Quintae tapped his cheek, right under the eye. "Good craft. Used the lines of the rocks, the fractures of the earth, the split and the seam." He skimmed the palm of one hand across the other. "Could not have done better."

"He's right." Drusil leaned in the corner, arms folded, watching the strange little man. "The craftsmanship's beautiful and the water over the rocks has crusted it up, hiding the cracks. I never would have found the entrance without him."

FORGED FOR DESTINY

"I did a great job finding it." Quintae patted the scarred side of his own head. "A great job."

"Sure," Valens said, rolling his eyes. "Good boy."

Just what he needed, one more overgrown kid looking to him for reassurance. That thought was chased down by a swallow of guilt. Raul wasn't an overgrown kid. He was Valens's son, or as near as he'd ever get, a good lad, strong and smart. If he seemed naive sometimes, that showed how much better he was than Valens, how much kinder than this rotten world. If heroes were real, then they looked like Raul.

Prisca walked in, along with Holy Cirillo. She and the High Priest of Yorl had been getting cosy the last week. Not the sort of cosy that would loosen her up, but the sort that led to even more plots and schemes. Prisca was slipping back into old habits too, but hers were the way of the courtier, not the warrior. Maybe the country would need that when all of this was over; someone was going to have to make Estis run smoothly, while Raul showed it which way to go.

"Are you ready?" Prisca asked.

"Ready as we can be." Valens patted his sword.

"Where's Raul?"

Valens shrugged, set his empty bowl down. He wished he had more to go with it. A hunk of bread, maybe. If he was going to die, he wanted it to be on a full stomach.

"You don't know?" Prisca snapped.

"Reckoned he deserved a day to do what he wants, before..."

"Before the thing we absolutely must have him here for?" Prisca's eyes narrowed. "Very clever. What responsible parenting."

"He knows when he's needed. He'll be back."

333

"And if he isn't?"

"It's Raul."

"Exactly."

They stared at each other, eighteen years of arguments and plans, hopes and disappointments, fears and resentments filling the air between them. The others stepped quietly back, all except Quintae, who sat scratching the side of his head, muttering about beautiful rocks.

Footsteps approaching around the bales. Valens gripped his sword. Prisca turned expectantly.

Pomponius appeared in his threadbare scholars' robes, a chicken hanging from his ink-stained hand.

"I brought that sacrifice you wanted," he said.

"And the papers?" Prisca asked.

"My scribes are out and about, ready to distribute them."

"Thought you were accountants, not scribes," Valens said.

"Times are changing." Pomponius smiled ever so slightly. "Ask me tomorrow what we are." He looked around. "Where's the boy?"

———————•———————

As Raul walked out of the dusk and into the warehouse, men and women turned to look at him; some he'd led in raids in the past few weeks, some he didn't think he'd ever met before. Like birds who had heard a hunter creeping through the woods, they fell quiet, the silence spreading from him. But while birds perched fearful and tense, these people looked at him and smiled.

FORGED FOR DESTINY

Raul did his best to return the smiles, then hurried through them, heading for the back. Past the last stacks of goods, he reached the hidden place where the inner circle were gathered, and behind him, conversation burst forth once more.

"Are you all right, Raul?" Prisca gave him the same look she gave when he got stuck on a tough part in a book. Maybe his smile wasn't so convincing after all.

"I'm fine," he said. "Ready to save the kingdom." He looked around. "Does someone have my sword?"

"Valens, help him look for it. We'll go prepare."

Prisca led the others past Raul, Drusil dragging Quintae along. A chicken squawked and flapped its wings as Pomponius carried it out.

"Here." Valens opened one of the bales, revealing Raul's sword and the box that held the magical moth. "All ready for you."

Raul stared at the box, remembered the words that had come with it: *Be careful who you trust*. He had trusted in a vision of who he was, what he was doing, in a dream of heroism. What he had seen since reaching the city was blood and destruction.

"I can trust you, can't I, Da?" he asked.

Valens, hunched over to pick up Raul's sword, paused where he was, back stiff, arm outstretched.

"I will always do what's right for you," he said, then turned to face Raul, the sword clutched close. He swallowed. "Reckon I might have done two good things in my whole life, and you're one of them."

"Love you too, Da." Raul smiled, but he still wasn't happy.

Too much squirming in his guts. "What about Ma? I mean, Prisca. I can trust her, right?"

Valens took a long, slow breath. Raul didn't like asking questions like this, ones that would cut like knives when a family member wielded them, but he had to hear the answers, had to be sure.

"Your ma has built her whole life around what you mean to her. Have faith in that."

"Thanks, Da."

Valens held out the sword. Raul took it, pulled it an inch from its scabbard, watched how the magical light caught the edge of the blade. This wasn't the sword he was meant to wield, the one left to him by Balbianus, the sword destiny had prepared.

"How can I be trusted to lead a people to freedom?" he asked softly. "First thing I did in this city was lose the blade that was destined to save Estis."

"It was just a sword."

"It was something you trusted me with." His voice rose as he waved toward the bales, to the people hidden behind them, dozens of people, scores of people, hundreds out there in the city, all looking to him. "Now they're trusting me with their lives, but what if I'm not a hero? What if I'm just some lad from an inn who can't sing notes right, who prefers reading to fighting? What if I can't protect you all, never mind save a kingdom?"

The corners of his eyes prickled and he clutched the sword like he was clinging to his own feelings, holding them tight so they wouldn't come spilling out, wouldn't shame him and his

FORGED FOR DESTINY

da. He'd given up his home in the Vales to come here, given up everything Yasmi offered for the sake of omens and prophecy, but what if he couldn't live up to the destiny his ma saw for him? What if he ruined it for everyone?

"Hush."

Valens laid his hands on Raul's shoulders, and Raul realised that he was shaking. He took a deep breath, and another, tried to find the calm that his da had, that reassuring solidity.

"You amaze me, lad," Valens said. "All this madness, everything that's been put on you, and you're worried about other people hurting?"

He brought Raul to one of the bales, sat him down, and crouched facing him.

"What happens tonight has been coming for eighteen years," Valens said. "And I believe it's going to work. Not because of the omens, though Prisca's found plenty of them. Because of you. All the stars in the sky are nothing compared with what's in there." One huge finger tapped Raul in the chest, on his heart. "Whatever else happens, you'll make me proud."

"What if I don't?" Raul tugged at the edge of his tunic. The thickness of the leather didn't feel like much protection.

"You could never fail to make me proud." Valens tapped Raul's chest again. "Look at me."

Raul met his da's gaze.

"Some good people are going to get hurt tonight," Valens said. "Some will die. The sad truth is, that's how it goes, even in the old stories. But it's better to risk that, to fight for what's right, than to spend your life living in fear. If we don't do this, then good people are going to suffer forever. If we do it, then maybe the world can change.

"Believe in yourself. Believe in your destiny. And while you're about it, know that we all believe in you."

A lightness spread through Raul's chest from the spot where his da's finger lay. It lifted him up, his back straightening, head rising, even his smile lifting. He could do this. He would do this. He had to do this.

"Thanks, Da."

He got up, walked over to the unravelled bale of wool, and picked up the moth's box. Whatever Queen Junia had meant, he could worry about it tomorrow. Tonight, destiny called.

"Son?" Valens said in a voice so soft it was barely his. Raul turned, and the light shone in the corners of his da's eyes. "I love you."

———————————— • ————————————

Quintae had built the altar out of two old storage chests, then carved the moon and dagger into the front. Prisca stood behind it, holding a slender knife with an inch of highly polished blade. In front the rebels knelt, breath held, waiting. Raul knelt among them, his sword at his hip, his da beside him, his entire body tingling in anticipation.

"Yorl's blind eye watch over you," Holy Cirillo intoned. "Avgar guide you. Selthin strengthen you. And may the spirits of all we have lost grant their fire to your hearts."

Prisca flipped the squirming chicken onto the altar. Her blade plunged down and, in a single swift move, sliced the

FORGED FOR DESTINY

bird open. It lay twitching as she plunged a hand in and pulled out its guts. She held them up and watched with haunted eyes as they slithered through her fingers.

"I perceive a path," she proclaimed, and Raul thought that he could see it too, the guts twisting like a woodland trail, like a tunnel through the earth. "It is shrouded in darkness and flame. I see a red eye in the sky and a new moon ascending. I see dawn, dawn of the day and of the age, and in its light we stand triumphant.

"Three warnings the omens give us." She pointed at lumps in the guts with the tip of her knife, and if Raul couldn't make out what she saw in that mess, he could hear her certainty. "Watch your neighbour, for you will need their blade before the night is out. Watch your flank, for danger hides in the unwatched shadow. And watch the fire, in your hearts and in your streets, for the blaze that runs wild can be your salvation or your doom."

The last of the guts pattered onto the altar. Blood ran down the lines of the carvings, drawing the outline of the pierced moon. Prisca pressed a finger against her left cheek, leaving a red mark like a third eye.

"It is rising," she said. "Let us meet destiny together."

Valens stood and raised his fist.

"For the new moon rising!" he bellowed, and they all leapt to their feet.

"For Estis!" they shouted as one.

Chapter Twenty-Seven
The Weight of the World

Raul followed Valens out of the narrow gap between the buildings overlooking Rack's Scar. Only a footfall from them the ground fell away and became a jagged, uneven cliff leading to the roaring river far below. One long stride, one false step, and he would tumble into oblivion. Valens showed no fear as he looked over that edge, then set his foot onto something below. His confidence gave Raul the courage to approach the edge, to feel a cold wind rush up to meet him, to look down into the wildly churning waters barely visible in the deep.

Prisca, Appia, and a dozen others followed Raul, their footsteps soft as a cat's tread. The shutters on their enchanted lanterns were narrowed so that only a faint light was cast ahead of them. Enough to illuminate their next five, ten steps, but not so bright that they would draw the attention of passing patrols. At least, that was what they had hoped as they slid

340

FORGED FOR DESTINY

through the streets of the city's darker, more crowded districts, where the shadows of close-packed buildings obliterated all hope of light. As they emerged from that winding warren, standing on the sudden edge of the city, the light fell on something new: a narrow trail down the side of the Scar.

Poised at the precipice, Raul looked up. A myriad of stars shone down on the city, as bright and hopeful as children on the first day of spring. The sky was full, but there was still something missing.

"Keep moving," Prisca whispered as Valens disappeared from view. "We don't have time to waste."

"Where's the Eye?" Raul asked.

"The Eye?"

"The Red Eye? It was meant to be the sign that the prophecy was about to be fulfilled, that we'll save the country. Where is it?"

Prisca froze on the cliff edge. Despite the thunderous roaring of the Scar, which echoed from the back of the buildings until it seemed to come from everywhere at once, he knew she'd heard him.

"The Eye is still there," Prisca said, in the voice she used near the end of a long argument with some stubborn drunk in the inn. "It will shine later."

"What if it doesn't? What if this isn't the time?"

"Of course it's the time. We're here, aren't we?"

Raul stared. He wanted her to be right, but . . .

A cloud shifted. Suddenly, a red spot appeared between the mountains, larger than the other stars, burning with a feverish light. Raul watched it rise in awe, felt the power of this overwhelming world, the force of fate falling upon him. He laid a hand on his rising chest, steadying his heartbeat as his world turned around that single shining point.

The Red Eye watched over the land of Estis, just as Prisca and Valens had watched over Raul. His parents had saved him when the country fell, and now a greater force was here to save the country itself.

"Watch the fire," he whispered, echoing the words Prisca had seen in her scrying. The eye was a fire burning in the heavens, like last night's embers unearthed from beneath the ashes in the hearth, ready to ignite the new day's fire. A flame in the hearts and the streets. One that would bring their salvation. It was Raul's duty to carry it into the palace, into the very heart of the enemy.

No, not his duty. His destiny.

"Happy now?" Prisca asked stiffly.

Raul nodded. "It's time."

He raised his hand in a salute to the Red Eye. Beside it, the cloud moved further, unveiling the slender curve of a new moon. Behind Prisca, the other rebels raised their hands, following Raul's gesture. Then they followed him off the cliff and down.

The trail was narrow, but more solid and even than it looked, no harder than following a goat track up a hillside, and he wasn't helping a farmer carry a lost ewe this time. True, the consequences of falling were far greater, but Raul didn't worry about that. The Red Eye watched over them.

Valens stood halfway down the cliff, silhouetted by the light of his lamp. Raul swiftly caught up with him and saw

FORGED FOR DESTINY

why his da had stopped. Hidden from above by a turn of the trail and a rocky outcrop, a cave opened into the cliffside.

They waited while the others caught up, soft patches of light moving cautiously down the cliff. Raul reached for one of his pouches, which held the bronze moth Queen Junia had given him.

"Save it until we're closer," Valens said. "No one's going to hear us out here."

He took a step into the cave mouth, but Raul laid a hand on his arm, held him back.

"I should go first," Raul said. "I'm the prophesized one."

Valens frowned, then nodded. Shadows cast by the lanterns hid his eyes from Raul.

"You're right, lad. You go first. I'll be right behind you."

Raul raised his lantern in front of his chest and walked into the cave, slowly at first, then with more confidence. It looked like a dead end but that couldn't be true. Destiny didn't allow it. Sure enough, amid the rocks at the back, hidden by a fold in the cave wall, a wide crack opened into the rock, a tunnel hidden by careful craftsmanship and the passage of time. He craned his neck, peered around the closest rocks, found the sign of the hooded eye carved into a shadowy crevice. More than mere craftsmanship had gone into keeping this concealed.

Lantern held out ahead of him, Raul crept in. He had to duck in some places, to avoid scraping his head across the ceiling, and turned sideways to get through the narrower parts. He looked back from time to time, remembering the message that Prisca had intoned, the warning to watch for the others,

343

because he would need them before the night was out. He saw Valens walking in a constant stoop, his body too powerful to fit within the constraints of the earth. He saw Prisca, two eyes gleaming as they pierced the darkness ahead, and a third, drawn in blood, a red eye to match the one in the sky, the sight that found such omens. He saw Appia, grim and determined, leading a string of figures whose faces were hidden to him, just one part of their brave force. Those people's faith, their expectations, closed around him as solid as armour, more certain than the hardened leather he wore. He gripped the handle of his lantern and kept walking.

No one spoke. In some stretches, the tunnel echoed and amplified the sounds they made, the footsteps and the deep breaths, someone sniffing, a clink as weapons shifted on a belt. In other places, it was as if the earth swallowed the sounds and an eerie silence shrouded them. Twists and turns carried them upward, toward the peak of the hill from which the palace overlooked the sprawl of Pavuno.

One final turn, and the tunnel opened into a cave. The cave itself turned, widened, and finally there were signs of human activity. Stacks of barrels, rows of crates, sacks heaped up against one side. Torch brackets with streaks of soot staining the walls above. Scuff marks on the ground. At the far end, the entrance to the cave had been bricked up. Double doors of thick pine planks and iron bands filled the only gap in that wall. Raul looked carefully around, peering into every shadow, wary for the danger on his flank. When he looked back, the tunnel entrance was hidden in the rough rock and the turns of the cave.

FORGED FOR DESTINY

"Time for the moth," Valens said.

Raul handed over his lantern, took the box out of his pouch, and opened the lid. Fragile bronze wings caught the magical light.

Valens pressed his hands against the doors, testing them. They didn't budge. He nodded to Appia, who stepped forward with one of her people, the two of them hefting woodsmen's axes. They braced, ready to swing, then looked at Raul.

He set the moth in his palm. With steady fingers, he drew out one wing, then hesitated. He looked at the men and women around him, come to risk their lives for the cause.

"Blood for luck," he whispered, the charm the older ones used before a fight.

"Blood for luck," they hissed back, tense smiles becoming confident grins.

Raul unfurled the moth's other wing. The shuffle of feet, expectant breaths, creaking leather, and rustling cloth vanished. He opened his mouth to give the command, but nothing emerged.

A nod from Appia. In absolute silence, the axes hit the door.

Chapter Twenty-Eight
Striking in Silence

One of the doors tipped, the planks around its hinges splintering beneath the axe blows. Pushed by Valens and Appia, it pivoted over the bar that had held it in place. The bar snapped and the door fell. In place of an almighty crash, Raul felt the air current sent out by the door's fall. It rushed across his hands, one of them clutching his sword, the other cupping the fragile bronze moth. Then the moment was gone in a swirl of dust, Valens pushed the other door open, and they stepped into a stone-lined corridor. The light from their lamps made shadows shift across the walls, swaying like the dancers at a harvest festival.

Prisca pointed to the left, then tugged at Valens's arm as he was about to head that way. Raul walked past, focusing on what lay ahead instead of on his parents. Unable to hear anything, he had to trust that the others would follow.

A short set of stairs led to a junction. Raul stopped there, peered cautiously in both directions. No sign of anyone.

Prisca appeared at his elbow. She looked both ways, hesitated for a moment, then pointed to the right. Raul ran that way, almost ran too far, caught himself as he was about to pass a doorway, and stopped to look inside.

It was a small room, its shelves filled with cups, plates, and bowls. A pair of servants stood at a table in the middle, polishing silverware with soft cloths. One of them was looking at the other in confusion and pointing at her mouth. Her lips moved, but no sound came out. The other one looked around, saw Raul, smiled, tried to say something. She too frowned, touched her throat, then her eyes went wide as she looked at his sword.

These were ordinary people, not invaders, not soldiers. Raul couldn't leave them here, where they might raise the alarm once he was gone, but he wasn't going to murder them. Instead, he pointed at the back wall. If they stayed there, then maybe he could bolt the room shut behind him, and then...

Valens saved him the trouble of working out what came next. He pushed past, two of the other rebels behind him. The servants stepped back, looking very afraid, and a silver goblet fell silently to the floor. Valens grabbed the servants, turned them around, shoved them against the wall, while others took ropes from belts to tie their hands. It wasn't gently done, but not cruelly either. Swift, forceful, practical, get the task done and move on. Raul still had so much to learn.

Prisca grabbed his arm, dragged him on. One of the rebels was at the end of the corridor, peering through a door that was open just a crack. A breeze brushed Raul's skin as he looked past her.

Through the door was a wide courtyard, cobbled, with stables to one side and the palace's central keep on the other. A pile of scaffold beams lay to one side, and an empty wagon next to them. Half a dozen soldiers stood around a brazier, its fire illuminating the pale trees on their blue tabards. They had sabres at their hips and several held spears or leaned them in the crook of an arm. One sat on an old saddle, which in turn perched on top of an empty barrel. They were laughing as they passed a wineskin around.

The enemy, laughing and joking while the country suffered. They reminded Raul of the warriors he had met in the Vales, who had threatened to hang him. Of the warriors who had attacked an innocent woman and stolen Raul's sword. Of the ones who had beaten the granary overseers just for trying to make the food last.

Holding the moth carefully close to his chest, he set his sword down and signalled to the others, tapping the sword to indicate warriors and holding up fingers to show how many. The rebels set aside their lanterns and gathered, weapons drawn.

Raul nodded to the rebel who had reached the door first. She pushed it open and he ran out past her.

One of the warriors looked up at the movement.

"Here, what's—"

The rest of her words were swallowed by the silence radiating around Raul. She grabbed her spear with both hands and her companions turned, some confused, some reaching for their weapons. Then the rebels were on them and Raul lashed out with his sword, catching one of the guards in the thigh.

FORGED FOR DESTINY

Fighting in silence felt like dancing in the dark. Raul could go through the movements, could follow the steps he had practised, but he could never be sure what else was happening. He constantly wanted to look behind him because he couldn't hear movement there, wouldn't know if someone was about to cut him down. But there were enemies ahead, spear tips jabbing, and they would skewer him if he turned away. He knocked a thrust aside, stepped in past the spear's head, but his opponent dropped the spear and drew her sabre. He felt rather than heard the ringing as their blades clashed, and the impact jarred his arm.

He twisted his blade, failed to disarm her, jumped back to avoid a lunge. Panic jolted through his chest as he almost dropped the moth; the task of keeping it safe was as debilitating as the silence. Far worse than fighting with one hand tied behind his back was fighting with one hand clutching this delicate, precious piece of magic, one more vulnerable organ he had to protect from his opponents' blows.

One of the Dunholmi was running, but Valens ran after, hacking him down before he got out of the silence. The others were all down, one of them slumping into the empty barrel, legs dangling out, limp and pathetic. Raul wanted to call upon his opponent to surrender, but how could he do that without words?

It didn't matter. Appia stepped over a twitching body, swung her axe. The last warrior fell, blood streaming from her chest, running in rivulets through the gaps between cobblestones.

In the stillness that followed, rebels snatched up the guards' weapons, weighed them against their own. Some ran to cover the doors and gateways off the courtyard. Prisca stood to one side, looking back and forth with her brow crumpled, arms folded in tight.

Raul tapped her on the shoulder, raised a questioning eyebrow. He needed to know where next. His heart was pounding, his every instinct urging him to keep moving, to run, to fight. She shook her head, tried to wave him away.

Valens appeared, blood dripping from his sword. He pointed at the moth, then curled his fingers in. Raul folded in one of the wings.

Sound returned. The rebels heard their own footsteps and stopped moving.

"What's the problem?" Valens whispered.

"No problem," Prisca replied, eyes darting back and forth.

"Then which way do we go?"

"I..." She shook her head. "You should know, you were here before."

"For a few weeks, eighteen years ago. You were here for years."

"I was. I just..."

"Has it changed?" Raul asked.

"No. Yes. Maybe..." Prisca pointed to a door. "This way. Hide the bodies first."

Raul unfurled the moth's wing and silence fell again. Rebels dragged the fallen guards into the corridor they had come from. None of them knew when more warriors would come this way, but no one was going to notice blood on the cobbles in this darkness, and hopefully, by the time the bodies were found, it would be too late.

FORGED FOR DESTINY

The rebels gathered by the door Prisca had chosen. She held up three fingers, then two, then one, then swung the door open.

Raul strode through, into a corridor with a curtain hanging at the far end. He'd almost reached the curtain when it was twitched aside and a warrior in chainmail stared out at him.

The warrior mouthed words that didn't emerge and stepped back. Raul ran at him, knocking the curtain aside, trying to reach the man before he could get out of the moth's effect.

He burst into a space twice the size of the inn's main room, with a fire at one end and benches lining a pair of trestle tables. The floor was strewn with straw. Horns and animal skulls decorated the low rafters. The warrior who had seen Raul pounded his fist on one of the tables, and though it made no sound, the other warriors there looked up.

No time to think, no chance to undo his actions. Raul lunged. The warrior tried to dodge but Raul had planned for that. His sword skewered chainmail and flesh. The absence of sound made the impact all the more vivid.

One of the other warriors slashed at Raul with a small knife. Raul lurched away, tried to drag his sword free, but it was stuck. He let go rather than let himself get stabbed, and Valens charged past him, hacking the warrior down.

The room descended into chaos as the rebels ran in, rushing to block the exits, to bring their opponents down before they could get over their surprise. A clay cup bounced off the side of Valens's head and shattered against the wall. Someone shoved the table in front of him and a sabre fell in the straw.

Raul snatched it up, looked around, saw one of the rebels, drawn from the congregation of Yorl, trapped in a corner by two armed Dunholmi. Raul ran over, screaming as he went, but though his voice ran raw up his throat there was no sound, no distraction, no chance for the enemy to face him. He hit one of them in the back of the head, and as the other turned, the Yorl worshipper cut him down.

Candles had fallen from the table and one of them set the straw on fire, its melting wax adding to the blaze. Prisca grabbed a jug off the table, quenched half the flames with ale and stamped out the rest, even as Valens parried a blow that would have hit her back.

One of the rebels fell into the fireplace, a horseman's axe buried in her shoulder. Greasy smoke and a smell of burning meat billowed through a room that was growing dimmer. Appia and one of her people hauled the body out, but the smell wasn't going away.

Raul charged one last guard. Again, the silent clash of steel, the judder of blades, bodies twisting, feet sliding on the straw. The guard snatched a candlestick off the table, flung it at Raul. He ducked, barely parried the next sword swing and the one after that, then struck low. The guard stepped back rather than lose a foot, and Valens's blade came in from behind, ending him.

No opposition left. Rebels stood at each of the room's exits, watching for danger. Appia pointed at the fallen candles and diminished fire, then mimed holding up a lantern. Two of her people nodded and ran back the way they had come.

Valens pointed at the moth in Raul's hand, made the

FORGED FOR DESTINY

closing gesture. Raul looked around in case anyone was doing anything noisy, then folded in a wing.

This time, he heard groans and whimpers, accompanied by the crackle of logs settling in the fire.

"You said this way." Valens looked at Prisca. His tone was sharp.

"It should have been this way," she replied. "They must have made changes."

"Funny, because I remember this room."

"Now is not the time." She pointed at one of the doorways. "We go that way, up the stairs to the throne room."

"You sure?"

"I'm sure."

"How sure?"

"Really, you want to do this now?"

"I don't want to walk into another mess like this."

Not all the bodies on the floor were Dunholmi. Two of the rebels lay dead. One of Appia's dockers was binding another's sleeve into a sling, to stop the limp and bloody arm hanging loose. Raul had to remind himself that, awful as the carnage seemed, it was a price worth paying.

"Perhaps the signs led Prisca this way," Raul said, keeping his voice calm and quiet. He was a leader now and he had to keep them all focused. Strange, to step so far out of his parents' shadow that they might soon stand in his. "Maybe we had to take these guards out so that they can't run to the governor's rescue."

"Those signs are as smart as you, boy." Appia handed Raul's sword back to him and passed a Dunholmi sabre to one of her men. "We're better armed now."

Three rebels were testing the draw on composite bows that had hung from hooks on the wall. They looked pleased with what they found. Prisca snatched the last remaining bow and a quiver of arrows, keeping her back to Valens as she strung the bow.

The rebels who had run off reappeared, carrying lanterns. They passed them to anyone with a hand free.

"Ready?" Raul unfurled the moth's wing and silence fell again.

He walked through the doorway and up a set of stairs, into a wider corridor than the ones they'd been in before. Torches burned in brackets fixed to the walls. The stars could be seen through unshuttered windows above a set of double doors. At the opposite end of the hall, past several open doorways, was a wide set of stairs.

Across the hall from Raul, an elderly servant stood, his arms full of firewood. He stared at the silent rebels. The logs fell from his arms but made no sound as Raul walked toward him. The servant pointed at Raul, then out the window, at the silver arc of the moon. Raul nodded. The servant sank to one knee and bowed.

Raul took hold of the man's shoulder, drew him upright, and bowed his own head in return. He mouthed the words "throne room," hoping he would understand.

The servant pointed at the stairs. Prisca was already halfway up them, bow at the ready, looking back impatiently. Raul went after her and the rest of the rebels came with him. The old servant picked up a log like it was a cudgel and followed.

They ran up the stairs, Prisca leading the way. Through

FORGED FOR DESTINY

a window, Raul saw the Red Eye, higher in the sky now, framed by the mountain peaks. He felt the world watching him through that one eye, and he knew that he could do this. They were almost there. One last push. A new moon rising, and the start of a new age.

At the top of the stairs was one last hallway with a pair of grand doors at the far side. Raul was rushing across it when he remembered, just in time, the warning the omens had given them: *Watch your flank, for danger hides in the unwatched shadow.* He turned his head, saw warriors running out of another doorway, silently screaming as they charged.

These men and women were better armoured than the ones the rebels had faced before, their tabards better sewn. The first of them swung at Raul, a left-handed blow that channelled all the momentum of the charge. Raul deflected the attack, stepped aside, let her run through the space where he had been. He used his own momentum to slash at her back, but she twisted, parried, lunged, then he was staggering into the chaos of a whirling melee. Someone jogged his elbow and he only just hung on to the precious moth. He saw a movement in the corner of his eye, ducked an attack at neck height, stabbed the man who had tried to decapitate him and this time found his mark.

The first attacker came at him again. She wore a captain's sash with its silver dagger, and she carried herself with unflinching confidence, a certainty that the world would yield to her. But as the Red Eye shone through the window, Raul felt that same certainty, the knowledge that nothing could stop him. He ran at her. Their blades met, locked. He didn't have her weight of muscle, but he was nimble. He twisted his wrist, brought his pommel up, caught her under the chin. She stumbled and he pressed his advantage, using swift strikes to keep her on the back foot, driving her away from the rest. Her foot crossed the edge of the stairs. She swayed, arms waving to keep her balance. Raul lunged, stabbed her through the shoulder. With her empty hand she snatched at him, grabbed his off arm, squeezed the hand that held the moth. He punched her in the face with his sword hand and her grip slackened. Her hand jerked, tugged at his, and as she fell, so did the moth. It hit the stairs, bounced, one wing buckled, the other snapped. As the captain flopped like rags down the stairs, Raul heard the crunch of her bones. All the sounds of the fight rushed back into the world.

He wheeled around. They were winning, but it wasn't done and there couldn't be any more delay. He charged, hacked a warrior down, ran another one through as he opened his mouth to shout for help. Arrows in the back brought down the last Dunholmi as she tried to run.

"What happened?" Prisca snapped.

"War happened," Valens growled.

He strode toward the doors at the end of the hall. Raul was quicker than him, rushing past, full of the thrill of the fight and the certainty that came with knowing his purpose, knowing his cause, knowing how many people were counting on him. Not just the rebels here but those who would be rising up across the city; those who would see the tide of freedom and rise with it; those who were weak or scared or vulnerable, who could not fight for themselves, who needed someone to fight for them.

FORGED FOR DESTINY

He flung the doors open and strode into the throne room. At the far end, a dark-haired man sat with one leg draped across the arm of the throne, reading a book and drinking from a skull goblet. He was dressed in fine armour and embroidered blue silks, a sabre hanging from his hip and a longsword resting against his seat. There were others around him: a grey-haired, stoop-shouldered man who scuttled away from the throne, dropping papers in his haste; a pair of servants backing fearfully toward the far wall. But the man in the throne didn't twitch. He set his goblet down and smiled.

"Count Alder," Raul called out. "Your time has come."

The count stood and raised his blade, Raul's blade, the ruby in its pommel catching the light. His lips twitched into a mocking half smile.

"I see that a new moon has risen," he said. "How marvellous."

Chapter Twenty-Nine
Wounds

Raul advanced slowly down the length of the room, his sword raised, his whole body held in a fighting stance. He could do this. He was ready. Alder might be more experienced, but so were most of the warriors Raul had beaten in combat. The prophecies said that he was going to win, that he would tear down Alder's rule and restore what had been lost. He just had to believe in himself.

"How old are you?" Count Alder gave a casual flourish with Balbianus's sword, held it out and down, pointing at the floor. His chamberlain and a servant watched fearfully from behind the throne. "Fourteen, fifteen?"

"Eighteen." Raul puffed out his chest, flexed his arm to show this mocking fop what a real hero looked like. "Old enough to love, to live, to fight, to die if that's what it takes to free my people."

"How noble of you. And touchingly dramatic; I wonder if you've been watching too many plays?"

Raul tensed. The count was mocking him, a tyrant with a

FORGED FOR DESTINY

sharp tongue trying to prove his superiority. But that didn't make him any less wary of the man.

"That would explain this." Alder held up his sword, turned it so that the engravings caught the light. "Too fine to fight with, too well weighted to be for display. You wanted to show off, didn't you, to get everyone's attention?"

"My sword." For a moment, dread ran through Raul. If Alder had Balbianus's sword, did that mean that destiny had turned against them, that their enemy had the advantage?

No. The sword was *here*. That must have been what the omens meant all along. Raul, the living essence of Balbianus, would retake the ancient king's blade and with it his kingdom.

A tingling energy surged through him, like when he was younger and Valens fed him honey from the hives they kept to make mead. He felt like he could take on the world.

"I am Balbianus's heir," Raul said. "That is Balbianus's blade, and before this night is out, I will reclaim his kingdom."

"Balbianus's blade? This?" Alder's eyebrows drew in, his brow furrowed, and then he laughed. "Of course. Now I see."

That mocking half smile was back and it made Raul want to attack him more than ever. How could he laugh and smile while his people killed and oppressed? Outside, blades crashed and arrows thudded, voices shouted commands and screamed in pain. Rebels had run to hold the doorways into the room, and violence sounded from every quarter. Violence that the Dunholmi had brought to Pavuno a lifetime ago.

"I . . ." Raul needed to say something but he was out of grand speeches. All he knew was that he had to tear this man down. "I hate you."

"It's nice that one of us cares." Alder raised the blade in salute. "Shall we?"

———————————•———————————

"I like a good duel." Alder flicked his blade out in a short, sharp strike, then a pair to the other side, testing the boy's defences. "Less taxing than a battle, you can focus on technique."

The boy was fast, his parries in place almost before Alder attacked. He had good footwork too, like a well-trained horse; nimble, instinctive, assured, his body shifting behind his blade, not letting Alder turn him or throw him off balance. Alder enjoyed a challenge, especially one so clear and contained. Kill the boy, end the conspiracy. Politics was seldom so beautifully simple.

He stepped back to see what the boy would do. As he'd hoped, that determination bled into overconfidence, a swift advance and then a strike before he'd finished closing the gap. Alder turned it aside.

It was a feint. The boy's blade darted, lunged, tore the silk of Alder's robes as it skimmed off the chainmail on his shoulder.

Alder winced at the impact of the blow but didn't pause to recover. Instead, he swung hard at the boy's sword arm, forcing him into a clumsy dodge and a stumble. Then Alder was on the offensive, striking hard, overwhelming him with raw strength. The ringing of blades echoed through the chamber.

Alder liked a challenge, but what he liked most was that he always won.

———————————•———————————

FORGED FOR DESTINY

Raul dodged, parried, tried to counterattack but had to revert to defence. He was driven back, turning toward the window as Alder's blows rained in. The count was using all his strength, and beneath the force of those blows Raul realised for the first time that Valens had always held back, never committed his full force against Raul. Alder was no Valens, but combined with the precision of his strikes, that strength was devastating.

Raul had strength of his own. A lifetime of carrying sacks of grain to the brewhouse and barrels from there to the inn, of helping neighbours plough their fields, fetching crops, cutting down trees. He summoned that strength, channelled it through the moves that Valens had taught him, all those lessons leading to this moment.

He ducked instead of parried, brought his sword up, went on the attack. Alder dodged and now his back was to the door. Raul advanced upon him, hacking to right and to left, driven by the memories of everything he'd seen, the petty cruelties of occupation, the brutalities in the city streets. That made him stronger. He was the one pushing Alder, forcing him to react to the moves Raul chose. Alder's sword was hammered down by one of Raul's blows, the edge of his blade almost touching the count's head. For the first time, the smile left Alder's face. A little more strength, one last push, and all this could end.

Raul roared and beat at the count's blade, a relentless attack instead of a calculated one, almost breaking through again, and again, and again, until his own muscles ached from the effort and surely his opponent's must too.

Alder's blade, *Balbianus's* blade, flashed out and caught Raul on his forearm. Pain was a sudden shock. Alder's wrist twisted, his blade turned Raul's, forced it out of his grip. The sword fell with a clang. Alder lashed out, Raul jerked back, stumbled, retreated, fumbling for the knife on his belt. Alder charged, shoved him over, and Raul skidded across the floor, to sprawl against the steps at the foot of the throne.

———————————●———————————

Valens stood in front of the double doors to the throne room. This was the widest way in, the best connected to the rest of the palace, and the hardest to hold. So that was where he belonged.

The hall was scattered with bodies already, blood painting the tiles. He could smell it, practically taste the sweat and iron in the air.

Another wave of warriors rushed up the steps. They were more organised than the first group and several of them had shields. Behind Valens, Prisca and the other archers loosed. One arrow thudded useless into a shield, one hit a warrior in the leg and she fell cursing. The others charged and Valens charged to meet them. No warning, no war cry, just his blade swinging, reaping a harvest of blood and screams.

It was like that last night again, facing the armies of Dunholm. Fabia had been with him then and she was with him still, the mourning ring pressing into the worn leather of the sword's hilt. He cut one man down, ran another through, flung the body back, knocking others down the stairs. He snatched up a shield just in time to catch the arrows that flew at him. Then he stepped back, out of sight of the archers, to hold the gap, to buy Raul the time he needed.

Valens knocked the arrows from his shield and took a deep breath. Another wave of attackers driven off, but they were getting stronger and the rebels were starting to tire.

"Fuck." Appia stood beside him, her face pale, one hand clutched to her bleeding shoulder. "We lost Hander and Kurl."

Valens looked at the bodies, spotted the two dockers she had named. He wanted to say that he was sorry, but this was war.

"We'll give them a good burial," he said.

"This scheme of yours had better be worth the price."

Appia leaned against the wall. One of her legs was trembling. Someone needed to bind her wound, but there was no one spare. Too few blades left, too much space to hold. She would have to wait until it was over. He hoped she had that long.

"Shouldn't be long now," he said

They only had to hold out long enough for Raul to take down Alder, to give them a tyrant's head or a captive, to seal the boy's place as a figure of destiny. Then the flames of rebellion being lit in the city would become a full-blown inferno. Then, at last, Fabia would have her revenge.

Valens hated this part of the plan, where they left the boy vulnerable. But it had been the capstone from the start. Without it, everything fell. He had spent a lifetime preparing Raul. He had to believe in his son now. He had to let this be a story worth telling.

363

He had to let it be heroic.

Still, he looked over his shoulder, saw Prisca in the doorway, eyes wide, one hand fumbling at her empty quiver. Saw down the hall to the throne. Saw Raul on the floor, unarmed, and Count Alder standing over him, sword outstretched.

Valens had thought that he was numb to any horror the world could throw at him. Now he knew that he was wrong.

He charged past Prisca, all his rage fixed on the count's exposed back.

Eighteen years he had prepared for this. It was time for a reckoning.

———————————•———————————

Alder held the tip of his sword an inch from the boy's throat. What was the best move, to kill him now or to save him for later? Would a public execution make a salutary lesson or a martyr?

"My lord!" Tur shrieked. "Behind you!"

Fools turned when they heard words like that. Alder flung himself sideways and a sword ripped through the space where he had been. He hit the floor, rolled, sprang to his feet, and whirled around, shoulder aching from the impact on the ground.

A warrior strode toward him, a vast slab of muscles bound in boiled leather, taller by a head than any of Alder's men. His face was twisted with old scars and fury, his eyes blazing with a hatred the boy had barely managed to imitate. He held an old Estian infantry sword and a shield bearing Alder's own silver tree.

FORGED FOR DESTINY

The warrior roared and swung that sword. Alder leapt back, felt the wind of the blade's passage inches from his guts. Another swing. He dodged, found himself against the wall, chainmail links pressing through the padded jacket into his spine. Another swing. He parried this one, both hands clenching the grip of that ridiculous engraved sword, and the force of the warrior's one hand almost wrenched the sword from both of his.

There was no hope in strength, but perhaps in speed. The warrior punched at Alder's face with his shield. Alder flung himself clear, around the warrior's off side. The shield's edge buckled and splintered against the wall. Alder brought his blade up. The warrior turned. Alder kept moving, stepping in close. Too close to swing a sword, but it threw the great slab of meat off balance.

As Alder stepped through and turned, he drew his sabre with his left hand, felt the weight and balance of Dunholmi workmanship. The sabre came up as the warrior's sword came down. Alder caught that sword on his sabre, arm braced, knees bent, held back his opponent's terrible strength for a moment as brief as a foal's first breath.

With all his remaining strength, Alder brought the other sword up and over.

———————————— • ————————————

The moment the fight moved past him, Raul was back on his feet. He ran to the centre of the throne room where his sword lay. The chamberlain was ahead of him, about to pick up the sword. Raul barged him aside, their feet hit the sword, and it slid away.

Raul slammed his elbow into the chamberlain's face. The man staggered, clutched his nose, spat curses about dark magic. Raul grabbed the sword and turned.

He saw Balbianus's blade slice through Valens's wrist. Saw the spray of blood. Saw sword and hand fall to the floor. A cold wave of horror washed through him, then one of blazing fury.

"No!"

Raul raced across the room.

Valens, his face pale, dropped his shield, stepped back, clutched his bleeding stump. He thudded to his knees.

Alder faced Raul, both swords raised.

There was a crash as their blades met, then another, and another. Blood pounded in Raul's ears and heat throbbed through his whole body. He attacked without thought, without restraint. He screamed with rage and struck with wild ferocity. The instincts that Valens had trained into him guided his blows as he let loose all his anger, all his pain, all his grief.

Alder grinned like he was still playing his cruel little games, still sitting on his throne with his grotesque goblet and his grovelling minions. He smiled.

Raul flung his whole weight into his attacks, his body becoming a weapon, the strength that would strike Alder down. He drove Alder back until the count was pinned against the wall again.

Alder sidestepped, stuck out a leg. Raul tripped, slammed face first into the wall. A blow hit him in the back, not the edge of a blade but the blunt force of a fist. The breath burst from him, pain taking hold as he was caught between the blow and the wall. Another punch. Another. The sword slipped from his fingers and he slid to his knees.

Alder took a deep, ragged breath and shook his hand, easing the pain from the knuckles. With his other hand, he brought his sabre around, rested it on the boy's shoulder, its wicked edge next to his neck.

That had been exhilarating, a greater challenge than he had expected. For a moment, facing that other ridiculous mass of muscles, he had almost thought that he might lose. Only for a moment, but it was quite a sensation.

"Lower the blade." A woman stalked into the throne room, pointing a bow at Alder. Her face was lined and grey streaked her hair, but she was still striking. The trembling tip of her bloodstained arrow gave away that she was no warrior.

"You must be Prisca Servita," Alder said. "Minister to a conquered king and now ringleader of a ruined rebellion. Unless you're going to tell me that he's the brains behind this."

He pointed at the massive warrior, who sat with his back against the wall, blood pooling around him as he fumbled one-handed with a belt, trying to tie off the stump of his wrist.

"Remove that blade from Raul's throat or I'll kill you," Prisca said. "Don't think for a minute that I wouldn't."

"I'm sure you would, I just don't think you'll hit. And if you do miss, it gets messy for him."

More movement behind her. Alder's guards came in. Several had blood on their blades. They looked from Prisca to Alder, saw the arrow pointing at him, waited for his command.

"Raul, is it?" Alder took the sword from the boy's shoulder. He doubted that Prisca was fool enough to think that he was doing so for her sake. "Stand up, Raul."

The boy got off his knees and turned to face them. His breath wheezed and he clutched his chest. He trembled as he stared at the one-handed warrior. A moment ago, he had been so fearsome. Now he seemed on the verge of tears.

"Did she tell you that you were the heir of Balbianus, Raul?" Alder slid an arm around Raul's shoulder, while his other hand kept the sabre at the ready. He leaned in close, like they were friends sharing an amiable drink, and he grinned as the boy shuddered. "That you had a destiny, that the signs foretold your coming, that you would liberate the kingdom?"

Prisca's eyes narrowed.

"I am." Raul nodded. "I will."

The boy looked at his shoulder. The skin was hidden, of course, beneath the hardened leather of his tunic, but Alder had read the papers these people planted. He knew what to expect.

"Birthmark's there, is it?" he said. "How compelling." He looked Prisca in the eye. "Did you find a child with a real birthmark, then build it all around them? Seems too risky. Children die. No, you must have made the mark yourself. Tattoo or branding, maybe some sort of magic? That's a painful thing to do to a child, but somebody has to pay the price, don't they?"

"Silence." Prisca drew the bowstring tighter. "He doesn't need your lies."

FORGED FOR DESTINY

Alder ignored her. She wouldn't risk shooting him now. Not with the boy so close, her hand so unsteady, the arrow's balance uncertain after being wrenched out of a body.

"You were chosen, Raul, but not by fate or destiny. By her." Alder pointed the sword at Prisca. "You were chosen to help her recapture what she lost, so that she could take the reins again. People need signs and symbols, whether they're true or not. Everything you've done here, Raul, has been a lie."

"No." Raul shook his head firmly. "I am the one. The lost prince. We saw the queen, she said..."

"So Junia is still alive. That is interesting. Probably the most interesting thing to come out of this night. Make a note, Tur, we'll deal with that later. But the thing is, Raul, queens lie as well as anyone. Better, even. It's part of their job."

"She wouldn't lie to her own grandson."

"Maybe not, but that's not who you are. Can you tell when something is a lie, Raul? I imagine you've been surrounded by them for so long, you'd never know the difference."

The boy's mouth hung open.

"Queen Junia," he whispered. "She told me to be careful who I trust."

Alder laughed. These people were perfectly ridiculous.

"What wonderful irony," he said.

———————————————— • ————————————————

When he was young, Raul had found a sheep's skull in a field, a remnant from old magic buried decades before. He'd strained to pick it up, it had been so full of dirt.

369

That was how his head felt now: a dead weight full of dirt.

He dragged his gaze up to look at Prisca.

"Is it true?" he asked.

"Of course not," she snapped, but the brittleness of her tone made Raul squirm.

He looked at Valens.

"Is it true?"

Valens looked away, swallowed, clutched his bloody stump and the belt he'd tied around it.

"I'm still...ah, fuck."

Valens grimaced, shook, tried to pull the belt tighter. Blood-slicked fingers slipped across leather.

"I'm still your fucking da," he hissed through clenched teeth. "I still love you. It's just..."

The words faded to a rasp, a ragged exhalation from a face crumpled by pain.

"You lied to me," Raul said.

The thoughts tumbled through his mind, too fast for him to process, that dead weight of dirt turning into a landslide that threatened to carry his whole heart away.

"You told me I could trust you, that you would always do right by me. You told me to believe in this." He stared at Valens, his trembling face pale, eyes downcast, unable to deny any of it. "You lied to me."

Raul stepped out from under Alder's arm and the count didn't try to stop him.

"You lied to me." He looked Prisca right in the eye and he knew that he was right. "You told me that I was special, that I had a destiny. That I was meant to save the kingdom."

FORGED FOR DESTINY

"I did what I had to." She lowered the bow, let the string slacken. "For Estis. For you. For all of us."

Raul clutched his upper arm, where the birthmark was hidden. Except it wasn't a birthmark. The lie had lasted a lifetime.

"I trusted you, loved you, and the whole time you were manipulating me, preparing me, turning me into someone who wasn't real. All this..." He waved his arms wide. There was blood on his hands, blood on his tunic, blood on the floor. "You had me killing people, burning down the city, leading our friends to their deaths, all based on a lie!"

"I did—"

"Shut up, Prisca," Valens growled.

Raul's arms hung limp. He had to get out of there, away from these people, from the lie that they had loved him. From the lie that was his whole life.

His feet were heavy, his legs numb, but he dragged himself forward, one footstep after the next, barely aware of anything but that movement. The world faded. People kept talking, but he didn't hear them. He shuffled down the throne room, past Prisca and Valens and all the guards, past Appia's corpse in the doorway, a string doll soaking in the blood around her. No one in the world cared enough to stop him. He stood at the top of the stairs and stared out a window. The Red Eye stared back.

Chapter Thirty
The Pain of Living

The mourning ring was dark against the pale skin of Valens's finger. A black band, smooth and featureless. A carrier of memories. A carrier of loss. On instinct, he tried to flex that finger, tried to rub his thumb against the ring, like he so often did. Nothing. The hand lay, unmoving, in a spatter of blood three long strides away from him. A part of him and yet not part of him. Almost in reach, yet as far away as anything could ever be.

How could he do that, losing the ring? It had been with him ever since the moment it was made, the jet carver chanting Fabia's name with every stroke of his tools, Valens watching in grim silence, swearing to himself that he would never let this token of her go. And now he had lost it, just as he had failed in the plan she had died for. It was out of his hands.

That last phrase drew a choked sound from him, half laugh, half sob, cut off by the pain as he moved his arm. He had seen wounds like this before, scores of them, hundreds of them, so many he couldn't count. The lost limbs of friends and enemies,

FORGED FOR DESTINY

of comrades and strangers. The wounds of survivors and those choking on their last blood-specked gasp of breath. He'd bound them with tourniquets, he'd wrapped them in scraps of cloth, he'd been the man to cut away the mangled part in desperate hope of saving a life, or to slide a merciful knife into a lost cause. He'd seen this so often in so many forms that it should have been nothing to him, yet it seemed strange once more.

The stump was an obscene red, raw as beef fresh from the butcher's block, bone protruding pale from the middle of the stump, a clean, flat end where it had snapped under the impact of the blade. A good cut. That was something. That increased the chance that he would live and that the wound would heal clean. No need for mercy's blade here, as long as he saw a physician soon. But what were the chances of that?

He looked around. The room was full of faces, more every moment, none of them friendly. The count and his chamberlain were directing their people, messengers running this way and that, guards forming around Alder in a tight knot. More stood watch over Valens, as if he could fight back now. He considered his prospects and that strange choking noise burst out of him. One way or another, this ended in death, but he had never been one to give in. Fabia wouldn't have stood for that. He shivered, tried to tighten the belt around the stump.

"Here." Prisca squatted at his side, holding out a bowstring. "That needs a better ligature."

He stared at her. She had brought them to this. She had planned everything they did to Raul, every lie they told. She was the reason Valens's son hated him. The reason he had lost the ring he promised never to let go.

"Get away from me," Valens said, cold and slow.

"Don't be ridiculous. You need to—"

"Get away from me or, by Yorl, I will use my last hand to beat you dead."

His pulse was rising, his breath coming faster. She stood, stepped back, the bowstring hanging from her hand.

"We can talk properly once you've calmed down."

How many times had he heard those words from her? Almost as many times as she'd got her way.

Somewhere in the back of his mind, he had been aware of Count Alder and his captains talking. Some corner of their conversation caught his attention and he leaned forward. They were talking about Raul.

"...only apologise, my lord, but the boy has run."

"Then he's smarter than he looks." Alder smiled. It was a soldier's smile, one that had seen things. "How did he get away?"

"He attacked my men on the stairs, caught them by surprise before they'd bound him, then leapt out a window above the stables. From there, we're not sure. I'll gather more men and send them to search."

"Don't waste your time. The boy doesn't matter, any more than the sword he held. He's a broken tool. We have the woman who wielded him. Send your men into the city instead. Tell them that there's to be no hesitation, no half-measures. Unless we want Pavuno to go up in flames, we must quench every spark of dissent tonight."

"Yes, my lord." A captain bowed, then strode away.

Another captain stepped up to take his place, watched with eagle eyes by both Valens and Alder's chosen guards.

FORGED FOR DESTINY

"Well?" Alder asked.

"Fifteen came in, my lord, as near as we can tell. Only the boy is still at large."

"How many prisoners?"

"Four, but three are badly hurt. At least two are going to die." The captain looked at Valens, who stared straight back. "Him too, perhaps."

"Wake my physician, have her tend to this one." Alder didn't look at Valens, just waved in his direction. "I want to keep the leaders for questioning."

"We have wounded of our own, my lord."

"And others who know how to tend wounds. The physician will help once she's done here."

"Our warriors were injured fighting for you, my lord."

"And if we don't deal with this smartly, far more of ours will suffer. Perhaps our whole country, if the North March rises again. The terrible arithmetic of war is not on our warriors' side tonight."

"My lord." The captain bowed and hurried away.

The chamberlain, hovering at his lord's elbow, watched Prisca with narrowed eyes.

"My lord, surely we should restrain her." The chamberlain's skeletal fingers twisted around each other. "Just in case."

"She's in no position to weave magic, Tur," Alder said. "Stop fussing and go check on my household."

"My lord." The man bowed his head and scurried away, with one last suspicious backward glance.

Valens looked at his stump, that twitching red piece of meat, that raw circle of pain. He could untie the belt, let the blood flow, let himself die. That might be better for all of them, though part of him screamed at the rest to live. Better for the rebellion. Better for the nation.

Better for Raul.

He picked at the knot of the belt, fingers sliding over leather made slippery with blood.

"Stop that," Prisca hissed, crouching again, leaning in.

"What's the point? They'll kill us anyway."

"No they won't. I've seen the omens."

"Omens?" Valens tried to spit at her but his mouth was dry. "Your omens are lies."

"Don't get precious with me. You know full well that I've used the truth to find our path as often as I've lied to shape it. We will live through this."

"Oh, *we* will, will we? What about Appia? What about the rest?"

"I concede, things have not gone according to plan, but as long as we live, there is hope."

"Fuck hope."

"Listen, Alder has two choices. If he executes us, then there is public spectacle, something to antagonise people, adding to the tally of resentments. But if he keeps the leaders of a rebellion alive, in his cells, then others will lay schemes to seek our guidance and eventually to liberate us. The fire we kindled tonight will burn on."

He stared at her. How could she think like this when the battle was lost and everything precious with it? How could she still calculate so calmly?

"Now," she said, holding up the bowstring, "will you allow me to tie a proper ligature?"

FORGED FOR DESTINY

There was commotion from the direction of the stairs, voices rising. The guards raised their weapons but the woman who came in wasn't another rebel. She was dressed in a nightshirt, her red hair scraped back in a knot, and she carried a basket full of jars and instruments.

"Where is this first patient?" she asked, then made a small bow, as if it were an afterthought. "My lord."

"Here." Alder finally turned to Valens and Prisca. "The one missing his hand."

The physician strode over and set her basket down. Prisca stepped aside. The physician took a firm hold of Valens's arm and looked closer.

Valens hesitated. His thoughts were spinning. Did he want to live or to die? What was he fighting for? Should he break free? Should he draw a knife and take one last enemy down?

One of the guards, crouching at his other side, settled the issue by kicking away the knife that lay beside him, fallen when he took off his belt.

The doctor tutted, turned to one of the guards.

"Fetch the low folding bench from my chamber. I need a proper surface to work on."

She laid a row of knives out behind her, then unrolled a cloth holding needles. She opened a clay jar and maggots wriggled inside. Those things reassured Valens. The woman knew her work. If he did die, it wouldn't be from a long fever or a rotting wound.

"Well, Minister Servita." Alder had sheathed his sabre and stood with a hand resting on its pommel. "This was quite a scheme. I admire its ingenuity."

377

"I don't know what you mean, my lord." Prisca stood as proud as Valens had ever seen her, head held high. "I simply followed the omens."

"If that were so, then I would have even more reason to execute you, to cut off this taste of the dark power that was Estis. But I don't think that will be necessary, do you? This has more of the human about it than the predestined."

"Do as you desire, my lord. I am ready to face the consequences."

Valens's heart beat faster. Was he ready to face those consequences? He had never been afraid before, but he had never stared at his own hand from a stone's throw away.

"Where's that damn bench?" the physician snapped. "The blood loss is telling. I need to operate before he deteriorates."

"Valens won't die," Prisca said. "And you won't kill us, my lord. You don't want martyrs, or to discard the insights we might provide."

"Then what will I do?" Alder asked, one eyebrow raised. In the cold of his heart, Valens had a terrible realisation that this man was as deadly with his wits as his words. He had outfought Valens and Raul. Had he outthought Prisca too, and she didn't know it yet?

"You will keep us prisoner and interrogate us. That will need to be a careful procedure: an old woman and an amputee might not survive a torturer's more rigorous arts. Still, our captivity will set an example to those considering resistance, a message that no one can escape your grip."

"Yes, that sounds smart." Alder nodded. "The sort of smart I might expect from a royal minister. I could tie myself in

FORGED FOR DESTINY

knots trying to decide whether it's the sort of smart I should follow, or the sort meant to bluff me into a mistake.

"Fortunately, I've already made up my mind. You will be imprisoned and you will be questioned, but there will be no show trial, no grand statement condemning your attempt to seize power. Some of your comrades will hang for rioting and looting or other mundane crimes, while you will quietly disappear. There will be no dramatic moment in which rebellion was crushed, no story to rally future revolts. No one will know whether you two are alive or dead, whether you are still in the country, sent to slave in the salt marshes of Dunholm, or staked out to feed the wolves on the mountainside. Perhaps a whisper will even emerge that you chose to collaborate, and when people speak your names, it will leave a sour taste in their mouths.

"I'm not going to stamp out your rebellion, Minister Servita, because stamping scatters sparks. I'm going to smother it."

"The boy escaped." Prisca's tone was sharp, the words abruptly blurted out.

"He did, didn't he? And any tale he tells now will include what a fraud you were. Even if he changes his mind later, the waters will be muddied, doubts spread. Did you foresee that, diviner?"

Valens looked at Alder, so relaxed, so casual, though he'd fought for his life only minutes before. Then he looked at Prisca, her face rigid, hands clenched on her belt. He didn't know if the cold he felt came from his wounds or from that expression.

Alder picked up Valens's hand, the one lying on the ground,

the one with the ring. The count turned it over idly, caught Valens's eye, and shook his head. Valens tried to stand up, to protest, but the hands of guards slammed down on his shoulders, and others grabbed his arms, pinning him in place. They thrust a wooden dowel between his teeth, reducing his bellows of rage to futile grunts. Tears ran down his cheeks as the ring disappeared from view.

A servant set a low bench across Valens's legs, the physician picked up her knives, and the real pain began. The pain of living.

Chapter Thirty-One
Choices

The street was quiet, like it had been since dawn broke. From the middle gallery of the theatre, looking out through a window above their main doors, Yasmi saw a dog chase a rat through the mud, and behind it, a pair of pigs snuffling for abandoned food. No people. Mercifully, no bodies. This time, the trouble hadn't touched the players. The sounds of fighting had stayed as distant as the terrible silence that followed.

A swift flew past, a fleeting moment of beauty, of graceful manoeuvre against a grey sky. Yasmi smiled, imagined the movements she would need to imitate that flight, to evoke the bird's presence onstage. Then it let out a piercing shriek and she shook her head, tapped the wood of the wall to ward off bad luck. There were better birds to be.

Her father emerged from the staircase, wrapped in one of his old gowns and a cloak. He yawned and stretched.

"Have you been here all night, my queen of the boards?" he asked.

"I wanted to make sure that we were safe, that no one was coming to cause trouble."

"Such a good girl." He patted her on the head and Yasmi smiled. "But are you sure you weren't looking out for a certain young scenery painter, and whether he might make it back to us alive? Might even return in triumph, the hero of the hour?"

" 'Return with blood on your blade or none in your veins,' " Yasmi recited.

"Ah, *The Glory of Golenat*, one of Tenebrial's middling pieces, but the speeches were good." Efron patted her on the shoulder. "Go rest, ready for tonight's performance. I'll keep watch for a while, make sure no mob is coming to burn down our palace of dreams."

"Thank you, Father."

Efron turned to look out the window, lips twitching as he went over his lines. Yasmi waited for a moment but there was nothing more from him: no words of comfort, no arm around her. Shoulders slumped, she walked away.

Most of the players were sleeping, and those awake were keeping themselves quiet, an unusual state for such boisterous folk. Boards creaked beneath Yasmi's feet as she made her way past the stage, down a corridor, to her room. One of her shutters was creaking too, and she strode straight over to shut it, thinking that she must have set the latch poorly for the wind to blow it open. Then a dark shape in the mirror caught her attention and she spun around, hand on her wolf mask, mouth open wide and ready to raise the alarm.

The shape was Raul. Huddled and silent, folded up smaller than she thought he could be, crammed into the gap between

FORGED FOR DESTINY

her bed and the back of the door. She pushed the door slowly to, revealing the bruised side of his face, the bloodstained leather of his clothes, the rag he was clutching to one arm. She slid the latch into place. She wanted to wrap her arms around him, to reassure him that everything was going to be all right, but he looked so like an injured animal, she feared he might flee from her touch. Instead, she crouched and slowly reached out a hand, until it rested on his knee.

"What happened?"

"I was meant to be the hero," he whispered. "I was meant to save everyone. Instead..."

He told her the whole story in broken, halting sentences, as far from the flowing beauty of a playwright's art as words could be, yet more moving than anything she had ever uttered onstage. Those words drew her in, and by the end the two of them were sobbing together, their backs against the door, her arm around him, wrapping him tight, protecting him from the world.

"It's not your fault," she said. "It's not your fault."

Those same words, over and over, but they didn't change anything. And through it all, dreadful as the thought was, she found herself grateful that her own people hadn't been drawn into this; that in spite of everything, she and hers remained safe. It was the thought of a monster, and perhaps she had played so many of them that she had become one, but it was at least an honest thought.

"What will you do now?" she asked as she helped him wash and bind the cut on his forearm.

"If I'm not really the hero, then I can't beat them," he said. "I'll have to run. Find somewhere to hide. I can't stay here and I can't go back to the Vales. They might hurt people there to find me." He leaned his head against her shoulder. "I wish I'd run away with you, like you asked, but I thought that my parents... No, not my parents."

She watched his heart breaking right in front of her. He sounded nothing like the boy she knew, his whole demeanour full of bitterness and anger. She couldn't stand to hear him like that.

"Whatever else they did, they loved you."

"It was a lie."

"No, it wasn't. I saw you break dishes, spoil beer, say stupid things, and it didn't matter what you did, they were still proud of you. Valens is no actor, but the way he looked at you, the way he talked to you, the way he encouraged you, it was the most real, touching thing I've ever seen. Even if last night took everything else from you, don't let it take that."

It was ridiculous, when the rest of his world had fallen apart and he sat there covered in blood and snot, but saying those words made her jealous. Efron's attention was reserved for the stage so that was where she went to earn his praise. Nothing like that could be said about Valens.

"You weren't there." Raul shook his head. "You didn't see, didn't hear..." He shuddered. "It doesn't matter. We lost. The stories were lies, the heroes aren't real. All that leaves is giving up."

Yasmi brushed the hair back from his forehead, specks of dried blood crumbling between her fingers. She felt as though she was being torn in half. A few days ago, all that she had wanted was for him to give up on his dreams of danger, to run

FORGED FOR DESTINY

away with her. But she hadn't wanted the broken boy who was left when his certainties fell away. Her Raul wouldn't give up and she wanted her Raul back.

"No," she said. "There are other ways. Just because you lost once doesn't mean the whole world falls apart."

"You don't understand!" Tears welled in his eyes. "There was a prophecy I was going to fulfil. If that's not true, then what am I?"

"Don't tell me what I don't understand." She slapped him across the back of his head and got to her feet. He stared at her like a puppy whose stick had been snatched away. "So you were lied to. It happens. That's not an excuse to abandon everything like a sulky child."

"If there's no prophecies, then there's no chosen one to lead us. Not me and not anybody else."

Yasmi crossed her arms to keep them from flailing about. "*Good.* People shouldn't be chosen by prophecy. That's the sort of nonsense that happens when Tenebrial gets too lazy to write his characters real motives. If this country's going to throw out the invaders, then it will be because someone chooses to lead, because they've got the courage to pick that path and take responsibility for themselves."

"Then how will we know that we're going to win?"

"You won't!" She flung her hands in the air. "Do you think, when I get out there in front of the crowd, that I know they're going to love me? Of course not. I hope they will, but I accept the uncertainty of the world and work for what I want. That's how you get anything worthwhile."

"I'm not like you." He jerked to his feet, his face screwed

up in frustration. "I can't just go out there and say, 'Let's give this a go, it doesn't matter if we fail.'"

"You think it doesn't matter? You think it doesn't break my heart when the crowd jeers? I might not be fighting for your noble cause, but what I do *means* something."

"I didn't mean—"

"No, I'm sure you didn't." She turned away from him, but there he was, bruises and all, staring back at her from the mirror, as upset at hurting her as he had been about anything else. The boy had no middle ground. "To do anything worthwhile in life, you have to take a risk. No amount of prophecy can protect you from that."

There was a knock on the door.

"Yasmi?" Efron's muffled voice said. "Are you all right in there? Is someone with you?"

"I'm practising accents," she called back.

"Very good. I've often said that your voice work could do with improving."

His footsteps faded down the corridor.

Yasmi hung her head. She heard sniffling from behind her, then Raul's hand came to rest softly on her shoulder.

"Are you all right?" he asked.

"Me? You, right now, are asking *me* if I'm all right?"

"Yes. Sorry. I feel like I've upset you."

She laughed. It was almost a sob.

"You read a lot of books. Is there a word for when someone says a thing that is at once perfectly right and perfectly wrong?"

He scratched his head, then smiled sheepishly. "You're going to tell me that it's 'Raul,' aren't you?"

FORGED FOR DESTINY

"How did you guess?" She turned to look at him. He looked away.

"Maybe you're right," he said. "Maybe what Estis needs is for someone to step up and choose to lead. But that someone isn't me."

"Why not?"

"Because I'm not the person they told me I was. I'm not the hero and the leader."

"Prisca got a lot of things wrong, but casting you in that role, it was one thing she got right. You fit it perfectly."

"I don't have what it takes."

"Of course you do. You're strong and skilled, kind and courageous. When you talk, people want to listen. You're even passably smart, when you remember to use your mind. More important than any of that, when you see people in trouble, your first instinct is to help them.

"I've played pretend princes, lords, and kings, I've seen what leads to triumph or to tragedy. Trust me, you're what a real leader should be."

"Surely there are other people like that?" he said. "Why does it have to be me?"

She closed her eyes, took a deep breath. She'd spent her life working with words. She could wind them together to tell the tale she needed, to spin a story the audience would believe. One day, she was going to be the one to write their plays, no matter what Tenebrial said, and audiences would go wild for them. But sometimes, a story wasn't enough. Sometimes you needed the truth.

"Every day, I go out there, and I act," she said. "I give the crowd the greatest performance they've ever seen. It's a kind of magic, using my passion to summon their praise, to hear the roar of applause, to have people come to me afterward and tell me how wonderful I was. Because when I hear that, it fills something in here." She tapped her chest. "For a moment, I almost feel whole."

He looked at her, confused but not interrupting, trusting that what she said was worth hearing. He wasn't going to judge her. She didn't need to prove herself.

"That's how I feel when you talk to me," she said. "Even when I've got my lines muddled or my costume's a mess, or when I'm obsessing over a stupid play while you're trying to save the world. You talk, and I feel like I matter. I feel like I'm someone worthwhile.

"I've seen it in other people's eyes too. If you tell them that they can change the world, then they'll believe you."

She squeezed his hand, and he almost smiled.

"I'm not saying that you have to do it," she said. "I'm saying that you can."

He walked over to the window and peered through the gap between the shutters. Somewhere out there, reprisals would be taking place. The governor's forces gathering the beaten rebels, building scaffolds, fetching their whips. The fist of the conquerors would squeeze Pavuno harder than it had done in a generation.

"It's too much," he said, pressing a hand against his back. "I can't do it alone."

Yasmi looked at him, this boy she had known her whole life and yet somehow not known at all; who she had spent a

FORGED FOR DESTINY

few days with each year yet who she felt closer to than half the troupe she lived with. If she'd been in his place, no words could have kept her from fleeing, but here he was, almost ready to take on the world. Almost the man she needed him to be again.

As her hands rested on the weirdwood masks around her waist, Yasmi realized she had never done anything real. When she was hurt, the wounds recovered between scenes. When she risked her life, it was in the certainty that she would rise again for the next performance. She could defy any woman or man as long as someone had given her the speech, as long as the consequences ended when the players took their bow. The masks were for hiding from the world, not fighting for it. But how could she ask Raul to make a choice that she wouldn't make herself?

Her fingers closed around the mask of the wolf. The fiercest. The boldest. The most agile.

"You won't be alone," she said. An audience of one, that would be enough, if the one truly believed in her.

"Really?" He gave her that smile, the one that was better than all the applause in the world.

"Really."

He started pacing back and forth. The room was so small, he had to turn back every three paces, and the absurdity of it made Yasmi want to laugh out loud, but the intensity of his movements held her back. She sat quietly on the bed, the wolf in her lap, watching him.

"I can't deal with the count now," he said. "And we can't free the city, the two of us. We'll have to find others, people who still believe." He frowned. "Except they won't believe, once they hear the truth."

"Then don't tell them the truth."

"I can't do that."

"Why not? You're still the hero, even if you're not the one they were expecting."

He shook his head. "Never mind that now. What matters is saving what we still have. I need to rescue Prisca and Valens."

She gaped at him. How was he still like this, smart one moment and utterly naive the next?

"You can't be serious."

"Of course I am. Prisca's the smartest person I know and she's got contacts all over the country. Valens can teach people how to fight. If we don't have prophecy on our side, then we need those skills instead."

"They're locked up in the palace."

"I didn't say it was going to be easy."

"They betrayed you!"

"But they're my parents." He clutched a hand to his chest, and there was such a wounded look in his eyes, it chased away all the arguments she had been mustering, all the reasons why he had to let them go. "It doesn't make any sense to me either, the way I'm feeling right now. I don't understand how they could treat me like they did. But none of that changes this." His hand became a fist, slamming against the cage that played prison to his heart. "Maybe they deserve to rot in a cell, or be strung up in the square, but I can't do that to them."

"You're going to get yourself killed." Though her head told her it was true, her heart didn't believe it. "You're going to get us both killed."

"You told me that life is about choices. This is my choice."

FORGED FOR DESTINY

"And it seems I've made mine." She flung open a chest in the corner of the room, started tossing clothes onto the bed. "If we're going to play at heroes, I need to find the perfect costume. And perhaps we should consider expanding our cast..."

Chapter Thirty-Two
Stubborn as a Goat

Valens crouched in the corner of the cell, staring at the bandaged stump where his hand had been. The wall was hard against his back, the stones cold and wet. They'd been wet before the rain had started falling outside the tiny, barred window. They were probably wet even in the smothering height of summer. That was the way cells went. Damp, with rats, but at least the rats would wait until he was nearly dead before they bothered him. If the throbbing in his stump kept growing, they might not have to wait long.

He brought his hand around, the one he still had. His off hand. His clumsy hand, no good for fine work or details. He tried to move it through the space where the other hand should be, to prove that the itching he felt there was an illusion, but he couldn't bring himself to do it. His fingers stopped at some invisible barrier. Only a ferocious will kept them from trembling.

This was stupid. It was a piece of empty air. He'd met plenty of veterans missing a hand or a foot, half a leg, a whole arm. Women and men with one eye, a blunted nose, a mass of scars where an ear should be. This was what war did.

But not to him. Never to him.

He pressed his thumb against his mourning ring, felt the cold circle of jet. Except that the ring wasn't there, and neither was his thumb.

"I failed," Prisca said, her voice flat as slate, from the far side of the cell.

"You think?" Valens hissed through gritted teeth, still trying to force his hand through that space.

"I thought that I had time, that I could finish our endeavour while my mind was sharp. I thought that I still grasped all the threads. But I must be fading. My plans were flawless once, and now—"

"Oh, shut up."

The words escaped him; he was too exhausted to hold them back. Prisca was Prisca. She was smarter, more learned, more important than he was, but there were no ministers in prison cells, no lords and leaders, no warriors anymore. No damn heroes.

"Excuse me?"

"Stop your whining. You got sloppy and we wound up here."

"You don't understand. The plan could have worked. It should have worked! But the years crept by, and my mind started to falter, and I didn't even see it."

"Old age, that's your excuse?" He snorted.

She shook her head. There was a weariness in her face, a

sadness like an old warrior remembering lost friends. For a long moment, it seemed like she had listened, like she would give him the silence he wanted. Then her chest heaved as if she was dragging a weight out of the deeps and words reluctantly emerged.

"Not age. Divination." She tapped the side of her head. "There's a reason why the stories show diviners as crazy old ladies living in the hills, spouting riddles and nonsense. Magic devours the mind, Valens. It hollows you out from the inside. The harder you push, the sooner it does its work. I tried to hold back, used bluff and cold reading and simple deduction when I could. But in the end, we needed the magic, and now—"

"You think I give a shit?" He waved his bloodied, bandaged stump. "Old age or magic or stupidity, it's still on you. I sacrificed eighteen years of my life and the trust of my son to your grand vision."

"And I sacrificed my mind, everything I am, everything I think. I can't trust my thoughts anymore. Do you have any idea how that feels?"

"Do you think I care?"

She stared at him, her mouth hanging open, and for that moment, he wondered if she really had lost her mind and with it her precious self-control. But it was another lie. That familiar expression returned, the hooded gaze that hid constant calculation.

"There is still a chance to save our people," she said. "Still a chance to be a hero."

"A hero." Valens shook his head. "There are no heroes, just stories to trick fools with. You've shown me that."

"Don't pretend you're giving up the fight. You don't know how. The whole time we've been away, you've been raging inside, burning for your chance to strike back. Now they took your hand too, and you're going to let them get away with it? You can lie to yourself, Valens, but you can't deceive me."

"Let them get away with it?" He laughed bitterly. "There is no 'them.' You're the one who took those years from me, took the only thing I had left to care about and made me turn him into a pawn of your politics."

"I didn't make you do anything. You had choices."

"I had orders, and you had the words that made them sound right. Words like hooks in my brain, dragging me back if I stepped off your path. Remember Raul's fifth birthday? I was going to run away with him, take him somewhere he'd really be safe. You talked me out of it. No more. If we live to leave this cell, I'm getting as far from you and your damn plans as I can."

"Fine, have another of your petulant sulks," Prisca snapped. "You'll get over it."

"No." He shook his head. "Not this time."

He sank back against the wall. The stone was hard and cold, but so was Prisca Servita. At least the stone didn't treat him like a fool.

Footsteps echoed down the corridor outside the cell. Chains rattled. The light of moving torches added to the brand burning in a wall brazier.

The warriors who appeared were big, solid, dressed in chainmail under the count's colours. Only their captain had the bearing of a veteran, that way of holding herself ready in every moment. Not paranoia. Preparedness. The others were too young to have been part of the invasion and the long grind that preceded it. They put more effort into their scowls, and the one with the manacles made an extra effort to shake them as he approached the bars.

"You." The captain pointed at Prisca. "Back against the wall, under the window. You." Pointing at Valens this time. "Come here."

In a play, this would be the moment where the hero showed his character, spitting words of defiance despite his helplessness. Efron, his hand wrapped in a paint-stained rag, would have stood slowly, his expression shifting through pain to courageous determination. He would have given a speech that stirred the hearts of the audience, before the guards dragged him off for a dramatic confrontation with the villain.

Heroes only lived through plays because the writers wanted them to. Real warriors had to act smarter. Valens stood, paused for a moment as the sudden shift made his head spin, and walked over.

"He's not the one you should talk to," Prisca said. "Take me."

"When Count Alder wants you, he'll send for you."

"I understand that—"

"Shut up and sit down." The captain glared at Prisca. Valens half expected her to keep arguing, trying to take control through the power of her words, but after a moment, she sat stiffly back down.

With a key as thick as her finger, the captain unlocked the cell. The door squealed as its rusted hinges were dragged

FORGED FOR DESTINY

open. Nobody had been taking care of this place. Nobody had needed to. There hadn't been prisoners worthy of the palace cells in a generation.

Valens held out his hands. Hand. The warrior with the chains closed a shackle around one of his wrists, then looked uncertainly at the stump.

"This isn't going to work," he said.

Valens and the captain exchanged a weary look. He'd had to supervise the young and the stupid himself, back in the day. It was a bad sign for their rebellion that their opponents had put the veteran in charge of the fool and not the other way around.

Except that the rebellion was dead already. Eighteen years of work, gone in a single night. That was a different sort of pain from his stump. Less immediate, just as overwhelming.

"Look at him," the captain said. "He's not going anywhere."

Valens imagined what she saw. A cripple, pale and sweaty, wondering whether the physician had closed the wound cleanly, whether he felt dizzy from blood loss or because a fever was setting in. Failing to hide the trembling of his remaining hand as the weight of a few links of chain dragged at it.

"The chamberlain said—"

"Tur's a twitchy little weasel who thinks half the North March is trying to cast a curse on him. Do you really think this one's going to hit you with the evil eye?"

The younger warrior laughed, hid his nerves almost as well as Valens hid his shaking. "Not likely."

"Well then." The captain locked the cell door, took the end

of the chain, and led Valens up the corridor, dragging him by his one manacled hand. "Come on. The count's waiting."

Why were young warriors always so damn eager? They marched along beside Valens like they were leading a captured general off the field, not some broken remnant of a lost war. At least Raul's puppy-dog enthusiasm came with a smile, not this absurd seriousness. They marched up stairways and along corridors, past servants whose fingers made signs against misfortune as he passed. Some of them were mopping up blood. Soon, there would be no trace left of how close the invaders had come to seizing their prize and how badly they had failed.

The guards brought him back to the throne room. The shutters were open, letting in fresh air and daylight, the songs of birds and the bustle of the city. There was a smell of smoke, but that didn't mean anything. There were thousands of hearth fires in Pavuno. On a windless day, the air of a city was as thick as cloud on a mountainside.

An anvil had been placed in the middle of the room. The guards tied the chains around it, turning them so many times that there was no give left and Valens couldn't stand straight. Given a choice between stooping and kneeling, he manoeuvred himself awkwardly until he could squat, only now realising that he needed his hand for things as simple as sitting down. The anvil was cold and hard against his back.

Voices approached from a doorway close to the throne. Count Alder strode in, followed by his chamberlain, two servants, three guards.

"...you already, Tur, we don't need all these warriors here anymore," the count was saying. "The trouble is out there, in the city, and if we don't stifle it quickly, then we'll be fighting fires for weeks."

"My lord, I really must ask you to reconsider," Tur said. "What if the rebels return?"

"Is that what you're planning?" Alder looked at Valens, and he looked as if he was about to burst out laughing. "Are you waiting for a chance to leap up and finish me off?"

Valens stared at him. He wasn't going to rise to the bait and become this man's entertainment.

"I'll be fine," Alder said. "Leave my usual guards. The rest go."

"Not even—"

"Now, Tur, or I'll haul their diviner out of the cells and have her curse you."

The count waved a hand, fingers wiggling, and Tur jerked back.

"Very good, my lord." He hurried away.

Alder stepped closer to Valens, looked down at him, lowered his voice like they were sharing a confidence.

"Tur's actually very good at his job," Alder said. "Just a little fussy. I expect you know the type?"

Valens kept staring, saying nothing, giving nothing.

"Maybe you don't." Alder took a step back. "I've been wondering about that. There was no Valens among the earls and ministers when Estis fell. You could have changed your name, of course, but if Prisca didn't feel the need, then why would you? And if you weren't a nobleman, then you wouldn't have had all these servants and advisors, wouldn't have dealt with the Turs of this world. At least, not in the way that I have."

Andrew Knighton

Alder squatted just out of Valens's reach. One hand rested on a long fighting knife, the other on the hilt of his sabre. He'd done away with his robes, but still wore the chainmail that had been under them.

That armour. He'd been ready for them. A spy inside their camp, or precautions after the trouble Prisca stirred up? The plan had been broken from the start.

"You were a warrior," Alder said, watching him with the steady, calculating gaze of a commander. "Old enough to have been someone who mattered in the war. A trusted guard, perhaps, or commander of a company."

Valens said nothing. Alder watched him, reading signs that Valens didn't know he'd shown.

"Not command, then. A veteran, someone the others followed. Someone they trusted."

Valens tried not to wince, but he remembered the faces of the warriors he'd left behind, the ones who held the line so that he and Fabia could get away. He'd told them he would be back. He hadn't told them that he meant in eighteen years. A lie in all but name.

"You didn't fight for yourself, did you? Not to preserve your rank and status. You fought out of duty." Alder nodded. "That's noble. I admire that."

Still Valens said nothing. He wasn't going to be tricked into something by this pretty man with his shiny armour and his sharply honed words. He'd had enough of smart people. Smart people were why he couldn't scratch the itch in his sword hand.

"I've seen war too, Valens," Alder said, patting his sabre.

400

FORGED FOR DESTINY

"I've led charges and retreats, had horses cut down from under me, felt the shudder as my lance met flesh. Felt the sting of a surgeon's needle too."

This pompous prick thought that he was a real warrior, like Fabia had been. Valens tried to touch the mourning ring with a thumb that wasn't there, and his whole body clenched, straining to move the lost muscle. This man might know how to wield a sword but he didn't know what being a real warrior meant.

"You've seen war, have you?" Valens growled. "You've gone hungry when the rations went short? You've slept huddled in a tree's roots in midwinter? You've dug the shit pits for an army camp?" He shook his head. "You don't know war and you don't know me."

He waited for the slap, for the angry words. Instead, Alder got up, walked over to the throne, picked up a jug sitting on the table next to it. He poured, not into the skull goblet that perched absurdly on the arm of the throne, but into a pair of clay cups. Then he returned and set one of the cups down in front of Valens. It held milk, good milk, creamy on the top. Valens's mouth was dry and the milk looked soothing, but he didn't touch it.

"You're right," Alder said. "You've been through more than I have, more than any man should. You deserve to be rewarded, not punished. Tell me about the rebel ringleaders, about where the books you stole are kept, and I'll make you comfortable. You'll finally get the retirement you deserve."

Valens snorted. "Why would I trust you?"

"Why not? If the worst happens, and I'm lying, then your life gets no worse, but at least you won't have to dig any more shit pits. And if I really am grateful, if I want to encourage others to cooperate, then you might find your feed bag more full than before."

"I'm not betraying anyone."

"That's fine." Alder took a drink from his cup, licked his lips. The milk looked awfully tempting. "Don't tell me about your people. They're probably all dead or fled. Tell me about the books instead. They can't matter to you, but they're very important to me. If I can get them back, and any other documents your group acquired, that will be enough."

Valens shook his head. They might have lost, but he wasn't going to let this man win.

"Don't tell me that this is about Minister Prisca Servita." Alder crouched again, so that they were level with each other, eye to eye. "She failed you, Valens, you and all the other good, loyal warriors you led here last night. She came up with some absurd scheme to get herself back into power and look how it ended." He waved his cup toward the side of the room, where Valens's own blood stained the floor. "Your chance to be heroes, and she failed you."

"There are no heroes." Chain links rattled as Valens reached for the cup. The milk was fresh, foamy at one edge. It smelled rich and refreshing.

"If there are no heroes, then why keep trying to act the part?" Alder asked. "The play is over. Leave that role behind and retire. It's not worth dying for a pile of books."

Valens drank the milk. Just a sip at first, then great gulps, washing away the bitter taste of the night before. He felt like he was rising from a stupor and his body cried out for more.

FORGED FOR DESTINY

The taste of it reminded him of their first year living in the Vales. He'd never been much good with goats, but he'd knuckled down and he'd learned how to milk the one they had. He'd taken a few harsh kicks from her but it had been needed for the baby. It had been worth it, to hear Raul's happy gurgle and to see him smile.

Valens had done one truly good thing in his whole life. Maybe he'd lost his chance now to see what sort of man Raul would become, but he wasn't going to do anything that might lead them to the boy.

He set the cup down on its side and rolled it away.

"There are no heroes," he said, "but there are stubborn old men, and I'm not saying another word."

Chapter Thirty-Three
No Time for Pity

Though he'd been overwhelmed from the start by the noise and bustle of the city, some part of Raul had assumed that it was like a wild animal, that it must have quiet moments when caution or exhaustion took hold. He had been wrong. Even in the aftermath of a failed revolt, with warriors standing baleful guard at every intersection, with blood in the mud and rebel bodies swinging in the wind off the mountains, still the city never fell silent. Wagon loads of hay, herds of sheep, carts of cabbages trundled to the market squares. Shopkeepers called out their wares and innkeepers set out their benches, ready for the lunchtime drinkers. A giggling child skipped past one of the guards, only to look back in fear when a spear butt shoved her on her way.

The city wasn't a wild beast. It was something far worse. Death had come, but the city, careless, lived on.

"Get your piece of a rioter's shirt," a man called out. "Torn from the body this past hour."

FORGED FOR DESTINY

Two women approached, peered at the scraps in his hand, their frayed edges crusted with blood. The women gave him a few coins, took their pieces of torn cloth. One scrap slipped from his fingers and blew off down the street and the man chased after it. The women watched and clutched their grisly trophies close.

Raul felt sick.

"Why?" he whispered, and his hands went white as they tightened on the rim of the basket he carried.

"There's strong magic in death," Yasmi replied. "Use the criminal to counter their crime. A hank of a murderer's hair to protect you from violence, a scrap of a rioter's shirt to stop a troubled friend running wild."

"But that's..." Disgusting? Impossible? How did the world know the difference between crimes against the oppressors and a hero trying to set his home free?

"People will cling to any hope. Don't stand there gaping, we don't want to be here when the guards come to stop him selling those souvenirs."

Raul followed Yasmi up the hill, trying to ignore the aching of his bruised back as they headed for the palace. Cold swept over him with the shadow of a passing patrol, the clop of their hooves a funereal beat, hunting-hound gazes gliding across the crowd. He looked at Yasmi for reassurance and what he got instead was distraction, as his brain once again struggled to match the person he knew with the woman he saw.

The sight of Yasmi shifting had always made Raul's eyes go wide with wonder, but today he had learned that her real gift was something more. As she changed into a bulky and faded dress, with pale powder in her hair and a few sketched wrinkles from Claudio's makeup brush, her whole demeanour had changed. She had become stoop-shouldered, hunched with age, her voice rattling like stones in her throat. She hobbled along the street, a wide-hipped woman so worn by the years that Raul felt uneasy whenever he saw a fragment of the real Yasmi, a glint in her eyes or a touch of softness in her voice, a familiar way of holding out her hand. Those gestures didn't belong to this body.

At the bottom of the last street up to the palace, Raul froze. The bodies hanging there, wrapped in chains and suspended from wooden poles, were all people he knew, people who had followed him into the palace the previous night. Closest was Appia, flies crawling across the blood clotted in her hair, across her blankly staring eyes and open mouth. Bile burned in the back of Raul's throat.

"Breathe," Yasmi whispered.

Raul stared. He remembered Appia's rough laughter, her calloused hands, her calculating gaze. He remembered her cutting down a warrior who would have killed him.

She was dead and it was all his fault.

No, it was Prisca and Valens's fault.

"Do you want to go back?" Yasmi asked.

Raul swallowed, turned away from the bodies. There were still other rebels out there: Drusil, Quintae, Pomponius, dozens more who had been part of the action outside the palace. Some of them must have hidden or fled, must have survived the bloody aftermath. He wished that they were all alive, though he knew that it couldn't be true. He might never

FORGED FOR DESTINY

know what had happened to people he called friends. For them, he couldn't even mourn.

"We have to make the deaths mean something," he said.

Raul couldn't read Yasmi's expression beneath her disguise, but she continued on her way and he followed.

The main entrance of the palace loomed over them, a dark mouth blocked by heavy gates, the teeth of a portcullis revealed by the rounded lip of the arch. Yasmi approached a wicket gate beside it, a smaller opening into the tower. Raul followed obediently, focusing on the instructions she'd given him: keep your gaze steady, keep your mouth shut, if you've got to fidget, then scratch something like a proper young man. Even with his hair roughly shorn off, his face dirtied, and a hood shadowing his features, he worried that someone might recognise him; at least with instructions to follow he felt a little less helpless. If he pretended hard enough, maybe he would look as innocent as he needed to.

Yasmi knocked and a shutter shot back, revealing a small, staring sliver of someone's face.

"What?" they snapped.

"I've brought the silks back," Yasmi croaked.

"What silks?"

"Shirts and sheets. Not yours, I'm sure."

"No one told me there were shirts and sheets coming."

"They would have been here two days ago, but someone set fire to the warehouse I buy my lime from, and then there was a shortage of pig fat, you've got to have the right fat for the soap or the silk gets this colour to it that's—"

"How do I know this is real? Those could be your clothes."

"Mine?" Yasmi cackled. Black varnish made half her teeth look like empty gaps. "You think I can afford these?" She took the lid off Raul's basket and pulled out a bright blue shirt. "Or that I'd dress my clumsy grandson in something this fancy?"

She shook the shirt at Raul, then flung it back in the basket.

"It's fine," she said. "We can come back another day. I'm sure that the count is in a good mood, he'll feel very forgiving about sleeping in dirty sheets."

"Wait, wait, wait." The shutter slammed closed, there was a clunk of bolts, and the wicket gate opened. "In you come."

They stepped from the shadow of the gatehouse into the gloom of its interior. Five guards stood around them, spears at the ready. Raul swallowed, held the basket against him with one hand while the other scratched the back of his neck. Behind them, the door thudded shut.

"Let me see in there." The guard who had answered the door took the lid off the basket and rummaged inside. "All right, it's just laundry."

"And now it's crumpled, you fool." Yasmi shook her head. "He's going to love that."

"You leave those here." The guard pointed at the knives hanging from their belts, simple tools for everyday tasks.

"You afraid I'm going to sneak to the kitchen and eat your dinner?" Yasmi cackled again.

One of the guards laughed. "Wouldn't do you any harm, Bottle."

"Shut up and take their knives. They can have them back on the way out."

Hands reached for Raul's belt, and a face he might have seen

FORGED FOR DESTINY

in the previous night's fighting peered under his hood. There was a thudding in his ears, like the hooves of a horse bearing down on him. *Thud-a-thud. Thud-a-thud. Thud-a-thud.*

"You're a filthy sod, aren't you?" The guard laughed. "Better wash yourself with those sheets next time."

"And waste good soap on him?" Yasmi snorted. "I'm poor enough already. Now come on, we need to get this delivered and get back to work."

From the gatehouse, they crossed a courtyard and passed through a narrow doorway next to the stables. The sights were familiar and yet strange, fragments from Raul's memories of the previous night, seen then only in shadow and torchlight and panic. The interior of the keep was more familiar, its passages of smoothly cut stone, but again, daylight through the windows played its tricks. That light should have made the world less menacing. Instead, it brought memories out more starkly.

"Down there, I think," Raul said quietly, nodding to a dark set of stairs. "We came up through deeper rooms, places for storage, but there were tunnels off them that could lead to the cells."

"If that's how you came in, will it be watched?" Yasmi asked.

"I think..." He ought to have an answer. After all, he was the one who had been down here. "I don't know. It depends on whether they've worked out how we got in."

Yasmi contemplated that for a moment, then looked around. These passages were quiet, the palace's servants busy elsewhere, or perhaps hiding in case more trouble came.

"Time to give up on tricks," she said. "No one's going to believe that a washerwoman got lost and wound up in the darkest depths of this place."

She straightened, cast off her shawl, and wriggled out of the battered dress, revealing her belt of masks and the short sword that had hung hidden by her voluminous skirts. Raul set down the basket, took off his hood, and accepted the sword. Without another word, they headed down the stairs, Raul taking the lead.

The stairwell was a windowless spiral, illuminated by a single burning torch halfway down. Raul lifted the torch out of its bracket and carried it with him: more light for them as they entered the dungeon, less light for anyone who came after.

The stairs ended in a windowless corridor, its walls streaked by the steady, eroding trickle of condensation. In one direction, the head of a well was just visible, a bucket and rope hanging from a wooden shaft. In the other direction, torchlight and voices seeped around a corner.

Yasmi unhooked the wolf mask from her belt. She stood looking at the back of it as if she was reading something there, perhaps the book of memories that every precious object bore.

"You don't have to do this," Raul whispered.

"Oh, but I do." The solemnity was chased from her face by that brightness she always held ready for the world. "My performances will be much more convincing once I've had a real adventure."

She pressed the mask against her face. Wood and flesh melded, shifted, became a furred head with a long snout. Grey cloth and blond hair became mottled fur and she fell forward, landing on four paws. She shook her beastly head, sniffed the air, then nodded and looked expectantly at Raul.

Gripping his sword tight, he strode down the corridor, the

FORGED FOR DESTINY

wolf at his side. Around the corner, they walked into a square room with a small table in the middle. Three warriors in blue sat on wooden stools. They looked up from their dice, one of them with an empty cup in his hand. Their faces, their uniforms, the torchlight, it was all too much like the previous night. Memories of Valens's hand and Appia's empty eyes froze Raul in place.

"Who the fuck are you?" One of them rose slowly, looking at Raul. Then his gaze fell to Yasmi. The wolf seemed to grow beneath his attention, from a rangy scavenger to a muscled and menacing beast. "Shit!"

The man turned, ran for a chain hanging from a hole in the ceiling. Yasmi leapt, caught him with his hand an inch from the chain, slammed him into the ground.

The others jumped up, overturning the table and their stools. Regret released its grasp on Raul. He lunged at one of the warriors, his sword an extension of his arm. The man had no armour and the sword slid into him, a shocking lack of resistance to the end of a life.

The other warrior drew a sabre, swung it in an overarm blow. The long, curved blade hit the ceiling, struck sparks as it grated across stone. Raul raised his torch in a parry and the sabre had lost too much momentum to cleave the wood. The weight of the dead guard's falling body dragged her off Raul's sword, and he whipped it around in a quick slash that opened the man's belly.

"Fuck," the dying man whispered, looking down at himself as the sabre fell from his grasp. "I mean...Fuck."

Raul ran him through. A mercy and a necessity, to make sure that no alarm was raised.

Yasmi was standing over the man she had brought down. Blood was running from his torn throat, his face mercifully pressed against the floor, where Yasmi wouldn't see the emptiness of his eyes. She looked at Raul, and even in the unfamiliar contours of the wolf's face, he saw a familiar grief. Grief for what she had done and for what it had done to her.

"It's going to be all right." He crouched beside her, set his sword down, ran a hand across her fur. "I promise."

She leaned into his touch. Her fur wasn't soft but it was comforting.

A ring of heavy keys hung from a hook in the corner of the room. Raul took them down, slid his wrist through the ring, tucked the end of his bandage back in, and picked up his sword. Holding the torch in front of him, he walked out the far side of the room, down another, narrower corridor.

The cells were old, rough stone, cold and damp, each one lit by a high window piercing the thick stone of the hillside, windows too small for any human to wriggle through, even if they weren't blocked by iron bars. The first two cells were empty, but as they approached the third, something moved.

"Raul?" Valens, squatting with his back to the wall, stared through the bars at the new arrivals.

The word "Da" stuck in Raul's throat, a sharp lump on which he felt he might choke. In its place came a grunt.

"You can't be here," Valens said, looking down the corridor in alarm.

"Of course he can." Prisca rose from a pile of straw at the far side of the cell. She walked over with confidence and dignity, as if there were no bruises on her face, as if none of the

FORGED FOR DESTINY

last night had happened. "He's a good boy and he comprehends his duty."

"No, I don't." Raul sheathed his sword, though he hadn't had a chance to clean the blade. "I don't even know what to call you anymore, but other people need you, so..." He held up the keys. "Which of these?"

"That one."

Prisca reached through the bars, tapped one of the keys. Of course she did. Of course she'd been paying attention to the little details from the moment she came down here. This was Prisca, cold and calculating, always planning her next move. How had he known that and yet not known what it meant?

He slid the key into the lock and the bolt slid smoothly back. The door swung open and Prisca stepped out.

"Thank you, Raul," she said. "And Yasmi too, unless you've befriended another wolf." Raul stood statue still as Prisca leaned up to kiss him on the cheek. "You've done terribly well so far. Do you have a plan to evade our captors?"

He stepped past her, into the cell, and looked down at Valens. The old warrior's face was clammy and ghostly pale, like a man in a fever.

"Come on," Raul said. "We're leaving."

"I don't deserve—"

"This isn't about you. It's about what other people need."

"I'm useless now." Valens held up his stump. "Don't waste your chance on me."

Raul squatted, face-to-face with him, a warrior himself now with a warrior's words.

"I'm sorry for your pain," he said, "but we don't have time

for pity. When you knocked me down sparring by the river, or when bigger kids shoved me over at the Vales fair, you told me to get back up and do better next time. So I'm telling you now, Da, get back up, and we'll all do better next time."

Valens looked down. His brow crumpled.

"Shit," he muttered. "Shamed by my own son."

He pushed himself upright, laid his remaining hand on Raul, who braced himself, ready to hold him up. But the wounded man's weight didn't follow. Instead, strong fingers squeezed Raul's shoulder.

"You're not the hero we made," Valens said, and lowered his head so that it pressed against Raul's. "You're the man you made for yourself, someone better than we could have dreamed of."

He stepped away and out of the cell. In its cold and clammy darkness, Raul took a deep breath and faced a decision that scared him. If he wasn't the man Prisca had twisted him into, then he could be the one people needed, however hard that was.

Chapter Thirty-Four
New Strength

Raul hadn't found the door himself. That had been Yasmi, remembering details from a previous visit to the palace, one Raul wished he'd known about when they were planning their attack. A sally port, Valens called the door, a way for defenders to get out during a siege and harass the attackers. Hidden from the outside, to provide the chance for surprise. One of the many deceptions that defence was built around. Not a weak point, because who would even know to attack it, who would approach unknowing along those perilous cliffs that flanked Rack's Scar, and how could they possibly approach that tower without being seen? As an exit, though, it was the one that would have the fewest guards and the best chance to escape unseen.

Or it should have been.

Raul crept along the corridor to the base of the tower. Yasmi, padding along two steps behind him, sniffed the air and let out a low growl. He looked back at her, then at Valens

Andrew Knighton

and Prisca, habit telling him that they would know what she meant, that his parents had all the answers. But they didn't speak wolf any more than he did.

Raul bit his lip, looked up and down the corridor. Should he ask her to change and tell him what she'd sensed? What he didn't know could kill him, he'd learned that all too well. But delay could kill them here too, and Yasmi's claws were half their fighting potential, not a thing they could afford to give up. He wrenched himself around, forced his feet to keep moving, slower, even more wary.

The corridor ended at a door, sturdy but not locked. There would be a guard on the other side, maybe two, a token force holding the tower room that led to the sally port. An easy shift for bored guards, they should be sleepy, inattentive. Raul lifted the latch as quietly as he could, then eased the door open, his whole body tensed, ready to fling the door back and leap into action the moment it made a sound.

"Here you are at last." Count Alder sat in a wooden chair, his back against the far wall of the room. His feet were up on a basket. In his hand was a skull goblet. "A weaker man might have doubted his own judgement, waiting here for your great escape."

Raul took a single step into the round room and held his empty hand back, signalling to the others to wait. With light coming through high windows, he didn't need his torch to see the warriors standing against the walls, all wearing captains' silver daggers. He tossed the burning brand to the floor and drew his sword.

"How did you know?" Raul asked.

"One of us is smart enough to recognise an obvious clue." Alder tapped the heel of his riding boot against the basket and Raul realised that it was the one he had carried into the palace. "You couldn't use that trick to sneak them out, or fight your way through the front gate before the garrison caught you. Valens's shoulders are too broad to slip through the privies or the outer windows, and after that, there aren't many options left. I've set guards at the others, just in case, but I was hoping you would come this way. It means I've understood you."

Alder swirled his goblet, took a sip. Wine, blood red, left its trace on his lip. It was as theatrical as anything Raul had seen from the players, a performance meant for Alder's own captains as much as the escapees. Like Prisca, the count was weaving a story from the threads that life gave him, building a legend with him at its heart.

"You like to hear yourself talk, don't you?" Raul said.

Alder still smiled, but something malevolent appeared beneath that look, a bee's sting hidden in the honeycomb. His shrug was carefully casual.

"Why not? Around here, people have to listen to me."

While they talked, Raul looked around the room. There were three doors out, but only one was bolted and reinforced. That had to be the sally port. Two warriors between Raul and there. If he was quick, he could maybe take one down, drive the other back. Then he just had to hold off the rest while his companions escaped.

Even as he played that out inside his head, he could tell how desperate it was. But this was a desperate moment and it wasn't getting any better.

"Are you still labouring under delusions of destiny?" Alder asked. "Or is this something else?"

"It's me standing up for my people," Raul said.

"How noble. Sadly, it's the sort of sentiment that gets young men killed."

Yasmi growled and stepped out beside Raul, fangs bared.

"My, if it isn't the brightest star in the firmament of theatre." Alder smiled his crooked half smile. "Though you seem to have forgotten the script. Rebellion won't get you to the royal court, except maybe in chains."

That growl deepened.

"Count Alder." Prisca emerged from the corridor. "Let us discuss what—"

"Hush, Minister." Alder pressed a finger to his lips. "Your time has passed. It's time for a new generation to be heard."

"You and I both understand that—"

"Quiet," Raul said, swallowing his own amazement that he could say it to her. "You've done enough damage."

Prisca blanched and her lips squeezed tight together. She folded her arms and stepped back against the wall, stiff as a statue.

"I like you, Raul." Alder leaned back in his chair, goblet resting on his thigh. "Why don't you come and fight for me? I can always use a warrior with a measure of courage, and I promise not to brand any kidnapped babies in the name of freedom."

"I'll die before I serve someone who turns his enemies into drinking cups."

"Turns his enemies into..." Alder laughed and raised the goblet. "You mean this?"

FORGED FOR DESTINY

"You're going to tell me that it's fake?"

"Not at all. This is the skull of my grandmother, the founder of the Alder line. She was one of the smartest, strongest, noblest warriors Dunholm has ever produced. If she'd been the firstborn, she would have been our greatest monarch too, but fate is fickle, isn't it?"

"You drink from your grandmother's skull?"

"How do you respect your heroes? Burn their bodies? Bury them in the dark to be forgotten? How barbaric." Alder shook his head. "We keep them close to inspire us."

He seemed absolutely serious, yet Raul couldn't escape the feeling that he was being mocked. How was he meant to make sense of a man like Alder?

"Tell whatever tales you like." Raul shifted his weight from one foot to the other, a small step closer to the sally port, and hoped that the others would follow. "I won't fight for people who go around conquering their neighbours."

Alder laughed out loud.

"Oh, Prisca, did you really raise him this naive?" His feet came off the basket and he leaned forward, staring intently at Raul. "Have you never heard of the Estian Empire?"

"I suppose, in stories and books."

"In stories and books." Alder nodded, set the goblet down on the basket. "A century ago, your country ruled half the known world. The descendants of Balbianus had conquered this continent with fire and steel. My ancestors' labour made yours wealthy, until we found the strength to throw off your yoke. I suppose they tell those stories differently in your books."

Though he hadn't known, Raul wasn't surprised. He could see how it fitted in the gaps of what he knew. A day ago, he might have been shocked, might have denied it, but what did history matter next to the lie that was his family?

"That was a hundred years ago," he said. "Were we still conquerors a generation ago, when you came to tear us down?"

"It had started again, and worse this time. Leaders like Minister Prisca here gathered minds from across the country at the Scholars' Spire, to turn the whimsies of folk magic into the power of essence. They shook down the walls of Schwartzwald, bent the paths of rivers to dry out Tuirllion and water the Winding Vales. Not just magic for warriors, life-saving charms and eternally sharp swords. Magic for *war*. Magic to reshape the world, in the hands of a nation that saw all others as its servants."

The count's hands clenched into fists as he spoke about the magic.

"Would you have let that continue?" he asked. "Would you have stood back while a savage empire rose again?"

Raul glanced at Prisca, who stood tight-lipped and pale. He remembered her fake prophecies and the books they'd taken. Lies and magic. Ruthless power.

"That's why you take the books," he said. "Why you limit what we learn. It's to stop the magic."

Alder slowly clapped his hands. "Smart as well as strong. You really should work for me. We could do wonderful things together."

"Whatever we did to you before, it doesn't justify what you're doing to us now."

FORGED FOR DESTINY

"If you're looking to retain your moral certainty, you should never have opened your ears to the truth. Perhaps you feel a duty to free your people, but I have a duty to tie them down. This land is rotten to the core, a country obsessed with power and domination. Even as it fell, its ministers were planning to raise a child on lies."

Raul felt heavy, exhausted. His back and the side of his face ached. His injured sword arm drooped, the blade pointing at the floor. He had seen so much in the past few weeks, heard so much in the past few days, felt so much. The pieces crashed against each other in his head, different worlds trying to take up the same space.

"I think that maybe there are no good countries," he said, looking for some hope to cling to. "Just good people."

"And you think you're one of them?"

"I don't know." It was a terrible thing to confess, but how could he be sure, after everything he'd seen and done? After seeing the bodies of people who trusted him, hanging dead in the streets? "But a friend has shown me that sometimes, if you pretend for long enough, the act becomes real. The mask sinks in."

Yasmi pressed her head against his side and he ran a hand through her fur. Perhaps it was her presence, perhaps it was the relief that came with admitting his own doubts, but he felt his old strength returning.

No, not his old strength. A new strength. The sort of strength Prisca showed, not the sort she told him to have.

"A new mask, then." Raul held out his hand. "Peace. Let's see what we can do together."

421

"Oh, Raul." Alder stood up and stepped around the basket. He smiled. "You're a terrible liar."

Alder's hand went for his sabre, but Raul's sword was already drawn. He lunged. Steel scraped across chainmail and the count buckled over, the air grunting out of him. Raul grabbed Alder's arm, twisted him around, brought the sword to his throat as the skull goblet clattered on the stones.

The rest of the Dunholmi froze.

"Silence," Raul snapped. "Drop your blades."

The warriors looked at Alder. The count's sabre hit the floor with a clang and theirs followed.

"Well played," Alder wheezed. "But what now? Are you going to lead me through the palace like this? Through the whole city? I'd bet my life against the accuracy of my archers, but I'm not sure you should play that game."

Yasmi, teeth bared, stalked toward the unarmed warriors, herding them into the corner. There was a scraping as Valens, one-handed, drew back the dirt-encrusted bolt on the sally port.

"Out," Valens said, pushing the door open.

Prisca looked so stubborn, so fixed in place, Raul thought for a moment that she might not move. He needn't have worried. She lurched away from the wall and out the door.

"You next," Raul said.

"No." Valens picked up a sabre with his remaining hand. "I'll guard them, give you time to get away."

"Dying now won't make you last night's hero." Raul was shocked by the sharpness of his own tone, more shocked to see how the words jolted Valens. "Get out."

FORGED FOR DESTINY

Shoulders slumped, Valens ducked out the door. Raul backed toward it, still holding the count.

"Yasmi," he said softly. "Time to go."

She growled, pawed the ground in front of the warriors, bared her teeth. In her eyes, he couldn't see the woman he knew, only the hunger of the wolf.

"Yasmi!" he barked. "Now!"

She glared at him.

"Please."

Those eyes softened. The yellow of the wolf became the green of the girl. With a swish of her tail, she darted out the door.

"I see." Alder stood straighter and his voice held its familiar smugness. "You hold us here with the threat to my life while your friends find horses and ride out of town. The sacrifice play. Does it feel better when you're sacrificing yourself, instead of being offered up by Prisca? Are you really that desperate for control?"

Raul sidestepped toward the door, almost lost his balance as his foot fell on the skull goblet. He lifted his heel, leg tensed. One sharp move and the skull would shatter. Alder had taken so much from him, this was the one thing that Raul could take.

With a flick of his toe, he rolled the goblet away.

"You can keep your family," he said. "But one day, I'm having my country back."

He took his sword from Alder's throat, shoved the count away, and ducked out the door.

Chapter Thirty-Five
The Country Boy and the Liar

The roaring off the River Rack buffeted Raul as he stepped out of the sally port. Yasmi stood on the narrow trail between the palace walls and the edge of the cliff, her mask in her hand, her hair blowing around her face.

"Come on."

She pointed along the trail to where Efron stood at the top of a rope ladder, watching nervously as Valens descended, one-handed, the ladder swinging under him. At the bottom of the cliff, in a rowing boat that bucked and strained at its improvised moorings, Prisca sat between Tenebrial and another of the players.

Raul slammed the sally port shut, jammed his sword between the door and its frame, kicked the pommel to wedge it in place. Even over the noise of the river, he could hear people shouting inside.

FORGED FOR DESTINY

He hurried to the top of the ladder. Rungs cut from old broom handles joined two lengths of sturdy hemp rope, worn by years of use, ends tied around the bar of a narrow window and a spur of rock that jutted through the path.

Valens dropped the last foot into the boat and steadied himself against its side. There was a banging from the sally port.

"Go, Efron," Raul said.

"Shouldn't I—"

"For the gods' sake, Father, go!" Yasmi exclaimed.

"Oh, very well." Efron huffed through his moustache. He crouched at the edge of the cliff, stretched one leg nervously over, then the other, and started descending. The ladder swung from side to side.

"Should we wait until he's down?" Yasmi asked.

There was a grinding sound. The sword protruding from under the door shook.

"No time," Raul said. "Go."

"You go." Yasmi held up a monkey mask. "I have another route."

She pulled the mask on. Grey cloth turned to brown fur as she hunched over and a tail uncoiled from her waist. Then she swung over the edge of the cliff and climbed, long fingers and toes grasping the edges of rocks.

Raul grabbed the ropes, set his foot on the first rung, and started his descent. The ladder swayed with Efron's movement, rope and wood scraping against the rock face. Hemp frayed. Knots groaned. Raul moved faster, his feet sliding off one rung to the next.

With a crash, the sally port burst open. The sword went

flying, spun into the gorge, and splashed down between rocks in the foaming water. A warrior emerged, looked along the path, then over the cliff edge, and she shouted, her words lost in the river's roar.

Efron landed in the lurching, shaking boat, and Yasmi a moment later, jumping lightly down the last six feet. Vibrations from one of the ropes ran into Raul's fingers.

There was a snap as one of the ropes mooring the boat broke. Tenebrial grabbed at the useless line as the boat swung away from the bottom of the ladder, one end gripped by the fierce current, the other bound at the foot of the cliff.

A Dunholmi captain crouched at the cliff edge, drew her silver dagger, its blade bright as starlight on a summer night. A swift slash and a rope parted. One side of the ladder gave way and Raul lurched as the remaining rope swayed.

A few feet to go, but not just down. Raul swung from side to side, trying to build up momentum, trying to swing himself to a place over the boat. Ropes and knuckles scraped against the cliff face.

The captain turned, her movements awkward on the narrow cliff ledge. She grabbed the remaining rope, raised her dagger.

Raul flung himself sideways, pushing with his feet. Even as he leapt, the ladder fell.

He hit the water, hit a rock below, burst through the surface gasping with cold and pain. A frayed rope end flicked out and he grabbed it, clawed his way along its length with desperate, clutching fingers.

A strong hand gripped his wrist, hauled him up and over, into the boat.

FORGED FOR DESTINY

"Now!" Valens bellowed.

Tenebrial cut the remaining mooring rope and the boat shot out into the River Rack, bucking and lurching in currents that twisted, spiralled, and foamed down the rocky chasm. Efron thrust an oar into the water, steered them as best he could, while the others clung on tight. Raul's teeth snapped together as the boat dropped off a short fall into the wider waters below, spun around in the current, somehow kept afloat, then picked up speed again. Ahead, the waters churned into a mass of foaming white, the rapids leading out of Rack's Scar.

Yasmi wrenched off her mask, became human.

"There!" she shouted, pointing to the side of the Scar. Efron jammed his oar into the current and Raul picked up another, rowed them frantically toward the side and the two figures standing there, dressed in the sturdy canvas clothes and heavy gloves of dockers.

The dockers scrambled across the rocks at the base of the cliff. One of them grabbed the other, and he leaned over, caught the edge of the boat.

"Out, quick!"

They clambered out. Valens, his wounded arm held close, struggled to keep his balance, slipped on the wet rocks. Raul caught him, thrust him forward, and followed. The dockers let go of the empty boat and it was swept away.

Raul scrambled over wet rocks, then along a narrow path and out onto the shingle beach below the Scar, just before the river junction. His bandage had come loose in the river and blood was running from his arm but there was no time to fix it now. Everyone was still with him, Efron red-faced and out of breath, Valens pale and breathing hard, the players anxious and uncertain.

"There." One of the dockers pointed to a sailing barge moored where the rivers joined. "The Dunholmi rely on their horses and roads. You can get a good distance before they realise which way you've gone."

"Thank you." Raul shook the docker's hand.

"It's for Appia. We won't forget her."

"Nor will we." Raul gestured to the others. "Come on."

"Wait!" Prisca said. "We can't leave now."

Raul stared at her, bewildered and frustrated. "We have to go before they catch us."

"No, we have to return to the city. There will be chaos, uncertainty over what we've achieved. Alder's hunt for us will give away that the—the—the rebellion is alive. We can use that to keep the fight going, to—to . . ."

She grasped at nothing with one hand, like she was trying to snatch words out of the air. From the look on her face, Raul would have thought that she was choking.

"Instigate!" The word burst out like a shout at a disobedient child. "We must instigate a full revolt."

"We'll be crushed," Raul said.

"No we won't." Her eyes blazed with a feverish intensity. "The pieces are in place, the momentum built, years of preparation and planning all ready in this moment."

"Your plan failed." Raul thumped his chest. "But as long as there's life, there's hope. Lives are what we have to save now, not the shreds of your stupid schemes."

FORGED FOR DESTINY

"Raul!" she snapped, and that voice cowed him, made him shrink like a child from his mother's disappointment. "I expect better of you. Show some ambition."

Everyone was looking at him. He pushed damp hair back from his eyes, took a deep breath, steadied himself. He might not be the chosen one, but he wasn't some innocent innkeeper's son from the Vales anymore. He had fought. He had killed. He had lied. He had taken the bold steps needed to challenge an empire and the desperate measures to save his people when their opponents' power proved too much. He might not feel like a hero and a leader, standing there bruised and dripping, his knuckles red raw, his heart pounding like a cavalry charge, but he could play the part.

Prisca was right, in spite of everything she had done, in spite of the pain in his heart whenever he looked at her. There were pieces of something good that could be saved. She was just very wrong about how to do it.

"We're leaving," he said. "If anyone wants to stay and fight here, that's their choice, but trust me, you'll find chances to fight elsewhere."

"Raul, please." Prisca pressed her eyes tight shut, as though she were closing out some terrible pain. "I can...I have the words, I can show you why we have to do this. Just, please. Give me a moment."

Her hand trembled as she reached for Raul, but he shrugged it off. He wasn't going to follow her plans any longer.

Shingle crunched beneath his feet as he walked toward the barge, the wind from the Scar chilling the back of his neck. A storm was coming in, clouds oozing like tar across the sky, dragging the rumble of thunder behind them. Spots of rain dotted the barge's boarding plank as he turned to see who was with him.

They all were. Efron and the players, coming to join their companions waiting on the barge. The dockers, running to deal with the mooring ropes and see them quickly away. Valens, smiling proudly at Raul as he passed him and headed up the plank. Prisca, arms folded across her chest, staring past him into a future that, perhaps for the first time, wasn't the one she had chosen.

Yasmi came last, and he took her arm, held her back before they boarded, leaned in close. She looked at him in amusement.

"I know that it's traditional to end the story on a romantic gesture," she said, "but shall we wait until the boat's moving?"

"I need your help," he whispered.

"Of course." Her voice changed, her expression growing serious. "Anything."

Raul looked out across the river, across farmland, across mountains scratching at the sky, a whole nation yearning to be free. He had a plan, crude and imprecise, no match for the web Prisca had woven around him. Unlike that plan, this one was his, a chance to fight on his own terms. That possibility animated him now—no longer someone else's puppet but a man moving under his own power toward an uncertain fate.

He looked at his companions, tense and huddled on the barge, soaked, scared, defeated. Count Alder was right about one thing. People needed signs and symbols. The deeper they sank into their troubles, the more desperately they clung to those signs to save them from drowning in despair.

FORGED FOR DESTINY

"I have to play a part," he said. "Something I know isn't real. If I falter, can you cover for me?"

"What is this, Raul?"

"Please, can you? I've seen you do it on the stage, fill the gaps when other people forget their lines, say things that make others seem more real."

"Of course. Yes. Whatever you need."

"And later, I need you to teach me how to act."

"The simple, honest country boy wants to be a professional liar?" She laughed. "I do like a challenge."

Yasmi and Raul strode up the boarding plank, then pulled it in behind them. The dockers flung the ropes onto the barge and waded into the shallows to push them off. Someone pulled a rope, the barge's sail unfurled, and the wind filled the canvas. With the storm on their heels, they sailed downriver, away from Pavuno, onward toward Rackmouth and Saditch, the waves of the Golden Ocean, wonders Raul had never seen. Places far from Count Alder's grasp.

Though they wouldn't be staying there.

Raul stood at the side of the boat, took off his soggy shirt, wrung it out into the river. He tightened the bandage on his arm, tucked the end back in, and his fingers came away bloodstained. When he turned back, the others were looking at him again, as he had expected. Everyone except Efron, who was busy at the rudder, and Prisca, who stared pointedly away. Several of the players looked at his arm, eyes running from the bandage to the scar higher up, the half-moon sign he had always believed was a birthmark. The brand burned into him by his so-called parents.

431

Andrew Knighton

"It's true, then," one of the players said.

"What does it mean?" another asked.

Valens looked away. Yasmi raised an eyebrow.

This was it. The point on which Raul's choice hung. He despised the lies and tricks that Prisca had woven around him. The last thing he wanted was to be like her. He wanted to be a hero, strong and proud, to save his people like in the stories of old. Those two characters, the scheming politician and the proud warrior, in the stories Raul knew, in the world he'd thought he lived in, they were opposites. But here and now, in a nation waiting for something to believe in, he couldn't be one without the other.

As he spoke, he felt like each word was a rock he must lift from the depths of the river.

"This is my birthmark," he said. "This is my destiny." He puffed out his chest, stood proud, caught Yasmi's eye, and she gave him a small nod. Across the deck, Prisca sneered.

"A new moon is rising, a bright sign of the future to come."

Chapter Thirty-Six
The Beginning

Ermet looked around to make sure no one was watching, then dropped a sprig of hawthorn into the post hole. It wasn't much, as acts of rebellion went, a drop of bad luck amid the Dunholmi's blessings, their strength and wealth and power. But then, Ermet wasn't much of a rebel. If he was, he might have resisted the labour levy called to build a lookout tower.

He might also have ended up dead.

"Come on, you lazy oaf," Nona called.

Ermet dragged his feet across the packed dirt to where the others were picking up the corner post. When they'd got together to build a house for Nona's son, the carpenter had carved a hearth fire into the bases of the posts, to bring warmth and welcome, and a bull's head to help the house endure. No one considered doing that for the Dunholmi, who stood watching, spears in hand, as the locals did all the hard work. Those Dunholmi probably would have beaten them for suggesting magic, even for a blessing.

There was a shout from down the hill, by the road up to the Winding Vales. The Dunholmi walked over to see what was happening. Given a moment unsupervised, the labourers laid down their tools and timbers.

The captain's horse, tethered at the edge of the wood on the hill's back slope, pawed the ground and snorted. Branches swayed. Ermet squinted as something shifted in the shadows of the trees.

A man stepped out of the woods, tall, blond, well built. He couldn't have been older than Nona's son, but he carried himself like a man who had walked half the world. A moon pierced by a dagger was painted in red on his leather tunic, and on those of the armed women and men following him. One of them was a giant who towered even taller and whose right wrist ended in a stump. A wolf padded along between them, teeth bared.

The blond man raised a finger to his lips. The labourers backed away, clearing a path across the hilltop. The blond man walked faster and so did his followers, swift strides turning into a charge.

One of the Dunholmi turned, opened his mouth to cry out. There was a hiss that ended in two swift thuds and he fell, arrows sprouting from his chest. The others turned, raised their spears, shouted in alarm. It was too late. The attackers tore through them, hacked them down, left nothing but dead bodies and last gasps.

"Take their armour and weapons," the blond man said as he wiped blood from his axe.

"Yes, Raul," someone said.

"The horse too, though we'd better keep it away from Yasmi."

Someone went to untether the horse, which was straining at its reins and staring in terror at the wolf.

"Pile up the timbers and burn them. Turn this tower of oppression into a beacon of hope."

"Yes, Raul."

The blond man walked over to the cowering labourers. A shiver of fear ran through Ermet as the wolf came to join him, blood on its paws, tongue hanging between its teeth.

"The age of empires is over," the blond man said, his voice strong and clear. He looked like a hero from the stories of old, handsome and noble, brave and strong. Watching him, Ermet wished he'd had the courage to do more than drop that sprig of hawthorn. "A new age is beginning, one of justice and freedom. Destiny calls to us down the centuries, demands that we make our mark on the world. Who among you will take up arms and join me in the fight?"

The story continues in...

Book TWO of Forged for Destiny

ACKNOWLEDGMENTS

Huge thanks to Milena Buchs, David Knighton, Ben Moxon, and Tej Turner for invaluable feedback on this story.

Thanks to the team at Orbit, in particular Stephanie Lippitt Clark, for all the help with this big step up in my career as an author.

And the biggest thanks to Milena for the support, encouragement, and inspiration.

MEET THE AUTHOR

Richard Wilson

ANDREW KNIGHTON is a full-time freelance writer and has published short stories, novellas, and comics in a range of venues. His fantasy novel *The Executioner's Blade* was described by Adrian Tchaikovsky as "a perfect balance of action and character wrapped about a delightfully twisted mystery" and by Anna Smith Spark as "a very enjoyable, fast-paced read." You can learn more about Andrew by visiting andrewknighton.com.

Find out more about Andrew Knighton and other Orbit authors by registering for the free monthly newsletter at orbitbooks.net.

www.ingramcontent.com/pod-product-compliance
Lightning Source LLC
Chambersburg PA
CBHW011241300425
25817CB00005B/19